The old man rested his white, blue-veined hands on the top of his magnificent satinwood desk and leaned slightly forward, as if to impress upon Elspeth Marriner the importance of what he had to tell her.

"My dear, thanks to circumstances beyond my control, I am going to send you out alone for the first time."

There was no need for further explanation. Elspeth understood fully the implications of Mr. Horelle's remark. For she was, although still on the sunny side of thirty, a veteran Watcher, one of that supremely select little group accustomed to whichever of the many parallel versions of Earth needed their services. Her blue eyes steady on those of the Chief Watcher, she said, "Where am I needed?"

SAM MERWIN, JR.
THE HOUSE OF MANY WORLDS

SF
ACE BOOKS, NEW YORK

THE HOUSE OF MANY WORLDS
Copyright © 1983 by Sam Merwin, Jr.
All rights reserved. No part of this book may be reproduced in any form or by any means, except for the inclusion of brief quotations in a review, without permission in writing from the publisher.

THE HOUSE OF MANY WORLDS copyright 1951 by Sam Merwin, Jr.
THREE FACES OF TIME copyright 1955 by Ace Books, Inc.
Magazine version copyright, 1953, by Better Publications, Inc.

All characters in this book are fictitious. Any resemblance to actual persons, living or dead, is purely coincidental.

An Ace Book

Published by arrangement with the author

ISBN: 0-441-34446-1

First Ace Printing: January 1983
Published simultaneously in Canada

Manufactured in the United States of America

Ace Books, 200 Madison Avenue, New York, New York 10016

CONTENTS

The House of Many Worlds   1

Three Faces of Time   169

The House of
Many Worlds

I

Elspeth Marriner fingered the sticky surface of the thick tumbler on the gimpy-legged table and wondered what in hell she was doing in the dingy little restaurant. As a poet, she reminded herself, it was her duty to have her feet in the mire as well as her head in the clouds—but this was going a little too far. Besides, the night sky outside was cloudless.

Seeking to screen out Mack's insistent and unsubtle prodding of the leather-skinned native he was plying with the hot and heavy liquid molasses that passed for rum in this incredibly backward little Carolina community, she concentrated on the strip of pale amber flypaper that dangled from the ceiling, which was less than six feet above her head.

At regular intervals the curved planes of its spiral surface glistened menacingly in the dim reflection of the green-shaded lamp that dangled beyond it from a dark-brown cord. Less regularly, trapped insects buzzed hysterical protest at such unmannerly death as faced them. She counted the flies she could see imbedded in its sticky surface. There were exactly fourteen, five more than had been present the night before. It was these five that were buzzing—the others were still.

Fourteen, she thought. Fourteen—the magic number that spelled sonnet. She began mentally to frame a sonnet to fourteen wretched flies, caught in a spiral of flypaper, five alive, nine dead. Surely even such unpleasant creatures merited some sort of memorial to their passing.

She lost the thread of her verse in the midst of a couplet—and her rhyme scheme with it. Her head was aching dully, just in back of her temples, either from lack of sleep in the course of the assignment or from the soggy fried food which was all this Carolina township had to offer, or from the drink and a half of blackstrap rum she had just consumed. Or perhaps her headache was the result of a combination of all three. If Mack didn't get her back to New York on the morrow she would . . .

She glanced covertly at the photographer, who was leaning on the soiled oilcloth table cover as if eager to absorb every illiterate word of the native's half-drunken blather. It would be pleasant, she thought, to do something that would wipe the conscientious eagerness from his too-hard too-old too-young gladiator's face. According to Orrin Lewis, the tough-fibered smooth-talking managing editor of *Picture Week,* who had teamed them for the Hatteras Keys assignment, Mack Fraser had once been a professional prize-fighter. Elspeth believed him.

Mack's nose was slightly flattened across the bridge, its end a trifle off center. His cheekbones were not quite symmetrical, as if one—the left one—had been shattered by a fist. His eyes habitually wore a sleepy look which, she suspected, came from the thin pouches of scar tissue on their upper lids.

She told herself sternly that she was being a snob, that she had no right to object to the fact that Mack had once made a living in the ring. But she could not help resenting the fact that he seemed determined to treat her as if, merely because she had not had to struggle out of some similar gutter, she did not quite belong to the human race.

". . . and I'm telling you, Mack," the native said in his soft brogue as the photographer signaled the bar for a refill, "that there's still some mighty odd things happening around here from time to time." He paused, and the Adam's apple vibrated beneath the scale red skin of his turkey neck. "We don't make much talk of it to outsiders as a rule." He paused again to chuckle and even sounded like a turkey. "Matter of fact, we don't make much talk of it among ourselves."

"What sort of odd things?" Mack asked quietly. He was leaning back in his chair now, apparently disinterested, since his fish was nibbling at the bait. Elspeth winced, thinking the pumping process painfully obvious. If she were Corey, or whatever the native's name was . . . But of course she wasn't.

Lacking a waiter, the bartender himself, a large lame individual with faded blue eyes and thick gray hair on the backs of his fingers, brought drinks over to the two men. Corey nodded and mumbled his thanks and lifted his fresh glass to Elspeth, who managed what she hoped was a smile as he downed half its contents at a single gulp. She shuddered at the sight, feeling as though *she* had drunk it, but on Corey it had no visible effect.

"It's like this," Corey went on, planting his forearms on the table after wiping his mouth with one dirty blue sleeve. "It goes a long long ways—some say to the bankers, and maybe even beyond."

"I've heard of *them*," said Elspeth, deciding she ought to say something in return for the courtesy of Corey's toast. "They used to do things to the beacon lights to force ships ashore on the Hatteras shoals and then loot them. Nice people!"

"That they weren't," said Corey, apparently taking her last two words literally. "And they did worse than loot. Some say they slew ten thousand men—aye, and women and little children. They could not afford to let any of them live."

"But what's this funny stuff—these 'odd things' you were starting to tell us about?" said Mack. His voice, Elspeth decided, was not actually bad. But it was rough around the edges, unfiled for subtlety or fine shades of meaning. On the whole it went well with its owner.

"Some nights the lights still shine," said Corey, placing his gnarled and brine-cracked lobster-pot hands flat on the oilcloth table top. His voice dropped a full half octave. "And when the lights are seen things happen. Other times there's darkness—darkness not even the stars can shine through when there's not a cloud in the sky. And that's worse."

"Not so fast, Corey," said Mack, his low forehead furrowed. "You say 'things happen' when these lights are seen. What sort of things?"

"Big things—bad things," the native said slowly, painfully seeking his words. "Things like wars and earthquakes and troubles to match. Times we don't get to hear of them until a long whiles after. But we know when they happen."

"And, Corey, why is this darkness you talk about worse?" Mack inquired, again leaning forward.

Corey hesitated and scratched his unkempt coarse black hair. He looked around the restaurant a trifle furtively and then leaned toward both of them, his voice low and hoarse as he said, "It's difficult to explain—but it is. You've got to see it when it happens to understand what I mean."

"You mean the whole locality—the entire area here—just blacks out?" Elspeth asked. Although their assignments—to come up with a romantic picture story about the Hatteras Keys and their inhabitants—had been a notable fizzle to date, she was in no mood for haunts.

"Not so you'd notice, miss," said Corey, regarding her as if she were a toddler who had failed to pass a first-grade test. "What I've been telling you is that Spindrift Key is the place."

He paused and Mack cut in with, "I think I know. Let's see, that would be the island just beyond the mouth of the inlet." He looked thoughtful, added, "I'm afraid it's too well groomed—too clipped looking—for this story we've been sent out on. Do you mean to tell me that—"

"What I mean to say is that's where these things happen I've been trying to tell you about," the native said, drawing himself up with a trace of dignified affront. Then, glancing down at his glass, which was again empty, he dropped his dignity and added earnestly, "Listen, you people may be outsiders but you've been mighty decent to me—mighty decent. I wouldn't tell you no lies, not so you'd notice it. I know what I know, Mack."

"But the place can't be haunted," Mack protested solemnly. "Hell, I cruised all around it yesterday with Elspeth here on our way to the outer shoals. It looks like a Southdown manor compared to the rest of these desolate places. And that big white house on it is well kept up. The lawns are clipped and the shrubbery—"

"Didn't say it was haunted," stated Corey, looking hopefully at his glass. "All I told you was that Spindrift Key is where things happened. It's where they've always happened."

"But somebody must live there," Mack said steadfastly. "The place is too well kept up."

"Didn't say nobody lived there neither," Corey told them. "The Frenchman lives there—him and his people. Always have lived there, as far as we know around here."

"Frenchman?" inquired Elspeth, more to keep from falling asleep than to contribute to the conversation. She was totally and desperately tired. Three days of traipsing to and around this rough-hewn primitive Carolina country with Mack were enough, she thought, to put any girl on the ropes.

"He's a foreigner anyway. And he's got a French sort of name—Horelle," said Corey.

Mack flashed Elspeth a quick, speculative look. Then, turning back to the native, he said, "Sounds like it might be worth a visit. Do you think this Horelle might be in tomorrow?"

"I can't tell about that," said Corey with a massive shrug. "Sometimes he's there—sometimes he ain't."

"But, Mack," said Elspeth in horror, "tomorrow we've got to get back to New—"

"But someone's got to be there," said Mack, as if she hadn't spoken at all. "A big place like that."

"I can't very well tell about that either," drawled the native. "Around here we leave the Spindrift Key folk pretty much to themselves. Always have. It suits them fine and suits us likewise. But there's times when the Key is just empty ground."

Mack straightened in his chair and looked briefly at the watch on his wrist. "It's only a little after nine," he told them. "Could you get us out there tonight, Corey?"

"Maybe I could," said Corey in a tone of deep reluctance. "It's a fact Horelle don't like visitors dropping in unexpected-like. I hear tell he's downright discouraging."

"Mack!" Elspeth said sharply. "I'm beat." They had risen at quarter of five that morning so that Mack could get shots of the sunrise over the keys.

"It's a story—maybe. And we're in no spot to pass one up," Mack told her firmly. The photographer was not to be denied.

To her considerable surprise and even greater disgruntlement, Elspeth found herself, nine minutes and a final drink later, standing with Mack outside the dingy little restaurant in the virtually unpaved main street of the little Carolina coastal town. Despite the fact that it was still early in the evening it appeared that most of the denizens had already gone to bed.

"No wonder they seem to have so many children," she murmured half to herself. "They have nothing else to do nights."

"Shut up," Mack said bluntly. "It's rough enough trying to get next to any of these natives without your insulting them. And if you hadn't run the Pipit into that ditch today we wouldn't have to have Corey take us out there."

"I said I was sorry," Elspeth replied irritably. She was sick of feeling like an inept and absent-minded idiot. Nor did it bolster her sagging ego that Mack's trim and gleaming little English-made vehicle was reposing in the town's one garage, thanks to a driving lapse on her part. She had spotted a flock of bright red cardinals while guiding the Pipit along a high-crowned country lane as Mack scouted the landscape for pictures. In the resultant slip from road to ditch she had managed to get the front wheels thoroughly out of line.

"I only hope whatever passes for a mechanic in this alleged town doesn't finish the butchery," Mack added unkindly. It was like him, Elspeth thought, to worry over a gadget like the Pipit. He was exactly the same about caring for his cameras. He was forever fussing with them, oiling them, testing them, taking them apart and putting them back together again. Elspeth, whose entire nature and interest lay in form, in people, in ideas and passion and the emotional responses they aroused, had a certain contempt for all machines. They were so—coldly tangible.

"Lord, I'm sleepy!" she said, and let herself yawn widely, making no attempt to cover it.

"My God, after the way you've been beefing about the beds at the local hostelry!" said Mack, and his white teeth gleamed in the starlit darkness as he grinned at her. "I should think you'd be grateful to me for giving you a chance to stay out of them for an extra hour or two. Women!"

"Your logic," said Elspeth icily, "leaves me frigid."

"Just as it found you, eh?" Mack chuckled.

Mercifully for their continued existence as a writer-photographer team, Corey loomed up out of the shadows of the ill-lit street before Elspeth could frame a suitably pungent reply. The native was rolling a bit as he came toward them, but Elspeth decided to give him the benefit of the doubt and put his unsteady gait down to his years on a fishing-boat deck rather than to the rum he had just consumed.

"That is all a bit daft," he remarked as he led them toward the shimmer of white moonlight on the water beyond the small quay at the far end of the street. "Still, you folk have been more than decent to me. If it'll give you any benefit I'm glad to be of service. Look out for the steps just ahead."

"Thanks, Corey," said Mack. He paused to negotiate the irregular steps down onto the quay, leaving Elspeth to manage for herself. Then, fingering the case of the infrared camera which hung from a strap over his shoulder, "We'll be more than glad—"

"We wouldn't want to miss a moonlight trip on the water for anything," said Elspeth quickly, gaining the quay without stumbling. She sensed by his tone that Mack was about to offer their guide money—and that Corey would be hurt beyond words if he did. By way of emphasizing her point, she jabbed an elbow into the photographer's short ribs.

"Dammit—be careful!" cried Mack. He glared at her in the moonlight and Corey stopped in front of them, glanced back with evident concern. Mack finally caught on and to her relief, added, "Sorry, I must have stepped in a pothole or something."

"Gotta watch your step in these parts, Mack," said the fisherman earnestly. " 'S tricky walking after dark."

His boat was tied to one side of the quay and the water lapped gently at its side. The moonlight did not hide its lack of paint and all-around battered condition. It smelled of stale machine oil and long-dead fish. Elspeth, who had considerable native grace for a tall girl, managed to scramble safely aboard and find a seat near the stern, across the cockpit from Mack, who was already seated and smoking a fresh cigarette.

"Light one for me, will you?" she asked. Illogically and in spite of the fact that she prided herself on an ability to deal with men on equal terms, she felt irritation at his not having offered her one unasked. Mack complied casually and reached across the cockpit to hand it to her without rising, thus forcing her to reach too. He was, she decided, a thorough-going boor.

At that moment Corey, who had been working quietly in the bilge, got the big flywheel spinning and the motor sputtered abruptly to life, seeming to shred the entire peacefulness of their surroundings with its sharp barking sounds. It coughed and sighed briefly, then caught and subsided under the fisherman's expert handling to a steady thrum. Corey cast off and they putt-putted out across the dappled moonlight that seemed to dance like a will-o'-the-wisp in front of them.

"That Spindrift on our port bow?" Mack inquired less than five minutes later. Corey denied it and offered the information that they would not lay eyes on their destination until they had rounded the black point that lay just ahead.

"Forgot about the point," said Mack apologetically. Elspeth decided he was trying to be subtle. They had studied the entire harbor layout from the Pipit just the afternoon before, and Mack was not dumb about things like that. He was only dumb where it counted, she thought.

"There she is," said Corey, pointing, after another quarter hour of silent progress as they rounded the point.

Elspeth, who had noticed the island earlier only as a civilized anachronism in the general desolation of their Hatteras surroundings, studied the dark lump of land before them with new interest. It was remarkable for its single low hill amit the flatness, for its obviously landscaped and well-pruned tree silhouettes, for the large white-pillared mansion that capped its rise.

"Mack!" she cried, suddenly excited. "There are lights!"

"Yeah," said the photographer. "Somebody must be home."

"That's not what I mean," Elspeth protested. "Didn't Mr. Corey just tell us that when there are lights on Spindrift it means that things are going to happen?"

"They's just the regular lights in the big house windows," said the fisherman without excitement. "They's not the lights I was meaning."

"What's different about *them?*" Elspeth wanted to know.

" 'Tain't easy to say exactly," Corey replied slowly. He hesitated, seeking words beyond the limits of his meager vocabulary. "The lights I was meaning are higher up—and they move."

"Could be St. Elmo's fire," said Mack casually. He had opened his camera case and was squinting through its infrared viewer. "Ought to be something for your story in this, Elly. It's the first new slant we've come up with for Orrin."

"Nothing like an unhaunted house to spice up a travelogue," said Elspeth with definite irony. She disliked having Mack speak of Orrin Lewis as "Orrin." Lewis still called *her* "Miss Marriner."

"Could be St. Elmo's fire," said Corey, picking up the conversation three sentences back as if nothing had intervened, "but it ain't. It shows up on clear nights as well as on rainy ones."

"These phenomena occur only at night?" Elspeth inquired.

"Whatever you call 'em, that's right," Corey told her. " 'Tain't easy to explain. There's a lot of things hard to explain about Spindrift. Take those house lights. They weren't shinin' last night. The whole place was as dark as my cellar."

"Maybe this—Horelle—was away somewhere and just got back," Mack offered. He stood up to take a shot of the Key.

"Sure—maybe," said Corey doubtfully. "But if he was, when did he go? And how did he get back here without being seen?"

"We'll ask him and tell you about it on the way back," said the poet. In spite of herself she was feeling increased interest in Spindrift Key and its strange inhabitants. It might be a boon to an otherwise dull story after all.

"I'll be waiting," said Corey and there was something in his tone that caused Elspeth to glance sharply at the dark shape of him, standing up front, his hands on the wheel.

He replied, without turning around, "Just what it says. I'll be waiting for you—'less I get word you don't want me to." He sounded as if he was not looking forward to his vigil.

"We'll bring you word ourselves if this Mr. Horelle asks us to stay any length of time," said Mack, putting his night camera back into its case. He sat down and this time lit two cigarettes, handed one of them to Elspeth. "Nice night to haunt a house," he said.

"Shut up!" she said snappishly. It occurred to her that they had switched roles. Now it was she who was genuinely interested in Spindrift Key, while Mack had become the scoffer. This annoyed her and she told herself she was acting the emotional fool.

"There's the dock," said Corey, pointing directly ahead.

They were sidling up to a well-groomed little pier whose base was lost in the shadow of a clump of poplars that rose like black lower fangs against the star-studded sky. Its white pilings gleamed their silent answer to the moonlight with the assurance of things well built and well tended.

"Funny," said Mack thoughtfully as Corey cut the motor to let momentum carry them in. "There are no boats."

"Never are," said the fisherman laconically. Elspeth and Mack looked at each other across the cockpit. There seemed nothing to say, nothing to ask. In a matter of minutes they would be close to the source of all knowledge about Spindrift—the Key itself.

Elspeth felt herself shiver although the night was warm. She tried to tell herself that it was merely fatigue. But inside she knew better. Corey's fearful legends of the island might be a contributing factor—but they seemed scarcely sufficient to cause the fear that gripped her. She could not have stated what she feared. She was simply scared witless.

Their bow thudded against the pier then—a prosaic sound. Corey scrambled up onto it and made fast the painter. Then he helped Elspeth ashore and she shook down her travel-rumpled tweed skirt while Mack, nursing his camera, climbed up beside them.

"Which way—Oh!" said Mack, spotting the neat white path that took up its hedge-lined existence at the shore end of the pier.

"That'll take you to the house," said Corey, who was engaged in stuffing his pipe. "Got nowhere else to go."

He chuckled at his own joke and Elspeth sighed. They dutifully thanked their Charon and slowly began to walk up the path. It led them toward a large clump of landscaped shrubbery whose nature was indistinguishable in the darkness, some fifty yards inland from the pier. There it took a ninety-degree turn to the left.

It was there, just around the curve, that the darkness came. It came without sound, without motion, without warning. One moment Elspeth was looking ahead at the lighted windows of the big pillared house ahead—the next she was alone in a world without light, without stars, without moon.

She cried out in alarm and it seemed to her that she was enveloped by an airlessness that must mean asphyxiation. Instinctively she stretched out an arm to where she remembered Mack, drew reassurance from the feel of his fuzzy jacket.

"Mack," she whispered, for somehow normal tones seemed wrong in the blackness. "Mack, what is it?"

"I dunno," he replied, his strong fingers finding hers and drawing her into the circle of his arm. "But, Christ, it would make one wonderful darkroom!"

It might have been more reassuring to Elspeth if his voice hadn't trembled when he said it.

II

It was, to Elspeth, like being enclosed in a globe filled with nothing. Even the firmness of the ground beneath her feet seemed not to be. Mack Fraser's arm and body were the only remaining tangibles—and for once in her life she was of no disposition to sneer at tangibles. She sorely missed them.

"What do you think it is, Mack?" she asked him, and her voice sounded small and very uneven and a long, long way back from her lips.

"I'm not thinking, Elspeth," said Mack, his own voice a little uneven. "I'm just standing here—waiting."

How long they had to stand here in the blackness Elspeth had no way of knowing. Without being able to see or to hear anything beyond the noises they themselves made, it was impossible to gauge anything. There was a bitter gathering coldness to the blackout that made her shiver and cling even more closely to her companion. She had no idea that muscular strength could be of any use in such an emergency, but she was suddenly and overwhelmingly glad that Mack was a strong man.

"Put your watch to your ear," she whispered. "You can tell from its ticks how long this is lasting."

"What good will that do?" Mack countered irritably. But she could feel the shift of his weight against her as he lifted his left hand. Then, after a long moment, he said, "That's funny. The damned thing seems to have stopped."

"Oh, fine!" said Elspeth. At least the failure of Mack's wristwatch was something on which she could take out the frustration that was making her want to scream out loud.

She didn't want to take it out on Mack, however—not just then. He might get angry with her and step off by himself. She could not bear the thought of being alone in this black nothingness.

Then, again without warning, as suddenly as it had come, the darkness was gone. Again they could see the white-shell surface of the path leading to the big white house with the white pillars atop the gentle rise of the hill that was Spindrift Key. The shells themselves again made crunching sounds under their feet. Above them shone the stars.

Spurred by an inner urge she did not at the moment understand, Elspeth studied them. They looked, to her untutored gaze, to be exactly as they had been before they—went out. The Big Dipper still hung in the same spot, and the neatly spaced jewels in Orion's belt had not slipped a notch.

"They're just the same," she said with a sigh of relief. She became aware of the fact that she was still glued closely to Mack's right side, that his right arm was still curled tight around her waist. She said, "Well, really!" and disengaged herself with gentle firmness.

He looked down at her for a long speculative moment. Elspeth was a tall girl, a good five feet nine in her stockings, and tall men had never bothered her before—quite the reverse. But she had resented Mack's height ever since they had been teamed together for this assignment by Orrin Lewis in Manhattan more than three days before. She disliked acutely the idea of having to look up to him.

"Very well then," he said, and his voice was as unreadable as had been the bowl of darkness that had enveloped them moments before. "We might as well go on to the house."

He strode off rapidly, and Elspeth found herself forced to scurry without dignity or poise to keep abreast of him. She cursed him silently for a heel. Damn his dirty soul, she thought, he knew she would not dare let him get far ahead of her lest the darkness come back. She wished, not for the first time, that she was the sort of conniving wench who instinctively made certain that all available men were not only willing but anxious to serve her.

She had ample comeliness for the purpose when she chose to do something about it. Some female poets, she thought, were creatures of surpassing ugliness—perhaps that was why they had turned to poetry for expression. Aware of their inability to arouse male passion, they turned to verse as a sublimation.

She knew, of course, that there had been a few who were otherwise. Elinor Wylie was one—and perhaps Elizabeth Barrett Browning, for all that her father's twisted pathological tendencies and her own reactive hypochondria had hardly enlarged her capacity for attracting the male. And then there was Sappho—but what did anyone at this late date actually know about Sappho—or, for that matter, about the fabulously pornographic Elephantis, whose verses had been kept handy on Capri by the aging Tiberius as guides for the fantastic *spintriae* Suetonius had so vividly described in his *Lives of the Twelve Emperors* . . . ?

"*Hey!* Watch yourself, Elly." One of Mack's long arms invaded her field of vision like a snake and grabbed her, realigning her progress on the path. She had been on the verge of blundering blindly into the perfectly clipped boxwood hedge on her right. Mack said, "How often do you get into these things, anyway?"

"Shut up," she told him. "I hate back-seat drivers."

"Some drivers seem to need them—to stay out of ditches—or even to stay on a path," he reminded her tactlessly. From then on she concentrated on keeping up with him.

The path widened in front of the house, whose square pillars rose at least twenty-five feet above them in simple serenity, colonnading a wide portico beyond which french windows gleamed in rectangular softness through the ruffled petticoats of their drapes. The lines and proportions of the house itself, enhanced by the dimness of the night, were even more impressive close at hand than when seen from a distance.

"Oh—it's perfectly magnificent!" breathed Elspeth, pausing to look up at its tall perfection.

One half of the large double front door was opened slowly by a girl who came toward them with the light behind her. As she approached, her features were cut in high relief by the flanking light from the french windows. They were as arresting, to Elspeth, as her figure, equally well revealed, was to Mack. Elspeth could hear the quick coarsening of his breath but forgot to be disgusted in her own absorption.

"Miss Marriner? Mr. Fraser? Welcome," the girl said. Her voice, utterly without alien or even local accent, was softly contralto. It sounded, somehow, as if it belonged to one who had the mastery of many tongues. The girl smiled and added, "We're very glad you got here. Won't you come inside?"

"Thanks—thanks very much," stammered Elspeth when for once Mack seemed too dumfounded to open his mouth. They entered a long high-ceiled hall, which appeared to extend right through to the rear of the house. Three quarters of the way back a circular staircase of white with dark mahogany railing curled upward airily in apparent graceful contempt for the law of gravity.

Soft Persian carpet covered much but not all of the low-gleaming fine parquet floor. Light sparkled with gentle prodigality from a crystal chandelier that hung from the low floral plaster relief of the ceiling fifteen feet above them. Dado and high-wall paneling bespoke the genteel tastes of a century twice gone, and a pair of authentic-looking old portraits in simple gold frames provided the only other decoration. Chairs and table were mahogany—old and beautiful.

Seen in the light of the chandelier, the girl who had come to greet them was breathtakingly beautiful. Her hair, which hung in loose heavy demi-waves to her shoulders, seemed to match the deep red luster of the mahogany behind her. Her figure, although she was not tall, was perfectly proportioned—a fact which the sleeveless white silk shirt she wore, parted to the waistline, burgundy shorts and *espadrilles* that made up the remainder of her visible costume, did little to conceal.

Yet, curiously, such extreme modern informality in this instance failed to clash with the surroundings. This old house was meant to be lived in—lived in and enjoyed like some fine vintage brandy, by folk of charm, beauty, and dignity. And the girl had all three qualities. There was dignity in the so-young face framed by the mahogany hair—dignity and a sort of timeless poise that were startling in one whose youth was so apparent.

"I'll take you to Mr. Horelle," she informed them softly as she led them through a door to their right, which took them into a library whose white-oak wainscoting, unstained but polished with loving care for generations, had assumed the patina of a treasured meerschaum pipe. "He has been waiting for you. I believe he is very anxious to talk to you."

"About what?" Mack asked bluntly. Ever, thought Elspeth, the diplomat, the meatball. When bigger feet were made to come crashing through more fragile greenhouses, Mack would be wearing them. But the girl in burgundy shorts appeared unabashed. There were quick little dancing lights in her off-hazel eyes as she turned to look quickly at the photographer.

"Mr. Horelle will tell you that," she said demurely.

Briefly Elspeth wondered why it was that so very many women—some of them creatures of undoubted intelligence, beauty, and breeding—seemed to find lurking within themselves such quick response for men as crude as Mack. It was, she thought, a refutal of every basic tenet of civilization; it was brutalizing, it was the crudest sort of feminine masochism . . .

They went through another doorway with a flat-curved arch and Elspeth stopped thinking about it barely in time to avoid walking into one of its fluted supporting pillars. They were now obviously in a sort of den or study at one end of the big house. It was an exquisite room—yet a thoroughly comfortable and practical one. Light hand-tooled leather with Florentine gilt work at its borders was inset in the vast satinwood desk. A huge globe rose behind it in a window embrasure to the left—and in a like embrasure to the right stood a celestial orb.

Directly above and behind the desk, which dominated the entire room, a large portrait hung against the wall. It was old—obviously, by the scarlet hues of its flesh tints and the ivory black of its shadows, a work of Gilbert Stuart. It depicted a surpassingly lovely young woman in white, a young woman clad in the neoclassic high-bosomed gown and ringlets of the early nineteenth century, a young woman who was both puzzlingly and hauntingly familiar to Elspeth.

"Don't you recognize her, Miss Marriner?" The gentle voice of the man who sat in the armchair behind the great desk brought her out of her reverie. She looked at him and saw that he was old and beautiful—beautiful as only the saints are beautiful—and very, very wise. The whiteness of his skin and hair, the blue underhue of his eyelids and the veins of his temples and the backs of his hands made Elspeth think of alabaster.

"Such pallor is a symptom—perhaps a failing—of great age," he told her, and she wondered fearfully whether he was telepathic or whether she had spoken her thought aloud. But the charm of his faint smile eased her embarrassment and canceled her fear. It was obvious that here was a very great gentleman.

"Our skin grows thin with time; our blood grows sluggish," he went on, and made a slight gesture of self-deprecation. "The effect of alabaster is not uncommon. But enough of myself. I believe Juana has explained by this time that I am extremely anxious to talk with you, Miss Marriner, and Mr. Fraser. Won't you sit down? And by all means smoke if you wish."

They sank into ancient leather armchairs that embraced them with the softness of clouds. Juana found herself a perch on a red-and-white leather hassock where she drew one slim tanned leg up beneath her. Dammit, Elspeth thought, the child *was* beautiful! That is, if she was a child. There was a timelessness behind her perfect poise that reminded Elspeth of Mr. Horelle himself.

"You *are* Mr. Horelle?" Mack asked then with his usual bluntness. "May I ask how you knew our names?"

"It is not much of a mystery," said Mr. Horelle, again with his faint and wise smile. "I received information that you would almost certainly find your way here. If you had not"—he paused, gestured casually with one thin hand—"there would ultimately have been others. But perhaps not soon enough—"

"I'm afraid I don't understand," said Mack, openly puzzled.

"I shall try to explain," said Mr. Horelle gently. "But first I must ask that you hear me out with open minds. For you must be aware by this time that Spindrift Key is not exactly what it seems."

"So we just found out, over in the village," said Mack. He lit a cigarette and regarded Mr. Horelle as if daring him to say something startling.

"I judge that you have lived here for many years," Elspeth put in hastily, seeking to avert an open clash between the men. "This house—this island—they are like a well thumbed book in these surroundings. They show the taste of generations of security, the lavish care of someone who—" She bogged down helplessly in her own words, felt her face grow hot. Mack was regarding her as if she were an utter idiot but Mr. Horelle merely nodded his appreciation.

"If I were to tell you how many years I have lived here you would not believe me," he replied quietly. "Suffice it to say that it has been a very long time indeed. And there were others before me—have been ever since Spindrift Key became a tangential point."

"What's that?" Mack asked aggressively, suspiciously.

"*I'm* the one who's supposed to be writing this story," Elspeth reminded him sharply. "You're here to take pictures. Let *me* ask the questions."

"It's a very good question, Miss Marriner," said Mr. Horelle gently. "Let me state first that Spindrift Key *is* a tangential point. I don't suppose that either of you knows much about the tangency of time—or parallel time-tracks, if you will."

Elspeth glanced covertly at Mack, was inwardly delighted to note that he looked baffled. She turned eagerly to Mr. Horelle and said, "But *I* know a little about it. It's a theory that whenever an important decision in world history is made the world actually goes both ways with different subsequent histories. Oh, *damn!* That doesn't sound very clear, but I'm afraid it's the best I can do."

"Tommyrot!" said Mack loudly and rudely.

"On the contrary," said Mr. Horelle quickly, "it happens to be absolutely true. Hold on, young man—open mind!" He held up a reproving hand and protests visibly bubbled up toward Mack Fraser's lips. "I know exactly what you are going to say—that if a tangent in time develops out of historical decisions, then it must grow out of minor personal decisions as well. It takes forces far greater than any one person can generate to split the space-time continuum in which our universe exists.

"A nova, the destruction of a planet, even such momentous man-made events as affect the life history of this minor speck of space-dust we call Earth—these things all leave their marks in varying degrees. For a while after their occurrence—the time span varies according to the shock suffered by the fabric of the continuum—a tangential zone remains through which, to those who know the secret of the key, it is possible to effect a transfer between worlds."

"But what has ever happened here—in this godforsaken place?" Mack inquired, unable to contain himself longer.

"Spindrift Key is thrice tangential," said Mr. Horelle with an undertone of quiet assurance that made denial an impossibility. "Almost four centuries ago an Englishman named Sir Walter Raleigh put ashore inside the Capes while en route back to England after founding a colony at Roanoke. He then decided that this island and the mainland behind it offered a safer and more generally favorable site for his colony. It was his plan to transfer it here before returning to England."

"And . . . ?" said Elspeth, her fascination growing apace.

"In one of our tangential worlds he was able to make his transfer. His colony survived and the entire history of this continent was altered," said Mr. Horelle. "In the world you come from conditions arose which caused him to postpone doing so. The Roanoke colony, left to its fate, perished."

A butler with a face as wrinkled and sad as that of a kindly hound-dog made a silent entrance and set a silver tray that held bottles, ice, tumblers, and soda on an ancient cherrywood table against a side wall. For a brief spell the talk was light and general. Then Mr. Horelle resumed his lecture.

"In January of 1813 the American privateer *Patriot*, Captain Overstocks commanding, was lured onto a reef by the so-called 'bankers' or pirates, who then made a highly prosperous business out of decoying ships to their ruin. The *Patriot* was running the then British blockade off the Capes with a safe-conduct arranged between the British admiral and Governor Joseph Alston of South Carolina. She was bound for New York."

"Alston!" exclaimed Elspeth, straightening. She looked again at the portrait behind the desk, recognized its subject as Theodosia Burr, only child of Aaron Burr and wife of Joseph Alston. "Of course," she said and her eyes grew bright as she nodded toward the picture, "that's some of the loot from the *Patriot*."

Mr. Horelle smiled ruefully and looked more than ever like an alabaster saint in the soft lighting. "I regret to say that it qualifies as pirate pillage," he informed them and sighed. "Many of the things in this house are likewise. My ancestors, some of them . . ." He made another deprecatory gesture.

"I'd like to take a color picture of it," Mack said alertly. He looked less combative, less disturbed, now that he was back on ground he could accept as real. But their host's next words put the furrow back in his brow.

"Actually Alston was only able to obtain his safe-conduct because he and his father-in-law were both trafficking with the British. There was a conspiracy afoot which planned for a double uprising in both the South and New England that could have altered the entire course of subsequent history. In your world the shipwreck prevented it. But in certain others . . ." His thin cultured voice faded out briefly.

Then, leaning forward over the desk, he told them, "And more recently, when a pair of brothers named Wilbur and Orville Wright were experimenting with heavier-than-air craft at nearby Kittyhawk, they made a number of their crucial plans and decisions in this very room. I believe you can compute the tangential potentialities of their discovery." He paused again.

"So," he concluded moments later, "Spindrift Key is perhaps the strongest tangential point on this continent. That it is a seasonal storm center is an added factor in its tangency. It is actually a multiple gateway to parallel worlds, its older tangencies maintained by the importance of more recent occurrences. I trust you understand me now."

"Sure," said Mack with his usual lack of tact. "I understand everything except—what in hell does it have to do with us?"

"Everything," said Mr. Horelle, mocking him politely. His half-smile returned. "You have been carefully selected, both of you, to undertake an extremely delicate and difficult assignment in another world. As a matter of fact, in coming here, you selected yourselves."

"I'm getting out of here right now," said Mack, rising.

"I very much fear you will find it difficult," said Mr. Horelle, still smiling. "You see, when you stepped ashore, a transfer was effected. You may have noticed some—odd phenomena."

"The darkness!" exclaimed Elspeth. She felt a rushing return of her fears. All at once the old room, the old man, the beautiful Juana, ceased to be decorative, friendly, or interesting. She felt as if she had been dropped suddenly into a chamber of horrors.

"You mean we're not on the world we started out on?" asked Mack staring at Mr. Horelle. "Phooey! I'm going back to Corey at the pier. Come on, Elly, let's get the hell out of this nuthouse. Thanks for the drink and the bedtime story, Mr. Horelle. I suppose you have Corey on your pay roll to get suckers out here."

"Go ahead," said Mr. Horelle dryly, ignoring the photographer's insulting tone. "However, I'm afraid you'll find that some changes have been made since your arrival on Spindrift Key. Perhaps Miss Marriner will await your return here. I'd like to discuss your assignment more fully with her. Juana—will you see that Mr. Fraser doesn't get lost?"

Mack looked at Elspeth, who had not risen. She was definitely intrigued and wanted to learn more about Mr. Horelle and his strange island—whether or not he was a liar. A story was a story, true or not, and this was a gorgeous one that stirred her poetic imagination. Besides, she had no intention of passing another night on a corn-husk lodging-house mattress.

"I'll go alone, thanks," said Mack bitterly, but Juana,

soft and far more appealing than a kitten, moved close to him and Elspeth could see his defenses visibly crumble.

"It may interest you to know," said Mr. Horelle with amusement, "that Juana herself is from a world not your own."

Mack looked the girl up and down and grinned crookedly. "If they make them like you, honey, show me the way. Until then I'll settle for you in the here and now."

To Elspeth's annoyance the gentle Juana did not bridle at Mack's vulgarity. Instead she laughed softly and slipped a bare arm through his and, as they passed through the arch into the library, said, "Remember, Mr. Fraser, I'm *really* out of this world."

"Just call me Mack, honey," said the photographer. Elspeth, still sitting in her chair, felt anger beyond all reason. Somewhere deep within herself she wished she too were small and lissome and darkly lovely instead of too tall and too fair with straight hair so fine it refused stubbornly to take a wave.

"If you can spare an old man some of your attention," said Mr. Horelle, "I would like to inform you as to certain factors of your assignment. I think you will find them important."

"Sorry," said Elspeth, bringing herself back with a wrench.

"It is always startling at first," Mr. Horelle told her, "but there are a few of us—a *very* few, by the way—whose job is to watch these tangential points. We call ourselves—alas, without much originality—the Watchers. Thanks to the fact that natural cataclysms have much to do with the creations of such points, few of them are population centers; few are even habitable."

"But exactly what do you *do*—besides watch?" asked Elspeth.

"In effect," said Mr. Horelle, "we do our best to look after the health and fortunes of all the shapes and forms of Earth."

III

The briefing, which was objective, detailed and complete, lasted until midnight, when Mr. Horelle, who sat shrunken and exhausted in his chair behind the desk, pressed a button that summoned the hound-faced butler. "I hope," he said, his voice almost inaudible, "that you will find your rooms comfortable. Also that you understand what you and your young man must do."

Her young man, Elspeth thought acidly. Mack had not yet put in his reappearance—nor had the fabulous Juana. But she said, "I hope so too. All I can promise is that we'll try."

"I can ask no more of anyone," whispered Mr. Horelle with the wisp of a smile. "I am sure that you have been wisely selected and will acquit yourselves admirably."

"I——" she began. Then, "It's a frighteningly important assignment," she said, and her panic returned with interest. Mr. Horelle merely nodded and his eyes were closed. Somehow Elspeth knew despite the questions banked within her, that the interview was at an end. She followed the butler dutifully to her room upstairs at the back of the house. Its grace and comfort were on a par with that of the lower-floor rooms. Once enfolded by the soft linen sheets, she found herself—to her amazement—drifting into slumber almost at once.

She was awakened at nine by a grave-faced maid who brought her breakfast and announced that she would be expected to start in an hour. In the bright sunlight her fears evaporated, as did her anger at Mack, and were replaced by a sense of high adventure. She did not even chide him about his bedraggled appearance when he came downstairs to join her and they walked to the wharf.

Another boat and boatman there awaited them—not Corey—and they were taken to the village, where a refurbished Pipit awaited them. Mack said, "You drive—I'm still sleepy. Try to keep out of ditches." He slung his cameras into the back, which already contained their other gear, suited action to words. He was snoring softly beside her when she tooled the Pipit down the lumpy main street. Other world or no, the village looked much the same—dismal, bedraggled, sadly in need of a coat of paint.

It was a couple of hours later and the sun was close to the meridian when he stirred, yawned, sat up and stretched. By that time Elspeth had the Pipit close to the border of South Carolina. Mack regarded her balefully through bloodshot eyes and said, "Can't you drive this thing without hitting every bump in the road? A man can't sleep with all this tap dancing."

"If you hadn't done whatever you did with Juana last night you wouldn't need sleep now," she said, corrosively virtuous.

"Some things are worth it," said Mack, and an infuriating sated-tomcat grin spread itself over his somewhat battered features. He yawned and stretched again without a trace of inhibition, then lit himself a cigarette.

"I still think we're both bats," he said. "Or maybe victims of one of old Horelle's perverted gags." He looked puzzled, fumbled in his breast pocket. He produced a worn pigskin billfold and pulled a sheaf of bills from it, eyed them dubiously. "I wonder if this damned stuff is any good," he murmured, squinting as he examined its alien engraving.

"It's good all right," said Elspeth. "I bought some fuel for the Pipit with it half an hour ago. Incidentally, it's a good thing this brutal beast of yours runs on kerosene—that's all they have here. The attendant thought you were dead."

"Okay," said Mack, looking at his watch. "Suppose I take over for a stretch. If you've managed to keep us on the road this long we're running on borrowed time. You can brief me on what we're supposed to do while I drive."

Elspeth pulled over and braked to a stop and they

changed places. Behind the wheel Mack examined the road and whistled. She said, "Let's see *you* try to avoid bumps on this pavement."

Mack did not stoop to reply as he got the Pipit going again. He said, a moment or two later, "I hope your poetic brain hasn't scrambled this deal too badly. I don't mind telling you I had a shock when I went outside last night and found the old boy wasn't fooling."

"You took a remarkably long time getting over it," said Elspeth uncharitably. Despite her fine free new sense of high adventure, she was still gnawed at intervals with jealousy over the photographer's satyr-like behavior of the night before. After all, he had yet to make any sort of a play for *her*.

"Past history," said Mack, adroitly maneuvering the Pipit past a particularly tricky stretch of highway erosion. "I wish to hell we were allowed to fly this thing. We could make New Orleans in a couple of hours. I learned that much from Juana. But I suppose flying is out."

"You suppose correctly," said Elspeth.

"I also suppose we're both good and fired from *Picture Week* back in whatever world we really come from," Mack added.

"Mr. Horelle says not," Elspeth told him. But despite her confidence in their ancient host she could not repress a tremor of inward worry. Life as a poet before Orrin Lewis hired her as a staff writer for *Picture Week* had involved a number of substitutes for eating—substitutes whose only variety lay in their degree of non-satisfaction and discomfort.

"He acts like he thinks he's God," said Mack. "Dammit, what a putrid highway! Well, how about giving me the dope?"

"Very well," she told him. Despite her lurking desire to be as unpleasant as possible to Mack Fraser, she was much too aware of the importance of their strange assignment to risk wrecking its completion through personal pique.

She proceeded to organize her thoughts, seeking to put in some sort of reasonable order the succession of incredible things that had happened from the moment darkness had engulfed them upon Spindrift Key. All at once she felt small and alien and, save for Mack, very alone in a strange world. She reminded herself sternly of Mack's scandalous behavior with Juana lest she grow soft and foolish.

Viewed in retrospect, she felt that Mr. Horelle, intentionally or otherwise, had been vague as to some facets of the job he had assigned them. "You have everything you'll need," he had told her with quiet assurance that swept away all possible doubts. "When the time comes you'll know what to do right enough."

Apparently, from what she had been able to gather, they were entering the affairs of the alien world as catalysts to help solve a crisis that was threatening the entire continent of North America with war. They were supposed to proceed in the Pipit to New Orleans, where they were to make contact with the agents of an American rebel leader named Reed Weston. Weston, a former Cabinet member, was the leader of a group of recalcitrant citizens whose headquarters were somewhere in the rugged Ozark country.

"Weston seems to be the man the country needs," Mr. Horelle had told her. "But if you cannot reach him with the Pipit before the week is out it will be too late. Events will have moved past any possible peaceful solution. You see, my dear, in an effort to reunite a sorely divided country the New Orleans government is plotting war with the Empire in Mexico.

"So Weston must get the whip hand, and quickly. You two can enable him to do so with the Pipit. But you must keep it on the ground until you reach him. Once its abilities are known, you will be lost. You see, in this world you are about to visit, there are no airplanes, no flying machines save balloons and uncontrollable rockets. Scientific and industrial development have been largely stifled in the name of autocracy."

It was hard going, adjusting herself so rapidly to a world utterly different from her own. But she had managed to absorb most of it—she hoped. If not, it was now too late for any return. She passed this along to Mack, who listened intently, his eyes on the road, his low forehead furrowed.

"We'll have to move carefully—watch our steps, Elly," he said when she was finished. "And for God's sake, try not to go winging off on any of those patented tangents of yours. Lord, that word again! I've been around a bit more than you have. Better let me make the contacts when we get there."

"You certainly did all right last night," said Elspeth—a remark Mack greeted with dignified silence.

She wondered again why he bothered her so. It wasn't love—it couldn't be. Not with a crude gadget-mad ex-pugilist who went dashing off after everything in skirts, shorts, or slacks that beamed a receptive eye in his direction. She resented the fact that she found herself thinking of him so much of the time, decided that the long-fabled peril of propinquity was, in this instance, a trifle too real. Something would have to be done about that. She felt grimy with the dirt of unplowed fields and tobacco plantations that lined the road in irregular alternation. Worst of all she felt herself unwanted.

Thanks to her lengthy session with Mr. Horelle the night before, Elspeth had not been especially startled by the discoveries of the morning—that of the strange boat and boatman who had brought them ashore from the Key, of the Pipit—repaired, refurbished and ready—of such apparent anachronisms as the filling station that gave nothing but kerosene.

There were other differences, of course, in the countryside through which they rode bumpily as the sun passed its zenith above them. Towns were fewer than in her own world, industrialization was less, cities according to the map which Mr. Horelle had furnished them were almost non-existent. And the road itself, not only poorly paved and conditioned but a high-crowned two-lane affair, would scarcely have qualified as a third-class byway, much less a highway. But highway it was—on the map.

Save when they were in one of the widely separated towns or villages, they passed an average of four cars every twenty miles. And not once was the skyline broken by the pylons of a high-tension line; not once did a silver transport plane gleam and drone its way across the bowl of light blue sky overhead. The people they saw from time to time appeared shabby and loutish. And for every prosperous-looking mansion or farmhouse they passed several score decrepit-appearing hovels, which seemed for the most part to be inhabited by immense Negro families, whose members regarded the Pipit with an air of sullen disinterest.

They lunched late in an archaic public house in Spartanburg, noting with some surprise the Portrait of President Wilkinson upon the room's one unwindowed wall. He appeared a languid somewhat hollow-cheeked citizen of surpassing homeliness. The food was plentiful and incredibly cheap but the saddle of mutton, which was the main dish, was so high as to be almost inedible, a fact which seemed not to disturb their fellow-diners.

"No air travel, no refrigeration," Mack said sourly, pushing away his plate with distaste. "I'd like to take the Pipit up and scare the whey out of some of these cretins." Then he brightened up noticeably as their waitress, a comely chubby brunette of perhaps nineteen worldly summers and with a single apparent purpose in life, ogled him while she poured a bottle of wine out into remarkably fine crystal stemware.

"Relax, mate, and take ten," said Elspeth when the girl had departed with a provocative flirt of what lay beneath her apron strings. "We have a long way to go yet if we're to reach Atlanta tonight."

"Yes, teacher," said Mack. When he paid the bill at the bar he seemed pleasantly surprised that the money Mr. Horelle had given them proved acceptable to the cashier. "This," he told Elspeth in an aside, "is a very soft snap."

"To date," said Elspeth, ostentatiously crossing her fingers. Until then they had discovered no symptoms of conflict brewing—no uniforms, no marching troops, no air of tension.

It was dusk when they reached a strangely altered Atlanta, a small city of no tall buildings and wide ill-tended parks. Elspeth was bone-tired and travel-worn and was glad to settle for an inside room at the rickety old American-plan hotel that seemed to be the best the town had to offer.

For a change, however, the table fare proved both good and bountiful and was served with deftness by polite black waiters. Tension was here all about them, tension that was to increase at a geometric ratio with their arithmetic progress toward the nation's capital, New Orleans.

A fat-necked and ornately dressed man was seated in company with two Christmas-tree females of uncertain age at the next table during dinner. He regaled his companions throughout the entire meal with a vicious diatribe against "that stinking traitor, Reed Weston, and his whole rotten subversive crew of anarchists."

Weston, he claimed further, was not only undermining the foundations of proper government as duly elected by the representatives of the people, was not only threatening to destroy all Columbian civilization with his revolutionary ideas, but was in the pay of the Mexican Emperor himself—and this despite the fact that the country which had borne him and given him wealth was faced with war.

There was more, much more, but it was all in the same vein and did not improve with repetition. Mack wagged his head in mock exasperation, and one of the overdressed woman at the next table smiled faintly at him. But she did not look again. Perhaps, Elspeth thought, because the fat man was pouring champagne freely.

Champagne and bulging vests . . . There was, perhaps, the germ of a poem in it. She drifted off on the wings of her own thought, seeking phrase, form, rhythm, that would give it clarity, mood, and bite. Which, she wondered, was more sad—the drab whose insensate thirst for the gay life could be slaked only through letting herself be pawed by such a gross and loathsome creature—or the fat man, ignorant of love save that which his money could buy.

"Come out of it, Elly," said Mack, shattering the pleasant lilac sadness of her mood. "We'd better turn in if we're going to get an early start tomorrow."

"Look who's talking," said Elspeth. But she went along to her room meekly enough. She was far too worn out—physically, nervously and emotionally—to let Mack irritate her further. She all but fell asleep in the weird dark-wood-and-copper horror that passed in this Atlanta for a bathtub.

She was awakened at six the next morning by a whistling voice from the desk downstairs that emerged from a speaking tube close to the head of her bed. This was, apparently, a world without telephones, although she had noticed what looked like a telegraph desk in the lobby the night before on her way to bed.

She was considerably pleased on getting downstairs to discover that Mack was not in the dining room, where an alert young Negro was serving breakfast to early risers. But he informed her courteously that Mr. Fraser had already eaten and was waiting for her in the garage across the street.

She limited herself to toast and coffee, paid the check and joined the photographer. He was deep in study of a large six-wheeled touring vehicle parked next to the Pipit. He acknowledged Elspeth's arrival with a nod and said, "Get a load of this buggy. Looks like a dinosaur."

"It's big, that's all," she said not comprehending his interest in what to her was merely a clumsy machine.

For this comment she received a lengthy technical lecture. It was as different from the Pipit as day from night. Mack lifted a hood that swung oddly on a pivot, showed her an engine that looked to Elspeth like any other engine. "The damned thing runs on ammonia," he told her. "Didn't you notice *any* of the cars we passed on the road yesterday?"

"Unh-unh." She shook her head. "But look—the Pipit has new plates." She regarded them with surprise.

"We wouldn't have got that far yesterday without them," Mack told her contemptuously. "Get in. We're going to make a try for Baton Rouge. We can lunch in Selma."

Feeling like a hopeless ignoramus, Elspeth obeyed. Not until they were well out of Atlanta did she straighten from her slump and utter the word, "Teeth."

"What's that?" said Mack, dodging a hole in the road.

"Teeth, teeth, teeth," she replied. "Didn't *you* notice?"

"Notice what?" He seemed honestly puzzled, risked a quick glance at her as if to reassure himself of her sanity.

"Look." She pulled from her handbag a small container like a pepper shaker with little holes under its hinged lid. "I found this in my alleged bathroom at the hotel. Apparently everyone uses the stuff here—it's got a government seal."

"So it's a monopoly," Mack remarked with a shrug.

"Maybe, but have you noticed everybody's teeth in this world? They're perfect. And we didn't see a dentist's sign in either Spartanburg or Atlanta. They may not have airplanes and telephones, but they've found something to keep teeth from decaying."

"I take it all back—you *have* got eyes," said Mack graciously. Elspeth restrained an impulse to box his visible ear.

"This could be pretty valuable back in our world," she said. "Apparently they just pour this into water and rinse out their mouths with it. That's what the directions say to do."

Toward noon, as they approached Selma, they discovered that railroad tracks ran parallel with the road. They were the first Mack and Elspeth had seen in this strange new world. After a while in the Pipit's rear-view mirror, Elspeth, who was driving, spotted the smoke from an approaching train. When it passed them at high speed it proved to be a gaudy affair with a rear locomotive which by its trail of smoke appeared to be jet- or rocket-propelled. It was painted bright red and the six cars in front of it formed a complete spectrum from orange to purple.

"She goes right along, doesn't she?" said Elspeth brightly, for which amiability she received only a look of contempt.

Elspeth wondered why Mack despised her so. Perhaps, she thought, he despised all poets. He was a crass materialist in many ways. Yet he could be as fussy about framing a photograph to perfection as any poet over selecting exactly the right word to give meaning to a couplet. He was, she decided, an iambic-pentameter type. She glimpsed the sweeping lawn of a great estate and forgot about him in the comforting sight of the emerald sward.

They lunched as planned in Selma beneath another picture of the languid President Wilkinson. Inevitably their fare consisted of southern fried chicken, mashed potatoes and biscuits. When she had eaten all she could Elspeth looked at Mack and sighed.

"Apparently a change in worlds does not mean a change in regional cooking," she said. "I'll wager this same fare is being served in five hundred thousand different southern restaurants in five hundred thousand different versions of Earth. It frightens me."

"It's probably a lot more frightening to the chickens

said Mack. He had been thoughtful and silent all morning. Now he added, "I'm liking this assignment of ours less and less as we go along."

"Afraid?" Elspeth inquired lightly. He shook his head.

"Just cautious. It's tricky enough to play a three-cornered mess like this one we've been tossed into when you know all the local angles. We're walking into it mighty cold—and green. We could make a fatal misstep and never know it."

"Look at the map," said Elspeth, nodding toward the opposite wall. It revealed a North America whose divisions were utterly different from those of their own world.

The United States, renamed the Columbian Republic, extended from Maine to Key West as before. Evidently, however, the Oregon controversy of a century earlier had gone against Columbia, for the Columbia River marked the Canadian border in the Northwest. And while Texas lay intact to the Rio Grande, most of Arizona, New Mexico, part of Nevada, and the southern half of California belonged to a Mexican Empire that extended all the way to the Isthmus of Panama.

"Wonder how that Mexican thing got started," mused Mack. "And how we became the Columbian Republic."

"Parallel time-tracks," said Elspeth smugly. "Things went differently 'way back when. Do you believe it now?"

"I'll have to until I wake up," he growled. She decided that the problem of adjusting to a tangential universe was proving hard on the rigidly logical Mack. For herself, she had long since given up trying to find logic. It was better, in this instance, to take things as they came.

They drove on and on through the Deep South that afternoon and early evening. They passed through Meridian, Mississippi, not long after leaving Selma, then headed southwest toward Baton Rouge over a road whose lack of excellence varied from township to township according to local whim and budget.

Once they were almost forced off the highway into a swamp as a long military convoy passed them at high speed en route for the Mexican border. The big multiwheeled vehicles were propelled by some jet drive similar to that of the locomotive, with exhaust vents flaring fiercely along their sides. In the trucks were green-clad soldiers armed with odd-looking weapons.

"They may not have planes," Mack remarked thoughtfully, "but somebody's been seeing they know how to kill on the ground. Some of those things they're carrying look rugged."

"No matter what world man lives on he always sees to it that he has the tools to kill his fellows," said Elspeth bitterly.

"If he doesn't his civilization perishes," said Mack quietly. "It's a story as old as Rome—a lot older."

They drove on through an afterglow until, within a few miles of Baton Rouge, they were stopped by a red light that was swung across the road in front of them. Mack, who was driving, pulled to a stop, and a suntanned young officer in a pale blue uniform with silver trim and insignia walked over to the Pipit. A pair of bucket-helmeted soldiers moved up behind him.

"I'd like to see your papers," he told them. "We're checking for rebels. A lot of them are trying to cross the river to Weston's camp."

Mercifully the passes and identification with which Mr. Horelle had furnished them were in order. Mack mopped sweat from his brow as the officer motioned them to proceed. "That's a neat looking car you have, Mr. Fraser," he said. "Is it foreign?"

"English," said Mack. "They make the best."

"Wish we had their know-how," said the officer sadly.

As they drove on Mack was even more thoughtful. Finally he said, "Did you notice the guns those soldiers were carrying? They looked to me like some sort of machine rockets. And our friend's pistol. Unless I'm crazy, that was a rocket job too. Funny that they haven't learned to fly . . ."

IV

Baton Rouge proved a delightful surprise. In place of the sleepy little river city of their own world, Mack and Elspeth found themselves driving into a metropolis far larger and far more impressive than the down-at-heel Atlanta in which they had slept the night before. The buildings they passed did not tower to skyscraper heights, but they were many, large and, almost without exception, magnificent.

"Why," exclaimed Elspeth, "it's like a never-ending garden party hung with Japanese lanterns!" Her fatigue faded before excitement as the Pipit moved slowly amid bizarre traffic composed of multi-wheeled vehicles. They were rolling along a broad sleekly paved eight-lane double boulevard with a mimosa-planted central park area. The blue blossoms shone white in the light of looping strings of lights hung from poles lost against the trees in a garland effect that continued for miles.

On either side the double boulevard was flanked by sidewalls forty feet wide reminding Elspeth of the Champs Elysées in Paris, and beyond them lay an apparently endless succession of great houses, palaces, and walled gardens. Baton Rouge was very evidently one of the major cities of the Columbian Republic. Elspeth felt a quick stir of inner response to its drama and beauty.

"It's a mighty well-guarded garden party," said Mack, his more prosaic vision caught by the large proportion of vari-colored uniforms that flashed brilliantly amid the more somber male civilian costumes and the gay gowns of strolling women.

"But it looks so—so Continental!" said Elspeth, her

whole self aglow. "It doesn't look American at all."

"It isn't—it's Columbian," said Mack. "Let's get to a decent hotel quick and nail ourselves a room. *If* we can find rooms. This town looks loaded."

As usual Mack was right. The first three hotels they tried were full to the gunwales and the fourth was evidently the supreme caravansary of Baton Rouge—Bienville House. Elspeth felt like the wreck of the Birkenhead, as she stood forlornly amid the splendors of the lobby while Mack consulted the room clerk.

Semitropical extravagance! she told herself after a cursory study of the opulent velour drapes that framed the Roman-arched-two-story windows. She did her best not to notice the superb features, figures and grooming of the women who paraded past in a constant stream, most of them hugging the elbows of slim-waisted young officers whose gaily colored dress uniforms were reminiscent of Napoleonic splendor. Even the evening dress of the non-uniformed males was colorful, with multihued cummerbunds, waistcoats, and lapels.

She wished Mack would get it over with so that they could continue their search for shelter in more modest surroundings. But to her amazement she heard the desk clerk, a black-browed individual with a professional smile, say, "We're most happy to be able to accommodate you, sir. It is only by the sheerest happy chance—"

"That's great." Mack cut off his effusiveness curtly. It seemed to Elspeth, when they crossed the lobby to the bank of elevators a few moments later, following a scarlet-clad golden-haired bellboy, that Mack was eying her furtively, even suspiciously.

But before she had the opportunity to do more than register this impression, her entire interest was caught up by an immensely tall white-haired officer, completely magnificent in blue, scarlet and gold, who entered the lift after them. Elspeth tightened her fingers on Mack's near arm and tried not to register her astonishment.

For the general or field marshal or whatever he was was almost coal-black of skin. For once even Mack was visibly startled—perhaps as much by the deference the white elevator operator and bellboy showed him as by the fact that a man of such obviously high rank should be a Negro. He smiled pleasantly at Elspeth, then at Mack, as the lift rose slowly.

"You must have had a long trip today," he said politely in a deep and beautifully rich bass voice.

"Oh dear!" exclaimed Elspeth woefully. "Do we look *that* terrible?" Mack, for once, was too stunned to speak. The man of ebony looked at Elspeth gravely.

"If you did I assure you I should not have remarked upon it," he said with a softness that robbed his reproof of its sting. Before Elspeth could manage to assemble and deliver a reply the lift stopped and he stepped out into the hall. There he turned, smiled again, and said, "I hope you both enjoy your stay with us."

Their stop was one floor higher up—the fourth—and, as they discovered later, the top story of the hotel. As the golden-haired bellboy, having put down their two suitcases on the corridor carpet, unlocked a high handsome white-paneled door, Mack asked him, "Who was that—the big chap with all the gold lace—back in the lift?"

"You mean you didn't know that was Marshal Henry?" The boy seemed utterly astonished. "He's here in the city to consult with President Wilkinson—about this Mexican War business. He's Chief of Staff of the Columbian Army."

"I don't care what he is," said Elspeth. "I thought he was a very charming gentleman."

"He's a very good tipper," said the boy pointedly as he opened the door. Elspeth entered first, took in at a glance the high-ceiled expanse of the room. Then, with a little sigh of sheer relief at the prospect of luxury, she swiftly crossed the soft carpet to fling open one of three french windows that opened on an attractively elaborate wrought-iron balcony. The leaves of a palm tree unfolded before her and beyond and below them she could catch glimpses of the flashing loops of light along the great boulevard.

Magic lantern city, she thought, then wondered whether *Goblin city* might not be more appropriate. She sought some phrase that would trap in the chill finity of letters the warmth and magic around them, the low-throated gaiety, the softness of the night air, the fragrance of millions of blossoms.

It eluded her and she put aside the effort, knowing that in time it would come to her. Dreamily she turned and drifted back into the room, feeling as if she were at least six inches off the floor and floating, floating . . .

She was jarred back to earth with a thud—by the sight of Mack, his jacket off, his tie pulled loose, his shirt unbuttoned halfway to the waist, stretched out casually in one of the huge room's several easy chairs. Arrogantly he blew cigarette smoke at the ceiling, eying her with a half-hidden defiance.

"Don't detonate," he told her, holding up a warning hand. "Listen. This is the only decent room left in the city. Of course I had to tell the clerk downstairs we were—er—together to get it. It seems that the marriage rules are a bit lax in this world. The clerk took one look at us and told me that it didn't matter—before I could lie about it and say we were man and wife."

Elspeth's eyes ranged quickly from his suitcase, already open on a rack next to hers just inside the door, to the luxurious bathroom visible through a half-open door to her right, to the immense platform bed whose four twisting walnut posts pointed with slim dignity toward the ornate floral pattern that adorned the plaster of the ceiling high above them. Mack's eyes followed hers.

"Roses," he said, looking up at them. "Sort of cute, aren't they?"

Elspeth blew her top. "Mack Fraser," she began with a full head of steam, "if you think for one moment that I'm going to go to—"

"Relax, my iron virgin," he told her with insulting blandness. "You can sleep on the couch if you elect to spurn the charms of my company. In view of the possibility of your snoring, it might be better that way all around."

"Oooh!" sputtered Elspeth, for once in her life utterly unable to find verbal expression. Mack contented himself with lying back in the big chair and turning on his most evil leer. He was too evidently enjoying her discomfiture.

All at once overcome with fatigue, to which were added the emotional and nervous and intellectual strains of the past five days, Elspeth collapsed on the carpet and burst into tears. She was dimly conscious of Mack, swearing but concerned, rising quickly to his feet and hurrying over to comfort her. As her sobs subsided Elspeth knew that the explosion had eased the tension within her. She also knew that her head felt stuffy and that her nose was red.

"Cut it out, Elly," Mack said helplessly, bending over to put his hands under her arms. "Please don't cry." He pulled her easily to her feet, hugged her to him briefly, then released her with an awkward pat on the shoulder. "I was only fooling. Elly—honest I was—except about the fact that this *is* the only decent room in the city."

"D-decent isn't exactly the word, is it?" she replied, sniffling. "Mack what are we going to *do?*" She felt a sudden intense desire to be dead. Now Mack would really have something on her. He fumbled in his hip pocket, emerged with a rumpled handkerchief, thrust it under her nose.

"Blow!" he told her firmly. Then, when she had complied, "Cheer up, it's not as bad as all that. Get into a robe and take a bath and you'll feel better. I'll take a trip downstairs and see if I can't pick up some books or something that will give us some idea of what we're up against in this screwball world. When you get through with your bath I'll take one. Then let's settle down to do some boning. And for God's sake don't worry about *me*. I'll sleep on the couch. I was going to anyway."

"Oh, Mack, you're so good and I'm so simply stinking," she heard herself say with considerable surprise. She stifled another impulse to sniffle and even achieved a watery smile. "All right, Mack," she said meekly. "I'll take a bath."

"That's more like it, Elly," he told her, reclaiming his handkerchief and stuffing it into his pocket as he moved toward the door. When he reached it he turned and added over his shoulder. "You won't be stinking after you bathe."

"You star-faced mole!" she snapped at him. He was grinning like a hateful ape as he closed the door behind him.

After a brief moment of defiant hesitation, Elspeth took his advice and got hurriedly out of her grimy dress and underthings. Once in the tub, an immense gleaming sunken affair, she felt the warm water wash away her travel dirt and most of the tensions within her, leaving her in a comfortable glow of fatigue. When she emerged Mack was already back from his foray downstairs. He waved a hand toward a wheeled cellarette adorned with bottles, ice and glasses.

"Help yourself," he told her. "It's on Mr. Horelle. And while I'm washing the rings out of the tub you might look these over. We've got to do a lot of homework in a hurry." He nodded in the direction of a fair-sized stack of books and periodicals which lay piled up on a straight chair near the door.

By the time Mack had bathed and rejoined her—looking unexpectedly scrubbed and little-boyish in a worn green-and-white flannel robe—Elspeth was already deep in concentration upon a brief popular history of Columbia that Mack had managed to purchase in the lobby. Her drink, barely sipped, stood forgotten at her elbow. Mack had to give her a couple of shakes before she became aware of him.

"Hey!" he cried. "Learned anything yet?"

"Oh!" She looked at him blankly for a moment before awareness returned to her. "Only that we have a ghastly amount to learn," she said. She made a vague gesture toward the other reading material he had assembled. "You might see what you can get out of those. I'll give you a précis of this as soon as I'm finished. It's the same world as ours up to eighteen fourteen."

"Then old Horelle wasn't kidding us," said Mack. He picked up the other books and magazines and settled himself in a chair. He seemed, Elspeth thought, to have become at least temporarily adjusted to the fact of their being on an alien Earth. It had taken concrete evidence to do the trick. Mack was not one to let a mere theory convince him.

Elspeth again lost herself in the history book. The differences in the past—and therefore in the present—were fascinating. The jump-off point appeared to be a Burr-Wilkinson conspiracy, which had been renewed in 1814 with belated but overwhelming success. In return for pulling the fledgling United States out of the war with England, the conspirators had, abetted by Spaniards and Creoles and New Englanders, managed to overthrow the Madison regime following Admiral Cockburn's burning of Washington, D.C., had quickly made peace with England

and founded the Columbian Republic.

In Europe the battle of Waterloo had come and gone while Burr and Wilkinson—entitled Founding Fathers in this book—organized their new nation along the hierarchal lines of the ancient Republic of Venice. In Columbia the franchise was limited to the property-owning few, slavery was permitted, and public office was unofficially but actually a matter of inheritance and appointment rather than popular election. Wilkinsons, Alstons, and the like were names repeated in prominent posts, generation after generation.

New Orleans was selected for the new capital—since the Columbian Republic's attention was focused upon the South and Latin America rather than on Europe. One of the conditions under which Great Britain had favored the great conspiracy was that its leaders, once in office, use every influence in their power to assist the breakup of the Spanish Empire in South and Central America and the Caribbean. However, it seemed doubtful to Elspeth that the method of accomplishment was one the British had expected or liked.

By 1820 both Mexico and all of South America, with the exception of Brazil, had been ripe for revolt—largely incited by Columbian money, arms, and pledged support. Swift frigates of the Columbian Navy, under the command of Commodore Stephen Decatur, had raided St. Helena, flying the rebel Mexican flag, had successfully salvaged Napoleon and sailed with him to New Orleans.

When the British government became aware of this coup the ex-Emperor of the French was already ensconced on a throne in the Viceroy's palace in Chapultepec, and all of the Americas below the Rio Grande were up in arms. Thanks to Austrian and Russian aid in Europe, the more-or-less United Americas had been able to beat off the combined British, French, and Spanish efforts to regain the lost territory.

The British had captured Boston and burned it, and the Columbians had retaliated by seizing both Montreal and Quebec—cities which were returned to their original owners when peace finally was signed in 1826. The Mexican Empire was firmly established as far south as the Isthmus of Panama. South America was divided up into one kingdom, Brazil, and the republics of Venezuela, Peru, and Patagonia. These divisions still remained, largely unaltered.

Columbia and Mexico, the latter under the rule of the erstwhile Duke of Reichstadt, had gone to war briefly in 1841 over the disputed territory of Texas, with the Columbians winning handily, thanks largely to the genius of Generals Pillow and Quitman. In 1850 the Russians, discovering gold close to their California settlement, had attempted to enlarge their holdings there by conquest. Mexico and Columbia, along with the British in Canada, had quickly joined forces to drive the minions of the Czar from the Western Hemisphere and had divvied up the territory among themselves.

Then had come peace until 1869, when the northeastern states, resentful of their waning importance in the Republic, made an effort to secede. The contest lasted five years and all but finished Columbia. But the South, the Midwest—tied to the South by the Mississippi waterway and the nearness of New Orleans—and the Far West had ultimately been able to prevail against the ten rebellious states—including New England, New York, New Jersey, Pennsylvania, and Ohio—following the decisive battle of Elmira.

Thoroughly crushed, the Northeast still played a secondary role in the nation's affairs, was famed for its summer resorts and its down-at-heel lost-causism rather than for its heavy industry. Columbia and Mexico had sent a combined expeditionary force to Europe in order to abet France in the first war of the West against the union of Turko-Austro-Prussian forces, which threatened to overrun the continent at the beginning of the present century. Abetted by Russia, the Allies had finally been victorious in 1906.

The second great East-West war had been against Russia, whose Czar had sought to destroy the Ottoman Empire and gain a Mediterranean Sea outlet. But the rest of Europe had united against him and driven the Russians back behind the Vistula. Since then the world had been living in uneasy peace.

Internal troubles in Columbia were serious, Elspeth discovered, despite the legitimist tone of the book she was reading. This although the slavery problem had finally settled itself. Compelled by world opinion to enforce humanistic legislation upon slaveowners, the Republic had discovered slavery to be economically impossible.

More and more slaves were manumitted to save their owners from bankruptcy as their support grew more expensive than the paying of salaries to unindentured workers. When at last the institution was abolished in 1901, passage of the bill that freed the few remaining slaves had been a mere formality.

There was virtually no color line save among the few oligarchical families that actually held tightly the reins of power. Freed slaves for more than a century had been winning high places in government, business, the arts and society; had proved to be invaluable citizens and producers.

But Columbia, thanks to its history and form of government, was too limited a Republic to endure without constant internal turmoil. And turmoil it now had in the form of Reed Weston, a one-time highly successful industrial inventor who had turned to bite the hand that fed him—or so the book implied.

Seeking to read between the lines, Elspeth thought she detected a profit motive in the revolt. Evidently invention and scientific progress—at least in so far as their practical applications went—were strictly limited by the oligarchy. This, she decided, would account for the poorly paved highways, the few cars, the absence of heavier-than-air craft—as well as the amazing weapons of the soldiers they had seen. The rulers of Columbia were not permitting the enrichment of their masses through large-scale cheap production of consumer goods—if it were possible in this culture. On the other hand, they were seeing to it that the military, their defenders, were equipped with the very best in weapons and transportation.

Apparently this state of affairs was more than Reed Weston could endure. He had, while high in the government, attempted to push through legislation that would widen the scope of unlimited private enterprise. He had acquired a considerable following, not only in the still-underdeveloped Northeast but in the very heart of the Republic itself.

When irrevocable Presidential veto finally blocked his efforts, Reed Weston had, the book said, basely resisted arrest and fled, first to the Black Hills of South Dakota, then to Missouri, where his legions of supporters had slowly and secretly gathered around him and had formed some sort of organization.

With a strong irregular army, he had moved south to the Ozarks, becoming thus an open threat to New Orleans itself. He insisted that President Wilkinson either withdraw his veto or resign and permit the unthinkable—an election open to every man in Columbia, whether he owned property or not. This, the book insisted, was nothing less than anarchy.

There was no mention made of the impending trouble with Mexico, but Mack, in his reading, had found plenty of material on that subject. After listening to Elspeth's summary he told her what he had learned about it.

"It's another grab like Texas," he said. "Southern California is the target this time. A lot of Columbians have settled there, and Wilkinson and his gang are screaming persecution. My hunch is that Wilkinson and this black marshal of his are planning to kill two birds with one stone. They'll heat up the country for a war with Mexico and come up with Southern California for a reward. And if this Weston doesn't give himself up they'll be able to pin a traitor tag on him and make it stick. Frankly, I wouldn't like to be in his shoes."

"That's our job, isn't it?" said Elspeth. "To get him a new pair of shoes?"

"Yeah," said Mack, stretching and yawning. "But I don't see why we have to go all the way to New Orleans. It seems to me we ought to be able to contact him a lot quicker from here."

"This is the summer capital," Elspeth told him, "the play city for Wilkinson and his friends. I'll lay odds it's too tightly guarded and screened. It certainly is beautiful."

"Yeah," said Mack with another yawn. "Let's turn in."

Although it was late when they got to sleep, Elspeth was awakened early the following morning. Beneath her window the dawn stillness was shattered by men shouting and the sounds of running feet. She got up and went out on the balcony and looked down, tying the belt of her blue silk robe as she did so and pushing the hair back out of her eyes. Below, through the green palm fronds, she saw a pair of soldiers in lavender uniforms chasing a civilian, who was fleeing desperately along the broad sidewalk.

"Stop, you bastard!" shouted one of the soldiers, raising an oddly designed weapon to his shoulder. When the fugitive failed to halt, the soldier pressed a trigger. There was a back flash over his shoulder, a ripple of heat in front of the flaring muzzle.

Where the running man had been there was nothing—nothing but, for a single flickering instant, an impression of still-running disembodied shoes. Then they, too, were gone.

The other soldier, apparently a noncommissioned officer, looked angrily at the firer, then carefully examined the spot on the sidewalk where the running man had vanished. He scuffed at a faint brown stain on the cement, then said, his voice tight with fury, "What's the idea of burning him here? You know how the lieutenant is about marking up these sidewalks. He'll have us—What in hell are you looking at?"

He turned quickly, followed the soldier's pointing finger—which was upthrust directly toward Elspeth on the balcony.

V

Involuntarily Elspeth drew back behind the shelter of the palm. But there could be no doubt about the purpose of the soldiers beneath. Suddenly terrified, she sought to peer down at them through the spear-shaped fronds of the tree, saw the one with the strange weapon raising its flared muzzle toward the balcony.

At that moment, mercifully, an officer appeared and moved swiftly to strike down the disintegrator—if that was its title—before it could be used again. He slapped the soldier sharply and cursed him in low but violent tones. The man achieved a ragged salute, pointed a finger up at the balcony.

"I'm sorry, sir," he said, "but that woman up there—she saw us use the dis—"

"You goddamned idiot!" the officer exclaimed. "This is going to raise all kinds of a stink. I gave you men strict orders not to use your . . ."

She lost the rest of it as the fronds rustled in a sudden breeze. Nonetheless, without understanding the issues involved, she felt a distinct impression of having witnessed something unpardonable; further, that steps were going to be taken directly to ensure her silence. Terrified, she ducked back into the big room, where a sleepy-looking Mack was sitting up, rubbing his eyes.

"What in hell's going on?" he asked her, yawning. "What was all that shouting outside?"

She told him as rapidly as she could. She had barely concluded when the speaking tube at the head of the huge four-poster whistled a summons. Mack regarded her for a moment with raised eyebrows, then got up off the couch to answer it.

He gave terse uncommunicative responses to his unseen collocutor, then let the mouthpiece slip back into its hole and ran his fingers through his hair. "That was the desk," he told her, frowning. "You seem to have got us into one sweet mess. A Captain Logan is waiting for you downstairs. He said something about its being a routine formality, but I don't like the sound of it. I don't like any of this setup."

"But, Mack, *I* haven't done anything!" Elspeth protested. A rising anger was beginning to submerge her fear.

Mack lit a cigarette and tossed the pack to her as she sank onto the edge of the bed. He shook his head and said thoughtfully, "They're giving us just fifteen minutes to get dressed and downstairs. I'm for getting out of here in five. So get hopping. If we do report they will probably tie us up for days—or longer."

"But if they're waiting for us in the lobby," said Elspeth anxiously, "how are we going to avoid them?"

"I'm trying to figure out a way right now," Mack told her quickly. "For God's sake get into your things. And don't go prudish on me now. We haven't time for it."

"Don't be a furry weasel," snapped Elspeth, gathering the shreds of her ego about her as she darted for the bathroom. By the time she emerged, four minutes later, Mack was already dressed after a fashion and in the act of closing her suitcase.

"But we haven't a chance," she told him. "Mack, you haven't seen this—this thing of theirs in action."

"We took on a job, didn't we?" countered Mack, poking a protruding corner of nightgown out of sight under the edge of her bag without regard for wrinkles. "Hell, we took Horelle's money, didn't we? We promised to make our contact in New Orleans today, didn't we? Come on—get moving."

He handed her one of the bags and then drew from his jacket pocket a flat deadly looking automatic pistol whose presence amid his gear Elspeth had not hitherto suspected. He caught her look of surprise, muttered, "It's a good thing I brought it along," and opened the hall door cautiously.

Evidently it was against Bienville House regulations to have soldiery openly patrolling the upstairs corridors, for their exit was unguarded. But as they reached the elevator bank Mack uttered an *"Oh-oh!"* and yanked her swiftly past and into the shelter of the stairwell just beyond.

They were barely out of sight when the lift light went yellow, showing an upcoming car, and a heavy metal grille clicked open. A pair of erect young men in well-cut civilian clothes moved away from them toward the room they had just left, walking in perfect purposeful step and in well-briefed silence.

"Do you suppose they're after us?" said Elspeth anxiously.

Mack nodded grimly. "No supposing about it," he said and then his eyes lighted up with inspiration. "Come *on,* Elly. I think I have an out." He moved swiftly and silently as an Indian down the wide marble stairs. Elspeth, following less silently, wished her bag were not quite so heavy.

"Stick right in back of me and keep your big mouth shut," he commanded when they reached the floor below. He peered out at the corridor and whispered, "I got a glimpse of this layout last night when we came in. If I'm right—and I'll lay odds that I am—we may get out of this yet."

He moved rapidly toward a door directly across from the elevators and knocked on it swiftly. Elspeth found herself admiring his ability to make instant plans and decisions, as well as to act on them in an emergency. At the same time she disliked herself for her admiration. After all, Mack was really nothing more than a well-trained male animal who could manipulate competently the trickeries of camera focusing. But could he write a sonnet or compose an original philosophic concept that would hold water? Could he paint a picture worth looking at or sculpt a passable statue? Could he compose a . . .

"For God's sake, snap out of it, Elly!" Mack's whisper was like a whip. "Of all times to go dreaming off into a—" It was his turn to snap out of it as, at that moment, one of the big double doors at which he had knocked was opened a few inches. Without hesitation Mack pushed himself aggressively inside, holding his pistol in front of him. With a jerk of the head, he motioned Elspeth to follow him and close the door after her. She did so numbly, mechanically parked her bag carefully alongside his just inside the doorway.

Only then did she look up—and gasp. To her utter surprise and consternation, the towering figure of Marshal Henry was facing them, clad only in pongee underwear. His impressively handsome black face gathered into a thunderous scowl as he slowly lifted his hands above his white head.

"Sorry to use these tactics, Marshal," said Mack with what was for him unusual politeness. "My young lady here had the bad luck to see some of your trained seals use a disintegrator or something on a fugitive in front of the hotel just now. They want to detain us and we haven't the time."

There was a long and, for Elspeth, a difficult pause as the enormity of Mack's plan became apparent to her. The huge Columbian chief of staff scowled intently at a side wall, seemed to have considerable difficulty in refocusing his attention on the photographer and the pistol he was holding.

"A disintegrator, you say—in front of the hotel?" He looked hard at Elspeth, then added, "Tell me what you saw."

She did so as briefly as she could, and when she had finished Marshal Henry nodded slowly and said, "You seem to have been exceedingly unfortunate, young lady. The disintegrator is an outlaw weapon." Then, to Mack, "But, young man, just how do you think your forcible entry here at gunpoint is going to get you out of your difficulties?"

"You're going to do that for us, Marshal," the photographer told him coolly. "You're going to see us safely out of this hotel to our car. So be a good chief of staff and pop into a pair of pants, won't you? I took a gamble on the boys downstairs calling your plain-clothes guards away to nab us and it paid off. But they're bound to be back in a matter of minutes. So may I suggest you hurry?" His words were polite, but there was no doubting the determination behind them.

Marshal Henry regarded Mack for another long moment, then permitted himself the faintest of smiles and moved with dignity toward a dressing chamber whose door stood open at the far side of the room. Mack moved right behind him, keeping him covered, very much on the alert for concealed weapons. But nothing untoward happened as the Columbian chief of staff donned a magnificent blue-and-silver uniform on whose chest a vast number of gay campaign and decoration ribbons glittered.

"I hope you don't expect to get away with this, young man," said the marshal, pausing as he reached the door. "I admire your nerve, but you're bound to be caught."

"Not necessarily, Marshal," said the photographer. "Shall we go?" He slipped the pistol out of sight in his pocket but held it so that it bore on the immensely tall chief of staff at all times. They rode down in the elevator without words, to the evident puzzlement of the operator.

Downstairs there was surprisingly little difficulty. The soldiery assembled in the lobby, including a quarter of young officers, were evidently too overwhelmed by the sponsorship of their chief of staff to put any overt obstacles in their path. But as they approached the outer door these men in uniform fell in silently behind and began to follow them.

"Tell them to get back and stay back," Mack whispered to the Negro marshal.

"Report to barracks for a weapons check," the huge marshal told them with the full voice of his authority. There was no need for further commands until they reached the garage in back of the hotel, where Mack told the attendant to get out the Pipit for them. The chief of staff regarded their newly washed vehicle with thoughtful speculation.

"I'm afraid you'll never make it," he told them quietly. "I shall have to summon a hue and cry immediately if only to save my own reputation."

"In that case," said Mack sarcastically, "perhaps you'd better come along with us."

Marshal Henry unexpectedly put back his magnificent head and laughed aloud. Then he said, "My dear old chap, then there would certainly be twice as big a pursuit. No, you'll have to take your chances. I may see you sooner than you think."

His teeth flashed a brilliant white salute, and Elspeth, already seated in the Pipit, wondered what his though could be. He continued to stand there, grinning at them with some vast inner amusement, as Mack scrambled into the driver's seat and got the motor going. They started and the Pipit's tires cut gravel on the court between garage and hotel.

"Mack, what are we going to do when—" Elspeth began, then gasped in quick panic as a file of lavender uniforms appeared no more than sixty yards in front of them. They carried flare-mouthed weapons that looked to Elspeth exactly like the disintegrator whose effects she had already witnessed.

"This!" said Mack as he gave a yank at the knob on the dashboard which released the Pipit's wings. "It's no time to hold anything back, Horelle's orders "notwithstanding."

Even as he spoke the Pipit's wings, hitherto on this strange world slotted neatly inside the top, slid rapidly out and into flight position. When he felt their tug the photographer pressed the superdrive button and the sturdy little English vehicle seemed actually to leap ahead with a new freedom. Its wheels left the gravel and automatically the engine pan dropped slightly to become a jet vent.

The bewildered soldiery were well behind and beneath before any of them could manage to open fire. Within a few tens of seconds the entire city of Baton Rouge lay a full mile below and seven or eight miles to the north of them. Its palaces and hotels and boulevards and gardens flattened out in magic geometry along the lazy curves of the great yellow river.

"How are we going to make contact?" Elspeth asked nervously. She was beginning to feel the emotional aftereffect of what they had just gone through. "Surely they must have some means of rapid communication—I saw what looked like a telegraph booth in Atlanta. And isn't someone bound to spot us between here and New Orleans?"

"Well, since we've been forced to show our hand—or rather the Pipit's wings—early, we'll have time for a diversion," Mack replied slowly, thinking his way. "We should be able to locate the arteries around New Orleans from the air and then come in by road from some unexpected direction. I don't see why we won't be able to make contact."

He paused, shook his head, added, "I wonder why that disintegrator, or whatever it was you saw, seems to get everybody so steamed up."

"Did you notice that it bothered the marshal, too?" Elspeth asked him.

Mack merely nodded and lifted the Pipit above a fortuitous cloud bank directly in their path. "It bothered him, all right," he said. "And it bothered the men you saw using it—*and* their officers. Come to think of it, our black friend did say it was outlawed. It certainly sounds deadly enough."

"It was horrible," said Elspeth, shivering. Through gaps in the clouds as they sped southward she could see the intensive development of the Lower Mississippi in this strange Republic of Columbia. From Baton Rouge to the capital itself the population was evidently very dense. It was almost built up into one huge city, with virtually no open country along the riverbanks.

They flew on, high and all but silent, above New Orleans and noted its immense sprawling expanse. Clouds sheltered them at frequent intervals, but Mack expressed little fear of being spotted in a world unused to heavier-than-air craft. He went on past New Orleans to the south. Elspeth, still suffering from reaction to the events of the early morning, relaxed uneasily and lost herself in contemplation of the cotton puffs of cloud beneath them and the birdlike shadows they cast on the checkerboard of earth still further below.

There was heavy ocean travel throughout the Delta channels and on the Gulf beyond. The smaller vessels were apparently steam-driven, but the more imposing ones, like the train and trucks they had seen the day before, were double-hulled rocket affairs that seemed to cover the waves at extremely high speeds.

"Funny they can't fly," mused Mack. "They've got plenty of other up-to-date gadgets in this world."

"Perhaps they aren't allowed to," said Elspeth a trifle vaguely. Then, "Mack, I'm hungry. We haven't eaten a real meal since yesterday noon. Where are you bringing us down?"

"North of Pontchartrain," said the photographer. "There seems to be some open country up that way with a number of little-used roads. We ought to be able to sneak into the city all right."

Either through planning or luck they made it successfully. They paused for luncheon at an old Creole estate in the suburbs given over to a restaurant, and for once were spared the routine fried-chicken-and-grits-and-biscuits of "orthodox" Southern cooking. Oysters in red-hot but delicately flavored sauce, red snapper papillon, jambalaya, fresh green salad, a sound red wine and the atmosphere of a vine-hung iron-balconied courtyard made Elspeth sigh her appreciation over sherbet and café-royales.

"I am ruint," she told Mack happily, "but it's worth it."

"Me too," he replied, rubbing his stomach. But he looked at his wrist watch and frowned. "We've got to get ourselves parked in the Hotel St. Louis before dinnertime and we're still a long way out of town. Come on—let's get going."

"You ought to be burped," said Elspeth, annoyed at the intrusion of practicality upon her satiation. They paid an unexpectedly modest check for their repast and took off again in the Pipit, once more restored to its road-running role.

Fortunately they were able to find a garage within a couple of blocks of the rear of the hotel, which faced a walled-off Canal Street. After leaving the Pipit there they walked slowly, in the hot afternoon, toward their appointed destination. Mack kept up a constant grumbling at having to carry both bags.

"Hey—what's this?" inquired the photographer when a door in the wall that barred off Canal Street opened for them as if by magic.

"Must be an electric eye or something," said Elspeth, glad that for once she had come up with a practical answer. Mack grunted unintelligibly and followed her on through, bumped into her as she stopped dead on its other side, then himself froze in equal astonishment.

"What the—" he exclaimed. The question was purely rhetorical. It was evident now why the city's chief thoroughfare was barred to motor traffic. It was an immense moving boulevard, arranged in eight lanes, four moving in each direction. The two central lanes on either side were considerably faster than those on the borders, and there was a stationary strip in the center, designed for passengers who wished to change direction.

"Doesn't look so wonderful once you've seen it," said Mack at last, turning away. Elspeth said nothing, for once her first moment of rapture had passed at seeing such a fantastic human dream fulfilled she was forced to agree with him.

The moving road extended for several miles, its sections separated by main crossroads. Far inland, beyond a number of vehicular overpasses, could be seen the lofty neoclassic dome of a huge white building, which Elspeth judged to be the Capitol of Columbia. At the river end of the moving boulevard rose another dome atop a complex arrangement of marble arches. This, she thought, must be some sort of memorial.

Despite its sweep and vastness of concept, the moving boulevard was disappointing. Like virtually every other public project Elspeth had seen since entering this world, it appeared dingy and ill-tended. One of the fast central lanes was working faultily as it rumbled past, and noisily protested its ill-health.

She wondered how often there were breakdowns, decided that she was thinking like Mack, and resented his influence. But she followed him dutifully along one of the slow outer lanes to the Hotel St. Louis, another ornately balconied structure with a high, almost cool lobby. The photographer went directly to the desk and asked a foppish octoroon assistant manager if there were a reservation and any message for Mr. Horelle. This was according to instructions.

The manager handed Mack a note and summoned a bellboy for their baggage without putting them through the routine of signing the register. Mack grinned mockingly at her in the creaky elevator. "Don't blame me if *you* have to sleep on the couch tonight," he said. "If there *is* a couch. Horelle arranged this."

"I could spit," she replied. But to Mack's loudly expressed disappointment they were ushered into a suite of five rooms—a drawing room, two bedrooms, two baths. It was roomier but not so lush as the single chamber they had shared in Baton Rouge.

The first thing Elspeth did was brush her teeth with the effective powder that seemed to be standard equipment in all hotel bedrooms. Columbia, she decided, was a land of contradictions—of recent slavery, of feudal customs, of no aircraft—but also of applied rocket power, miracle toothpowder and disintegrator guns—to say nothing of moving streets.

" 'Hail Columbia, Happy land,' " she sang as she struggled with her hair and wondered when, if ever, she would manage a decent wave. She discovered herself out of cigarettes and wandered into the drawing room, where Mack was reading one of the books he had purchased in the Bienville House the night before.

"Help yourself," he said, waving hospitably at a pack beside him. "Incidentally, I ordered some drinks sent up. Thought we could use them."

"Is that all we have to do now?" she asked him.

"The word is to sit tight here until Weston's mob makes contact," he told her. "It seems the government is making things hot for them just now."

"Do tell!" she replied, slightly annoyed at his lack of courtliness. There was something just a trifle *too* casual, *too* intimate, about his lack of manners. It was almost as though they were . . .

The arrival of the man with the drinks cut short that perilous line of thinking—for which she was moderately grateful. Elspeth mixed herself a highball and, while the photographer did his own honors, studied him covertly.

Certainly propinquity had failed to improve his somewhat battered features. His nose was as far off center, his eyelids as laden with scar tissue. But even so, she thought, he might be passable—even his voice—if he weren't so damnably materialistic-minded. Which of course put him beyond the pale.

She tried to forget the fact that he had extricated her at great risk to himself from a highly combustible situation that morning in Baton Rouge. Then she caught him looking at *her* and felt herself blush and turned quickly away. A shrill piping sound from somewhere outside caught her attention.

It grew slowly louder, reminding her of scores of fire sirens stuck on one very high note. She moved instinctively toward the balcony. But Mack, rising quickly, caught her roughly by the arm and said, "Careful. Remember what happened this morning."

"It's not likely to happen here," she replied, almost shouting to make herself heard above the crescendo of high sound that now seemed right in the room with them. Freeing herself forcibly, she went to the balcony and stepped out upon it.

There was an armored motorcade approaching on one of the fast lanes that moved toward the Capitol. It was made up of small rocket cars, then trucks, then big self-propelled weapons. In its center was a large gleaming rocket car, and standing proudly erect within it was a tall military figure, magnificent in blue and silver, bowing and saluting the crowd assembled on either side of the moving boulevard. As he drew nearer Elspeth saw that it was Marshal Henry and that the crowd was cheering him madly.

Mack grasped both her shoulders to draw her quickly out of sight, but not before the field marshal came abreast of their balcony. As he did so his distinguished face lifted and his teeth gleamed white in a smile while he lifted his plumed kepi in a direct and unmistakable salute.

"He *saw* us!" gasped Elspeth when they were again inside the drawing room. "Mack, we've got to get out of here. I'm scared."

"It's worse than that," said Mack, kicking gloomily at the carpet. "The big bastard knew we were here. He didn't look up by accident. We're sitting ducks."

Both of them jumped, for at that moment there was a sharp rap on the corridor door.

VI

They stared at one another through a brief but pregnant moment of silence. Then Mack motioned Elspeth imperatively toward her bedroom, crossed swiftly to his own bedroom on the opposite side of the drawing room. The knock was repeated sharply twice as he emerged almost running and released the safety catch on his pistol while in motion. He held it ready and stood well back from the corridor door when he opened it.

A tall angular young man, scarecrow-lean and with a sallow face that seemed impervious to the hot Louisiana sun, came in and then stopped short at sight of Mack and his automatic. His light blue eyes flashed panic signals and he turned nervously to Elspeth, who stood in her bedroom doorway, watching. Then he turned back to the photographer with a helpless gesture. He laughed uneasily, stroked a thin mustache that outlined his upper lip.

"Really!" he exclaimed, and his accent sounded more British than that of any Britisher Elspeth had ever heard. "*Really*, old man, take it easy. I'm van Hooten. I'm here to direct you to Reed Weston."

Elspeth dusted off a smile of greeting and broke it out for their visitor—but Mack motioned her back with his left hand before she could take two steps toward him. Keeping the newcomer carefully covered, the photographer peered quickly out into the hall, satisfied himself that van Hooten was alone, then slammed the door shut and bolted it. He studied their Anglicized invader with narrow appraisal and said, "Haven't you forgotten something—van Hooten?"

"Eh? What's that you say? Forgotten something? Surely

you're spoofing." Van Hooten spoke with crisp uncertainty and again achieved a laugh. His height matched that of the photographer almost exactly, but his build was so much slighter and his posture so much more erect that he seemed a far taller man.

"I'm waiting," Mack said ominously. Elspeth felt her stomach muscles tighten in sympathy as the photographer pushed his pistol closer to the abdomen of the intruder.

A spark of sudden enlightenment glowed in van Hooten's pale blue eyes. "Oh of course!" he exclaimed. "How utterly stupid of me! Wilkinson, isn't it?"

"You don't sound exactly sure of it," said Mack. But he appeared satisfied. At any rate, he slipped the automatic into the waistband of his slacks and extended his right hand in greeting, adding, "We've not been waiting for you very long. Thank God you're prompt."

"Prompt—*haw!*" exploded van Hooten, eying Elspeth with overt curiosity. Then, to both of them, "As a matter of fact, I'm bloody damn early. Just fool's luck, my catching you here a bit ahead of the game. There's the very devil to pay just now. Raids, tipoffs, a regular housecleaning."

"In that case we'd better get out of here as fast as possible," said Mack thoughtfully. He was studying van Hooten, and seemed to be having considerable difficulty in assessing him. He took a cigarette himself, tossed the pack to Elspeth, accepted the flame of van Hooten's expensive-looking gold lighter. He said, "We had a bit of trouble ourselves in Baton Rouge this morning."

"Bit of a muck, eh? Heard about it," said their eccentric contact. "It's all over the place. Must have been a delightful rumpus, trapping the dear old marshal in his scanties." He turned to Elspeth and said directly, "You may call me Everard, my dear."

"And you," said Elspeth, who had no desire to be stampeded even into enmity by this orchidaceous creature, "may call me Miss Marriner—a privilege I permit only my most *intimate* friends."

"Haw-*haw!*" exploded Everard, but his eyes were like ice. *"Very* amusing indeed, my dear."

"If you two will stop clowning for just a moment," said Mack with a Job-ish expression, "we have good reason to believe Marshal Henry knows we are here. He lifted his cap to us just now when he went by in the parade."

"But it's the talk of the town," said van Hooten, dismissing the fact of their discovery with the graceful flick of a well-manicured hand. "Everyone in the know has been expecting you for days now."

"But Marshal Henry knows we are here in this hotel—in this suite," Mack said doggedly, bridling at the other's frivolity. "I think it's time to move on—and right away."

"But that simply can't *be!*" said Everard, who seemed to talk habitually in exclamation points. "I mean, it actually isn't possible that the marshal should have—"

He was interrupted sharply by another knock on the corridor door. Once again Mack moved swiftly to answer it, pistol ready in his hand. But this time it was only the room-service boy with the check for the drinks, which he had forgotten to bring with him on his earlier trip. Trying not to show his relief, Mack paid the check, tipped the boy, waved him on his way.

He turned on van Hooten, looking grim. "You know where Reed Weston is. Your job is to get us to him. *Do* it."

"As a matter of fact, it's not quite so simple as all that," said their appointed guide with an air of resentment. Then, with a shrug, "But I suppose we *had* better hop to it if we wish to get out of here. Your duffle all packed and puckered?"

Elspeth and Mack were ready to move on in a matter of minutes. Just before they braved the perils of corridor, lift, and lobby, Mack said, "I suppose they expect us to provide the transportation?"

"But, that's the teetotal idea!" exclaimed Everard, again looking shocked. "You have simply *no* idea of the appalling uproar you dear people caused at Baton Rouge this morning when you lifted your little old car right into the air—*brrrrrrrppppppp*—and under the very muzzles of the marshal's personal bodyguard! The wires have been really buzzing with it ever since."

"All right then," said Mack, who was becoming even more misanthropic than usual under the impact of Everard's highly effeminate effluvia. His lips were tight to invisibility as he led the way out of the hotel. Once more Elspeth found herself carrying her own suitcase. But Mack had to have one hand free on his pistol and she sensed that

Everard was scarcely the type to offer help with anything heavier than a lipstick container.

They emerged from the Hotel St. Louis and walked to the garage without hindrance or incident of any kind, much to Elspeth's surprise and relief. She consoled herself, as they crept at half speed over the unevenly paved streets in the faithful Pipit, with the thought that she was apparently not going to spend the night in a prison cell. But all the same, the luxury of the hotel and its concomitants of bath, good food, and comfortable bed made her regret their hurried departure.

Sitting on the front seat between the two men, she let her imagination rove over the possibility of a bit of verse anent the creature comforts so summarily abandoned. She gave it a working title of *Champagne and Suds* and decided it would be a simple little quatrain, a sort of lament, with none of the abstract frills and murky hidden meanings of free verse. It should rhyme tidily, she decided further, and consist of three quatrains with an unexpected little rhyme break in the middle of each line.

The beat—she experimented with a couplet—should be basically simple, even iambic, a meter she usually shunned like the plague. In more thoughtful compositions she could not abide that basis of doggerel—but then this was not really a thoughtful idea. It was not even much emotionally—just a fragment, a thought nonetheless universal for being so light.

She began to consider what things she missed most when she no longer had them. There was, of course, that dreadful thing of Kipling—in which "a woman is only a woman, but a good cigar is a smoke." Barely realizing she was doing it, she began to think about men and women—or, rather, about women and men.

The three quatrains became a sonnet, then three sestets, for the mood of her composition would never carry the stateliness of the fourteen-line form. And of course, the mood itself began to change on her. She could, she decided, get in a lick or two for her own sex. Perhaps. The word "perhaps" was in itself important. She considered ways and means, finally achieved

> . . . *a man, perhaps, although a sigh*
> *Is all collapse of each and all my loves*

Has left me. How much more dearly I
Prefer the myth that liquor dies with cloves
Or that my firm-fleshed skin will never dry
Nor my poor hands grow thin, force me to gloves.

It was complex and scarcely light any more, but it would do very nicely for the third sestet. She rather liked the aa-bb-cc of the inside rhyme scheme against the ab-ab-ab of the final syllables. But she was still left with only the caboose of her poem. She began to build her idea-structure laboriously back through a second sestet toward the first

She was rudely jolted out of her creative abstraction when Mack, without even a warning grunt, reached rudely across her to take a map which Everard van Hooten had pulled from his pocket. The Pipit was parked at one side of a broad palm-lined avenue on the southern outskirts of the great city and the afternoon sun was already well down in the western sky.

Mack muttered unintelligibly as he perused the map. His forehead corrugated in its familiar frown while he studied their course. Finally he looked up and said to van Hooten, "It takes us awfully close to the Rio Grande. How come? I thought Weston was supposed to be up in the Ozarks."

Van Hooten dismissed this with another of his patented graceful gestures. He said, buffing his nails assiduously on the flaring lapel of his jacket, "Oh, poor Mr. Weston has to keep moving his headquarters around." Then, dropping his too-British voice to a whisper. "Confidentially, he has arranged a secret meeting with an envoy of the Emperor. He's running himself ragged."

"Ummm," said Mack with what Elspeth decided was his usual garrulity. Then, after studying the map further, he handed it back to Everard. "All right if you say so. We'll give it a try anyway."

Said Everard, flashing his nervous grin, "Tell me, are you actually going to take this miracle bus of yours right up into the air—with all of us in it?"

"Once we're clear of the city and it gets a bit darker," Mack informed him. "Otherwise we'll be days on the road and probably get picked up by a Columbian patrol."

"*Good*ness!" exclaimed van Hooten, and Elspeth could

actually feel him shiver against her side. "This *is* a bit of a thrill, isn't it, old man?"

"Are you British, Everard?" Elspeth asked him.

He turned to regard her, his sallow countenance alight with joy. "But of course not—hardly!" He added, "And how utterly divine of you to have said so. I come from outside of Boston, you know, and in that region we value our British ancestry *most* highly."

Elspeth tried vainly to suppress a yawn that all but cracked the hinges of her jaw. The strain of the last week, the continued presence of danger all about them, had combined to induce in her a sudden and unfightable fatigue. She remarked, "If you two supermen don't mind too much, I'd like to curl up in the back seat for a nap."

"But of course—you poor dear!" said Everard, opening the door and getting out to make room for her to effect the transfer. Mack, barely turning his head, said, "Good idea, Elly. You may need it. I may want you to drive later while I nap myself."

She gave him one of her special Mack looks and scrambled gracelessly into the back of the Pipit. Mack got them under way almost at once, but Elspeth made herself reasonably comfortable on the broad seat cushion—and of course immediately ceased to be sleepy any more. She lay there, watching frequent palms and increasingly less frequent buildings flash by. She speculated on what was going to happen next.

Strange world or no, Everard simply didn't ring true. She discounted his blatant effeminacy, of course. But even so he seemed a most unlikely sort of secret agent to be operating for either the stalwart idealistic Reed Weston or the aristocratic Mr. Horelle. And his actions negated any idea that he might be working for the Columbian Republic.

His effeteness, she decided, could be traced back to the fact that he came from the inbred Northeast, whose best blood had been siphoned off in the cutters of a civil war almost a century earlier. But his loquacity made him a most unlikely selection for secret missions—unless, of course, he were far more clever than he seemed and employed his gush of asinine chatter as camouflage in preference to the gaunt secrecy of silence.

Mack, she knew from numerous small symptoms, was

also dissatisfied with Everard—but he was perforce accepting him as the sole presently available instrument of escape from the trap closing around them in New Orleans. And now Everard wanted to lead them almost to the border of Empire territory—along with the Pipit, an almost incredibly valuable piece of property in a world that knew no airplanes.

It was hot, and not even the speeding Pipit could stir a breeze in the hot late-afternoon air. While they were still on the ground Elspeth did manage to doze off, sweatily uncomfortable, into a series of unpleasant dreams in one of which an immense ebony field marshal with a disintegrator blasted Mack Fraser, who had a purple bee tattooed in back of his left ear.

She flung herself between them, but was just too late to save either of them. Her dust and Mack's and that of the orchidaceous one—suddenly no longer Mack—eddied and whirled and intermingled as it rose slowly into an orange twilight, and the ebony field marshal grew in height to match theirs and his teeth flashed like rows of mammoths' tusks as once more he aimed the dreadful flare muzzle of the disintegrator at them. This time it meant . . .

She awoke with a horrid start, and for a moment it seemed that her dream was reality. Then she realized that they were actually flying through the dusk with the sunset ahead and a trifle to starboard. She shook herself and shivered, for it was blessedly cool after the New Orleans swelter. Briefly, as the half awake will, she pondered the apparent reality of her dream.

She stretched and yawned and pushed back her hair. Then, fully awake, she fumbled for her handbag, found the Pipit's light switch and pressed it. She gasped at what her short nap had done to her already scrambled grooming.

"Turn off that light," snapped Mack. "We're too low."

She did so but not before she had again seen the purple bee. It was there—half hidden by the neat fringe of his haircut—behind Everard's left ear. She must have subconsciously noted it earlier and recalled it while asleep. A silly sort of adornment for such an exquisite as Everard to indulge in—but she supposed it was one of the absurd foibles the Everards of this and all other worlds delight in. She wondered why it had disturbed . . .

And then the alarm bells began to toll once more—

inside her head. She saw, as clearly as if she had an X-ray that could read whatever secret papers Everard carried, why he wore the purple-bee tattoo. She knew what he was and where he intended taking him.

They altered course then, causing the sun to shift further to starboard, and the tattoo vanished. Apparently it had to be seen from just the right angle—with the light coming from beneath and very flat. Otherwise, even with the shortest of haircuts, it would not be visible at all.

The bee—ageless symbol of the Napoleonic Empire—and purple, the Imperial color. She should, of course, have realized its implications at once—or at any rate in conjunction with van Hooten's unsuitability as an agent for either Weston or the Republic and his insistence upon taking them so close to the Border.

But in her world there was no Napoleonic Mexican Empire, and New England was not a drained-out defeatist area of small opportunity for a young man—if Everard actually qualified as a man. It was entirely understandable from a psychological viewpoint. Unable to endure the conditions of life in his home, unable to feel sympathy for the rude vigor of the Reed Weston revolt, he would have been drawn to the Empire as to a lodestone. And what more natural than that the Empire should put him to work as a secret agent?

Elspeth saw it as clearly as if Everard had told her—but what to do about it was something else again. If Everard were armed, as he probably was, he would take advantage of any diversion she might make and force them to fly to Mexico. Or he might have a disintegrator weapon himself. He would not use it on both of them, for they were the only persons in this world who could fly and, even more important, land the Pipit. But used against either one of them it would be tragic enough.

So Elspeth sat there and battled her suddenly galloping nerves and wondered what to do. In this she could not rely on Mack. Everard was far too sensitive not to see through at once any double talk she might make in an effort to warn the photographer. And Mack's sensitivities were by no means so acute.

They flew on toward the Southwest in the gathering dusk and Elspeth desperately sought a plan of action, for she was going to have to act both soon and effectively. She rummaged in her handbag in search of something that would do double duty as a weapon.

It held nothing. The pencil of rouge with which she tinted her lips was of too small a bore—especially since Everard had seen Mack's pistol—to bluff him. A hairpin would not unlock this puzzle. She lifted the bag to discard it in its uselessness.

Of course—the bag itself would do. It was a rectangular affair constructed about a frame of heavy metal with sharp corners. British-made, there was nothing flimsy about it. If she could manage to bring one of its corners down sharply on one of Everard's temples it ought at least to stun him briefly.

She eyed him tensely, gripping the bag tightly, seeking the exact moment and spot to strike. She would have but one real chance and that would have to be good. Chills were rising through her body like smoke rings from a Red Indian's signal fire.

Suddenly he flung an arm over the back of the seat and turned toward her, his face alight with excitement. "Isn't flying simply *too* tremendous?" he offered enthusiastically.

"It can grow very dull once you're accustomed to it," she replied and noted with some surprise that her voice was steady.

He uttered some further banalities, to which she managed to muster equally banal replies. She wondered when if ever he was going to turn around once more. At last she saw a cluster of lights ahead and asked him what city they were approaching.

"Jove!" he exclaimed. "That must be Dallas. See, Fort Worth lies just beyond. Dreadful sinkhole, that cowtown. It—"

Elspeth struck then, swiftly, hard, with a prayer in her heart. Her aim was true—the corner of the bag caught him just above and in front of his left ear as he leaned slightly forward, the better to see the view out the window beside and ahead of him.

There were a surprisingly light shock of contact and a dull *thock* as Elspeth's blow hit home. She had a horrid moment of choking fear in which it seemed as if she could not have struck hard enough to accomplish anything at all. Her panic endured while Everard continued to lean forward.

Then slowly his trunk began to slip. His knees hinged as his hams slid off the seat and he crumpled against the corner of the cabin, his head lolling drunkenly. A dark trickle began to crawl slowly from his left temple down toward his cheek-bone.

"What the hell!" said Mack, looking at Everard, then at Elspeth, who was crouched in the back, her handbag raised to strike again if necessary. His eyes popped as he saw her. Apparently he thought she was out of her mind.

"Turn on the autocon," she told him. "We've got to tie Everard up and search him. He's an Imperialist spy."

"You're crazy if you—" Mack began. Then his eyes narrowed and he pressed the automatic control switch and turned on the cabin light. The air was steady under the Pipit and she flew on toward Mexico. He dragged the unconscious Everard up onto the seat and, with Elspeth's aid, got him into the back and laid him out.

"That was quite a wallop you handed him," said the photographer unemotionally. "What makes you think he's a spy, Elly?"

She told him. Although she had to explain the significance of the bee, Mack did not laugh at her, somewhat to her surprise. Instead he regarded her gravely and said, "Thanks. I've been smelling something odd about Everard ever since he barged into the picture—and I don't mean his perfume."

"Mack!" said Elspeth with horror, "you don't suppose I—."

"You didn't kill him," said Mack, unperturbed. "Come on—before he comes to—let's see what he's got on him."

They found a flat little weapon, something like a pistol in shape but very different in detail if not in purpose. It was in a cleverly concealed holster built in where the watch pocket of his trousers should have been. Mack regarded it dubiously. "Of course it's not proof," he said. "Wonder what it does."

"Don't try it here," said Elspeth, practical for once. "It might burn a hole in the Pipit. Mack, he's coming to!"

She gasped this last as a surprisingly steady hand suddenly gripped her wrist and she found herself staring into a pair of malevolent ice-blue eyes whose viciousness went beyond anything in her previous experience.

VII

"Tell me—why did you hit me?" Everard van Hooten asked softly. His voice was still low and well modulated, but its pink-tea tones had been replaced by the malevolence that showed in his eyes. It had the softness of a snake's hiss.

"All right," said Elspeth frankly. "It was because I caught sight of the purple bee tattooed behind your ear." She struggled a little, seeking ineffectually to break Everard's grip on her wrist, added, "That meant you were directing us into an Imperialist trap."

For a long and painful moment the cold blue eyes continued to bore into hers. The unexpectedly powerful fingers continued to bruise the flesh of her wrist. She moaned a little, said, "Mack, he's hurting me! Make him let go."

"All right, van Hooten, cut it out," Mack commanded, and the pistol in his hand rose in preparation for a chopping blow. Everard caught the photographer's gesture out of the corner of an eye, permitted himself a slight shrug, then released Elspeth with a wry smile of resignation to his fate.

"Oh, very well then," he said with apparent good humor. "I'll try to be good. I shouldn't have lost my temper just then, but the young lady made me so *darned* mad."

"You aren't really mad at her," said Mack unexpectedly. "You're only mad at yourself for letting her knock you cold." His insight surprised her and she felt a sudden glow of pride in her recent achievement. But then she caught sight of the dark blood still trickling down the van Hooten temple and pride vanished before a desire to be sick. She had always loathed violence and physical force of all descriptions.

Everard gave vent to a dry little laugh. "I don't suppose that there's much sense in seeking to dupe you two charming people now," he said and mopped the blood from his temple with his sleeve kerchief. He regarded the resultant stain with evident distaste.

"You did very well up to a point," Elspeth told him with a degree of sympathy. "I suppose it was bad luck rather than any failure of yours that betrayed you. But the answer from now on is a resounding no."

"Oh, very well then," Everard repeated with a tone of resignation. He seemed to be still the exquisite if no longer so offensively so. He regarded them thoughtfully, added, "I shall now put my cards on the table. You may find my offer more interesting than you think."

"We might," said Mack, watching him carefully, "but the answer would still be no."

"Gad, one of those inflexible characters," sighed the fair Everard. "But I'll show you my cards, nonetheless. Yes, I work for the Mexican Emperor. We received word some days ago that Reed Weston was about to acquire something exceptional from the East. So of course when word of your remarkable escape from Baton Rouge reached New Orleans this morning, we knew that it was time to act."

"It seems to me that you would be more at home on Reed Weston's side of the fence in view of the situation between Columbia and the Empire," Mack said speculatively. Without taking his eyes from van Hooten, he handed Elspeth his automatic and added, "Keep him covered with this every minute, especially if he pretends to go to sleep, Elly. You can do better than I from the rear seat."

"Gracious!" exclaimed Everard. "Careful codgers, aren't you?" He again indulged in his inimitable shrug, then went on with, "However, I can't really say that I blame you. To return to our previous line of converse, Fraser, my affairs aren't quite that simple—nor are those of the Empire. Granted, our rulers have no intention of losing a war to the Columbian Republic. Still, we cannot find much to favor in Reed Weston and his rag-tag-and-bobtail anarchists and agitators.

"We would like to have Weston on our side in the coming struggle. In this way we could better manage to hold his ambitions within reasonable bounds. Then, too, he—or, rather, his group—has developed some weapons that might prove decisive if turned against Columbia.

"Naturally, since this flying machine of yours seems to be one of the things that is important to Weston, we decided it must be important to us. And frankly, dear people, after traveling in it I have no doubt at all that your Pipit—quaint name that—will not only win us any war Columbia may elect to wage but will probably prevent any such war from occurring."

"And it is your idea that we should stop this war by turning our Pipit over to the Empire—just like that?" said Elspeth thoughtfully.

"But of course," said van Hooten, apparently surprised at her question. "That's why I'm here."

"By the way," Mack asked him quietly, "just how did you manage to make contact with us so neatly?"

"Oh, really!" Everard's tone was patronizing. "We have our Empire cells, of course, planted within both factions north of the Border. Hence the obtaining of your itinerary and password and the preventing of Weston's agents from fulfillment of their assignments was scarcely a difficult matter to arrange. Actually, some of our agents in the Columbian service will receive decorations from President Wilkinson himself for their work in exposing Weston's spies."

"Well, you're certainly frank about it," said Elspeth, wondering whether she didn't actually prefer the false van Hooten she had unmasked to this cold-bloodedly efficient machine. "You wish us to work for a *pax Mexicana.*"

"Is it really so important?" Everard inquired with still another shrug. "It will be someone's peace, come what may. In the years ahead it will scarcely matter. And the Empire is in a position to reward you far more extensively for your services and that of the Pipit than any other faction involved."

He looked from one to the other and his eyes narrowed slightly. His voice acquired a flavor of honey as he added, "Money, of course—all you will ever want and more. And there are other possibilities only an Imperial regime can offer—say your choice of some of the finest estates in the Empire, assured position, a title. We pay well those who work in our service."

Elspeth, in spite of herself and to her considerable horror, was tempted. She had a sudden vision of what her life would be like as a great and noble and rich lady in a magnificent colonnaded white palace—say in the hills of Guatemala—surrounded by servants, by every conceivable luxury, by fertile lands whose harvests, sowed and reaped by human chattels, would provide for her in magnificence for life. The poetry she would have time to write under such conditions, the . . .

"By the way," said Mack with a notable lack of enthusaism. "How does it happen, van Hooten, that such a number of fine estates in the Empire should be without owners?"

Everard made a deprecatory gesture, followed by his shrug. "Oh, people die," he told them airily. "And of course those who die without issue or heir—well, occasionally their estates revert to the crown."

"I see," said Mack. Then, stubbornly, "But *how* do they die—and why?"

Everard's offhand casualness was visibly shaken by the photographer's line of questioning. But he said, "Naturally, even the Empire is not Utopia. However, neither of you will have a thing to worry about, not with your knowledge of this flying device—and doubtless of other things unknown to us."

"Oh, fine," said Mack sharply. "Great! Now tell me—where do we find Reed Weston?"

"And why should I know that?" countered van Hooten, openly laughing at the photographer.

"Because you knew how, where, and when to find us," said Mack. Elspeth, who was beginning to understand him better, sensed the terrible anger gathering within him and felt a sort of reluctant admiration stir within her. He was completely strong, so utterly incorruptible, so . . .

All at once she snapped out of it with a jar. "Mack!" she cried. "He's stringing us along—playing for time! We'll be over the Border before long and our fuel load won't last forever. Turn north, Mack! Turn north now."

Van Hooten proceeded to call Elspeth an unspeakable epithet with a venom that struck her almost like a physical blow. At this Mack made a quick motion as if to lay his fists on the Imperial agent where they would do the most good.

However, he managed to get control of himself instead, and wordlessly snapped off the autocon and took over the steering wheel himself, banking the Pipit in a sharp right turn. At this threat to the fulfillment of his mission Everard stirred rebelliously. Elspeth jabbed the muzzle of Mack's automatic hard against the back of his neck.

"Better sit still," she told him firmly. "Killing you would be a pleasure." Then, to Mack, "How about Fort Smith? We *know* that it's a Reed Weston base. Do you think we can make it on what we've got in the tanks?"

"Not a chance, Elly," he replied, shaking his head. "We'll have to hit earth somewhere and soon. Keep your eyes open for an unoccupied highway, will you?"

"Right," said the girl, wondering how she could do so and still keep dear Everard under control. But somehow she found herself able to manage.

They brought the Pipit down some forty minutes later on a deserted stretch of one-strip highway, somewhere between Fort Worth and a large town to the north—non-existent in Mack's and Elspeth's world—known as Wilkinson City. The fuel gauge already registered below zero and both of them were edgy.

Everard, on the contrary, seemed to have relaxed into a state of blissful content. He had spoken only briefly and politely from the moment Mack announced that they would have to hit the earth soon. In fact he had scarcely moved save to light, smoke, and discharge through the window an occasional gold-tipped monogrammed cigarette.

The Pipit was rolling uneasily up a long, very flat hill—an apparent rarity in the endless flatland around them—when a sudden bright glow above its top caused Elspeth to hope that they were approaching some sort of community in which they could purchase the fuel that would enable them to continue their air journey to Fort Smith.

But Mack, giving the wheel a sharp turn, suddenly turned the Pipit to the right and off the road, jouncing them right through a shallow ditch and part way across a lumpy field. At Elspeth's involuntary cry of protest he said, "Those lights are moving, Elly—and moving our way. For the love of Pete, watch Everard, will you?"

"I'm extremely comfortable, thank you," said van Hooten. The smile with which he accompanied the words—it was unmistakably present in his voice—was invisible as Mack cut the lights of the Pipit. He brought the sturdy little vehicle to a jerky halt.

He had scarcely done so when the first pair of headlights—they had a distinct yellow sodium glow that was, to Elspeth, oddly sinister—topped the crest of the gentle rise. As it came down the road, followed by other similar two-eyed monsters, it seemed to be moving straight down on the Pipit, jet exhausts flaming brilliantly in the darkness.

For one instant, despite her sharp awareness of Everard as a potentially deadly threat, Elspeth's attention was irresistibly attracted by the terrible yet majestic spectacle of the heavy military convoy as it sped along the highway and past them, no more than a hundred yards away.

The Columbian tanks and trucks and armored and supply vehicles and self-propelled rocket chargers moved with a hissing of powerful jets that drowned out the rumbling roar of their heavy wheels on the road. Evidently the caterpillar tread, like the airplane, was not a feature of the Columbian world. But the wheels which supported the vehicles were ugly, powerful and complex in construction.

In the glare of the sodium headlights and the lurid flare of the jet exhausts, the uniformed men, riding the trucks and ensconced atop the larger armored cars and tanks, looked literally like demons from some ghastly underworld. And the snouts of the weapons themselves, without exception pointing rearward, and tarpaulin-covered as protection against exhaust flares and dust, were as alien and deadly in appearance. The entire long convoy appeared unworldly—as indeed, Elspeth thought, it was.

"Goddammit, Elly, I told you to watch him!" Mack exploded suddenly and wrathfully. Elspeth, who had become utterly entranced by the eerie spectacle of the convoy, became aware with a sickening sense of guilt that Everard had vanished from the Pipit. The open door on his side of the little vehicle told its story all too plainly.

Quickly Elspeth slid into the seat vacated by the Imperialist agent and slammed and locked the door and closed its non-shatterable glass window, told Mack to do the same on his side. Thus they were reasonably safe from any counter-attack while waiting for the convoy to pass.

Mack muttered a full roll call of curses and derogatory remarks anent females in general and female poets in particular until Elspeth felt guilt give way to resentment. Then she asked him sharply why, if he were so alert, he hadn't given her warning of Everard's flight. Also, whether he still had the spy's pistol.

"The low-down degenerate so-and-so must have picked my pocket!" the photographer almost shouted when he discovered that the strange little weapon was missing. "Come on, we've got to get out of here before he manages to get that convoy aware of us. Hang on and let's get going."

It was a rugged take-off and a dangerous one for several reasons besides their shortage of fuel. Among them were the darkness, the rugged terrain, the possible proximity of Everard and his alien weapon, the nearness of the Columbian convoy. But the Pipit again proved her worth by getting up off the ground without mishap and, more important, apparently without drawing notice from the soldiery riding southward along the unlit highway.

"If the fuel gives out we're gone geese," said Mack grimly. But they managed to top the hill easily and, at a safe altitude, spotted the tail of the convoy in the act of surmounting it and—with relief—a small city no more than five miles ahead of them.

They came down beyond sight of the soldiery and managed to reach a fuel station on the outskirts of what proved to be, according to map and sign, Burrville. The Pipit's motor gave a final despairing cough as they rolled up in front of the pump.

The station attendant was curious about the Pipit, but Mack once more safely passed it off by explaining that their vehicle was of new British make. They got their tank full and decided to spend the night in Burrville if they could find lodgings in reasonable safety.

As if to make up for their troubles since early morning the night passed without incident. They had no trouble getting a suite of surprisingly clean and modern rooms in a clean and modern hotel. On a card hanging from the drawing room door of their suite hung a sign with the legend—

You Want It? We Have It! If We Haven't We'll Get It—Ask Us!

"Texas," said Elspeth, smiling, "is evidently Texas no matter what world it's in. Want a nice redhead, Mack? Just ask."

"You're about as funny as Everard," said Mack, scowling. "Listen, Elly—let's turn in and get some sleep. For all we know tomorrow may be worse than today."

Elspeth got her second decent night's sleep since leaving New York—her first since the departure from Mr. Horelle's mysterious house of many worlds. Once again she was up before Mack, who seemed to be feeling the rigors of their expedition increasingly. She ordered breakfast sent up for both of them and passed the time until its arrival reading the newspaper that had been stuck beneath her door during the night.

It was a highly lurid gazette, its front page sprinkled with bright green headlines in large type. There was a lead story about a young lady who had ridden in from her ranch in some sort of an automobile and had run amok in the night-club belt after a prodigious amount of imbibing. This was not in itself remarkable, save for the fact that the young lady wore only a ten-gallon hat and a pair of cowboy boots while on her spree.

There was a feature about a famous Parisian actress, who declared the mountain lions of Texas as the only fitting pets and playmates for a woman of true spirit. She had promptly been presented with a half dozen of the large and ferocious beasts—for which she was bringing suit against the donors on charges of shredding not only her nerves but her wardrobe and apartment *décor*.

There were a pair of sports pages in which Elspeth found little of interest. Then came a few items of news, hung beneath their respective date lines in a single inside column. It was the second of these that brought Elspeth out of her chair in a hurry.

It stated in brief and obviously censored language that Reed Weston's Norman, Oklahoma, headquarters had announced a visit by envoys of the Mexican Empire, and claimed that this proved definitely the rebel Weston's utter and complete perfidy where the welfare of his native Columbia was concerned.

Mack had emerged from his bedroom, yawning and rubbing his eyes, by the time the waiter arrived with the food she had ordered. He at once got to work on an amazing Texas breakfast of red-hot steak *á la ranchera, huevos rancheros,* frijoles and chile con carne, washed down with chicory-packed black Mexican coffee.

"Take a look at this, Mack," said Elspeth when he had eaten all he could hold. "It should shorten our journey considerably."

Mack read the item, laid it down, slammed it with the flat of a hand. "So he's still moving south. Well, that's swell for us. On the strength of spotting that and after ordering this breakfast you're in good again, Elly."

"I couldn't care less," she retorted acidly. Mack merely gave vent to a snort and went back to his room to dress.

They drove out of Burrville without incident and took off shortly after leaving the city limits from a lonely and flat stretch of road. Thanks to Everard's map, Mack had small trouble plotting a course for Norman. Elspeth, sensing that their incredible assignment was all but concluded, to say nothing of feeling clean, rested, and refreshed, was lighthearted as they sped above the checkerboard of the country beneath them.

"It's odd," she said to Mack when they had been airborne about an hour, "that the paper said so little about the war."

"I don't believe," Mack offered, "that many people in this world believe war is actually coming. They've managed to live for a long time without it."

"Then there probably wouldn't have been war anyway," said Elspeth, studying a swallow-shaped cloud perhaps a mile under them. "I mean, even if we hadn't brought the Pipit."

"There probably would have been—and still will be if we fail to fulfill our mission," said Mack sternly. "These people lack experience of war, so they don't know they're almost in one. Only folk like Mr. Horelle and this Everard seem to understand."

"I'm glad he got away," said Elspeth impulsively.

"I'm not," said Mack, "even though I'm damned if I know what we could have done with him—except maybe kill him."

"Mack!" exclaimed Elspeth, shocked at his violence. "You don't mean it—*do* you, Mack?"

"Never more so," said the photographer. "That Everard is about the most dangerous bloke I ever met— and I won't feel safe in this world so long as he's still around. He may look and talk like a prime pansy, but believe me, he's cute and he's tough."

"Ummmmm," said Elspeth. She didn't want to talk any more—she wanted to get back to her sense of well-being. They flew on in silence until, close to their destination, Mack uttered a startled exclamation and peered out the window on his side.

"For the love of heaven," he whispered, "look at that!"

He banked the Pipit so that Elspeth was able to follow his gaze. Some nine thousand feet below, in the concave flat center of a hill-ringed valley, was a large clearing, surrounded by low buildings that seemed to blend with the landscape around them.

In the center of the clearing, held upright by elaborate metal scaffolding, rose a gigantic silver bullet around which men were moving with the labored slowness of worker ants. Its size was immense, judged by the late-morning shadow it cast, which reached almost to the row of buildings to its west. It looked as unlike something from the Columbian world as it did like anything from the world of Elspeth and Mack.

"What is it?" the girl asked curiously.

"I may be crazy," said Mack, "but it looks to me like a space ship."

"A space ship!" Elspeth echoed inanely. She peered at it more curiously, aware that she was staring at a near-fulfillment of one of man's oldest dreams. Then, as they sped on past, she asked, "Does it look to you as if it would work?"

"Can't tell from here, Elly," he told her, "but it's mighty impressive. 'This Reed Weston must be *something* if his boys have built that in this scientific scrambled egg of a world."

Elspeth thought more about it as they landed on one of

the roads leading to Norman. Horelle had told her nothing of such a development. He had, in fact, been a little vague about Reed Weston and his plans, beyond saying that they needed the Pipit desperately. The idea of travel to the planets, perhaps to the stars, was suddenly and deeply stirring.

"You know, I'm beginning to find this exciting," she said dreamily while Mack sped the Pipit along the highway to the city.

"Yeah," said Mack. "More than I like—Look *out!*"

He braked violently, just in time to avoid crashing into a large armored vehicle which had suddenly pulled across the pavement in front of them. In quick order they were arrested and were driven to a business-looking sort of building by a wordless and highly efficient soldier. Mack tried to protest, but they were told politely but firmly to shut up, were hustled into a large office in which a tall man in uniform stood behind a desk.

His skin was coal-black—his hair snow-white. He was Marshal Henry, Chief of Staff of the Columbian Army!

VIII

Elspeth felt sudden and sickening sense of failure. They had managed to come so far in this alien world—and they had endured so much. She glanced quickly, covertly, at Mack for encouragement, but the bleakness of his expression sent her already sagging morale plummeting to a new low. It was all too evident that he, like herself, realized their travail had been all for nothing. The appearance of Marshal Henry here in Reed Weston's headquarters was as much a wallop to him as to herself.

"Please sit down, my young friends," the black marshal said politely, leaning forward to rest his knuckles on the desk. "I'm sorry that this is so much of a shock—but please remember, you gave me quite a shock yesterday morning." His white teeth flashed again as he smiled.

"I'm sorry—I'm afraid I just don't get it," said Mack, sinking weak-kneed into one of the large overstuffed leather armchairs with which the big office was liberally equipped. Speechless for once in her highly articulate life, Elspeth followed the photographer's example. On top of the surprise of his presence here, Marshal Henry's manner toward them was so unmistakably good-humored. It didn't make sense . . .

"Your confusion is understandable, of course," said the marshal to Mack. "If I had not permitted a certain regrettable love for the theatrical to overcome my good sense yesterday afternoon in New Orleans, we might have been able to make the trip here together. As it was, my agents were exactly five minutes too late at the hotel. But since you have managed to find your own way here—let me assure you you are welcome."

"But, Marshal Henry," said Elspeth, so perplexed she all but wailed, "Whose side *are* you on? We thought—" She stammered, aware of the thin ice upon which she was treading. "I mean, from what we've heard—"

"I think I can pretty well guess what your thoughts must be," said Marshal Henry in his deep and richly pleasant tones. "Unfortunately we had neither time nor opportunity to talk together either yesterday or the evening before. I was on my way to a conference with the President's personal secretary in my suite when we met in the elevator."

He paused, shook his head, added, "And yesterday morning conditions were scarcely propitious for lengthy conversation. Incidentally, Miss Marriner, I am deeply indebted to you for the information that the Presidential Guards are actually using the disintegrator. The knowledge hastened my move here, of course."

"Is—whatever it is—outlawed?" Elspeth asked quickly. "I can still see that poor man's feet running even after they had disappeared." She shuddered.

"It is outlawed by every recognized civilized government in the world." Marshal Henry spoke with a lurking anger that made his eyes gleam almost red. "It was done—arming the guard—not only without my knowledge but against my direct orders."

"But as Chief of Staff of the Columbian Army—" Mack began.

"As Chief of Staff of the Columbian Army I am—or was—a figurehead, Mr. Fraser," said the black marshal with a sardonic half-smile. "Do you think for a moment that the tight little group that runs this Republic is going to give a nigger like me any real authority?"

"Oh, I'm so sorry," said Elspeth, feeling a rush of sympathy for the marshal. "But in a way I think I'm glad. It means you are on Reed Weston's side really."

"Reed Weston and I have been good friends for a very long time," said the marshal, his anger fading before the affection he felt. "I have done all I could to support his ideas—as much as my oath to the Republic permitted me. But, Miss Marriner, until the accident of your seeing the disintegrator in use yesterday gave me proof that the Republic had violated its oath to me, my help has been extremely limited."

"Marshal Henry," Mack inquired sharply, "if you were on Reed Weston's side all the time, why didn't you help us escape from Bienville House yesterday morning?"

Marshal Henry looked sadly at the photographer, then shook his head and sighed. "If there was anything more I could have done for you, please name it, Mr. Fraser. I could have had you arrested and disarmed without danger to myself at any instant between my rooms and the garage. Incidentally, seeing your car suddenly take to the air over the heads of those guards"—he shook his head again—"was one of the happiest moments of my life."

"I'm sorry," said Mack, for once apparently contrite. "And thanks for being so patient with me. We ran afoul of an Imperial agent named van Hooten in New Orleans or we'd have been here ourselves some time yesterday evening."

"Van Hooten—Everard van Hooten?" Marshal Henry asked. At Mack and Elspeth's nods his eyebrows shot upward. "An Imperialist spy? I've heard of that young Northerner as a cotillion leader—for all I know I may have seen him here and there—but how could anyone give such a fop credit for being anything else?"

"Elly—Miss Marriner—spotted him first," Mack said charitably. "It turned out that he had a purple bee tattooed behind one ear. That was the giveaway."

"Thank you again, Miss Marriner, for information which may prove to be of vital importance in the struggle ahead of us," he said, bowing gently to Elspeth.

"It was—it was just luck both times," said the girl, feeling her face grow embarrassingly hot. "I've fouled up a lot more things. Ask Mack—Mr. Fraser. He knows." As usual, when embarrassed and unable to flee, she took refuge in the world of her reverie. She studied Marshal Henry, the marvelous arrangement of the planes of his face, the vast strength of body beneath the simple gray field tunic, the ebon gloss of skin, the white hair, the perfect ball of his head.

"*Miss* Marriner," Marshal Henry's voice, usually so softly modulated, revealed its training to command.

Elspeth emerged from her reverie with a start and murmured something inconsequential about having let her attention wander.

The marshal forgave her with a kindly smile, said, "Before you meet Reed Weston I want to tell you something about him—sketch in a bit of his background. Otherwise you might fail utterly to understand him, which must not happen. I believe you are both new to Columbia and are therefore unacquainted with many of its problems and people and states of mind."

"I'm very much afraid that is true," said Elspeth apologetically. "Yes, we *are* very green."

"But potentially very valuable," the marshal informed them. He had lighted a long thin black cigar and was smoking it while seated upon a corner of his big desk. His was, Elspeth thought, a personality both intensely likable and immensely impressive—a most unusual combination to find in one person. Character and compassion seemed to come through his very pores, yet she could sense an innate hard core of toughness that gave her no doubt as to the fact that here was a born soldier, a born leader of men.

He went on to say. "You must first understand that Reed Weston is the son of a swag-grabber. These swag-grabbers were avaricious and generally unscrupulous men who invaded the northeastern states after what *we* call our Civil War—*they* prefer to think of it as the Second Revolution—during the inevitable period of demoralization that followed the Elmira surrender."

"These swag-grabbers bought or stole land, votes, money—everything they could lay their hands on. As a rule, since they controlled the state legislatures during the period, they managed to make their thefts legal simply by altering the laws to suit. It is the memory of the swag-grabber and his misdeeds that causes the Northeast still to feel resentment against the rest of the nation. Frankly, I know no one today who blames them for feeling so.

"It so happens that Reed Weston's father ferreted out a brilliant young New York inventor named Edison—Thomas Edison, I believe—and forced him to sell all his patents for a song. Later they proved of incredible value—our electric lighting, our basic rocket-power patents, our metal alloys, for instance, are still dependent in large degree upon those 'stolen' patents.

"Young Edison, utterly embittered, shot himself not long after his patents were force-purchased. Harlan Weston—Reed Weston's father—became immensely rich out of them. Thus Reed Weston was born into one of the greatest fortunes Columbia or any other country has ever known. He is still incredibly wealthy in spite of the fact that he is today virtually an outlaw. His patent royalties still roll in from all over the world.

"However, Reed Weston"—Marshal Henry paused long enough to flick a three-inch ash from his cigar into a hole with a metal rim set in the corner of the desk itself—"Reed Weston has suffered all his life from a sense of guilt. It derives, I suppose, from the way in which his father obtained his great wealth. He has always felt a burning desire to make sure that such injustices can never happen again."

"I understand perfectly," said Elspeth when the marshal paused again. Mack, who was frowning in deep concentration, merely uttered a grunt of agreement.

"Good. I have tried to be clear about it," said the marshal. "Now Reed Weston, perhaps as a result of this sense of guilt for his father's sins, is at times a most impatient man. He is capable of being badly hurt by what he considers the failure of some of those about him to live up to his ideals.

"For instance, he was terribly hurt when the Wilkinson government refused to accept in toto the national reforms he knew were needed. He was disturbed again this morning when I got here and told him of the violation of civilized law on the part of the government by use of the disintegrator."

"Any man who wants to make changes in the world has got to be tough—perhaps tougher than the rest of us," said Mack in his rather flat normal tone.

"Reed Weston is tough—make no mistake about that," replied the black marshal. "But he is a man unavoidably driven by his inner compulsions. And he is also a great scientist—probably the greatest in the world today. As a very small boy he made up his mind to dedicate his life to justifying his father's thieveries by living up to the Edison tradition."

"If he's responsible for that space ship we got a look at

when we were flying in just now he really is a wonder," Mack remarked, lighting himself a cigarette.

"Your flying over the Mars was reported to me," said Marshal Henry with a flicker of concern. "As a matter of fact, that's why I sent out a patrol to bring you here. We were highly concerned about what might have happened to you after we lost your trail in New Orleans yesterday. Naturally we wanted to make sure it was you in that amazing flier of yours. Now—well, your recognition of the Mars for what it is makes you more important than ever to us."

"Marshal Henry," said Mack, "I'd like to ask you some questions—may I?" The marshal nodded, flicking another ash from his cigar into the desk hole. Mack, frowning, went on with, "There's one thing here I don't understand. If you have all this rocket power and even space ships, how is it you don't have airplanes?"

"Airplanes?" Marshal Henry looked his puzzlement from one to the other of them.

"Heavier-than-air compression-powered flying machines," Mack explained. "The Pipit, our little job, is a convertible dual-purpose automobile-airplane. It looks silly alongside the Mars. You have these disintegrators, a whole flock of amazing rocket machines and weapons—but no planes. Why not?"

Marshal Henry rose from the desk and walked the carpet with long-legged strides, casting an occasional thoughtful glance at the photographer and the girl. Finally he put out his cigar, lit a fresh one and resumed his seat on the desk corner. He said, "To ask that you must come from very far away indeed."

"We do," said Elspeth. "I thought you knew about that. But it doesn't answer Mack's question." Instantly she felt fright at her temerity in speaking so aggressively, but the marshal only smiled faintly.

"I know very little about you—except that Reed vouches for you," he told them. "As for—Mack's question, I think that perhaps I may know the answer. Some of the factors are sociological, some economic, some military, I suppose. But it is my belief that the basic cause is our failure to develop a sufficiently light and powerful engine to drive the sort of craft you mean. We have for a long time obtained tremendous power and tremendous speeds, but only from the heaviest sort of rocket drives.

"Perhaps we got our power and great speed for trains and trucks and ships too fast—too soon. Our ships can average fifty knots, the best of them. Our trains are twice as fast. We have never had need of any other sort of power, I suppose. That is why your flying machine—the Pipit, is it?—comes as such a thundering surprise to us here. Why, when I saw it sprout wings and fly . . ."

His voice faded off and he shook his head slowly. Mack put his cigarette butt down a metal-lined hole in the arm of his chair. He said, "Marshal, do you mean to say you don't have an internal-combustion engine here?"

" 'Internal combus—' " The phrase was obviously new to him. But then his face cleared and he said, "I think I know what you mean. I believe Reed Weston has done some work on such a motor—but without much success to date. It required too much shielding for the results obtained."

"When do we meet Reed Weston?" Mack asked bluntly.

The marshal glanced quickly at a clock set in the wall behind the desk. He said, "Reed Weston should be here in exactly three minutes." He paused, added, "I presume you are both curious as to why you are here—your real purpose." His voice grew grim. "I believe you have been sent here to prevent Reed Weston from leaving this planet forever."

"Good God!" Mack exploded, coming up out of his chair. "You mean he's about to leave Earth? But in that case, where is he going? The other planets—"

"Mars is completely habitable for humans," said the marshal. "Reed actually visited the Red Planet last year in a small space rocket and found conditions generally satisfactory."

"How did he get back here?" Elspeth found that she, too, was on her feet, vitally interested in the strange and unexpected turn of the conversation. "I mean, if you—if no one here has any planes, how did he land?"

"He didn't—on Mars," said the marshal. "He and his crew circled the planet twice and were able to take atmosphere samples, spectroscopic, photographic, and other readings of the surface. They landed back here by parachute. Reed broke his leg."

"My God!" exclaimed Mack. "So now he's going back there to stay, in that monster rocket we saw from the Pipit?"

"He's taking the sixty best brains and bodies of Earth along with him this time," said Marshal Henry quietly. "I feel honored that there is a place for me aboard. But thus far I have refused to go. I feel that my place is right here, where I am needed more. So is Reed's."

"Apple juice!" said a new voice rudely. A stocky and dynamic little man with an immense bulldog head, flaming red hair, and staccato stride, voice, and motions moved swiftly into the center of the big room as a door shut softly in back of him. "You'll be needed a lot more on Mars, John," he added definitively.

"John Henry"—the name rang bells in Elspeth's memory. She had, of course, read the old legends of the great John Henry, the mighty black riverman of her own world. And here, in this alien orb, John Henry was a latter-day reality.

To Elspeth he towered over Reed Weston, and his size was no mere matter of bodily height and breadth and girth of chest. She superimposed upon his reality a mental image of the legendary John Henry of her own world, watched through half-closed eyes as the two images melted into single clear focus.

She realized then that Reed Weston was talking angrily to both John Henry and Mack, flapping his short arms as he spoke.

". . . and now you tell me that the corrupt and criminal fools have put disintegrators into the hands of their own *condottieri* with orders to employ them at will. I ask you, why should I or any man of reasoning intelligence want to remain on such a world? What better chance is left than that of creating a new and better world on a planet where such idiot killers do not exist?"

Elspeth found herself again on her feet. Within her was the memory of the sad wisdom of Mr. Horelle, of all that Mack and she had endured on this mission, of Marshal John Henry, of the evil Everard, of the long motorized columns of soldiers and their counterparts south of the Border, moving north toward inevitable deadly collision. It had to come out of her, and it did.

"We offer you the need of hundreds of millions who want only a chance to follow the ways of peace and progress," she said. She knew she was shouting and didn't care. "We offer you the job you seek to flee from, even though in your heart and the hearts of those who would flee with you, you know self-forgiveness cannot lurk.

"You can never flee from yourselves; you can never forget the ruin of those left at the mercy of men like President Wilkinson and a hungry empire by your desertion. We offer you a new chance to find peace with yourselves upon a world that needs you too sorely to let you go."

Reed Weston, who had been studying her while she talked as if she were some strange and rather unpleasant new animal, blinked rapidly and shook his red head. His voice, when he found it, was heavy with irony.

"And just how, Miss Marriner, are you proposing to show me a way of putting this mad world at peace?" he countered. "Against disintegrators our weapons are worthless. Nothing we know of can remain organically existent within a thousand yards of them. And we have nothing to prevent them from coming within a thousand yards of us."

"I have seen the weapon these young people have brought us," said Marshal Henry quietly. Mack's eyes lit with sudden hope.

"We've got what will fill the hole in your inventory," he said with conviction. "You must have some idea of who sent us and why we are here."

"I do," said Reed Weston and for once uncertainty was present in his voice and manner. "I was—informed of your journey and its purpose." He paused, lowered his head, then lifted it to reveal his broad lumpy brow. "Otherwise would I be listening to you at all in a moment like this? But you have come here too late—forty-eight hours too late. The use of the disintegrator, which you yourself saw, Miss Marriner, should convince you of that."

"Just what is the disintegrator—and how does it work?" Mack inquired.

"It is the projector of a beam of intense heat," said

Reed Weston patiently. "We have nothing to stand against it. It will eliminate a human being almost instantaneously at close range. At longer ranges—up to a thousand yards—it may take a second to work fully. But in that time a man is long dead. And it will disintegrate tougher organic substances in only a little longer time."

"I should think it would melt the barrel that fires it," said Mack thoughtfully.

"The compound that composes and charges it does not take effect until its basic charge reaches the muzzle of the weapon itself. That is the reason for its odd design. It is a molecular process, much too involved for explanation now. And it is a combination of very simple elements—so that it is an easy weapon to manufacture once the secret is known. Too easy! No, Mr. Fraser, you have come here too late."

"I still think we brought you a way to victory—if you will only use it," said the photographer stubbornly.

"We have already won our victory—over space," the inventor replied. "We have *our* way out of this horror. The most brilliant scientific and philosophical brains of Earth have already agreed with me that it is the *only* way out."

"You won't be alone on Mars long," said Elspeth. "We flew over your space ship coming here today. We saw quarters for hundreds—perhaps thousands—of men around it. We saw hundreds of men working on the Mars itself." She paused to clear her throat.

"When you and your fine-feathered friends take off for a new planet and leave these men behind to face the wrath of a government planning to convict them of treason, do you really believe they won't build another ship—either for their own escape or for their new masters? Do you really think so, Reed Weston, mighty intellect that I am informed you are? If so you are a fool."

She felt a certain detached amazement at the sound of her own voice. But there were still words to say, phrases to make, ideas to express. Assembling her thoughts, she went on.

"Do you think, Reed Weston, that you will be regarded as an object of faith or honor by the men and women you have deserted in their hour of greatest need? Do you think that, Reed Weston?"

"It is a difficult question—a most difficult decision," said Weston. Then, more firmly, "We have decided that it is better to begin anew on a new planet where men and women of good will can be free to work and live and think and breathe and love rather than be tainted by the general corruption of this world."

"And how *should* men and women work and live and think and breathe and love?" Elspeth countered. "As they can, as they must, as they *do*—or by some theory conceived in comfort and security, a theory suitable perhaps to a few selected souls? Do you think your children, if you have any, will fit neatly into a pigeonholed set of shelves? Nonsense! They'll be acquisitive little pioneers, out for all they can get. They'll have to be—if they wish to survive on a new planet.

"Furthermore, the world will follow you—*must* follow you. Agreed, at least some of the men who worked on the Mars will know enough to build another ship without your guidance. Even if not, other men will find the way. You will find, ultimately, that there is no escape from Earth, even in space. Your scheme of a tight little hygienic heaven is a myth. *Face* it!"

"Bravo!" cried a new feminine voice from somewhere to one side of the room. "That was terrific, Elspeth!"

Startled, Elspeth looked around for its source. A small very lovely young woman stood just inside the door, carrying a sealed message in one hand. She was modestly—even demurely—dressed in dark skirt and crisp white blouse, her deep-red hair drawn back neatly in an inconspicuous roll at the nape of her neck.

But no demureness of costume could hide the curves of her figure; no plainness of hairdo conceal the soft enchantment of her features. Had Elspeth needed more for recognition, the gleam that lit in Mack's eyes at sight of her would have been enough.

"Juana!" Elspeth said, honestly surprised and actually glad to see someone she knew. "Where on earth did you come from?"

IX

Mack, of course, was overboard and sunk without trace. Elspeth needed but one quick sidelong glance to see that he was vibrating almost visibly to Juana's unexpected presence. Also that the girl, while overtly ignoring the photographer, was doing considerable vibrating of her own. Once again Elspeth was snapped back into the present focus by Reed Weston.

"Words—mere words!" the rebel exclaimed, regarding her with a cold sardonic expression. "Perhaps you and your friend here do have a gadget which makes earth-flight no problem. But what good is a mere gadget, no matter how novel or effective, against the creeping dry rot of intrenched hoggishness that has closed *this* world to honor and is now doing all in its power to sterilize it against ideas or any form of creative thought?"

Elspeth again glanced covertly at Mack, but saw that she could scarcely expect help from him at that moment. She was pierced by a bitter shaft of resentment, not only at Mack and Juana but at Mr. Horelle, who must have been responsible for the presence of the lush little auburn-head in Norman at this extremely crucial moment.

"At least," she told Reed Weston after briefly rallying her forces for a solo endeavor, "I think you ought to take a look at the Pipit—the 'gadget' as you call it—before you give up on its possibilities of use in this world. We have come a long way and our journey has been both difficult and perilous."

"I'm sorry, Miss Marriner, I didn't mean to be rude," said Weston, and for the first time since his entrance into the room he smiled. It was a quick, nervous lip smile, but it served to reveal to Elspeth some fraction of the magnetic charm that had helped to make him a vital leader in this alien world.

"Unfortunately," he went on more calmly, "we are laboring under a sword of Damocles whose already thin thread has frayed until it now hangs by but a single strand. Furthermore, time is running out on us. Already the Columbian Army is advancing upon the Mexican Border from Brownsville to Ventura—and already the Imperial forces are advancing upon it from the south. War may break out anywhere at any moment."

He paced the carpet jerkily, then swung to face her and continued his monologue. "Once war *does* break out—as it now must—our brief period of grace will be automatically over. Columbia, in spite of the corruption of its leaders, is none the less a mighty world power. It has other armies already moving to encircle our few strongholds here in the freedom area."

Weston paused briefly to light a cigarette, went on with, "Columbian agents as well as Empire spies have been planting their subversive seeds for months among our people—and both of them can tap treasury funds we cannot hope to match. No, Miss Marriner, we must leave this nation, this Earth, at the first possible moment!"

"But, Mr. Weston"—to Elspeth's surprise it was Juana speaking in her liquid accents—"I do think, if only as a favor to me, that you should at least *look* at this machine Mr. Fraser and Miss Marriner have brought you."

"You really do, Juana?" Reed Weston's expression softened as he looked at his secretary. Then he shook his head at her and added in tones of mock reproof, "You know, my dear, you are something of a mystery to me. Every instinct I possess but one tells me I ought not to listen to you. Remember, I know very little about you despite your vouching." Then he sighed and concluded with, "But if you say so I'll do it."

Elspeth found herself rejoicing unashamedly in the inner lift she received from the jealous resentment that flamed high and quickly beneath the scar tissue on Mack Fraser's upper lids. But Marshal Henry, who had remained quietly in the background during most of the argument, stepped forward once more.

"Reed, I can vouch for this machine of theirs," he said with his quiet, irresistible force. "Remember, I saw it in operation only yesterday morning."

"Was it only yesterday?" inquired Elspeth with rhetorical irrelevancy. "Why, it seems ages!"

Reed Weston regarded her blankly, then said, "Very well, let's take a look at it now." He led the way from the office with Marshal Henry and Elspeth close on his heels and Juana and the bemused photographer bringing up the rear.

The Pipit, looking demurely and innocently earthbound, sat in lonely isolation at the far end of a sparsely populated gravel parking lot, its windshield twinkling a greeting at them in the sunlight. Reed Weston, his hands clasped behind his back, marched twice around it, surveying it with the dubious interest of a man who finds a meteor reposing on his front lawn.

Finally he came back to the others and, following an unbelieving look over his shoulder, said, "Do you mean to tell me that this—this whatever-it-is—flies?"

"Oh quite—certainly," said Elspeth. She punched Mack and gave him a none-too-gentle shove in the direction of the driver's seat. He skidded a step, regarded her with resentment, then drew himself up with dignity and climbed in behind the wheel. Elspeth sighed her relief, turned to find Marshal Henry looking down at her thoughtfully.

"I believe I'd like to try it too," he said. Then Juana, to Elspeth's slight annoyance, said likewise, and both of them climbed in after Mack, leaving her alone on the gravel with the scowling Reed Weston.

He was still studying the Pipit, muttering to himself and shaking his red head. Finally he looked hard at Elspeth and said, "I don't believe it, you know. It's impossible. The combined . . ."

Just then Mack started the motor, and the rebel leader stopped talking to run quickly to the Pipit. He lifted the hood and regarded the engine in motion for a long moment. Then he dropped the hood back, reset the clamps, stepped aside and motioned for Mack to go ahead.

Mack ran it for a hundred feet on the gravel to pick up speed, then let out the wings and took off sharply from the ground. Reed Weston followed him, his frown gone, his eyes popping, his mouth half open in sheer surprise, as Mack put the little vehicle through its air paces.

Elspeth was far from awe-struck. On the contrary, she was angry. "The crazy damn fool!" she muttered, thereby drawing an annoyed glance from the rebel leader. She knew what Mack was doing—he was showing off. Not for the benefit of Reed Weston and Marshal Henry but for Juana. She hoped he wouldn't crack up and wreck the demonstration after all they had gone through to arrange it.

She should have known better where Mack and machines were concerned. After a five-minute flight the photographer brought the little car-plane easily to earth, retracted its wings and pulled to an easy stop directly in front of Reed Weston. At once the rebel leader was wrenching at the near door handle, urging the others to make room for him inside.

This time Elspeth watched the demonstration with Marshal Henry at her side. The marshal looked slightly gray beneath his ebony skin. He sucked in his breath and shook his head as the Pipit took off once more.

"It's the most amazing thing I've ever seen," he murmured, as much to himself as to Elspeth. "Think of it, an automobile that can fly—and that can be handled so easily!" Then, focusing his attention directly upon Elspeth, "Miss Marriner, I think that you have saved a hemisphere—perhaps a world. Tell me, what fuel does this Pipit of yours use?"

She told him that it flew on ordinary kerosene, just like most of the non-ammonia-using vehicles in this strange Columbian world. He listened to her attentively but kept one eye on the Pipit while Mack was running it through its paces. He was palpably relieved when the photographer brought Reed Weston safely back to earth.

"What do you think of her, Reed?" the black marshal asked of his chief as the latter emerged reluctantly from the sturdy little vehicle.

"Think?" cried the redheaded rebel leader. His face was aglow and his teeth gleamed suddenly in a grin that threatened literally to split his cheeks. *"Think!"* he shouted. "Why, with this wonderful craft in production we have Columbia, the Empire, the World itself in our hands! Miss Marriner, I can only apologize humbly for my doubts." He bowed briefly over her hand. "Rest assured I am now a fervent believer."

Mack clambered out then and assisted Juana from the Pipit as though she were composed of the same components as an old-fashioned lace valentine. This, Elspeth thought uncharitably, although the dark redhead moved with the lithe assured strength and poise of a ballet dancer—or perhaps a female hockey player.

But Mack had little more time with Juana that day. Reed Weston was at him from then on, questioning, hypothesizing, chivvying, bullying—Weston and a small corps of engineers and experts hastily assembled from sundry other projects. The photographer had to call on all his knowledge of and instinct for machinery to explain to these specialists the principles and materials upon which the Pipit was built and functioned.

To her considerable surprise, Elspeth found herself lunching in a pleasantly functional woman's commissary with the glamorous Juana. Even more surprising and annoying was the fact that she found herself unable to help liking the girl, who gave her some sorely needed and low-voiced briefing upon various facets of being an interworld agent.

"Perhaps," Juana told Elspeth bluntly over an excellent charlotte russe, "we aren't always discreet about romance. But we're like sailors or traveling salesmen—we have so little time for it anywhere that we have to grab what we can. Maybe I shouldn't have let Mack lead me down the garden path, or vice versa"—she dimpled with all the irresistible charm of a knowingly mischievous child—"if it hadn't been plain to see that you two were so poorly suited to one another."

"Just a moment!" cried Elspeth, making a desperate grab for both her breath and her wits. "When you say 'we' I take it that you're putting me on the same team with yourself—and with Mack also in the line-up."

"But of course," said Juana, looking honestly surprised. "Take it from me, there is no road back once you're in it—

even if you wanted to go back, which I simply can't believe. Mr. Horelle wouldn'd have sent you here unless you were with us. After all, it *is* the most important and exciting and honorable work in all the worlds. No, Mr. Horelle would not have summoned you unless he were sure."

It was on the tip of Elspeth's tongue to say that Mr. Horelle had not "summoned" either Mack or herself. However, she thought better of the comment before it left her lips. After all, she still had nothing but the vaguest of ideas as to what forces had been at work—were still at work—where she and Mack—yes, and Juana—were concerned.

So instead, she remarked, "And just how long have you been doing this—this sort of interworld hopping, Juana? You look awfully young to be a veteran."

"You learn fast in this field—or else," the other replied. "Of course I'm older than I look—even if I'm not as old as you."

"Ouch!" said Elspeth, wincing. "I suppose I asked for that."

"Why, did I say something wrong?" Juana inquired naively. Then, while Elspeth was counting slowly to ten, "I don't come from this world, of course—*or* the world you and Mack come from. Mine's in a bit of a mess just now. I guess I got into this business through Tod. He was my fiancé."

"*Was?*" the poetess inquired. She found it difficult to associate tragedy of any sort with a person as young, as vibrantly alive, as comely as Juana. But Juana nodded matter-of-factly.

"Yes, Tod was called for this sort of work right after he graduated from college. We were going to be married that autumn, but—well, he wasn't lucky. Or perhaps he didn't learn fast enough. I was determined to find out what had happened to him and bring whoever was responsible to justice. Oh, I was all ready to call in the cops, the G-men, the T-men—everything."

"Yes?" said Elspeth, faintly puzzled but intrigued.

"Well, I guess Mr. Horelle was afraid I might upset the ever-loving balance—you know, 'never underestimate the power of a woman' sort of thing—so he had me brought to Spindrift Key and explained what had happened to Tod and what the work was. He had a letter to me from Tod, a letter asking me to carry on for him if I didn't want to settle down with some other man in my own world."

"Your Tod must have been quite a fellow," said Elspeth sympathetically. Juana nodded and unexpectedly her eyes filled.

"That he was," she said. "So much so that I've never found another man I wanted to marry on any of the worlds I've visited." She laughed mirthlessly and tossed back her long mahogany hair. "But I have my share of fun, and I really feel as if I'm doing something. It isn't a chance many girls get—or many men either."

"You're quite a girl yourself, Juana," said Elspeth and found herself meaning it.

"But I'm not, really," the other replied earnestly. "I just run errands and fill in at small jobs like being Reed Weston's secretary and entertain visiting firemen. It's all right, but I have no real gifts—like yours for poetry."

Elspeth thought that Juana had a good many more gifts than she realized but forbore saying so. Instead she had coffee with the other-world girl and then went back with her to Weston's office, where Marshal Henry was temporarily working. He smiled up at them from behind a small stack of papers atop the big desk as Juana ushered her in and closed the door behind her.

"Miss Marriner," he said, rising and motioning her to a chair, "you and I seem to be deputed to do some negotiating. Reed has left the matter in my hands, and your—er—Mr. Fraser is going to be very busy this afternoon. He informed me at lunch that you were fully qualified for the task. Before we begin, however, I must repeat what you already probably know—that time is of the proverbial essence."

Had the marshal not used the word "proverbial" to soften his cliché Elspeth might not again have noticed him as a person. Until he spoke she had been utterly wrapped up in and befuddled by her absorption in her emotional life and the strange new existence that had opened up for her since she and Mack had been given the routine Hatteras Keys assignment by Orrin Lewis less than a week before.

But because she was word conscious she looked at him then, saw him not as a living legend but as a man. She smiled back at him, then frowned as she sought the thread of his words.

"But, Marshal Henry, *we* have nothing to negotiate. We came here on assignment to turn the Pipit over to Reed Weston."

He rose again, towering over her, and scowled as he ran a big hand through his white hair. "I don't mean to be dense," he told her, "but I don't understand at all. You and Mr. Fraser have come here at considerable trouble and risk. You have brought with you a device that is little short of a miracle—a device that may enable us to fulfill all our ideals as well as bring peace to Columbia. You have brought with you the knowledge to teach us how to manufacture this device ourselves. Yet you say there is nothing to negotiate, Miss Marriner."

His voice grew deeper, rougher, bringing her out of the near-hypnotic reverie that had overcome her. It was, she thought, the Afro-American music of his voice, the rhythmically controlled power of his every move, the . . .

She had begun instinctively to put her thoughts into poetic phrase, to seek the liquid meter that would fit the marshal, that would catch the essence of this ebony demigod, would capture his very being in words, as a fly is caught in amber. But the phrase, the meter she sought, were still stubbornly elusive when the marshal's use of her name woke her up.

"Are you ill?" he inquired solicitously, reaching for the carafe at his elbow. "Shall I send out for a drink—or a doctor?"

"No—no, thanks," she said, a trifle faintly. "I'm—all right. I'm afraid I have a bad habit of wandering when what passes for my mind gets to working. You see, Marshal, I'm a poet."

"Which is all very interesting," he told her with a trace of irony that was somehow not unsympathetic, "but fails to get us much further with our negotiations. Surely you must expect something. After all, you may have saved us from certain defeat."

"I'm sorry," she said and knew the warmth rising within her was dangerous. "We were sent here to deliver the Pipit and await further orders. We were not told to demand payment."

"You *are* an unworldly person, Miss Marriner," he said, regarding her as if he half expected her to vanish. Then, with sincerity that brooked no suspicion, "But I think I like you very much. I think I even trust you." His eyes became grave and he added, "I wish I could fully share Reed's assurance that the Pipit will win us the peace we want." He sighed, looked at his hands.

"He is either riding the crest or deep in the trough," the marshal went on slowly. "You saw him before and after he rode in the Pipit. Before, he wanted to flee Earth, after, he was sure he had all the reins in his hands."

"Why do you doubt his assurance?" Elspeth asked.

"Because, while I know the Pipit offers a solution to many of our problems, it does not solve them all. I fear, unless we find some way to check or find a shield for the disintegrator, the best we can expect is a costly stalemate. We are not dealing entirely with fools, Miss Marriner."

"What will you do if you can't find a way of stopping the disintegrator?" Elspeth asked. Marshal Henry opened his hands.

"The only thing we can do—run a colossal bluff," he told her. Then he smiled and said, "But I would rather discuss a more personal possibility."

Elspeth agreed, some moments later, to have dinner with Marshal Henry that evening. It was already dark when one of Reed Weston's huge staff rocket cars braked to a halt in front of the women's quarters to pick her up. The poet, who was awaiting the marshal in a dither composed of equal portions of excitement, newly roused emotions, and a clinging sense of faithlessness to Mack, emerged promptly and moved to enter the rear of the vehicle.

"In front, please," said the chauffeur, opening the door. She got in and they roared off in a flare of jets, away from the cantonment. Puzzled and concerned, Elspeth said, "But where is Marshal Henry? I thought we were to—"

"Here he is," said the driver, laughing and tossing back a sort of parka he was wearing to reveal the ebony visage of the former Columbian chief of staff. "I didn't want a lot of bodyguards following us around, so I arranged this little surprise." He chuckled like a boy who has just successfully planted a tack in the principal's chair. "They'll be out of their minds until we get back," he added.

Elspeth found her first trip in a rocket car much like a jaunt on a Percheron after being accustomed to Shetland ponies. The big vehicle bucked and blasted—yet held the road with astonishing firmness under the marshal's skilled guidance. They drove some forty miles south to a fine secluded rural restaurant he knew, and on the way they passed the gracefully towering silver spire of the Mars, gleaming like a gargantuan needle in the early moonlight.

Over the meal Elspeth said thoughtfully, "Seeing the Mars almost makes me wish we had not broken in here today to alter Reed Weston's plans—his dream of space—"

"His dream was already shattered or he would never for a moment have conceived such a plan with conditions what they are," the marshal told her firmly. "Your arrival here was the machination of Fate if ever I saw it machinate."

"I'm not joking," she said, but for all that she smiled. He had such an appealing boyishness for all his greatness and importance. Then she added, "You must have had some inkling of who we were—of our coming at any rate—when you spoke to us in the hotel lift in Baton Rouge. And of course when you helped us to escape and when you smiled at us on the balcony in New Orleans."

He looked at her for a long moment with an intensity that almost frightened her. But when he spoke his voice was low, almost a whisper, as he said, "If you'll forgive a supposedly responsible citizen for being a damned fool—I'm afraid it was you."

"Oh my dear!" she exclaimed and all reason was washing away in the emotion that flooded her. "Oh my dear!"

She was still walking in a rosy glow that defied the night shadows when at last they left the inn and re-entered the huge rocket car for the drive back to camp. The moon was already low in the sky as Marshal John cut in the twin motors, and Elspeth found herself fascinated by the long shadows the trees scattered about the innyard cast on the grass that surrounded them.

One, she saw, had a double shadow. It amused her to speculate upon what set of natural conditions could have caused it. And then she saw the shadow move, just as her companion cut in his sodium headlamps. She peered at the tree as they went roaring past it and, in the glow of the lamps, caught just a glimpse of an outlined profile, a remembered profile.

"John," she said. "You remember that spy—the one we had trouble with—Everard van Hooten? He's back behind that tree. He must have been watching us."

The marshal uttered a magnificent curse but drove on. Then he said, "Look back as long as you can—for any sort of signal. If they were going to trap us at the inn they already would have."

Elspeth swiveled around in the seat and peered over the back of the open-topped rocket car. Seconds later she saw it—the golden stem and green flower of a rocket. She informed the marshal, who said, "Now keep your eyes open ahead."

Again in a matter of seconds a rocket flared—this time a red one. "I see it," said the marshal. "Looks as if they've got us boxed. I'll never forgive myself for getting you into this."

There was no sense in cutting the lights, with the jet flare to betray them in the darkness. The marshal handed her a weapon and gave her brief instructions on how to use it. It was an air-needle gun, good, he told her, up to a hundred yards. Elspeth saw that it was much like the weapon Everard had carried the evening before and had recovered from Mack's pocket.

They had gone less than a mile when the road block loomed up in their lamps. The marshal did not slacken speed—rather, he increased it. "Going to try to crash through. Hold on," he told Elspeth. She crouched low in the seat, wondering if, after all, the whole incredible experience were a dream.

The jar of their collision informed her otherwise. She was rocked and bumped and finally tossed clear of car and road to land with a jarring thump high up on the side of a bank. To her amazement the gun was still in her hand.

Marshal Henry, standing in full light in the middle of the road, was a magnificent if somewhat ragged figure. Blood was flowing from a cut in his scalp, and three men, looking like ugly little gnomes, were crowding around him.

"Who was with you? . . . Where'd he go? . . . Better talk quick." The questions poured thick and fast until one of the gnomes spotted Elspeth as she got to her feet and yelled. Then he turned to run for her, waving his gun.

She tried to work her own weapon, but her aim was poor and before she knew it the man was pulling her down into the road. He smelled of garlic and the rough surface of his jacket scraped her face. She heard him yell, "Hey, guys, it's a girl, no less!"

She screamed and then a whole sudden spate of new sounds broke out around her. She did not lose consciousness but her awareness was fading when her captor was pulled roughly from her and she found that she could again see.

Two of the pygmies lay crumpled in the road, their skulls smashed like pumpkins, blood and brains staining the asphalt of their pillows. One of them was still stirring feebly and his eyes glowed like dying fireflies in the hideous yellow sodium torchlight that illuminated the scene.

Then she heard her recent captor scream like a horse with a broken leg. Horrified but unable to tear her eyes away, she watched the marshal, now more torn of uniform and bleeding from fresh cuts on his face and neck, pick up his enemy in both hands as if he were a fox furpiece, shake him violently to stop his screaming, then break his back across one knee and toss him carelessly away.

"Don't be afraid, darling," the marshal said, coming to help her up. "Most of this blood isn't mine. Let's see if these dogs have a car here that will get us back to camp."

That was the last thing Elspeth remembered about that night.

X

Beginning late the following morning, events began to move more swiftly in Columbia, and Reed Weston's Norman headquarters was the focal point of activity. There were increasingly rapid exchanges of messages and messengers, not only with Weston's other headquarters but with Columbian and Imperial leaders. From a time of increasing gloom and forced patriotism it had become a time of mounting excitement.

Elspeth, who found herself up and about some thirty hours after her shattering experience with the marshal, saw little of Mack in the days that followed. The photographer seemed to be incessantly tied up either with the technicians or with Juana, who continued to play a silent but omnipresent role in the background. Elspeth was present, however, by request of Marshal Henry, at meetings with both Columbian and Mexican plenipotentiaries, who wished to know something of the qualities and uses of the Pipit.

It was the black marshal himself, still slightly patched, who took over both meetings when the officials had finished questioning her. "Miss Marriner," he told both groups, "has given you an idea of the Pipit's uses as a means of peaceful transport. You will shortly see a demonstration of its potentialities for war.

"Our engineers, already engaged in preparing its manufacture on a vast scale—vaster than anything yet attempted in the world—will give you estimates to prove that this flying marvel can be made at a price far lower than that of any existing locomotion.

"It is, however, my especial job to make plain to all of

you that the Pipit's war uses are potentially even greater. Armed with rocket weapons, it can sweep down upon any desired point from above and without warning. It can land and evacuate an army or merely destroy and escape unharmed. I know that you gentlemen today are in possession of no weapons to stop it.

"Orders have already been issued," he concluded grimly, "to send the Pipit so armed to destroy immediately and utterly the headquarters and headquarters personnel of either Columbian or Imperialistic forces which again employ the illegal disintegrator. And rest assured, gentlemen, we have agents able quickly to inform us of the use of that weapon on any scale. Now, sirs, if you will be so good as to follow me . . ."

When he had finished with the last of them and they had departed for their bases, a quiet, thoughtful, and shaken group of men, Marshal Henry turned to Elspeth with a sudden and softening smile and said, "Did I preach them too much of a sermon, Elly? Do you think I put it over?"

"You done wonnerful—jus' wonnerful, Johnny," she told him. Then, seriously, "You were grand. Now what do we do?"

"From now on we sit and wait—and keep on learning how to manufacture Pipits. Keep your fingers crossed, Elly. They'll be coming back to us soon enough—with their hats in their hands."

"I hope you're right," Elspeth told him. "But when I asked the question I was thinking of us, not of high politics."

"You continue to amaze me, darling," Marshal Henry told her, taking her arm gently and leading her out toward his car. "You should know by this time that there is no such thing as 'high' politics. But I think I know just the place for us to celebrate our private and personal victory dinner—and this time we'll let the bodyguards tag along."

"Sissy," she told him, but she was careful to smile when she said it.

Three more weeks passed in hectic succession while the negotiations followed their inevitable progress. For Elspeth they were weeks oddly dreamlike in essence—yet for all that oddly satisfying. Whether the emotion she felt for Marshal John Henry was love or not she neither cared not bothered to analyze. Whatever it was it pervaded her, packed her every waking moment with a satisfying emotional excitement her inner being had not felt since her first adolescent crush. And behind this reawakening there was always the stirring accompaniment of great events in the background.

Never in her comparatively obscure life on her own prosaic world had Elspeth known the supremely human glory of being an important person. There she had been merely a young woman—moderately attractive, yet considered a bit odd for her poetic leanings, a bit frightening to most men for her intelligence.

Here and now, thanks to Mr. Horelle, she was part of the very core of a bloodless revolution that might be altering the very face and fate of a globe. She sat in on meetings with great scientists, with ambassadors, with industrialists and military leaders. Furthermore, these great folk listened to her avidly.

She and Mack were persons of mystery, of origins they could not reveal but of resources that commanded respect. She continued to see little of Mack, of course. He had been drafted for the task of superintending the big push of tooling up for Pipit manufacture on a large scale, as well as of rushing to completion a few hand-built models.

She saw Juana often, of course—since the redhead had been assigned to be Marshal Henry's secretary. And Elspeth found her affection for the girl growing steadily, especially since her own emotions were no longer directed Mackward. But now and again she received a shock from her erstwhile rival.

One evening toward the close of the three weeks, an evening when she and the marshal had been out late testing the moonlight, Elspeth came home to find Juana curled up in the one armchair her room boasted, smoking a cigarette. The younger girl regarded her with open curiosity—and with something more disturbing in her glance.

"You've been out with my boss again," she said. It was a statement, not a question.

"Right," Elspeth said dreamily. She kicked off her shoes and lay back on the bed, linking fingers at the back of her neck. "I think he's perfectly perfect, Juana. He's so big and so humble, so strong and so gentle, so slow talking and so quick thinking."

"Check on all counts," said Juana. Then, "But, Elly, be careful. You won't be in this world much longer, and if you let yourself get emotionally involved you may impair your usefulness."

Elspeth regarded her uninvited guest and sensed trouble behind the limpid hazel eyes. With a spark of intuition she said, "It isn't just that, Juana. There's something else, isn't there?"

"Of course there is," Juana said slowly. "I feel like a prime crumb to say this, Elly—but dammit, he's a Negro."

"Somehow I never suspected you of *that*," said Elspeth, feeling an odd sense of disappointment. The idea of this sort of cheap race prejudice in anyone connected with the incredibly wise Mr. Horelle had never occurred to her. She felt a little ill.

"You're wrong—the things you're thinking about me, Elly," Juana said evenly. "There are a number of worlds where color doesn't matter, but this is not one of them. Nor is yours—nor mine, heaven knows."

"Then it's time something was done about it," said Elspeth, still hot under the neckline.

"I wish you knew how hard we all have worked for it—*are* working for it," Juana told her. "On world after world—even back before Mr. Horelle had charge! But progress is so stinkingly slow. Which is why I'm sticking my hot little neck out and trying to warn you, Elly. You look just like a girl who's falling in love—and you mustn't. It's not your job."

"I'm sorry I blew my top," said Elspeth. She sat up and reached for a cigarette, tossed the pack to Juana. The sincerity in that lovely voluptuous little face defied doubt. As she inhaled she was suddenly able to see herself as this girl must see her, as Mack . . . But quickly and sharply she told herself that she no longer gave a damn about Mack or what Mack thought of her. He had no business having any opinions at all about her.

"Perhaps," she went on finally, "I'm in love with an idea rather than with a man, but you'll have to admit he's gorgeous."

"Strictly for the birds," said Juana, and they both grinned. Had they been a few years younger they would have giggled. A few minutes later, cigarette finished, Juana rose to leave. At the door she said, "Have your fun, Elly—you have a right to it—but don't let the current carry you away. You're needed."

Elspeth nodded and frowned thoughtfully at the closing door. She felt suddenly a little begrimed. Falling in love had always come as easily to her as breathing. At various times she had oozed emotion over a math teacher—she hated figures—a pimply delivery boy, a small bird that had nested outside her window, a lady athletic coach at school, a Canadian lacrosse professional, a writer with a most unusual straggly pink goatee, a famous actress who had been kind to her on an early newspaper-interviewing assignment.

But love itself was something that had not come easily to her—it had not come at all as yet. Within herself she had always held in reserve something indefinable, something which she had never intended to give up until she knew herself to be honestly and irretrievably a lover—a lover beloved.

She thought, lying there, that she had almost certainly been the worst sort of a triple fool to have so withheld this part of herself. But even as she gave utterance to this silent self-condemnation she knew that it was as much a part of her as her eyelashes. It was something she had not been able to help, something she would never be able to change merely by wishing.

Yet Juana had done a great deal for her. The redhead had showed her that her current emotional upheaval over Marshal John was not the real love for which she had waited so long. She *was* infatuated with the idea of Marshal Henry—perhaps with the man himself. But she did not love him. And in pretending to she had done him a grave injustice.

She turned out the light, stripped off her clothes quickly and crept raw between the coarse linen sheets of her cot. Somehow the rough surface against her skin, replacing the silk of her nightgown, helped to salve a sorely torn conscience.

Being unworldly and utterly honest, she looked for a

chance to tell Marshal Henry the truth about her feelings the next day. But the marshal was not there. He had taken off hurriedly to deal with a snag that had developed in the negotiations, was en route to Brownsville. He had left her a brief note. It read:

> *Elly*—*If I could think of anything to compensate for the loss of your presence—a flower, a jewel, a bit of verse—I would leave it with this note. Unfortunately, darling, I can think of nothing but you. So be patient until I return. Times will not always be as difficult for us.*
>
> *John*

Elspeth looked at it again, then at Juana, who had handed it to her. Impulsively she handed it back for the girl to read. Juana studied it, reread it, then passed it to Elspeth without a word. But her large dark eyes were suspiciously bright.

"Does this mean trouble?" Elspeth asked.

Juana hesitated, then nodded. "I'm afraid so. The Columbian leaders are making outrageous demands, based on having the disintegrator. I'm waiting for a message right now. We may have more of a job on our hands than we figured."

"Then John Henry was right all along," Elspeth told Juana. She went on to explain the fears he had expressed after Reed Weston's first flight in the Pipit, and concluded with, "I do hope it isn't going to be serious—really serious."

"So do I—or rather we," Juana replied quietly. "It's balled things up rather—so be ready for anything. See you later."

She strolled away toward her office, and Elspeth, feeling utterly at a loss, wandered around until she managed to hitch a ride with one of the headquarters chauffeurs to where Mack was working. To her surprise, she was driven right past the long factory shed, where the Pipits were in process of manufacture, to the larger plant surrounding the space-rocket launching field. "He's over there," her driver informed her, pointing. "I can't drive you any closer."

Mack, sleeves rolled up, his eyes clear, his face tanned,

one cheek grimy, was glowering happily at a set of blueprints in a special steel shed that adjoined the rocket-launching platform. Surrounding him were a group of leathery-skinned engineers.

"Hi, Elly," he greeted her, and once more she was surprised by the unexpected charm of his lopsided grin. He seemed genuinely glad to see her. He looked, she thought, a little thin, and she felt an unexpected but wholly maternal desire to chide him for not taking better care of himself.

Then he was beside her, his brawny arm across her shoulders, introducing her to the others. "This is my sidekick," he told them. "Elly's slumming."

"I am *not!*" she replied with dismal lack of wit. "I've—well, it's just that I've been rather busy myself."

"That we know," said Mack, chaffing but not jeering. He drew her aside with a nod of apology to the others, walked her out onto the great flat launching area. "Heard the news? I just got word from Juana. There's a jam in the works and we're cutting out of here tomorrow. We've got another job on our hands if we're to make this one work."

"You mean—we're leaving this world?" she asked, unbelieving in the face of what had to be fact. Mack nodded.

"We're just about washed up here anyway," he said. "You and Juana and I. The Pipits—Reed Weston version—are already in full production, and I've just about got these spaceship plans to a T. It's a good thing I got some engineering under my belt when I was young and foolish. Some of the techniques these chaps have developed are miles ahead of ours. I've been treading deep water for a month now."

"But where are we going?" Elspeth inquired, desperately curious and upset. Everyone but she seemed to have some knowledge of what was happening. "Back to Spindrift Key and Mr. Horelle?"

"Eventually, I suppose—if we're lucky," Mack told her, lighting a cigarette and as usual forgetting to give her one. "Juana has the info—just got it, I gather. From what she told me I think we've got another job before we finish this one—on still another world. It seems our assignment here dovetails into a situation there or something."

"Holy cow!" said Elly inelegantly. This took a bit of

getting used to. She was not at all certain that she could withstand the various wrenches and upheavals involved in adjustment to yet another version of Earth so soon—to say nothing of playing an active role in a fresh major crisis.

Then she looked up at Mack, saw his serene readiness, realized that their roles had been reversed. It was she who had embarked upon the assignment lightheartedly, while Mack had had difficulty in fitting himself to the parallel time-track theorem. She understood now why Juana had visited her the night before, had warned her not to get in too deeply with the marshal, had deftly exposed the fraudulent roots of her love. Her respect for Juana rose another notch.

"All right, Mack," she said, putting her hands in her jacket pockets. "When, where, how, and why?"

"Juana has the orders," Mack repeated. "We tee off for Natchez tonight. I have a hunch we'll move from there."

"Just give me my cues," said Elspeth. "I think I'd better get back to what are laughingly called my lodgings and pack."

"Swell," Mack told her. "We'll probably fly down in the Pipit. And don't let your poetic soul go chasing after a trick cloud formation or a flock of birdies on the way. We want all of your celebrated poetic wits at this stage of the game."

She stared hard at the lower part of his face, squinting a little. Mack blinked, finally blurted, "What in hell's the matter? Something wrong with me, Elly?"

"Your mouth," she replied ungently. "It's far too big." With which she walked back to her car and chauffeur, feeling so well pleased with herself that she tripped and all but fell over a small stone in the launching field.

But on the way back to headquarters her thoughts were not pleasant. So the assignment was going on and they were to travel to still another Earth. She sought to consider the hows and whys without attaining constructive results. In the end she sighed and leaned back against the cushions, closing her eyes.

Mack was going too. Juana of course had seen to that. The big lug carried and fetched like some outside bird dog at every crook of her little finger. Yes, Mack, who had reacted in such ornery fashion to forced entry into the Columbian world, was muzzled and sitting up, paws in air, all but pleading to visit another alien world—because the lush little so-and-so had flashed a soft dark eye in his direction.

She opened her own eyes and said some most unladylike words, for she knew now that she was hooked inextricably in the interworld parade. It was, she thought, an unforeseen and dismal fate for a young lady who had once said "Rabbit" for good luck before opening her eyes on the first day of each and every month.

She did not see either of her co-agents until early that evening, when, after a wretched and lonely afternoon, she assembled with them and their luggage and a Mack-trained Pipit driver in the parking lot. Perhaps because of the chauffeur Mack said little during their flight to Natchez, and Juana was carefully casual in such remarks as she chose to make. It was well after midnight when they boarded a rocket train in the ornate but barnlike Natchez station, and by that time Elspeth was so tired and unhappy that she had almost lost interest in all tangential worlds.

XI

Elspeth did not awaken from the sleep of exhaustion that overwhelmed her aboard the train until their swift rocket-powered transport slowed jerkily to a stop at St. Louis. She moaned and rolled over in her bed, and an outflung arm struck the wall of the compartment beside her. This contact restored her suddenly to full consciousness. She sat up, yawning, and rubbed her eyes.

The train did another stop-start lurch as it rounded a curve, all but tossing her against the wall. Apparently while the rocket drive could get them under way smoothly and with immense acceleration, braking to a stop was a far rougher business.

Elspeth peered through the small round window placed at the head of her luxurious bunk and saw that they were in fact in the process of entering a city. Outside the sunlight was brilliant and the watch on her wrist informed her that it was almost noon.

They had proceeded to the Natchez station by devious routes after landing the Pipit—even though it was obvious that some sort of safe-conduct had been arranged for them by agents of the Watchers. Luckily their train was awaiting them, its rockets damped but ready. They had been quickly bundled aboard its final car, a brilliant affair of indigo, white, and silver, liberally plastered with coats of arms. This car, Juana informed them, was to be their residence throughout the brief remainder of their first stay in the Columbian world.

At that moment Elspeth had again hated the smaller girl. Juana seemed as gay and high-spirited as a teen-ager boarding a vacation special after a dreary term away at school. Mack had been hot and tired and thoroughly out of sorts, and as for herself, Elspeth had felt utterly wilted, inside and out.

There had been plenty of cause—the long strain of their perilous assignment and the sudden knowledge that, on the brink of its successful conclusion, even more work lay in front of them—not to mention Elspeth's emotional uncertainty over her relations with the black marshal. But, cause or not, an involuntary glimpse of herself in a station-concourse mirror had put the final crusher upon her morale. She had looked, she discovered, at least as badly as she felt.

"Let's take over the last three staterooms," Juana had suggested as an obsequious blond-haired porter ushered them into the ornate car that was to take them—where?

A full two-thirds of its length in front was taken up with vestibule, aisle, and a half-dozen large staterooms, neatly lined up along one side. The final third of the car was a combined observation lounge and buffet, fitted out with every luxury conceivable in the Columbian world. The *décor* was baroque but charming, and featured lacy mahogany grillwork, gold leaf and ivory-leather chairs on deep-piled indigo carpet.

"This is Minister of Finance Alston's own private car," the tall heavy-set steward had informed them in a rich accent as he stowed their belongings expertly in the rooms they selected for themselves. He had seemed to be inordinately proud of the fact.

Mack, Elspeth had noticed with interest, refused to give up possession of a heavy-looking leather attaché case. He had even kept it stowed tightly between his legs when they adjourned to the buffet lounge for a nightcap after the train got under way. She wondered vaguely what it contained, but had been too spent to inquire. There would be time for that later.

"What in hell are you so happy about?" she had inquired of Juana bluntly over the top of her glass.

For answer Juana had hummed an unfamiliar little phrase of song—something light and colorful and with a beat utterly unfamiliar to Elspeth. Then Juana had said, putting the sparkle of her highball in the shade, "We're going to *my* world this time. *Home!*"

"What sort of a place is it, baby?" Mack had inquired, showing definite interest. Damn him, Elspeth had thought, he was probably expecting it to be full of Juanas.

But Juana had merely laughed and told him, "You'll find out soon enough for yourselves, dear ones."

"When are we going to make the—the change or whatever you call it?" Mack had inquired, his curiosity, unslaked, merely veering onto another path.

But Juana had chosen to answer that one, saying, "We make transfer at the next tangential point—somewhere in Kansas, I believe—close to Topeka. I think the cyclones have something to do with it."

"That's right," Mack had mused. "Come to think of it, Hatteras is quite a storm center too."

"If you lovely, lovely people will deign to excuse me," Elspeth had said then, barely covering a jaw-cracking yawn, "I'm going to place this beautiful pagan body of mine sandwich-fashion between a pair of sheets. I'm a wreck and I know it."

Their good nights had been casual and disinterested, even to this somewhat tired bit of wit, and Elspeth had retired, bruised in body, spirit and, above all, ego, to her stateroom. She had been fully determined to lie awake all night just to spite herself, as well as to abrade the fifth-wheel feeling from which she was suffering—to cure which it was her purpose to relive every moment of her romance with the black marshal. She had got as far as the New Orleans balcony episode when slumber roadblocked and ambushed her—and this time Marshal Henry failed to rescue her.

Now it was noon the next day and they were coming into a large city. She wondered what town it was and then caught sight of a huge track-side signboard advertising a St. Louis lager and surmised quite correctly their whereabouts. It was here, according to Juana's information of the night before, that their private car was to be shunted onto the rear of another train—this one bound for California. She decided to get up and see what was going on. Also, she was ravenously hungry.

Mack and Juana were already in the lounge—Mack in his striped robe, Juana poured into a breath-taking negligee—when Elspeth, feeling about one-quarter groomed, emerged from her stateroom fully dressed. There were appetizing aromas of bacon, toast, and coffee in the atmosphere, and the steward, whose name was Soames, greeted her with a smile that looked almost genuine.

"Hi, you people, you," Elspeth said to both of them without discrimination. "You're looking stinkingly well fed and pleased with yourselves." She noted with rising curiosity that Mack still had the attaché case thrust between his legs.

"May I prepare you some breakfast, Miss Marriner?" the beaming Soames inquired politely. Elspeth shook her head.

"No—no breakfast, thanks," she told him with one ear cocked to hear the clamoring demands of her stomach. "What can you fix me in the way of a full meal?"

What Soames proceeded to fix within the limited confines of his shining little copper kitchenette proved to be nothing short of miraculous. First upon his menu was a thick hot soup of a cream-beef-chicken-and-claret base that was unlike anything in Elspeth's memory but was incredibly delicious. He followed this masterpiece with a thick and tender small steak, charcoal-broiled, soufflé potatoes, asparagus hollandaise, a tossed green salad and, for a finisher, a rich zabaglione accompanied by a steaming café-royale, rich with brandy.

"These female poets with their ethereal appetites!" murmured Mack *sotto voce* as Elspeth downed the last of her salad. Soames, grinning to see his work so appreciated, removed it in favor of the zabaglione, whose semi-liquid yellow richness he spooned from a small tureen.

"Quiet, Mack!" said Juana sternly. "Can't you see this woman is hungry?"

"I think that for her it's just a snack," said the photographer. Elspeth gave him a Mack look, but forbore to speak.

She took three spoonfuls of the zabaglione and began to realize that, although it was miraculously good, she was not going to be able to eat any more. She apologized to Soames and suggested to Juana and Mack that they help her get rid of it. When they turned her down with mock scorn she announced, "Soames, if you think for a moment I'm going to let this get away, you're out of your mind. Put it in my stateroom and I'll get to it later."

The steward grinned and took it away as ordered and Elspeth sat back, at peace with the world and herself. She lit a cigarette and sipped her café-royal, letting its warmth and strength flow through her. Mack leaned toward her across the car and said assiduously, "Elly, are you sure you wouldn't rather have a large black cigar?"

"*Mack!* You'll make her sick," said Juana sharply. "Stop being so mean to Elly."

"That's my Mack—the only Mack I know," Elspeth informed her. She transferred her attention to the photographer, nodded toward the attaché case still between his legs. "By the way, Mack darling, I'm curious. Are you attached to that thing by an umbilical cord, or what?"

"Oh, for God's sake!" he said crustily, then smiled as Juana snickered. "I'm not supposed to let this out of touch—literally," he explained. "It holds the space-ship blueprints and a sample of the trick fuel Weston invented. It seems he developed some sort of atomic release our next world is going to need."

"Incidentally, friends," said Juana, sitting up straight and tucking her perfect little legs under her, "since we're already high-tailing it across Missouri I might as well brief you on what's ahead. We'll be working against a deadline."

Mack and Elspeth settled themselves to listen and Juana went on: "In the first place, this dear old world of mine we are about to enter is a free-wheeling jam that makes our little Mexican-Columbian fracas look like a game of battledore and shuttlecock." She paused and looked thoughtfully straight ahead.

"Okay," she resumed. "Here it is. There are two whole sets of wars in the making—not wars involving mere nations or even hemispheres but the entire world. It has happened a couple of times before and we've pulled through somehow—but this time, if it starts, it may mean the end of civilization, maybe even of life itself."

"Must be nice people where you come from," said Mack pursing his lips.

"Shut up, stupid," said Juana amiably. "It isn't the people's fault. Nor is it their leaders'. What happened in my world—unlike this world we are leaving—is that our science went galloping ahead so fast it left our culture hopelessly behind. As a result everything got out of whack. It was like giving a disintegrator to a nine-year-old boy.

"For instance, our medical techniques got so good that the world population has tripled in a little over three generations," she went on. "Result—chaos except in a few spots, mostly in the Western Hemisphere. Asia is the big threat. They have more than a billion people combined with ancient ideas of statism—ideas they have dressed up in new clothing. At the moment we have them checked in Western Europe through technological superiority—so they have transferred their aggressions eastward.

"China, Malaya, Japan, and Indonesia have fallen to the Asiatic dictator, and India is in a ferment. He offers the usual revolutionary panaceas to the so-called common man, then turns him into a slave to his system. The scheme is older than the pyramids, but it seems as if people never will learn."

"And just how is the space ship supposed to help?" Elspeth inquired.

"Hold your ponies," said Juana pertly. "I'm coming to it. The President of the United States—he's the third Roosevelt to hold that office—has summoned a conference of the so-called Atlantic Powers and South America in San Francisco in an effort to increase their awareness of the menace to freedom from Asia.

"It is not going to be successful. The European nations are concerned only with their own front yards, and South America is resentful because the United States has thus far focused most of its attention and money on maintaining the barrier in Europe. Something is needed not only to shock the world out of its trauma but to offer it a new hope of release from its population dilemma."

"I think I'm beginning to understand," said Elspeth, frowning. "You believe space flight will do it?" She paused, added, "But how will that straighten things out for Reed Weston?"

"Listen," said Juana with quiet authority. "With what Reed Weston has learned about Mars' habitability, it should do the trick. It's a thousand-to-one shot that Mars will be habitable in my world—this world we're coming into. It's our job to put the contents of Mack's attaché case into the hands of President Roosevelt himself—and to see that he realizes its value."

"But what about the stalemate or whatever it is here in Columbia?" Elspeth asked stubbornly.

"I was coming to that," said Juana. "The big hitch in the local negotiations is that while the Pipit gives its owners mobility in a military sense it does not stop the disintegrator. Well, it just happens that on my world they have what Mr. Horelle believes is a shield. We trade our space flight and fuel for this."

"How come they've got it on your world and not on Weston's?" Mack asked, frowning in thought.

Juana shrugged. "There's a lot of luck as well as necessity in scientific discovery, Mack. It just happens my world has it—as probably a lot of other worlds do too. So the Watchers were able to hold our missions together by a simple reswitch of schedules."

"You mean we were going to this world anyhow?" Elspeth asked. Juana nodded. Mack frowned again.

"How much time have we got?" he asked.

Some of Juana's assurance seemed to fade. She said slowly, "Just one week—that's when Reed Weston must have his answer or else."

"Sounds like a large package," said Mack doubtfully.

"It is, of course—but it's not impossible," Juana replied with quiet confidence. "You two are not yet aware of the resources the Watchers possess. And there is a plan, naturally. President Roosevelt happens to be extremely devoted to his daughter—and his daughter is intensely ambitious in a literary way. In short, she wants to be a poet." Juana's dark eyes came to rest on Elspeth.

"I'm not sure I understand this!" exclaimed the latter with a sudden sense of panic. "How is her wanting to write poetry going—"

"It will," said Juana, smiling. "You see, you are going to arrive in San Francisco as an extremely well-known *avant garde* lady poet from England. Don't worry, that's already arranged." She nodded toward a book on the table at her elbow and said, "We have even managed to have some of your poems published by an English house in this world of mine we are about to enter."

"But that's unbelievable!" gasped Elspeth. She rose and took the book from the table, leafed through it with trembling fingers. Incredibly, although paper and binding were of a type unfamiliar to her, her verses were there, the so-slim little end product of so many hours and days and months and years of soul-searching thought and work.

She turned to the contents page, felt sudden nostalgia quicken within her at the sight of the titles—*My Love Is Yesterday, Luisa, Irish Sea, The Slender Wing,* and all the so-well-remembered others. Slowly her surroundings faded and she was no longer on this alien train, speeding inexorably toward an alien destination in an alien world.

She was once again, through a rollback of time, in the company of a black-haired young ruffian named Kevin, who had made violent and romantic love to her on a windy afternoon in an ancient ruin of a castle keep overlooking St. George's Channel. She was again straining to follow the flight of a swift gray-blue swallow as it darted and soared amid the chaste spires and brick chimney tops of a green-and-white New England town. She was once again back amid an incredible cluster of brilliant . . .

Mack whistled, long, loud and shrill, said, "For Chrissakes come out of it, Elly."

She did, apologetically as always, laid down the little volume and smiled sheepishly at Juana, who smiled back sympathetically. "I'm sorry," she told them. "But seeing my work just now brought back memories I was unable to escape."

"You're fortunate to be able to wrap yourself in dreams," said Juana, and drew a look of utter incredulity from the more practical Mack. Juana ignored it and went on with her briefing of Elly. "You'll be interviewed by the press within an hour of your arrival. From the moment the stories appear things will take care of themselves."

"And what about you two in this picture?" Elspeth inquired.

Juana laughed. "Oh, we're your entourage," she explained. "I'm your personal attendant—take care of all the mundane details your poetic soul refuses to handle. As for Mack"—she twinkled a sidelong glance at the photographer—"he's going to be your secretary. It seems you can't abide to work with women. Incidentally, we travel with you everywhere. Get that, Elly—*everywhere!*"

"Hold on," said Mack, his face red beneath its tan. "Do you mean *I* have to traipse around as Elly's personal stooge? Good God! Not only am I nobody's secretary, but I don't know the—"

"*Mack!*" Juana quelled his outburst. "Elly will be our one direct contact with President Roosevelt. She's the star of this act, and can you think of a better excuse for lugging that attaché case with you everywhere than as a private secretary?"

Mack muttered and fumed volcanically for a while, then subsided. Finally he said, "But when your President gets this space-flight data what's he going to do with it?"

"He is going to offer it to the United Nations," Juana replied, "the moment it is successful. It will not only give the billion and a quarter people of Asia a chance, but will focus all the world's hope, rather than their hatred, on America."

"Why don't the damn fools try birth control?" said Mack.

"Emotionally and religiously they simply aren't geared to it," replied Juana. "That is perhaps their greatest tragedy."

They continued to discuss aspects of the assignment as the rocket train sped across the plains of Missouri. Later they played cards, had cocktails and dinner. They had barely finished their salad course when they passed through Kansas City.

"This go-wagon makes time," Mack remarked.

"She makes almost two hundred over a straight flat stretch like this one," Soames informed them as he put a trio of enticing fruit compotes on the table. "She's only slow up the river."

After dinner, at Juana's suggestion, Elspeth read some of Christine Roosevelt's poems. They were, as she had expected, neither good nor bad—typical verses by an intelligent well-bred reasonably well-educated girl with a slight flair for word rhythms.

If the President's daughter had ever felt an unorthodox emotion there was no hint of it in her neatly scanned iambic, trochaic and anapaestic lines. This, Elspeth sensed, was a well-disciplined young lady. And to Elspeth both discipline and lady-ism were the sworn enemies of true poetry.

She wondered how on earth—whatever Earth this was— she was going to find anything kind to say about such facelifted doggerel. She decided to concentrate upon being nice about a neat turn of phrase here and there amid the mediocrity. In toto Christine Roosevelt's verse was inconsequential—not bad nor anything else.

"I had a hunch you'd find you had a job on your hands," said Juana, correctly interpreting Elspeth's expression from her armchair on the other side of the lounge. "Incidentally, Elly, I read your verse too—and was impressed. You don't write crud."

"What a ghastly word—and thought!" said Elspeth, laughing in spite of herself. She tapped the book of verse by the President's daughter. "But as for this—don't worry. I'll manage."

"You can always call on your secretary if the more delicate nuances elude you," said Juana, her face perfectly straight.

"Quiet, please," snapped Mack, "for the benefit of those who have expired." He lapsed into the dazed surliness that had enveloped him since Juana had informed him what part he was to play in their forthcoming incursion into her world.

As the evening wore on Elspeth found herself baffled by the relationship between Mack and Juana. Whatever it had been—and she knew it had been plenty—it was strictly business now. She had an idea, from the way both were behaving, that it was Juana who had slammed the door. Mack seemed to be the unhappy one.

She thought it served the big tomcat right. But being woman and intrigued with the photographer despite herself, she could not quite restrain a faint sense of resentment at Juana for having so casually won and so cavalierly discarded him.

It was close upon midnight when the train once more went into the series of lurches that announced it was slowing for a stop. Soames, the steward, appeared from somewhere, wearing his overcoat and carrying a small black bag. "I'm to leave you alone in the car on the side track and stay forward with the rest of the train?" he asked Juana.

The redhead nodded. "Right, Soames, and thanks for taking such good care of us. You'll find the car all right when the train comes back to pick it up in"—she glanced at her jeweled wrist watch—"exactly seventeen minutes. Good-by, Soames."

She opened her bag and handed the steward a bill of large denomination. He bowed to all of them and moved forward out of sight through the corridor. Juana's lips tightened and she seemed to stiffen when the train finally halted. "Transfer time," she said.

"What do we do?" Elspeth asked her, frightened.

"Relax," said Juana, taking a deep breath. "Don't ask me how it works. You went through it once and know as much as I do. Better move all your gear back here." She nodded toward their luggage, which Soames had piled neatly at the front of the lounge. "The new car may be of different design forward and things might get lost."

Elspeth discovered that her handbag was missing and went to her stateroom to get it. As she opened the door she could look ahead to the front of the car, could see the receding rocket flares of what had been their train moving slowly ahead on the siding. It gave her an unpleasantly lonely sensation.

She found her bag stuck in the washroom where she had left it, and slung it over her shoulder. Then she noticed the silver tureen of zabaglione which Soames had left for her. A taste of it, she decided, might help to settle the queasiness that had settled in her stomach since the train had begun to slow down.

Elspeth lifted the silver lid and reached for the silver ladle within the bowl. Then she stood frozen, staring down into it. The bowl was empty.

It had not been washed. There were well-scraped traces of foamy yellow clinging to its curved sides and to the ladle. And similar traces on one of the three small dessert cups on the tray beside the tureen. Someone had eaten every bit of it.

It must have been Soames, she thought. But it *couldn't* have been Soames. Had he wanted some, he'd have made more for himself. Mack might have eaten it, but he had professed an ardent dislike of all shapes and forms of Italian cooking, from antipasto to *caffè espresso*. And somehow she knew Juana wouldn't have . . .

Like Goldilocks, she thought, and the Three Bears—and for the first time she wondered if the little bear had felt a fear to match the rising tide of panic within herself. Of course the little bear had had his father and mother along for security, while she had—Juana and Mack.

With this thought she hurried from the stateroom and back along the corridor to the lounge. She wanted to tell them what had happened, to find out if either of them knew anything about it. She had just passed the pile of luggage when the darkness came.

XII

All in all, the black vacuum could scarcely have endured for more than two or three minutes. But to Elspeth, already fighting panic over the mysteriously eaten zabaglione in her stateroom, out of physical contact with either Mack or Juana, it seemed like a lifetime of Dantesque horror. She was further startled by an unfamiliar drumming noise until she discovered that it came from the chattering of her own teeth. Fighting the inner and outer chill that seemed about to overwhelm her, she forced herself to stand perfectly still in the blank void, wondering what cosmic changes were happening about her, feeling cold sweat bead her forehead.

Then, as suddenly as it had come, the darkness was gone. There was Mack, looking in her direction with an expression on his face that seemed to ask what that damned chucklehead had done now to foul things up. There was Juana, also looking her way, her dark eyes wide with concern. In the gush of relief she felt at being once more able to see them, in her interest in their changed surroundings, Elspeth completely forgot the panic that had shaken her so completely in the stateroom minutes before.

Gone with the darkness were the gingerbread, gilt, ivory and azure decorations of Minister of Finance Alston's private car. In their place was a subtly severe modern lounge section of glass and stainless steel and carefully grained blond woods, and carpet and upholstery of pastel tweed. Lighting was, for the most part, soft and indirect, and at the partition which divided observation lounge from forward stateroom section stood a curved satinwood bar, backed by a glittering array of glassware and bottles and a brilliantly colored mural in sophisticated imitation of a Hopi Indian primitive.

"It's like making an aircraft-carrier landing at sea," said Juana, exhaling her relief and then lighting a cigarette with fingers that caused the lighter flame to dip and tremble. "No matter how many times you make it safely you're always glad to get through it okay—or so some of the boys have told me."

There were sounds of a train backing toward them, followed by a slight jar as the coupling was completed. Then, acquiring impetus more slowly but far more smoothly than in the rocket-driven train, they got under way once more. Less than thirty seconds later an ebony-hued steward in starched white jacket was moving toward them from the corridor, smiling and inquiring if they had any preferences as to the staterooms they wished him to make up for them.

"Wonder whose car we drew this time?" murmured Mack, looking about him in speculative fashion. "My, things certainly have changed!"

"I believe it belongs to one of the wealthier members of a family named Vanderbilt," Juana told them. "They're quite big stuff in this world—finance, sports, politics, the works."

"Likewise in our world," said Mack. "I did a feature once on their sixty-room summer shack in Newport. But I never dreamed I'd be roughing it in one of their private land yachts."

They decided to simplify matters by selecting staterooms that corresponded to those they had occupied in Finance Minister Alston's car. Elspeth found hers to be even more compact and comfortable and well arranged than its predecessor. She looked for and noted the absence of the omnipresent dental powder of the Columbian world. Alone in front of her mirror, she felt a quick pang of homesickness for Marshal John—followed by a twinge of recurrent panic over the empty tureen of zabaglione.

But the very thought of that elaborate sterling-silver tureen, she decided, was anachronistic in this neatly modernized world. It belonged with Reed Weston and Marshal John and, yes, with the viciously effete Everard van Hooten, to the picturesque world they had so recently left.

THE HOUSE OF MANY WORLDS 125

As she strolled back to the lounge to rejoin Mack and Juana she wondered why, at such a time, she should have thought of Everard at all.

Their new steward, whose name was Marcus, proved fully as courteous an attendant and an even swifter and defter drink mixer than Soames. Yet, sitting on soft tweed upholstery and sipping a tall frosted rum punch through a long straw, Elspeth again felt her tensions and worries tauten within her. They had only six days left in which to accomplish their vastly complex mission.

She thought of Marshal Henry's precarious position and hated the fact that there was nothing to do but relax and rest until they reached San Francisco. But it did not prove exactly restful. She and Mack pounded questions at Juana about the locale of their new assignment until the little redhead smilingly begged off on the grounds of fatigue and departed alone for her stateroom and bed.

Looking after her, Elspeth shook her ash-blond head and said to Mack, "There goes the most amazing person I have ever met."

"You can say that again and again," said Mack softly into his drink. "You have no idea *how* amazing." A dreamy cat-plus-canary film overspread his countenance.

Elspeth felt a sudden surge of desire to grab the photographer's short heavy hair with both fists and pull it out in clumps. However, she somehow managed to restrain herself—or perhaps her bringing up did it for her. Instead she said savagely, "You don't seem to be doing so well in that quarter yourself any more, sugar plum," and, picking up the two volumes of poetry, took off with what she hoped was a fair imitation of haughty disdain for her own stateroom.

It was her intention to put in at least another hour of swotting over the poetry of Christine Roosevelt, but the motion of the train was satin smooth and the rum drinks apparently more potent than their bland texture had suggested. It was a mere matter of minutes before she fell asleep, barely remembering in time to switch off the convenient little wall reading lamp at the head of her bunk.

Elspeth felt fed, rested and more than ready to face the problems of two new worlds as their train pulled into San

Francisco late the following afternoon. Her tension and fears had faded with her awakening that morning, and a mounting excitement over the experiences that lay ahead had seen to it that they had not returned.

A glance at Mack, sitting upright in his chair, showed her that the photographer too was thoroughly keyed for whatever might lie before them. Despite the impassiveness of his rather battered face, it was there in the slightly aggressive set of his shoulders, in the careful reserve of his movements as he studied in an opposite-wall mirror the cut of the clothes he was wearing. They were not quite a perfect fit, but they had a smart cool-weather look that would have been alien in the hot Columbian capital.

Juana appeared, to Elspeth, incredibly well poised for a young woman returning to her own world after long absence, but unuttered emotion glowed in her large dark eyes, and during the day she had been given to unusual periods of silence that increased in direct proportion to their approach to the West Coast city.

Having registered these opinions to herself, Elspeth was in the act of contemplating her own appearance—in a rakishly cut dress of gray flannel with a diagonal white stripe and a soft-brimmed white felt hat that put unexpected but definitely intriguing shadows beneath her eyes, an outfit furnished like Mack's new garments and Juana's by the generous owner of the car—when sudden sounds of a violent scuffle somewhere forward brought her quickly to full attention.

The train was in the act of pulling into the terminal, and Marcus, the new steward, had been checking over the compartments and preparing to disembark their gear. Elspeth heard his soft southern voice cry out in sudden alarm, heard the thuddings of a number of hard fist blows, followed quickly by an unpleasant noise that was half gurgle, half scream quickly cut off.

"Hi-*yi!*" shouted Mack, leaping from his chair and moving swiftly forward through the corridor in the direction of the sounds of fracas, still carrying the attaché case. Peering after him, Elspeth saw him reach the door of the stateroom from which the fight noises seemed to be coming, turn in to enter the room on the run, still shouting.

Elspeth did not see or register accurately much of what

happened in the next few seconds. A fist lashed out through the door without warning, nailing the onrushing photographer with impeccable precision full on the point of the chin. Mack's head flew back with such sudden violence that Elspeth screamed, afraid that his neck was broken. Arms flailing, attaché case and all, he was literally flung back across the corridor, which he momentarily filled with his bulk.

Just at that instant a slimmer male figure seemed almost to fly out of the contested stateroom, to race quickly forward toward the next car. In view of the confusion he left in his wake, it was utterly out of the question for either of the girls to get as much as a clear view of his back. And before either girl could reach Mack, who was leaning against the corridor wall, his eyes glassy, the interloper had slammed the door of the private car behind him and vanished.

Mack, Elspeth decided, must have kept his grip on the attaché case by sheer reflex action. Certainly he was completely out on his feet. He looked at both Juana and herself, as they rushed up, without a trace of recognition, then began slowly to fall forward away from the wall. Elspeth could think of nothing to do but push him back against it by putting her left hand against his chest, thus holding him upright while she tried, foolishly, to fan him back to life with her handbag.

Juana, who had produced unexpectedly a small but very wicked-looking automatic pistol, which she handled in a highly professional fashion, darted past the pair of them into the compartment. She was still inside when Mack, with the first stirrings of consciousness, took an awkward round-house swing at Elspeth, knocking her white felt hat half off her head.

For some reason this made her furious and effectively smothered the sympathy she had been feeling. "You big blind baboon!" she shouted. "I thought you used to be a fighter. Can't you even stay out of the way of a fist?"

Mack shook his head and peered at her, but his eyes were still clouded. "Sonuvabitch hit me—when I wasn' lookin'," he mumbled. With which he attempted to take another poke at Elspeth, who lost her head and brought her handbag hard against the side of his head. For some reason this seemed to clear it and he looked at her and blinked.

"What happened?" he asked stupidly. Elspeth stepped clear of him, as he seemed once more steady on his feet, and Juana called them from the open stateroom. Marcus, it appeared, was in far worse shape than Mack.

Juana was calmly putting her pistol away in her bag when they entered. "There's no sense in trying a pursuit," she said calmly, although an unusual vertical furrow marred the smooth surface of her brow. "He's got clean away by this time. Come on, Mack, give us a hand with poor Marcus. Whoever it was certainly laid it on him."

She helped hold the poor unfortunate steward's gory head steady while a still-dazed and thoroughly chastened Mack did the heavy job of stretching Marcus out on the bunk. The black man was badly messed about. Blood was welling from a two-inch cut under his right eye, and even his dark skin could not hide signs of further battering. By using the towels and water handy in the stateroom lavatory, they managed to get him pretty well cleaned up and the blood stanched before he opened his eyes and moaned.

"Donno who done it to me," he said when he was sufficiently recovered to answer questions as to what had happened. "I jes' come in here to see the room's in shape for Mr. V. when—*powie!*—the lights go on all over the place."

"Did you get a look at him, Marcus?" Mack asked eagerly. "Even an impression will help."

"All I know is that he sure could hit," said the steward. "I thought he'd pulverized me fo' sure. An' my neck—it feels like I jes' stepped down from a necktie party." His face clouded and he looked ready for tears. "I sure am sorry to have had it happen. I guess I jes' wasn't doin' my job right, folks."

"You were fine, Marcus. It wasn't your fault, whatever happened—you can depend on that," said Juana soothingly. "Now, unless you want us to call you a doctor or an ambulance let's forget it ever happened. Okay, Marcus?"

"I donno about that," said the steward, looking relieved. "I'm not like to forget it. But I'll be all right, Miss Juana."

"Swell," said Juana, "but don't take chances. Just in case you do have any aftereffects . . ." She handed him a bill of very large denomination—a type of money new to Elspeth and Mack—and the three of them went on belatedly about their business of getting off the train.

Juana handled matters with brisk efficiency once they reached the platform. She acquired porters and a taxicab and informed a trio of reporters who had turned up to meet the celebrated English poet that they would interview any of the press who cared to see her later at the hotel. She did not waste a word until the three of them were safely installed in a broad-windowed suite on an upper story of a caravansary whose hill setting overlooked the incredible nature-and-manmade magnificence of San Francisco Bay.

Then, leaning back in an armchair and lighting a cigarette, she curtly interrupted Elspeth's rhapsodic delight in the view and Mack's mutterings about having walked into a sneak-punch with an unexpectedly stern and forthright little diatribe.

"I neither understand nor like what happened just now on that train," she informed them. "One of the greatest advantages we of the interworld service have—and one of its basic reasons for absolute secrecy—is that we can move into whatever world needs us most without warning elements that might conceivably be able to oppose us effectively granted time to prepare."

"In other words, you're afraid your Asiatic friends may be ready to play rough," Mack said thoughtfully. "Funny, I got that impression when you briefed us on the situation last night."

"But how could they know?" said Juana, looking baffled. "There can't have been a leak. Even if there had been one, no supposedly sane person would believe it. That's one of our greatest protections—no one except the initiate ever has."

"There has to be a first time, honey," Mack said softly.

"*Oh!*" Elspeth sat up straight on the windowseat and one of her hands flew to her mouth. She had just remembered the incident of the zabaglione. She told them about it.

"It's possible," said Juana, frowning again. "Though if it happened, it's the first interworld stowaway in history so far as I know. And if it did happen it only makes things worse."

"You mean that it will open up the tangency points to anyone who wants to change worlds?" Mack asked, rubbing his chin, on which a large purple bruise was putting in its appearance.

"Hardly." Juana dismissed this suggestion with a gesture. "It is not that simple. But any so-and-so smart enough to jump worlds without guidance or training is smart enough not to have missed my briefing yesterday in the train. Which means he'll be smart enough to know how to contact our enemies here and try to sell them our story."

"I wonder who it is—and why," mused Elspeth.

"We'll probably find out soon enough, never fear," Juana said dryly. She rose and shook down her skirt, looking absurdly little-girl-dressed-up in the process. "All right, kids, let's get set for the big act with the press."

Under the circumstances it was a considerable ordeal, but when at last it was over Juana informed Elspeth that she had played her role of visiting English poet very well. Elspeth pushed a strand of dark blond hair back from her forehead and released a grin that had been lurking deep within her. "I never knew I was such a ham," she said. "I actually loved it."

"You use the word ham that way in your world too?" said Juana. "Funny. Do you suppose people like us carry our slang from world to world?"

"Speaking of ham—I'm hungry," said Mack, looking sullen but relieved at having got away with playing the part of Elspeth's personal secretary—which had taxed his histrionic ability to the bone.

They dined in a magnificent restaurant atop the hotel, with a panoramic view of the city and bay which far surpassed in sweep that from the window of their drawing room six floors below. Elspeth felt wide-eyed and young at the attention they drew from headwaiter and lesser servitors—with herself its focal point. Being a celebrity—even a manufactured one—had its points, she decided.

And the view was incredible. San Francisco was a great city in her world and Mack's—but nothing like this. The tracery of lights along the bridges, the towering skyscrapers, the blaze of suburban cities across the bay . . . Breathtaking was the only word for it.

Elspeth wondered how it could be put into poetry. Surely the spectacle must have inspired thousands of versifiers in this magnificent new world—some of whom must have caught fragments of its grandeur in words and rhythm. She would like to approach it from another way, the way of infinite relative smallness.

Perhaps some early giant of legend—a giant who played among the tall sequoias like a child among saplings—might return from his wanderings to find this vast city sprawled over one of his former playgrounds, might feel dwarfed for the first time in his life. He might even—But she decided it was pretty corny.

Unexpectedly someone in a full-dress party two tables away recognized Juana and they were suddenly in the swirling center of a swarm of revelers. Elspeth found it hard to keep up with the rapid-fire chatter, the clang, the shared allusions. But Juana acquired a new glow and interpreted for them with practiced ease.

After all, as the visiting poet from abroad, Elspeth was in character as a vague and remote creature. And Mack, as a mere secretary, was not supposed to talk, although one or two of the girls glanced at him speculatively from time to time during the ninety-odd minutes they spent as members of the party. Elspeth fell prey to a pang of jealousy and detested herself for it.

Later, back in their suite, Juana kicked off her slippers and massaged her tiny feet thoughtfully. "I speeded things up a bit there, I think," she said. "That heavy brunette is a senator's daughter and a great pal of sweet Christine. I have a hunch you'll be hearing from the gal herself by tomorrow noon."

She frowned, released her foot and reached for a cigarette. "I wish I knew for certain who pulled that hassle on the train this afternoon—even more what his contacts are—and his motives. Unless he's clever as hell it's going to take him a little time to make connections, especially since he'll be using that Columbian funny money. He might land in jail for passing the stuff, but I'm afraid that's too much to hope for."

Elspeth once again found herself thinking of Everard— as she had thought of him when she found the zabaglione missing. He was clever, he was tough, he had reason to hate Mack and herself. They had not only wrecked his assignment, they were also menacing the war upon which his emotional and material welfare depended.

"I wonder," she began. The others looked at her expectantly and all at once she felt intuitive and foolish. "It's nothing," she told them. "Merely a zany fancy. I'm going to turn in."

They rose in midmorning and breakfasted *en trois* in the drawing room. The city beyond their window was curtained thickly with fog. It was, on the whole, an oppressive and miserable morning. Mack brooded over his attaché case like a human bulldog, and Juana and Elspeth scanned the papers. It did the poet small inner good to find herself described as a "colorlessly incisive and typically British blonde whose conversation seems to consist chiefly of unrhymed and occasionally profane monosyllables."

"On the nose!" said Mack with a nasty chuckle when Juana read it to them. Elspeth told him, to no avail, to close his large rhinoceros mouth, and turned sulky. Mack got out his heavy pistol and checked its workings. He had the whole thing apart when the telephone rang, making them all jump.

"Miss Marriner's apartment," Juana said smoothly. She listened briefly, then winked and nodded at the others. Mack finally got his weapon reassembled with a succession of metallic clicks.

"Yes, I feel certain Miss Marriner would be honored," said Juana. "Of course she never goes anywhere without Mr. Fraser and myself . . . Fine, I do hope that won't be too inconvenient . . . Certainly. We shall be ready at four."

Hanging up, Juana put her hands on her hips and did a bump grind. "This is it, kids," she told them, grinning. "The President and sweet Christine are staying at one of those monstrous places out on the peninsula. We, it seems, are very much wanted. They're even sending a car for us at four o'clock. Yipe! What a relief! I just dropped ten years somewhere."

"Careful, child," said Elspeth. "That would put you well under the age of consent."

Juana grimaced at her, thumbed her nose at Mack and did an off-to-Buffalo into her own bedroom. "If I'm to visit the President, I'm going to be sure my seams are straight," she informed them over one shoulder.

Mack headed for his room, hesitated, then came back and picked up the attaché case. Elspeth sat still a moment, putting her thoughts in order. She was going to have to go it alone without a single slip from here on in. All at once she was frightened—and not of Everard or Asiatic agents. This was just plain stage terror.

Four o'clock took a long time coming, but the phone rang almost on the dot with the announcement that a car was waiting downstairs to pick up Miss Marriner and staff. Mack enlisted the aid of the elevator man to tote their suitcases, but he carried the attaché case to the lift himself.

Just as the elevator doors opened in the lobby, one of the passengers, a middle-aged woman of pasty complexion, gave a groan and began to topple in a faint. Involuntarily Mack moved to help her from the elevator. At this the other passenger, a heavy-set man with a blue chin, stepped forward and, wordlessly, yanked the attaché case from Mack's startled grasp.

There followed a confused tussle, in the course of which the "fainting" woman hit the operator over the head with what seemed to a loaded umbrella, Mack slugged the heavy-set marauder, and the attaché case was bashed open.

Seconds later both heavy-set man and middle-aged woman were lost amid the crowd in the lobby, while a curious swarm blanketed the view of their flight. Standing on tiptoe, Elspeth tried to look over the tumult and follow their attackers' escape route. She caught a quick glimpse of them darting through a revolving door into the fog—while an elegant and too-familiar figure covered their retreat.

"Everard!" she cried.

Mack cursed. "The dirty bastards got away with my fuel sample," he growled. "Well, what do we do now?"

XIII

"Get back upstairs—quickly," snapped Juana. "The Presidential car is going to have to wait." Swearing under her breath in a monotone but with characteristic efficiency, she herded them into another elevator, brushed off dismayed hotel employees, and somehow, in less than a minute, restored them, frightened and disheveled, to the security of their suite.

"The dirty bastards really did it," muttered Mack. He shook his head as he surveyed the wreckage of his precious attaché case and indulged in further explicit profanity. His tie was half out of sight under one wing of his collar and a button dangled from his jacket by a single thread.

"Every time—just when it looks easy," mourned Elspeth, "it seems as if things go wrong."

"You'll get used to it, Elspeth," said Juana absently. Standing in the middle of the carpet, she was biting her lower lip in deep concentration.

"Dammit!" said Mack in irate frustration. "I had a hunch the weasel meant trouble from the beginning. But if I'd known how much . . ." He shook his head and cursed again. "These loving plans are worse than useless without the fuel. And without the sample it may take them years to get it. Everard's cooked our goose."

"For God's *sake,* stop using those tired clichés!" snapped Elspeth, whose nerves were not only on edge but their beam ends.

"Shut up—both of you," said Juana, frowning. She had gone to the telephone and was in the processss of dialing a number herself after getting an outside line from the switchboard. She had insisted upon such a phone before taking the suite.

Getting her connection, she said tersely, "Juana Brooks . . . forty-seven . . . this world . . . blue emergency." She then gave a concise and well-organized account of what had happened—including a complete description of their two elevator attackers. She mentioned Everard, listened briefly, then looked across at Elspeth with her eyebrows lifted. "Everard," she said. "Can you give a description?"

"You're goddamned well right," Mack broke in before Elspeth could assemble her thoughts. "Five-eleven. No, make it five-eleven and a half. About one-sixty—light brown hair—light blue eyes—very fair skin, almost sallow—hairline mustache on upper lip—"

"Also a bit of a swish," interrupted Elspeth, surprised at the accuracy of Mack's memory but determined not to show it. "Keeps a silk handkerchief up his left sleeve—accent very British, at least while he was with us. *And* a purple bee tattooed just behind his left ear."

"That ought to do it," said Juana, who had been repeating their words verbatim into the mouthpiece. Then, ignoring them in favor of her unseen collocutor, "Have you orders to cover the situation?" She listened for several seconds, murmured, "Got it—I understand perfectly," put the phone back on its cradle and turned to face them. "This is a real rabbit punch and no fooling," she told them quietly, hesitated, then added, "Now here's the pitch. You two are to carry on. Get fixed up and go along in the Presidential car as we planned. Elly, play Christine Roosevelt but keep moving in on the President, every chance you get—but slowly and carefully. If you have any doubts about making a move, don't move. Arrangements are being made to put all of us up in one of the guest cottages on the estate.

"And don't forget this. When you've talked enough poetry to make Christine happy, tell her you've always wanted to meet General Curtis—you saw his picture somewhere and think he's fascinating. Try to make arrangements to meet him somewhere tomorrow where Mack and I can talk to him. Get him to come to the cottage for a drink with Christine maybe. Curtis is a red-hot guided-missile man and he is also very close to the President. If you have to, tell Christine you're mad to do a big poem about rockets and the magic of space flight. Have you got all that?"

"I think so," said Elly, working her memory overtime. Once more she was feeling like someone walking through a nightmare that simply had to come to an end soon.

"You'd better," said Juana, in whom crisp and ruthless efficiency had replaced all traces of languorous charm. Then, turning to the photographer, "Mack, I want you to give me those blueprints—but take the attaché case with you. Here, you can fill it with these." She picked up the newspapers they had been reading, handed them to him, took the precious blueprints, and stowed them away carefully in her handbag.

"And I want both of you to talk, talk, talk about the assault in the elevator as if it were utterly inexplicable. Nothing was taken, mind you. After all, why should anyone want to rob a poet? This will focus attention on you, get you both noticed. Now beat it, both of you, while I try to square this—and good luck."

"But how about you, Juana?" Elspeth asked, worried.

"And how about those blueprints?" inquired Mack.

"Don't worry, either of you. I'll be okay," said Juana with a serene confidence that brooked no denial. "I'll be along later on—sometime after dinner tonight probably. You might arrange things so that I can get to the cottage without too much red tape. In the meantime, I'll get after the disintegrator shield—whatever it is. We're in a honey of a jam and we've all got to play our parts perfectly or we shan't get out of it. Now scram!"

Once again the three of them rode down in the elevator together. Mack nursed the briefcase as if it were a two-pound baby. They had still to wade through considerable confusion in the lobby—a natural aftermath of the hugger-mugger—but they managed to get outside to the waiting limousine without much trouble. There, on the sidewalk, Juana left them with a faint grin and a finger salute.

"Lordy, what a wonderful person that little girl is!" said Elspeth when they were driven smoothly out into traffic behind the broad back of an expert chauffeur.

"Ummmmm," said Mack thoughtfully. Elspeth glanced sharply at her partner, saw that he was looking out the window in a sort of abstraction, a slight frown on his face. He added, his voice low, "She's a lot more woman than little girl."

"All *right!*" said Elspeth testily. "I wasn't thinking of *that*, you old goat."

Mack turned to give her a twisted smile. "Oddly enough," he told her, "neither was I."

The fog lifted with knifelike suddenness when they passed the rim of the city hills, and they drove the magnificent miles to the peninsula in a warm bath of golden afternoon sunlight. They passed smoothly through trim small towns and hamlets, through areas of broad shaven lawns and carefully landscaped greenery, caught occasional glimpses of great estates resting securely in their settings of hedges, flowers, and trees.

"D'you know, Mack," Elspeth said suddenly, "I think I like this world. It's alive and imaginative—and young."

"It's fast, but it seems happy," said Mack with unexpected insight. "It would be a dirty shame if it were all spoiled."

"That simply stinking Everard," said Elspeth. "Remember, back in Columbia, when I said I was glad he escaped?" Then, as the photographer nodded, "I don't feel that way any more, Mack."

For the first time in her life she was beginning to learn the real meaning of personal hate. She had known dislikes, of course—some of them violent—but in general they had been of an abstract or at most inanimate nature. What she was feeling now was something utterly new to her, something she could tell she was never going to forget. And it gave her new insight into many people whose behavior had simply puzzled her before.

"*Hey!*" cried Mack, pulling away from her in mock alarm. "Don't bite a hunk out of *me*. I didn't steal the fuel sample. All I ever got was a smack on a very glass jaw."

"Sorry, Mack," she said. She laughed a little mirthless laugh, then forced herself to relax the muscles at the corners of her mouth. "I'm afraid I feel pretty were-wolfish about poor dear Everard. Why didn't we kill him when we had him in the Pipit?"

"That's my girl," said the photographer approvingly. "But we couldn't—then. We didn't know enough." Elspeth was still pondering this somewhat cryptic statement when the limousine stopped before a wrought-iron gate in a long brick wall, a gate which was promptly opened by an alert-looking pair of young-old men. One of them queried the driver briefly, then they were passed on through.

A quarter of a mile farther on, past more lawns, landscaped groves, and artfully cut hedges, they halted again beneath a large white porte-cochère in front of an immense porticoed mansion built in neoclassic style. There another pair of Secret Service operatives looked them over closely, after which a youthful butler in ribbed waistcoat, blue tailcoat, brass buttons and breeches came out and entered the front seat of the limousine.

On broad crushed gravel they were driven around the immense house and perhaps two hundred yards beyond it to a comparatively small white cottage, which nestled in dark cedars on a gentle bank above a shimmering blue-gray lake. Here the butler took their luggage—save for Mack's now-dummy attaché case—and ushered them into the cottage. His manner was somewhat apologetic.

"Mr. Gardienne told me to tell you that he hopes you won't mind being so far from the main house," he informed them. "But with the President's party here . . ." He paused politely to express his regret, added, "Whenever you are ready, Miss Marriner, Miss Roosevelt is waiting to see you. You can reach the house directly by crossing the side lawn." He pointed the way and left.

"Slumming!" said Mack. "I love it!" He prowled around the low-ceiled luxuriously appointed living room with its well-equipped bar and fireplace. It was a "cottage" only by comparison with the many-elled neoclassic monster house across the lawn.

"This work does have its little compensations," said Elspeth with a sigh. Not only did the cottage boast three luxurious bedrooms, each with its own bath, but in the rear were a small dining room and serving pantry as well.

"I don't know quite why it is, but every time I get in a place like this where all I want to do is loll around I seem to have a job to do," said Mack mournfully. He sank into an armchair, put his feet up on a hassock, lit a cigarette, grinned lazily. "This time is the exception. *You've* got the job, boss-woman. So get on your horse and gallop off to it."

"Don't remind me," pleaded Elspeth, who was too

nervous at the prospect of what lay ahead of her even to feel up to swapping insults with the photographer. She went into her bathroom, checked dress, hairdo and make-up, did what little she could, and emerged with a sigh. Mack had a quick straight drink ready for her—she noted that he had poured himself an interesting-looking highball—which she downed nervously before setting out across the side lawn to the great house.

Christine Roosevelt proved to be a complete surprise. Instead of the assured, mentally corseted young lady her poems had led Elspeth to expect, the President's daughter proved to be a tall, sensitive, rather shy girl, much younger looking than her pictures, a girl whose lack of assurance made her almost diffident during the opening gambits of their conversation.

"It was terrific of you to come here to see me, Miss Marriner," she said after maneuvering Elspeth into what appeared to be her own private drawing room on the second floor. Around them the house was literally larded with a feeling of movement, of importance, of comings and goings and low-pitched conversations, of the presence of far more people than it had been built for or was accustomed to contain.

"I've read your poems, Miss Roosevelt," Elspeth said blutnly when they were seated over a tea tray. From memory of her own past shyness she knew that the quick kindly incision was the best method of piercing the barrier between them.

"They stink, don't they?" said the President's daughter with an attack of diffidence that caused her to look away toward a lofty window hung with old-gold damask drapes.

"No, they don't stink," said Elspeth quietly and with all the sincerity she could muster. "But they aren't poetry yet."

"Oh! Do you think they ever *will* be?" Christine asked eagerly, her shyness vanishing in the face of even such negative interest. Her rather plain face was alight with sudden hope.

"That," said Elspeth, "is entirely up to you. I don't want to sound bromidic, but if you want to write poetry you've got to cut yourself loose from the world you were planted in and find or build one of your own."

"But how *can* I?" the girl asked almost tragically,

brushing a wisp of near-silver hair back from her high narrow forehead. "I mean, being a President's daughter and all . . ." She made a hopeless little gesture. Elspeth felt a flood of sympathy for her and spoke as gently as she could and with sincerity.

"You can find your new world within yourself—you must if you are ever to find it anywhere," Elspeth told her, and then they were off. To the surprise of both of them they found they were only two years apart in age. They were still at it hot and heavy when a tall rather portly man with white hair and a face which showed intense fatigue entered the room without knocking.

"Dad!" cried Christine, rising and giving him a hug. "When did you get out of conference? I thought those Yugoslavs—"

"Old Chichi's gout acted up and they called it off," he said with a sudden and utterly infectious smile. "So I hightailed it right out here. I got out of the conference, but I still want a drink. Just you and me, how about it, Chris?"

"But, Dad," protested his daughter. "I have Elly—Miss Marriner—here. Don't be so rude."

"Just leaving," said Elspeth, smiling and moving toward the door. The President clapped a hand over his forehead and stepped in front of her to bar her path.

"Miss Marriner, you'll have to stay if only to cover my embarrassment," he said, extending a large and friendly hand. "Are you telling my daughter how to write poetry?"

"She's tremendous, Dad," said the President's daughter. "I'll ring for a drink for all of us." She suited the action to the word. In the meanwhile the President frankly studied Elspeth.

"You look a lot better than your pictures," he told her with intonation that robbed the remark of any unkindness. A look of quick concern crossed his face. "But didn't I hear something about your being attacked in town on your way here?"

"It was nothing," said Elspeth in what she hoped was a tone bound to draw further questions. It worked, and for the next half hour she was busy explaining the incident for the two of them.

At the end of that time a secretary in striped pants entered and whispered in the President's ear. He sighed, put down his glass, said, "They've caught up with me, kids."

He rose, shook hands with Elspeth, added, "Is there anything I can do to make your visit with us more pleasant?"

Elspeth gathered herself, said bluntly, "As a matter of fact, I'd like very much to meet General Curtis, if I might."

"*Et tu*, Elly?" said Christine in mock despair.

"He's a wolf," the President informed her with a smile.

"He's also the best rocketman in the world, I hear," said Elspeth. "I want to pump him dry. I'm dreadfully keen about the possibility of space flight. One of my reasons for coming here was the hope of seeing White Sands. I may base my next poem on it."

"Curt isn't much on poetry, so far as I know," said the President, "but he's really jet-propelled where rockets are concerned."

"*And* anything in skirts, slacks, or shorts," said Christine dryly. "But if you *must* meet him, Elly, I can probably arrange it."

Her brashness paid off. Not only did she meet the dark and gallant General Curtis when she went back to the big house for dinner, but she was actually seated next to him at table. To her surprise, he proved to be utterly serious when she suggested that there might be inspiration for a man's efforts to escape his planet and fly the reaches of space. His black eyes narrowed as he considered it.

"It demands poetry—and an engineering miracle," he told her. "I only hope we both get a chance to know space first-hand before we die. But we have a lot of bridges yet to cross."

"You sound awfully discouraged, General," said Elspeth with what she hoped was something approaching dimpled charm. "Perhaps, if you're not too busy, you could come to my cottage for a cocktail before lunch tomorrow—you and Christine. I might be able to mix something that will help you cross those bridges."

"That, Miss Marriner, you already have," said the general with an answering smile. He looked unexpectedly youthful; only the faint weathered lines of his neck and the gray at his temples hinted at his age. He was almost too handsome, but there was steel beneath. Somewhat to her dismay, Elspeth felt herself drawn to him. She wondered if she were retrogressing to a point where she fell for anything in uniform. First Marshall Henry, now General Curtis.

The date was arranged with Christine after dinner. A new movie was about to be shown in the private projection room which Mr. Gardienne had had built in his basement, but before they went downstairs a servant approached Elspeth with a message on a tray. It was from Juana, asking her to come to the cottage at once.

Elspeth made her apologies, reconfirmed the morrow's date, slipped out and across the lawn. The moon was already high, and the entire magnificent estate seemed to be tipped with silver and splashed with lampblack shadows. It had been a pleasant evening, glamorous if not thrilling. Elspeth decided she was getting blasé. Interworld travel seemed to involve some very high living.

But she forgot high life once she was again with Mack and Juana. The latter was smoking a cigarette tensely, and Mack was again checking his pistol. Before explaining what had happened, Juana asked Elspeth for a report on her own activities.

"So far—excellent," she said when Elspeth had finished. "I only hope my end went half as well." She frowned, tossed her cigarette in the fireplace, and moved beyond it to a table upon which was a small leather-covered dialed box that looked something like a portable radio but was far more complex.

"I got part of the answer to the disintegrator, anyway," she went on, adjusting the dials and studying the waverings of twin needle indicators. "It seems they don't know about asbestos back in Columbia. You get used to these anachronisms of the various worlds—or think you do—and then when one turns up it surprises you anyway. The military here has a new cloth of it—woven with some sort of polarized bakelite—that will stand up to five thousand degrees Fahrenheit for a couple of minutes. It's a secret, but we ought to be able to get it in return for our rocket plus fuel."

"*If* we get back the fuel," said Elspeth unhappily. "I'd give a lot to know where it is."

"We *know* only one thing," Juana said, adjusting the dials and again studying the twin needle indicators. "Your friend van Hooten—and he seems to be the champ heel of two worlds—has not turned in the fuel sample to his new principals—as yet."

"How can you be sure?" Mack asked doubtfully.

Juana indicated the leather box with the dials. "This is a very special device," she said. "We call it the transferometer."

"What is it, Juana?" Elspeth inquired.

"It's an interworld detector of sorts," Juana told them. "I won't give you a technical explanation—I couldn't if I wanted to, kids, and, anyway, there isn't time. But each world in each tangential universe has its own atomic table. You might say that each universe exists in the gaps in the quantum rhythms of the others.

"When you undergo a transfer you are actually undergoing an atomic change. Otherwise no transfer would be possible—you'd be keyed to one world only. This transferometer can be keyed to the A-scales of any of the known worlds. They are all listed, numbered, and tabled, of course."

"I get it," said Mack, concluding the job of reassembling his pistol. "By tuning in to the world we just left, you can locate any object from that world in this one—like van Hooten, say."

"It's not quite that simple." Juana shook her head. "However, both van Hooten and the fuel sample are native to the Columbian world. And this indicator registers that fact."

"How does that help us find them?" Mack wanted to know. "If Elly has this General Muckamuck coming here tomorrow noon for cocktails we've got to have that fuel sample ready."

"Come here, Mack," said Juana, crooking a finger. "You, too, Elly." They crowded up behind her and she showed them a perpendicular white line across the chief dial. "This white line represents our location—on an axis vertical to the Earth.

"This little blob"—she pointed to a small spot of light above the center of the white line—"is this actual spot in relation to that axis. For all practical purposes, that's us right now. See how that left-hand needle is steady on center? That means we're registered correctly."

"But how does that find us Everard?" Mack inquired. "And what is the other needle indicator for?"

"That is keyed to organic substance—in this instance from the Columbian world," Juana explained. "In short—Everard."

"But the fuel sample?" said the photographer. "How—"

"The needle is not rocking back and forth," Juana explained, "which it would be if the two were separated. Now—" She pressed a button beneath the chief dial and a horizontal red line appeared, intersecting the white one. On it, too, was a blob of light, and it almost coincided with their location.

"That again is Everard," said Juana quietly.

"Mighty cute," said Mack. "How wide is its range?"

"On the needle indicators a thousand kilometers," Juana informed them simply. "On the main dial—ten."

"Then our friend must be getting warm," said Mack.

"He is," said Juana with a trace of tenseness. "We got our first fixes on him and the sample back in town and I came out here as soon as we found he was heading this way. It's my hunch he has to have both the blueprints *and* the fuel sample, or else. He is working for people a lot tougher than the Emperor now."

"What I don't get," said Mack, "is why he's lugging the fuel sample around with him."

"Obviously because he doesn't dare part with it and it's neither bulky nor heavy," Juana replied. "He has probably told them—whoever they are—that the elevator attack was a complete bust. He wants to swing the whole deal on his own. Cute cobra."

"But how can he get at us here?" Elspeth asked.

"By the lake," said Juana, nodding toward the cottage door. "He's coming in that way. He—or rather his new employers—have this estate thoroughly cased."

"Where *are* the blueprints?" Elspeth asked anxiously.

"Look, the lines—" Mack began, pointing at the dial.

He was interrupted by a drawling pseudo-British voice from the doorway, a voice that echoed Elspeth's question with, "Yes, darlings, where *are* the blueprints? Precisely the question I was *just* going to ask myself."

Everard, clad only in dripping shorts but wearing a heavy money belt, was standing there. And in his hand was an odd-looking bell-muzzled weapon that caused Elspeth to cry, "A disintegrator! He's got a disintegrator!"

XIV

"You're so absolutely utterly right," drawled Everard. "And nothing, darlings, would please me more than to give you a demonstration, although I believe Miss Marriner has already seen the weapon in action. However, there will be no need for such a—shall we say, performance? We shall—if one of you will just put the blueprints into my hot little paw. Would you mind very much?"

He turned the vicious weapon with apparent casualness, so that its ugly disked and slotted bell muzzle pointed first at Elspeth, then at Juana. Mack he ignored, seeming confident the photographer would make no move as long as he had the women covered. Despite the Corinthian floridity of his speech, there was no mistaking the ugly purpose that lurked beneath.

Juana looked coolly at the transferometer dials, then snapped off the instrument and turned slowly to study Everard. She said without a trace of tension in her voice, "You took quite a risk, leaving your clothes across the lake. If any of the guards should happen to find them—" She shrugged prettily and added, "But I'm very glad you brought the fuel sample with you in your belt. It saves us a lot of trouble tracking it down elsewhere."

"My very dear young lady," said Everard charmingly, "the blueprints, please. I feel certain that our mutual friends here"—with a bow toward Mack and Elspeth—"have told you something of the uses and effect of this little gun I have with me."

"But of course, my dear," said Juana, mocking Everard's pseudo-English drawl and smiling her defiance of the whitening of his knuckle over the trigger. "I'm simply devastated about the space-ship blueprints, Everard—really I am. However"—she sighed prettily and reached for a cigarette—"it just so happens they are where no one—not even clever, clever you—can get them. You see, my dear, I put them in the mail—registered—this evening before coming out here to wait for you."

She lit her cigarette with steady hand, and Everard, after eyeing her narrowly while she did so, said, "Tsk, tsk—a pity indeed! Then I suppose there is simply nothing to do but wait." He moved to a chair and sat down without relaxing his guard.

"It won't work, Everard," said Elspeth, coming out of the chill of fear that had held her wrapped in ice since the moment she had sighted the Bonapartist agent and his disintegrator. "You can't stay awake that long. And you can't kill us with any hope of getting the prints. How did you get in here, anyway?"

"I swam, of course," said Everard, looking slightly bewildered at the apparent stupidity of her question. Then, catching its true meaning, he tsk-tsked again. "Oh—the guards. Heavens, how dull of me! This little dis-gun of mine took very good care of them." He patted the barrel fondly.

"When their disappearance is discovered there will be a search," said Mack ominously. His eyes had not left Everard's since the latter's dramatic entry. "You'll never survive that, and you know it. Even with that blowtorch of yours."

"Why not give up?" Juana suggested persuasively. "Turn over the fuel sample and the dis-gun to us. I have already arranged for your transfer to a world where your—er—talents will be more appreciated. Suitably equipped, of course."

Everard's face went stiff and gray and his light blue eyes glowed with what Elspeth realized, to her surprise, was fear. He said too quickly, "Oh no, not that—*never!* How do I know *what* kind of a world you'll put me on? If I had had the faintest idea, when I stowed away on the train, that you were going to—to change worlds I . . ." His voice trailed off in a sort of ague.

"If you had known, you wouldn't have come along?"

asked the photographer, leaning forward slightly.

"Don't be absurd, my sweet," said the pseudo-Englishman with a trace of his usual bravado. "I'd have used this, of course." He again patted the barrel of the disintegrator and smiled unpleasantly. "I'd never have dreamed of letting you board the train at all. But had I used it in New Orleans I should scarcely have had a chance of making my escape."

Elspeth started, gave vent to a little cry that came from somewhere deep within her. Her start caused her to knock over her handbag, which had been resting upon the right arm of her chair. Involuntarily she bent over to pick it up.

Through pure reflex action Everard's pale blue eyes darted in pursuit of her motion toward the bag on the floor. And Juana, catlike, unerringly selected that moment to shoot through her own handbag with her efficient little automatic. The sharp *splat* of the shot, deafening in the low-ceiled room, drowned the more sickening thud of the steel-jacketed slug striking human flesh as it tore its way through Everard's bare torso.

Her full lips tightly compressed, Juana fired a second time, and again her aim was accurate. Jarred and numbed by the impact of the bullets, Everard swung his arm wildly toward the redhead, lifting the disintegrator as he did so. Mack leaped forward from his chair with a savage growl of fury and flung himself full length at the vicious intruder.

He crashed into Everard with the clean impact and ferocity of a jungle panther, rolling the chair in which the Columbian sat clean over on its back and jamming his victim against the wall beyond it. The sinister-looking disintegrator described a slow arc in the air and hit the carpet with a dull *thock*. On hands and knees, Elspeth scrambled for it and picked it up.

Straightening, she looked around her at a scene of utter horror. Everard was half sitting, half lying on the floor against the far wall, beyond his overturned chair, his eyes glazed and dull. Blood was welling in a double cascade from the twin holes in his chest, and there was a lesser cascade trickling down his chin from the corner of his mouth.

Mack, still growling like an enraged wild animal, was busily wrenching the heavy money belt from around Everard's waist, ignoring the blood. The photographer was apparently unaware of something that registered on Elspeth with the impact of a blow to the face. Juana—Juana wasn't.

A portion of the base of her chair was still there, sheared off cleanly, the surface shining with a glossy reflection that was almost like porcelain, as if it had been suddenly subjected to heat so intense that the wood itself was transformed. Against the wall beyond was an odd brown stain. Elspeth had a sudden sickening memory of a similar stain on the sidewalk outside of Bienville House in the Columbian Baton Rouge.

Mack rose, the money belt in his hands, turned slowly and, following Elspeth's horrified stare, saw what had happened. He looked at the disintegrator in Elspeth's trembling hands, then back to where Juana had been sitting seconds before. Elspeth nodded, herself unable to speak.

The photographer turned slowly back to the dying Everard, a look of thoughtful speculation on his face. Then, carefully, he took a step backward and, moving in like a football player, booted him with all of his force, square in the middle of his classic features. "I only wish the sonuvabitch could feel it," he said.

Elspeth found herself in hearty emotional agreement with the photographer and felt only the briefest of qualms at her own brutality. She sank into the chair behind her and covered her face to shut out the ghastly sight of that porcelained chair stump and the brown stain on the wall.

There were many running footsteps outside a few moments later, and Elspeth looked up reluctantly to see a quartet of plainclothesmen and a couple of uniformed army officers in the doorway. She let Mack do the talking this time. She still couldn't speak.

"This bastard," said Mack, nodding toward Everard's shattered body, for the Columbian was dead by this time, "was the leader in that attack on us in the hotel lobby this afternoon. Elly—Miss Marriner—spotted him then." He went on to explain that van Hooten must have swum the lake after eliminating a couple of guards on the far side that he had entered the cottage carrying his incredible new weapon, had rayed Miss Brooks to atoms after being shot by her.

"There's Jua—Miss Brook's pistol on the floor by the

chair she was sitting in," he concluded, nodding toward where it lay on the carpet, sliced cleanly in half, like her handbag near it, by the disintegrating ray. "As for our visitor's weapon—Miss Marriner is holding it."

Things happened with tumbling haste after that. The transferometer had been destroyed by Everard's blast at Juana, so Mack and Elspeth did not have to attempt to explain either that fantastic instrument or its uses. But when it was discovered that two guards on the opposite side of the lake had vanished without trace or explanation, when the disintegrator was closely examined, when Everard's clothing was found neatly folded and hidden beneath a bush close to the edge of the water—then they began to be believed.

"It seems very strange to me that you, of all people, should have been selected as the target for this fantastic attack, Miss Marriner." It was a Major Leach of Army Intelligence talking. "I don't mean to decry either your poetry or its literary value, but it is hardly of a nature to incite violence. Really, it doesn't make sense."

"Of course it doesn't, Major," said Elspeth frankly. She had managed to battle her way back to something like full rationality and self-control by forcing herself to remember that Juana had given her life to enable the two of them to complete their assignment. Now, of course, it was up to them both to make sure that the little redhead had not tossed away her life in vain.

So she added, evenly, "This attack tonight—coming on the heels of the hotel raid this afternoon—has merely precipitated things."

"What sort of things, Miss Marriner?" It was a soft-voiced lynx-eyed Secret Service inspector who asked this question.

Elspeth went on to explain that she had been sent to San Francisco on a secret mission of vital importance, that she had already arranged to reveal at least a portion of it to General Curtis on the morrow, in company with the President's daughter. She suggested that it was imperative that she and Mack see both General Curtis and the Chief Executive as soon as possible.

"They sure do things different on the other side," she overheard one of her questioners mutter in an aside.

"Imagine—a poet—and a she-poet at that! Well, judging from that dis-disin—that whatever it is, she's sure onto something. Wonder how many of the damn things the Commies have?"

"I can answer that," said Elspeth quite calmly. "None. The one van Hooten had tonight was stolen from us. However, I'm glad to be able to turn it over to you. You'll find it—effective—if used wisely. If not, it means all-around ruin."

After this there followed what seemed to Elspeth an interminable wait. However, by the hands of a small gilt banjo clock on the wall of the anteroom where they were held, it was still short of eleven o'clock in the evening when she and Mack were ushered under guard into a room assigned to the President.

He was standing in front of an unlaid fireplace, his hands clasped behind his back, his regard frankly questioning, thoughtful, polite. In the room with him were only two other persons—Christine and General Curtis. The general was examining the disintegrator, shaking his head as if he could not quite believe it.

"It is my understanding that you wish to see us—on matters quite different from those you discussed with my daughter this afternoon," President Roosevelt said quietly. Then he smiled. "And from what I have been told just now, I have a feeling we are just as anxious to see you—or at least, by their actions, our mutual enemies seem to feel so."

"Mr. President," said Elspeth directly, "what would you say if we were to put in your hands the means and techniques for mastering space—not ten years from now, not one—but just as soon as you can build both vessel and fuel according to tested specifications we can supply you?"

"I'd say—I'd have to say that I'm very much afraid I cannot believe you," the President told her. He turned to lift an eyebrow at General Curtis. "Right, Curt?"

"Five minutes ago I'd have gone along with you, sir," said the general, still studying the Columbian weapon. "After looking this thing over I'm at least willing to listen. But I'd like to know why *we're* getting the break—if we *are* getting it. I'd like to hear more about that."

"My secretary, Mr. Fraser," said Elspeth, nodding toward Mack, "has with him, thanks to the permission of your staff, a sample of the type of fuel that will make space flight not only possible but economical—comparatively cheap. It was stolen from us in the hotel attack this afternoon, but, thanks to the fact that the agent who stole it kept it on him, was recovered when he raided the cottage this evening.

"Miss Brooks"—for a moment her voice wavered as she thought of that gay, buoyant many-sided loveliness so utterly and ruthlessly eradicated—"Miss Brooks, in view of the earlier attack in the hotel, had already sent the spaceship blueprints and specifications from San Francisco by registered mail before she—was murdered. She did not have time to tell us to whom the package was addressed, but presumably it was sent either to herself or one of us. At any rate, knowing her, I know the package will arrive."

"Let's have a look at this miracle fuel, Fraser," said General Curtis, stepping forward, the disintegrator still in one hand. He extended the other and without a word Mack handed him the packet. After receiving a wave to go ahead from the President, the general retired to a far corner of the room to unwrap it and scan the printed material it contained.

"I don't pretend to understand any of this, Elly," said Christine, coming forward and taking both her hands, "but I know you're a very wonderful person. You can't have done anything wrong."

"Thanks, Chris, I haven't—not in this business at any rate," said Elspeth. Then, sadly, "But you had no chance to meet the only really wonderful one among us. It was Juana Brooks who put the whole thing over."

"Would any of you care for a drink?" inquired the President, moving toward a portable bar. "I know *I* would."

Mack stepped in quickly to relieve the Chief Executive of the mixing and serving duties, and Elspeth and Christine Roosevelt sat down on a sofa together, talking trivialities in spurts. It was a time of waiting for all of them, a time during which each was lonely despite the presence of the others.

Suddenly General Curtis gave vent to what sounded like an Indian war whoop. He jumped out of his chair and lifted his arm high as if to hurl to the carpet the papers he had been reading. "Of all the complete and utter damned foolishness!" he shouted. He might almost have been doing a war dance in his frustration.

"Something wrong, General?" President Roosevelt asked sharply.

"I should say so—sir," said the general, regaining a measure of self-control. "Only what's wrong is all of *us!* Do you know what this is, sir? It's a method—not only instructions but a sample—of making atomic fuel out of plain sodium! Furthermore, it defines a way of polarizing and shielding a sodium drive just about forever. And what's more, sir, without even testing this sample I'll lay a hundred to one it will work. Where have our great minds been? What have they been *doing* in their damned labs?"

"Good lord!" said the President, sinking slowly into a chair. He passed a hand over his brow, stared curiously at Elspeth, then at Mack. "I don't suppose," he said almost wistfully, "that you could tell us more about this? You and it didn't come out of thin air, did you?"

"Hardly, Mr. President," said Elspeth in response to both questions. "But we do want something from you." She was conscious of Mack's approving gaze as she put in her request for a heat-ray shield. Before the President could answer, General Curtis, who had been listening with keen attention, broke in:

"I was wondering, sir, why Miss Brooks' handbag—or what was left of it—contained some of the formulas for our new antinapalm fabric. So were the Secret Service." He turned to Elspeth, added, "You mean the shield will work against *that?*" nodding at the disintegrator, which he had put down on a table.

"That was our understanding," said Elspeth quietly. She knew that none of this could be real, that she was simply walking through her allotted dream paces. "Please, we need it. It's vitally important. If we don't get it, Miss Brooks will have died for nothing."

General Curtis spent the next half hour studying the disintegrator, then the fuel formulas, then staring hard at the far wall, rubbing his chin, while the others waited for his decision. Finally he looked at the President and said, "Damned if I don't think it might work at that—pending verification by our scientists, of course. *Brother!* Am I go-

THE HOUSE OF MANY WORLDS 153

ing to show up those long-hairs with this stuff!"

"Then you think we can let them have what they want?" the President asked hopefully.

"I don't see why not, if these space-ship specifications and blueprints pan out," he said. "Confidentially, I'm glad to have an antidote for this damned disintegrator. It's something like our new super flame throwers, but a hell of a lot more effective. Now, sir, with your permission I'd like a drink."

The following morning—none of them went to bed that night—the blueprints arrived, and again General Curtis spent his time being torn between admiration for the Reed Weston ship and chauvinistic self-reproach over the backwardness of American scientists. It was on his recommendation that afternoon that President Roosevelt, in one of the greatest gambles of history, told the Congress of Nations assembled in the presidio that the United States at last had the secret of space flight within its grasp, that the road to the planets would soon be open for human expansion.

"It will not be an easy road," he told them. "The road of the pioneer has never been easy. It may prove to be an impossible road, although, from information I now have, this I do not believe. Man will conquer whatever he must—no matter how alien, how vast, how puny, how fearsome or how difficult it may be. Sometime, perhaps when he has won the stars, he may even conquer himself.

"Furthermore," he went on, his voice rising magnificently, "as soon as we have completed certain experiments now successfully under way, we shall turn our information over to the United Nations to be shared by all who would share the planets."

Elspeth, sitting in a special seat in the balcony, barely felt the tap on her shoulder. She jumped, turned, smiled up at Mack and General Curtis. Mack said, "Come on, Elly. We're on our way to White Sands. You wouldn't want to miss the finale?"

They were driven to a vast airport on an artificial island in the bay under one of the amazing bridges. There they were bundled into a vast and deadly looking army jet transport, which resembled nothing they had seen on either their own or the Columbian world.

It took off with a shattering roar that soon faded to a faint scream, more felt than heard as it reached supersonic speed. Southeast they sped, over the towering Coast Range and the even loftier Rockies beyond, scaling the snowcapped mountain barriers with almost insolent ease. Elspeth felt almost as if they were already in space. She said as much to Mack, who was sitting beside her.

"It takes seven miles a second to get clear of Earth," he told her pedantically. "That's four hundred and twenty miles a minute. I doubt if we're doing much over twelve miles a minute—if that. Still," he conceded, "that's moving right along for turbines."

"Mack!" she said and to her surprise she found that her hand had somehow crept into his big near fist. "Mack, I'm scared without Juana. I feel like—oh, I don't know—I feel lost. How are we supposed to get *out* of this world without her?"

"I know what you mean, Elly," he told her with what she supposed was meant to be comfort. "I feel the same way, of course. If we're stuck, we're stuck, though, and it's a good thing we've both got plenty of jobs and connections ready-made. Still, it isn't *our* world." He paused, frowned, patted her hand.

"But somehow I don't think they'll leave us here," he concluded. "They seem much too well organized."

"But how will we know whoever comes for us?—if they do send someone," Elspeth asked. She knew she was being a fine old panic-bag, but she couldn't help it. She had to voice her fears, unbottle them. "How do we know it won't be another Everard?"

"We don't," Mack said harshly, and all at once his eyes were shadowed and the lines around his mouth deeper. "But if another Everard does turn up and we spot him this time, we'll know what to do with him."

"Juana knew all the ropes—was always in touch," said Elspeth. "We're like Hansel and Gretel—babes in the woods!"

"She knew the ropes," said Mack. "If we're going on with this we'll have to learn them, that's all, Elly. You'd better try to get some sleep." He lowered his shoulder to support her head.

THE HOUSE OF MANY WORLDS 155

Somehow she did manage to sleep while the big plane cut across Nevada, across Arizona, across part of New Mexico. She was aroused by a sudden move on the part of Mack, and opened her eyes to find him leaning across her to peer out the window. The plane was banking in a sharp turn as it prepared to make a landing.

Below them was spread an amazing spectacle. It was desert—desert as far as the eye could reach—desert like portions of the classic Sahara, with little hills and dunes and ridges that looked like the ripples in some vast sea of sand.

But there were men here too, and the marks of men were upon the desert. Elspeth saw square mile after square mile of buildings—low, long, efficiently laid out. Barracks, houses, shops, hospitals, even churches—acre upon acre of glass-roofed workshops. The streets were aligned with geometric precision, and upon them crept small black bugs that must be automobiles.

Close by the desert city was its airport. Its hangars and landing strips looked oddly nonobjective after the neatness of the city itself. And some miles beyond the airport could be seen the still vaster launching grounds, extending far into the dusk.

"It reminds me of Norman in Columbia," Elspeth told Mack.

"Not much," said Mack. "They have the plant here, but they haven't got the ship. *We're* bringing them that." There was a certain fierce pride in his speech and it found ready echo in her heart. Come what might, they were delivering the goods for Juana.

"Enjoy the trip?" General Curtis was bending over them. He had spent most of the journey forward in the pilot's compartment. Elspeth suspected he had been doing the bulk of the flying.

"Wonderful!" Elspeth told him, and Mack nodded.

"Better belt in—we're landing," he told them. Then, "Word just got here that some big-shot scientist from New York will be here to meet us—or rather you, Mack. He wants to talk to you about this sodium fuel of yours."

"I'm no nuclear physicist—hell, I'm no physicist at all," said Mack. "But I *have* seen the stuff work. I'll do what I can."

Elspeth had one of her psychic hunches as she fastened

her broad-webbed belt about her waist. That scientist from New York meant something special—what, she didn't know, or why—but she did know that he was going to be important to them. She steeled herself for any sort of surprise.

But she was totally unprepared for the surprise she got on landing. The chunky bespectacled "big-shot scientist from New York"—the man who came forward to greet them with a pleasant smile on his face—was none other than Orrin Lewis, her editor and Mack's back in their own world, the man who had sent them on the original assignment to the Hatteras Keys for *Picture Week*.

XV

"So when the bad news about Juana came through last night I thought I'd better transfer over to get you two out of this," said "Dr." Orrin Lewis, regarding Mack and Elspeth owlishly over the top of his highball. It was early evening, and they were relaxing in the living room of the small frame house that had been assigned them on "Scientists' Row."

"Incidentally, this is one of the goddamnedest of all the worlds I have ever visited," the editor went on, his broad low forehead furrowed with thought. "I don't do much transferring any more—getting too old for it—and it's my first visit here." He paused, looked at his glass, then shook his head. "What a monumental pyramid of paradoxes!" he exclaimed.

"They have more so-called peace organizations than any other world in this stage of development, and yet they manage to fight more wars. They have more medicine and doctors and hospitals—and a lot more sickness. They have more religions and church members—and more damned sinners."

"Don't the last two usually walk hand in hand?" Elspeth asked her employer.

"Touché!" said Orrin Lewis, smiling. "Both are symptoms of the same sickness, I suppose. Well, we're giving them an outlet to the planets. That ought to take care of some of their excess energy. I'm telling you youngsters, this one's a real problem."

"And when the planets have been exhausted?" Mack inquired.

"Who knows? We're at a tangent here, of course. We'll have to follow developments in both worlds—and on other tangents."

"The job is endless, isn't it?" said Elspeth thoughtfully.

"Endless!" said Orrin Lewis.

"And it was through you that we got into this," said Elspeth.

"That's a big part of my job—selecting recruits. They are always teamed on early assignments. Later, like Juana, they learn to work alone or with other teams as the need arises. I don't mind telling you she's one we're going to miss."

"Amen," said Mack unexpectedly but sincerely.

"Tell me," said the girl to Lewis, "what happens if a person on one world meets her—or his—counterpart on another?"

"That's bothered me too," said Mack.

"It does happen," said Lewis. He smiled at Elspeth. "For instance, Elly, there's a *you* on this world. You're a very famous expatriate poet in London."

"Then that book of poems was *hers* as well as mine?" Elspeth was shocked. Her poetry was so definitely a part of *her*—of whatever *this* Elspeth Marriner was. But Orrin Lewis shook his head.

"No, parallels simply don't run that close," he told her. "We had your verses specially printed for Christine Roosevelt. I took care of that little job myself."

"May I ask how Mack and I happened to be picked for this work—this job?" she asked. Mack's eyes echoed her curiosity.

"You have a right to know," said the editor. He paused, obviously marshaling his thoughts, then said, "Our ideal transferee must be young—only a strong young personality could hope to survive the sudden shifts, not to mention the dangers. Then we *must* have integrity—and then a certain breadth of view and adaptability. Beyond that we select specific people for specific jobs.

"Both of you, for instance, are young. Both of you have integrity. Mack, you tend to be a bit unmalleable at times. Elspeth, you too much so. You complement one another very well, which is one reason we always send our neophytes out in pairs. You either quickly acquire the qualities you lack in this business or you don't last long.

"To handle both the Columbian problem and this one we needed someone with at least a knockabout experience in applied science. You have that, Mack. And to reach President Roosevelt we needed a poet to get at him through his daughter—that was your special attraction, Elly. Frankly, I think you've both done damned well.

"And now I've got to turn in." He rose, looked at his watch, put down his glass. "We'll be leaving early tomorrow. We're flying to the Topeka transfer point. There we part company, but a pickup has been arranged to get you to Reed Weston." He paused, added, "Incidentally, *Picture Week* will be expecting a damned good feature on the Hatteras Keys. You are to return to Spindrift Key as soon as your work in Columbia is concluded. And that about winds it up."

"I've got a question, Orry," Mack said stoutly. "I want to know why it's so important to doctor up these other worlds."

"You have, Mack," said Orrin Lewis, "with your almost infallible super-simplicity put your well-grimed forefinger upon the very crux of the question."

"Huh?" said Mack, looking blank.

"He means you hit the nail on the thumb," said Elspeth.

"Correct," stated Orrin Lewis. "It so happens that if any of the tangential worlds is irretrievably damaged—or destroyed—it will have a cataclysmic effect upon the entire quantum fabric which holds the various universes in a statis of sorts.

"If this world, for instance, should manage to blow itself up it would leave a gap in the fabric of existence itself—a gap whose filling would jar the devil out of each of the myriad other worlds that co-exist with it. You know how thunder works. It's a vague analogy, but roughly the same. It is the job of the Watchers and their aides to see to it that no such catastrophe occurs."

"It's almost terrifying," murmured Elspeth, thinking about the magnitude of the entire scheme.

"Terrifying? It's a job," said the editor reassuringly. "Once again, I'm expecting a damned good picture story about the Keys. I still have to answer to the publisher, you know."

"You'll get it—won't he, Elly?" said Mack, and Elspeth felt grateful for the photographer's expressed confidence in her.

Lewis looked at them thoughtfully, said, "Be on your toes. Your job here is not yet done. And, Mack, have you been taking pictures?"

"A few," said the photographer, reddening a little. "I've been pretty busy in other directions, Orry."

"Well, take all you can from now on," Lewis told him. "If the film here is useless in your camera, get a new camera. The Watchers need all the records they can get. Got enough money?"

"Juana held the purse," said Elspeth, suddenly realizing that they were virtually broke. Orrin Lewis drew out a bulging wallet, tossed a fat sheaf of alien bills on the table in front of him. "This ought to cover any and every emergency you run into," he told them, then looked thoughtfully at nothing and added, "If the two of you together ever become as good as Juana Brooks was alone you'll—well, you'll both be doing more than your jobs. Good night—and good luck."

He turned abruptly and left them, but not before Elspeth caught a glimpse of the mist on his spectacles. Mack stood there, looking at the glass in his hand. Suddenly he hurled it into the stone fireplace, listened to its final tinkle before turning away. He was a little unsteady as he walked toward his own bedroom.

Elspeth, for once, knew enough to keep her mouth shut. But there were tears trickling down her cheeks as she gathered up the money Orrin Lewis had left for them, folded it carefully and stowed it safely away in the purse in her handbag. After all, if Mack couldn't take care of practical things, someone was going to have to . . . .

Orrin Lewis woke them early, yet they had barely time for a single cup of coffee before they were driven in a jeep to the airfield, where a sleek swept-back air force plane awaited them, already warmed up. They made Topeka Airport in amazingly rapid time, there transferred to another motor vehicle, which drove them to the station, where they boarded the last car after bidding farewell to the editor.

It was no luxurious private car this trip, but a smelly old coach of unfamiliar design. Shortly after noon their car was uncoupled after being shunted onto a siding, and they waited alone together for what they knew was coming. It was bright sunlight until the blackness came, but when it came it was just as dark as before.

"I'll never get used to it," said Elspeth when it was over.

"Me neither," said Mack, whose grammar, under the impact of engineer argot of three worlds, was becoming noticeably mongrel. He looked at her and by his eyes she knew that again he was aware of her. Somehow the fact pleased her, although she knew her thoughts should be turning toward the black marshal awaiting her at Reed Weston's headquarters.

They were picked up above Natchez this time by a Weston armored patrol and driven at breakneck speed to Norman. There the black marshal had only time for a quick grin and hug—they were in Weston's office when they met, were not alone.

He said, "Lordy, I'm happy you're back, honey. You just made it by hours. What happened to my secretary?"

"She was disintegrated—by van Hooten. He's dead too," Elspeth said dully, her happiness in seeing and touching Marshal Henry fading before the memory mention of Juana recalled.

"I'm sorry," said John Henry, and somehow, in his deep voice, the simple phrase meant more than the most florid expression of sympathy on the part of any other. Then, straightening, he said grimly, "But if she helped bring back a shield for the disintegrator, I'll see to it myself that she didn't die in vain."

"She was the whole show," said Elspeth miserably, feeling close to tears now that letdown was upon her.

"I've got to run a test immediately," the black marshal told her gently, sensing her mood. He lifted her chin, smiled down at her, added, "When this is over things are going to be different."

"I know," she replied in a near whisper. He did not, she thought, know *how* different they were going to be.

The test of the shield fabrics they had brought back with

them from San Francisco was run off and proved successful beyond all hope. And two mornings later, shortly after nine, a Reed Weston air cavalcade took off for New Orleans in four Pipits—shining new copies of the original little vehicle that had brought Mack and Elspeth to Spindrift Key.

Mack was flying one of them, which contained Reed Weston and two of the scientists who had planned to accompany him into space. Marshal Henry himself flew the second, which carried rebel high brass. The pilot who had flown Mack and Elspeth to Natchez flew the third, which contained more brass. Elspeth handled the fourth, which held the three leading legal lights of the rebel entourage.

All of them, Elspeth noted, were clad in simple khaki uniforms—with shirts open at the neck and decorations and insignia of rank held to a minimum. Elspeth herself, at Marshal Henry's behest, was similarly attired.

"This—is rather fun, isn't it?" the gray-haired and utterly eminent jurist sitting beside her said, relaxing the death grip on his briefcase as they leveled off at altitude.

"You were going to Mars—and you let a little flight like this bother you," gibed Elspeth to put all of them more at ease. "We'll be landing in New Orleans by eleven o'clock."

"It's—it's a matter of getting used to the idea," said another legal light from the rear seat. "It's so new."

"Relax and enjoy it," said Elspeth. "The water's fine."

It was a perfect sunny day and their altitude made the heat unnoticeable. They flew in a loose diamond formation southeast to the Mississippi, then followed the densely populated course of the great brown river toward the capital, cutting bird-fashion across curve and bayou in direct line.

They landed according to plan at ten fifty-five in the vast plaza in front of the Capitol at the western terminus of the great moving boulevard that was Canal Street. Immediately an honor guard of khaki-clad Weston men, who had entered New Orleans in advance according to treaty agreement, moved up in a hollow square to surround the four Pipits. They were, Elspeth noted, heavily armed.

The party that had flown down lined up in front of their Pipits, and Elspeth, looking around her, found herself dazzled by the splendor of the pageantry in the plaza. It was far and away the most brilliant military spectacle she had ever seen.

Imperial and Columbian leaders, in red, in blue, in green, in yellow, in white, their uniforms encrusted with gold and silver braid, buttons, medals and ribbons, cast coruscating reflections as they stood in an immense cluster in the sunlight on the Capitol steps. It was like some great review of Napoleonic times. Come to think of it, Elspeth realized, there *was* a Napoleon involved.

On one side of the square a Columbian honor guard was lined up in toy-soldier array—their lavender uniforms almost matching in magnificence those of their superiors on the steps. Opposite them an Imperial escort was aligned—equally gorgeous in scarlet. Behind them, fenced off by a double cordon of soldiery and police, were the people. Hundreds of thousands of them crowded against the barrier of the guards, other tens of thousands clustered in windows or on rooftops.

At first, as she compared the casual khaki of her own group with that incredible panoply on all sides of them, Elspeth felt ill at ease. But when the deep-throated roar of the multitude rose as they spotted Reed Weston's carrot top, when it went on endlessly and rose until it threatened to crush her eardrums, she realized how shrewd the Weston folk had been.

In that glaring heat the workmanlike simplicity and comfort of their costumes provided a contrast to the pomp that surrounded them that no competing fuss, feathers, and gold could possibly have done. Catching Mack's eye in the second rank beside her, Elspeth shouted on sudden hunch, "Was this Juana's idea?"

He nodded and replied, "On the nose, Elly. Told me she got it from something that happened a few years ago on a battleship back in her own world. Don't they look hot and droopy in all those stiff collars and junk?"

Juana, Elspeth decided, might have rated herself a mere messenger girl and visiting-fireman entertainer, but she suspected that the dark beauty must have been a lot more important. The heat of the plaza pavement seemed to undulate in waves as the little Weston party walked slowly across it toward the Capitol steps.

From then on things became a bit confused for Elspeth. She stood by in a sort of dream while interminable speeches were made by all important parties concerned. She got an impression of President Wilkinson, tall, sallow, unwholesome, accompanying his address of concession with awkward little gestures—the word "surrender" had been scrupulously avoided by all parties.

She recalled later seeing some woman—a mere inhuman black speck—fall from a window high in a building on one side of the plaza. She remembered Reed Weston, incisive and assured in his moment of triumph; the Mexican Emperor, a plump red-faced little man, making extravagant motions with his arms as he spouted a rapid-fire string of Spanish words in a near-soprano.

And she would always remember Marshal Henry, calm, assured, deep-voiced, natural, the greatest idol of them all to the assembled hundreds of thousands. What he said she could not hear, thanks to her position in back of the speakers. But even so she could sense the quiet confidence of the black marshal in the reactions of the immense horde he was addressing.

Later—much later—she had a brief moment alone with him. It was in some sort of a conservatory off the main ballroom in which a huge peace party was at its height. In some way he managed to have her brought there, to have the doors guarded by trusted aides. Her hands seemed to fly automatically into his, to lose themselves in his great strength.

"Elly," he said, and his deep voice was a trifle husky from the strains of the day, "Elly, is it true you are leaving us?"

She tried to speak but could not, for emotion was high within her. She could only bite down hard on her lower lip and nod.

"But why?" he asked her. "Why, when we are just beginning?"

"I have to," she said, and speech, rediscovered, came with a gush. "I know I shouldn't tell you, but I know you'll keep it a secret always. I'm not from this world at all—neither is Mack nor the Pipit nor was Juana. We came from somewhere else to help you, and now we have to leave for still another world. We're just like you—under orders."

"You're feeling all right?" he asked her anxiously. "The heat, the excitement, the—"

"Dammit, I'm fine except that I feel horrible!" She almost shouted at him. "Don't you know what parallel time-tracks are?"

"Parallel time-tracks?" he looked startled, incredulous, then almost frightened in turn. Finally he nodded slowly. "Yes, Elly, I think I do—in theory at any rate."

"But it's not theory—it's *true!*" she wailed and burst into tears against the vast armor of his chest.

Elspeth felt an odd end-of-the-world sensation as she and Mack trudged up the path together to the lovely old mansion atop the gentle rise and were ushered by the hound-faced butler into the patinaed study, where Mr. Horelle, looking more like alabaster than ever, still sat behind his ancient desk.

He greeted them with a smile of genuine warmth. "You have done extremely well. The other Watchers and I are more than satisfied—we might even say we are proud of your work," he told them. "In time you will more than make up for our tragic loss." He was referring to Juana and both of them knew it. But this was the only reference he made to the girl of whom he had obviously been so fond. He was a very old and a very wise man, who kept his many memories locked within himself.

He queried them about their adventures, eyed Mack's pictures—especially of the Mars—with keen interest through bifocal glasses that seemed continually to be slipping down the thin bridge of his nose. It was not until after dinner, a simple but perfect meal of red-snapper soup, filets of turkey, and fruit, that Elspeth asked him a question which had been troubling her increasingly of recent weeks.

"Mr. Horelle," she said, "I feel as though we have, with luck and the help of the Watchers, been of some aid to two other worlds. But what about our own? It has its share of problems."

"In fulfilling your assignment," he told them, "as magnificently as you both have, you have helped all worlds. But surely you know the answer to your own question. What is the chief problem of your world at present?"

"Our population is outstripping our ability to produce the goods they need for decent living," said Elspeth, frowning. "But, Mr. Horelle, I'm afraid I don't see how any of the—"

"*Got* it!" cried Mack. "Elly, those assembly lines, those super factories, that mass production, those interchangeable parts Curtis told me about on his world—if they aren't the answer I'll eat my infrared camera for desert."

"I hardly think you'll be threatened with any such gastric calamity," said Mr. Horelle, smiling through his white beard at the photographer's quick enthusiasm. "Of course that's the answer." He paused, looked keenly from one to the other of them, registering the maturity, the growth, the other changes his wisdom read.

"Yet I think you may find that you have brought back with you something even more important," he went on. "Something vastly more personal, of course. That again you must learn for yourselves."

Elspeth slept soundly that night between soft Irish linen sheets. And when she awakened she knew that she had been transferred again. Her surroundings remained the same—apparently this old house and its Key were unaffected by transfers—but she could sense it in herself. Perhaps her subconscious retained a memory of the darkness. At any rate, she *knew*.

Mack knew it too. He said nothing about it at breakfast but she had become too closely attuned to the photographer during the months just past not to sense much of what he thought and felt without need for words. They were lingering over cigarettes when a pert young housemaid came in and informed them that their boat was waiting at the pier. Elspeth found herself wondering from what world the young girl came.

The sunlight was fresh and bright outside. There was dew on the grass and the birds were singing and the insects just commencing their diurnal chants. She and Mack strolled slowly down to the wharf and there was Corey awaiting them with his smelly old power fisherboat. "Told you I'd come back for you," he said with a twitch of the lips that apparently passed for a smile. "Took you quite some while, though. Have an interesting time?"

"You have no idea, Corey!" Elspeth told him. Seconds later they were putt-putting out toward the point around which lay the little Carolina town. It was their own world and the poetess felt a great sense of peace and security wrap itself around her.

Even the ugly town itself looked beautiful. It was good to see the highway sign at the head of the pier with its crown and lion and unicorn; it was good to see the local constable in his round-topped bobby's helmet, gnawing his mustache ends as he stood, thumbs in belt, in front of the local green-grocer's shop. It was good to know that she was back in a world in which what had briefly been the United States of America was now a vital segment of the benevolent British Commonwealth of Nations.

"A President is all very well," said Mack as they walked toward the garage, bags in hand, "but I'll take Queen Bess. It's more—permanent somehow."

"I know," Elspeth replied. "I liked President Roosevelt, but still, he lacked something our Queen has. It's hard to define." She shrugged and gave it up, glanced at Mack, saw that he had stopped dead at the garage door. Following his gaze, she saw that, by some interworld magic, the Pipit was back.

It was wearing a number of dents and bruises that had not been present at the start of its journey to the Columbian world. But it was wearing them proudly, as it should. The garageman came up, looking relieved. "Scared me near out of my wits," he told them. "First the car disappears, then you folks do. And then, blimey, back she comes—and so do you! Well, all's well that ends well, I always say. She's fit as a fiddle; just needs a coat of paint. I ain't had time to give her that. Your bill, sir."

Mack slung their gear into the back, paid off the baffled garageman, who was still scratching his head when they drove out onto the lumpy main street. Corey, who was approaching the bar-restaurant in which their adventure had begun, waved a vigorous farewell as they drove past him.

Out of town, Mack took the Pipit up and they flew along the east air-traffic lane toward New York. Illogically

Elspeth found herself filled with sudden nostalgia for the cure-all tooth powder of Columbia, for Marshal John, for Christine Roosevelt, for the dramatic hills and bridges of San Francisco.

She glanced covertly at Mack, saw that his eyes, too, held a faraway look. She knew of whom he was thinking, had too much respect for the subject of his grief to interrupt it. She wondered if he or anyone would ever grieve for her so deeply.

"Wonder what old Horelle meant last night when he said we'd got something more personal out of it," the photographer said.

"The same thing Orrin was talking about that first night at White Sands," she said. "Integrity."

Mack uttered a short, sharp, and very masculine curse word. But integrity was there, had always been there, in his face. Perhaps it was now a trifle more pronounced. Elspeth smiled silently to herself at the physical intimacy Mack's curse word had implied. His using it in her presence, even unconsciously, meant a great deal. The bond was already forged between them, whether he knew it or not.

"Think you can write Orry a decent story to go with my Key pictures?" he asked.

"I think so," she said with quiet confidence. "I wonder where he'll send us next."

"You and me both," said Mack, and with a sudden swift pang Elspeth thought of Juana and her surmise that perhaps such agents as they might carry their slang from world to world.

Three Faces of Time

Prologue

The old man rested his white, blue-veined hands on the top of his magnificent satinwood desk and leaned slightly forward, as if to impress upon Elspeth Marriner the importance of what he had to tell her. His wise, deep-set eyes fixed themselves upon hers with a calm, yet compelling urgency.

He said, "My dear, thanks to circumstances beyond my control, I am going to send you out alone for the first time."

There was no need for further explanation. Elspeth understood fully the implications of Mr. Horelle's remark. For she was, although still on the sunny side of thirty, a veteran Watcher, one of that supremely select little group accustomed to risk their lives transferring as trouble shooters to whichever of the many parallel versions of Earth needed their services.

Usually, it was Watcher policy to operate in teams of two or more—working in close collaboration with the carefully screened and chosen agents in residence on the worlds to which they were assigned. On her previous missions for Mr. Horelle, Elspeth had worked with a man named Mack Fraser, an ex-prizefighter turned magazine cameraman. Although her relationship with Mack had been a chronically stormy one, she was used to Mack and sensed, with a pang of inner regret, how helpless she was going to feel without him.

But she knew better than to admit this unease to Mr. Horelle. In his wisdom, she knew he must already have foreseen her feelings and discounted them. Her blue eyes steady on those of the Chief Watcher, she said, "Where am I needed?"

Elspeth, fair, sensitive, a poet, felt deep gratification at the slight trace of a smile that moved the old man's lips. She had said what he wanted her to say. He passed a parchment-hued hand over his tall forehead before beginning the briefing.

Then he said, "My dear, I am assigning you to a newly discovered and quite remarkable version of Earth. Your mission will be neither military nor political this time—I am sending you merely to observe." His thin fingers caressed the celestial globe on one side of the great desk.

"We have been extremely slow in discovering the world of your destination," he went on, "perhaps because it and the worlds in close parallel to it have been concealed from our instruments by an odd cosmic cloud that partially shut off the sun's rays in your new world's particular plane."

"Heavens!" Elspeth exclaimed. "It must be a backward sort of world."

"It is," said Mr. Horelle, again with the trace of a smile. "Yet I feel certain that its backwardness is of a nature that will prove especially fascinating to you. *Antique*—that is the name of your assigned planet for reasons you will shortly understand—has been in a sort of cosmic deep-freeze for two millenia. It has, in short, lost almost two thousand years of its history."

Fascinated, Elspeth said, "Why, it sounds almost like traveling backward in time!"

"You will be transferring to a world that is actually equivalent to the latter part of the first century of the Christian era," said Mr. Horelle, obviously enjoying the fullness of Elspeth's response. "The disaster that retarded its development utterly destroyed life on the two-score planets closest to its continuum.

"Yet, in broader perspective, this appalling catastrophe has its fortunate facets," the old man continued. "Naturally, we must profit by its discovery—an ancient world that is actually contemporaneous with our modern worlds. If I were still capable of making transfer, I assure you I should not miss the opportunity I am offering you."

Elspeth could only nod as she considered what might lie ahead of her. Here, she thought, was a world for poets—poets and lovers rather than engineers or tradesmen. Here was the world of Horace, of Ovid, of Virgil and

Catullus. . . . She felt a surge of immense inner satisfaction sweep through her.

Mr. Horelle brought her out of it with, "Unfortunately, we are not fully aware of all the possible implications in the mere existence of such a parallel planet. They may not prove to be entirely pleasant or profitable to the worlds as a whole. So, my dear, I want you to be on the alert for any anachronisms, to let your intuition as well as your judgment guide you should you sense anything wrong or out of place."

"I understand." Elspeth nodded. "I take it I am to go to Rome." And, when Mr. Horelle nodded, "Where do I make transfer—on this side of the ocean?"

Again Mr. Horelle smiled. "Hardly," he said, "unless you literally wish to paddle your own canoe. I have already arranged for you to fly to Sicily. Your transfer point lies there, halfway between Messina and Mount Etna."

Elspeth nodded. The whole business of effecting transfer between worlds was a delicate and sometimes dangerous one. As Mack Fraser once remarked, in his meat-and-potatoes way: "It's like being a naval aviator—no matter how many carrier landings you make, you never really get used to it."

Mr. Horelle's house, situated on a small island just within the barrier of Cape Hatteras, was one of the key transfer points in the Western Hemisphere—for the important doings of mankind, as well as the forces of nature, were instrumental in making transfer points possible.

As Mr. Horelle had told Elspeth and Mack Fraser when the two of them, ostensibly on a picture-and-article assignment for *Picture Week,* were first conducted to Spindrift Key, ". . . if a tangent in time develops out of historical decisions, then it must grow out of minor personal decisions as well. It takes forces far greater than any one person can generate to split the space-time continuum in which our universe exists.

"A nova, the destruction of a planet, even such momentous man-made events as affect the life history of this minor speck of space-dust we call Earth—these things all leave their marks in varying degrees. For a while after their occurrence—the time span varies according to the shock suffered by the fabric of the continuum—a tangential zone remains through which, to those who know the secret of the key, it is possible to effect a transfer between worlds."

To this, Mack Fraser had wondered: "But what has ever happened here—in this godforsaken place?"

And Mr. Horelle had explained, to both of them, "Spindrift Key is thrice tangential. Almost four centuries ago, an Englishman named Sir Walter Raleigh put ashore inside the Capes while en route back to England after founding a Colony at Roanoke. He then decided that this island and the mainland behind it offered a safer and more generally favorable site for his colony. It was his plan to transfer it here before returning to England."

"And . . . ?" a fascinated Elspeth had asked.

Mr. Horelle's reply was, "In one of our tangential worlds Raleigh was able to make his transfer. His colony survived and the entire history of the continent was altered. In the world you come from, conditions arose which caused him to postpone doing so. The Roanoke colony, left to its fate, perished.

"Then, in January of 1813, the American privateer *Patriot,* Captain Overstocks commanding, was lured onto a reef by the so-called 'bankers' or pirates, who then made a highly prosperous business out of decoying ships to their ruin. The *Patriot* was running the then British blockade off the Capes with a safe-conduct arranged between the British admiral and Governor Joseph Alston of South Carolina. She was bound for New York . . .

"Actually, Alston was only able to obtain his safe-conduct because he and his father-in-law, Aaron Burr, were both trafficking with the British. There was a conspiracy afoot which planned for a double uprising in both the South and New England that could have altered the entire course of subsequent history. In your world, the shipwreck prevented it. But in certain others . . ." He had let it hang.

Then, leaning toward them across his magnificent desk: "More recently, when a pair of brothers named Wilbur and Orville Wright were experimenting with heavier-than-air craft at nearby Kittyhawk, they made a number of their crucial plans and decisions in this very room. I believe you can compute the tangential potentialities of their discovery.

"So," he concluded, "Spindrift Key is perhaps the strongest tangential point on this continent. That it is a seasonal storm center is an added factor in its tangency. It is actually a multiple gateway to parallel worlds, its older tangencies maintained and reinforced by the importance of more recent occurrences . . ."

Elspeth thought back to the moment, in this very room, which had so altered her life. Since becoming a Watcher, Elspeth found little time to write poetry or magazine articles for *Picture Week*. Instead of writing drama, she lived it—at times with danger and ugliness, at times with a full awareness of incredible beauty and the sense of serving other peoples in other worlds.

Yet none of the other worlds to which Mr. Horelle had assigned her, seemed to Elspeth to offer such a full meed of interest and excitement as this so-called *Antique* to which she was being sent. Looking at Mr. Horelle, she said, "Whom do I get in touch with upon my arrival?"

"I think you willl find the agent in residence both familiar and interesting," said the old man. 'His name is Pliny—Pliny the Elder—and I understand that, while he does not fully understand the theory of interworld transfer, he is both intelligent and disposed to be cooperative. I believe you will also find him a gentleman."

Mention of the word "gentleman" caused Elspeth at once to think of the man who had served as her partner on her previous assignments for Mr. Horelle and the Watchers—for Mack Fraser was apparently everything but a "gentleman." She said, bluntly, "Mr. Horelle, why isn't Mack going with me on this assignment?"

"Chiefly," he replied, "because Mack is needed elsewhere. Yours is essentially a cultural assignment. You speak the classic languages and know their history and their art."

"I wonder," said Elspeth, "which of the schools of Latin pronunciation will prove to be correct."

"Almost certainly, neither of them." Mr. Horelle smiled his faint smile again. "Actually, I should very much like to know myself whether *ae* is pronounced *eee* or *eye*. Perhaps, on your return, we can discuss the matter."

Elspeth sensed that she was being dismissed. While Mr. Horelle never discussed his age, he was almost incredibly old; it was necessary for him to conserve every precious ounce of energy he possessed. She rose and said, "I shall look forward to it. And thank you, sir, for such an assignment."

His thin lips curved again and he lifted one alabastrine hand in farewell salute. He said, "Remember, my dear. Be on the alert for anachronisms. We really know very little about this world. And above all, take care of yourself."

"I'll be careful," she said. She knew that, like herself, Mr. Horelle was remembering Juana Brooks, the brilliant little beauty who had inducted—and conducted—Mack and herself through the complexities of their first polyworld assignment—and had paid for it with her life.

To a very real extent, Elspeth had dedicated her life in an effort to fill Juana's shoes with the Watchers. Nor was her value lessened by the very real humility she brought to her job. She recalled the dark, vivid Juana, and the disaster that had destroyed her. It had come from a degenerate man out of a degenerate world, a man who had not hesitated to use that deadliest of all hand-weapons, the disintegrator. He, too, had died. But his death had not restored Juana Brooks to life.

Elspeth said farewell to the hound-faced butler who had served Mr. Horelle and Spindrift Key for more than four decades. She left the fine old white mansion, standing atop its gentle rise of well-landscaped lawn. Always, when she departed from this place she had come to love best in all the world, Elspeth wondered whether she would live to revisit it.

Walking to the trim little jetty, where a power boat waited to carry her to the somewhat dilapidated village that hugged the western shore of the inlet, Elspeth admitted to herself that she was going to miss Mack Fraser—even while she despised herself for making the admission.

She could envision every seam, every pore, every feature of his homely-handsome face. Thanks to his somewhat shadowy early experiences in the prize ring, Mack's nose was slightly flattened across the bridge, its end a trifle off center. His cheekbones were not entirely symmetrical, as if one of them—the left one—had been shattered by a fist. His eyes habitually wore a sleepy look which, she suspected, came from the thin pouches of scar tissue on their upper lids.

Why women found him attractive, Elspeth had never been able to figure out to her own satisfaction. But they did and Elspeth resented the fact far more than she should. *Conceited tomcat,* she thought, recalling that Mack had quite casually stood her up on their last supposed meeting in Manhattan.

She was going to miss his toughness, his steadiness, his meat-and-potatoes resourcefulness. She was going to miss him a lot more than she cared to admit to herself.

Yet it was going to be a test, a chance to prove herself—her first solo assignment. What had Mr. Horelle told her: to keep her blue eyes well peeled for any anachronisms in this strange new—or rather old—world she was to visit? She resolved to keep her ears open as well.

As she entered the power boat, she tried to remember some of the things she had read about Rome in the first century of the Christian era. Although, following the wild eruptions that succeeded the Claudian Caesars, the Flavians, led by Vespasian, had brought order out of the chaos that followed Nero, pagan Rome was still a difficult and dangerous place. She was going to have to depend very greatly upon the agent in residence, Pliny the Elder. She wondered if he were as complete a stuffed shirt as she had always supposed.

She lit a cigarette and dropped the match into the warm water of the inlet, thinking, *Rome, get ready. But ready or not, here we come.*

I

Elspeth Marriner reclined on a low couch of ivory and ebony and tried to forget that, if she stayed in this strangely backward world, she would have to wait at least fifteen hundred years for a cup of tea. The jug of Marsala which Gnaius Laconius had forwarded by his body slave, Cratus, was raw against the chords of her throat—especially when compared regretfully to the fine Falerno locked in the wine room of the villa's basement.

Yet she was bound to drink it in common courtesy to Gnaius Laconius, who leaned gracefully against one of the exquisite neo-Corinthian pillars of the portico as he recited an ode he had composed in her honor. His tan toga, edged lavishly with maroon embroidery, matched in hues the pale tan and dark red of his face and hair.

With a gesture that suggested passion while not disarranging any of the chain of ringlets which framed his upper face, he declaimed in fluid Latin, *". . . whose very breath, soft as the summer's night, sparks passion in my body with the speed of light . . ."*

There it was, she thought—another of the odd anachronisms that cropped up occasionally in the work and words of Gnaius Laconius. While half-listening to the rolling hexameters he was uttering, she considered somberly the puzzle he had become to her.

Mentally she reviewed his lapses. There was the evening at Berenice Agrippina's palace when, in the course of a conversation on medicine, he had mentioned a surgeon's scalpel—a device this world had yet to see or possess the steel to make. There was the afternoon in the forum when, languidly pretending an interest in things military with young Decimus Juvenalis, recently appointed to his army tribuneship, Gnaius had used the phrase, "swift and deadly as a war rocket." Decimus Juvenalis had looked puzzled, then let it pass.

And now, "speed of light." She eyed the poet narrowly, seeking other alien traces. But Gnaius, with his flat curls, his effeminate gestures, his carefully affected lisp, his redolence of Asiatic perfume, his demi-drunkenness, seemed the typical aristocratic poetry-buff of Vespasian's reign as Emperor of Rome.

Yet his appearance was a mask. Intuitively she must have known it from the first. There was an exotic quality to his verse itself, despite its careful crouching within the poetic limits of the era, which suggested a rigid restraint, hinted at knowledge of other forms and phrases and concepts beyond those of this world.

Truly, Elspeth's mission to an Earth, retarded by cosmic disaster and delayed some nineteen hundred years behind its myriad sister planets, was turning an odd corner into an even stranger street. For Gnaius had not once given her an indication that he was an agent of the Watchers, those tireless guardians of the delicate balance between parallel time-tracks. And she had given him ample opportunity to do so. Watching him, listening to him, she felt all at once afraid.

Her assignment was cultural rather than diplomatic, economic or military. Discovery of this backward world, known among the agents as *Antique*, offered a priceless opportunity for study of the ancient world at first hand—of its customs, language, poetry and daily existence without the filtering of subsequent opinion.

A poet of considerable progress before she became enmeshed in the work of the Watchers, endowed with a fine classical education, Elspeth had been an obvious choice for the job. She had entered into it with zest and relish, eager to walk among living parallels of the giants whose thoughts and works had remained fresh for two millenia.

She had felt a pang that discovery of *Antique* had not come earlier—when Virgil, Horace and the delightfully wicked Ovid, coming hard on the heels of Varro, Catullus and Lucretius, had brought the age of Augustan poetry to its magnificent fulfillment. But the arid era of the Claudian emperors was ended, the age of Martial and Juvenal about to burst into satiric flame.

She had met young Decimus Juvenalis, a young man of twenty-four whose gloom of countenance but rarely lighted with the warmth of inner delight, and found him more engrossed in the military advancement of his career than in the poetry which had, on so many hundreds of parallel worlds, already won him lasting fame.

Under Watcher sponsorship she had talked with Martial, currently voyaging on the lower Nile, before his departure, had been given the opportunity of reading manuscripts in the finest libraries of the eternal city, had even found opportunity to mingle in the social life of Rome. It had seemed the most glamorous of milk runs.

She discovered that Gnaius Laconius had stopped reading and was peering forward slightly, regarding her with an intensity of yearning that caused her to lower her gaze, to sip her wine, then to look out over the portico balustrade at the panorama of the magnificent city.

The villa, like Lamia, her body-slave, had been generously assigned her by Pliny the Elder, who had been selected a resident agent for the Watchers in this anachronistic world. And if Lamia, from Elspeth's twentieth-century point of view had definite drawbacks, the villa did not—save of course for such conveniences as inside plumbing and electricity.

Perched on the steep southwestern tip of the Cispian Hill, between the Vius Patricus and the Clivus Suburbanus, well inside the walls of the old city, it seemed to rise from the tops of the frieze of evergreens that nested in the slope below. Its portico looked across the succession of flat rooftops to the incredible grandeur of the palaces that rose like fairy castles from the Palatine.

Dark green and white—evergreen and marble. Although Elspeth had been resident in the villa now for more than two months, she found the vista still difficult to credit. Rome, under Vespasian, was rebuilt from the holocaust that had attended Nero's wretched reign. Soon it was to attain the ultimate glories of Hadrian. Truly, she thought savoring without pleasure the aftertaste of the Marsala, the modern versions of the city she had known were pallid carbons of Rome in full vitality and glory.

Gnaius, who had rewrapped the scroll of his manuscript

and capped it with a peevish snapping sound, said petulantly, "I fear you have not been listening, Marina."

Emerging from her reverie with a start, Elspeth—Marina Elspetia for the present—felt her face go hot while she foundered for some polite way out of the predicament. She began, "The beauty of your tribute caused my mind to mount a dream." *How corny,* she thought, and wondered how to go on in the same vein.

There was no need to continue. Shedding his usual diffidence, Gnaius Laconius sent his manuscript scroll rolling across the flagged tile of the floor. His arms pinioned her to the couch. His perfume, intermingled with the sourness of his breath, all but overwhelmed her, as he brought his face close to hers.

He said, "I must possess you or I die."

She resisted an impulse to utter a slang saying of another later day with a *Drop dead then.* Instead she said, "Gnaius, what's come over you? You've never acted like this before." She decided with wry self-detachment that she was getting cornier and cornier.

"It is only because you have never given me an opportunity to express the feelings that send the blood coursing through my veins at every thought of you, fair goddess," he replied reproachfully.

An alarm bell in her head rang a cash register. There was another one, she thought, adding it to her previous tally. What right had anyone in Vespasian's Rome to know about circulation of the blood? Her experiences in parallel worlds had inured her to all sorts of anachronisms—but this, she decided, was beyond acceptance.

She said, "I'm no goddess and I'm perfectly capable of being unfair," after allowing him to brush her cheek with his lips—which she suspected of having been stained red with betel juice or some such primitive cosmetic.

Elspeth was a little puzzled; Gnaius had won himself quite a reputation by his indifference to the dark charmers of the city. It was rumored that his interests lay elsewhere. She sought in vain for a reason for this unexpected behavior.

Standing over her, he was almost a foot taller than the average Roman. He might have been a Goth from the forests of Germany, but his features were cast in far less rugged mold.

When she rose he looked frightened at his own temerity—as if he expected her to scold. She patted his cheek, looked into his soulful brown eyes, and said, "I shan't pretend I'm not flattered, Gnaius, but I fear I must have time to consider your suit."

He looked like a condemned man granted a reprieve. He said eagerly. "Then I shall see you tonight at Berenice's?"

"Perhaps," she told him, though she had every intention of going. The son of the Emperor, and Berenice's lover, would almost certainly be present. Titus Flavius Sabinus Vespasianus had just returned from a journey through the northern provinces that had lasted almost four months and had carried him as far as Britain. After reporting to his father, he was due to make his first appearance in society. And Elspeth was frankly eager to meet and talk with a Roman Emperor-to-be.

Elspeth summoned her maid, Lamia, a sparkling little creature, while Gnaius smothered her with melting glances of love. His body-slave, a sawed-off Hercules from Mauritania, named Narvo, brought his master's toga, an ornate affair, and draped it properly around him.

"Until tonight, fair goddess," said the poet with a bow. He tossed the end of his toga over his shoulder with an elaborate bravura and strode from the portico toward the inner rooms of the villa, the atrium and the street entrance. His sandal bottoms made faint scuffling sounds on the tile floor as he moved.

Lamia eyed her mistress speculatively. Neither her inferior stature—the top of her blue-black head came barely to Elspeth's breasts in level—or her inferior station seemed to have infected the slave-girl from Pamphylia with the slightest notions of respect. She said, "You'd do better with the slave than the master, mistress." She proceeded to qualify this statement with some, to Elspeth, appallingly frank information.

"I'll keep it in mind, Lamia," she murmured when the garrulous little slave at last stopped speaking. She paused, her brows lifted curiously, as she sensed an air of excitement which the Pamphylian seemed to be having difficulty in repressing. "What is it?" she asked bluntly.

"Madam," said Lamia, her eyes rounder than usual, "there's a messenger awaiting your audience in the smaller atrium. I put him there to be out of the way of your company."

"You should have told me first," said Elspeth, faintly reproving. Then, "What is it about him that interests you so, Lamia?"

Lamia wriggled like a burlesque dancer from another world and said breathlessly, "He is tall and fair and looks a barbarian—but he comes from Aventine district beyond the Palatine and his accent is strange."

"Show him out here—at once," said Elspeth.

"Yes, madam," the girl said patiently. She withdrew, returned a moment later to usher in a tall bronzed fair-haired man who looked about as much at home in tunic and toga as a longshoreman in a white tie and tails. As he came out on the portico, the newcomer tripped over a dragging corner of his outer garment and uttered a distinct and thoroughly twentieth century, "Damn!"—at which Lamia giggled and slithered sinuously back into the house.

He stood rigidly in front of Elspeth and spoke in low-voiced English with a distinct Irish brogue, saying, "Miss Marriner, with the compliments of Commander Mestres."

Elspeth felt both fright and relief at the sound of her native tongue. She murmured, "Thanks," and took the envelope he offered her, scanned it quickly. It had been hurriedly written and said:

Dear Miss Marriner—Sergeant Carhart, the bearer, will back up my request for your presence as soon as possible. As you will understand soon enough, I am unable to visit you at present, to make known the present urgent situation of which Mr. Horelle wishes me to apprise you. Since it is important we cooperate I must therefore ask you to come to me, returning with Sergeant Carhart if possible.
Sincerely,
R.G. de Mestres
(Commander)

Elspeth read the note twice, feeling a chill at the prospect of unknown and rapidly approaching action. Out of life-long habit, she sought to read the character of Commander de Mestres from the written word. By his name, she decided, he must be French. Probably some sort of career military man, his prose rigidified by decades of service paper-work. A man with a soul of starch, she thought, as she moved to a brazier and held the note over the flame till it was burned to ash.

"You walked!" she asked Sergeant Carhart in English, still speaking softly lest sound of the alien tongue rouse the curiosity of Lamia or one of the house-slaves.

At his nod Elspeth tapped her lower lip with a forefinger, said, "Wait here while I summon my chair." Then, at his expression of contempt: "It's part of the act, Sergeant. Women like the one I'm supposed to be simply don't walk in Rome. And if you'd kept your eyes open coming here you'd know why."

Again he nodded. Then, blurtingly: "Madam, I never seen anything like it. What sort of a place is this, anyway? If I'd known when I volunteered . . ." His voice trailed off.

Elspeth laughed, said, "I'll be with you directly. We'll have to move fast because my time is limited. Wait for me in the atrium—the room where you were before." And, as his face stiffened, she said, "I'll keep Lamia busy so you needn't be afraid."

"Yes, ma'm," was the reply. Then, as they moved to enter the house proper: "That maid of yours—what was she after, anyway?"

"Probably just what you're thinking," said Elspeth. She went serenely on, deriving a childish amusement from shocking the sergeant.

A quarter of an hour later Elspeth was being carried in her litter down the steeply sloped Clivus Suburbanus, with its close-packed rows of apartment houses, toward the Forum. Sergeant Carhart, bewildered but determined not to show it, strode resolutely alongside.

As they progressed somewhat erratically through the densely populated street—scarcely more than a broad alley by twentieth-century standards, but paved with well-worn blocks of reddish sandstone—she saw through the litter curtains a plump dark girl in a bright orange stola brush against the sergeant. She let her stola fall open at the neck as the sergeant paused to let her pass, revealing the mark of her profession hanging from a chain about her well-fleshed neck, and murmured classic Latin phrases.

Sergeant Carhart yelped and pushed past her, his face turning brick red at the abusive jeers that followed him. He risked a sidelong glance at Elspeth, caught her watching eyes and turned from red to purple. He muttered, "What kind of a place is this?"

She beckoned him close, whispered, "You're in a pagan world, Sergeant." Then, in a torrent of Latin, she directed her slaves to proceed more rapidly with the litter. She was showing off and she knew it but enjoyed it. Almost three months had passed since she had been able to converse with anyone in her native tongue.

They passed along the wider Avenue of Castor, with its brilliant mosaic pavement. Ahead, still out of sight, thanks to the number and size of the buildings around them, lay the Tiber with its magnificent stone and marble bridges. On their right rose the round eminence of Capitoline Hill, topped with its ancient temple to Jupiter.

To their right the magnificent structures of the Forum merged into the seemingly endless palaces, temples and public buildings of the Palatine. While they lacked the airy slimness of Manhattan skyscrapers, there was a broad-scaled grandeur to their tiers of columns upon columns that was equally impressive. And, since from this viewpoint their marble and granite surfaces concealed entirely the ground of the hill on which they were built, they gave the effect of being one single tremendous and complex building.

Calling the sergeant to her side, Elspeth said, "Quite a spectacle, isn't it, Sergeant? A lot more than the history books give us."

Grudgingly reluctant to be impressed he replied, "Yeah—but I don't see how they ever found time to build it. Not the way they seem to keep themselves busy around here."

"Sergeant!" said Elspeth in delighted reproof, and had the pleasure of seeing him turn the color of a salmon steak.

They skirted the Circus Maximus, passed a crumbling vine-grown gate of the ancient Murcian Wall, reaching a less densely built portico of the Aventine Hill and the ill-tended wall of one of the palaces of a Claudian favorite, long since sequestered and allowed to languish in disuse. At Sergeant Carhart's request, Elspeth alighted from her litter. Telling her servants to await her return, she followed her usher to a ring-handled iron gate whose dark surface was bright with rust.

"Headquarters," he said simply, then rapped. A peephole was opened and a voice inquired in execrable Latin, "Who goes there?"

"Me, you motheaten son of a Senegambian baboon," was the sergeant's gentle reply.

"Pass, friend," said the other in English. The eyehole closed with a groan of tired metal and a small door within the gate itself opened in creaking protest. Elspeth stepped through it and gasped. She was inured to the often sudden contrasts that resulted from interworld transfers, but this one had been utterly unexpected.

The immense courtyard in which she stood belonged to the world called *Antique*—but everything within it was grimly reminiscent of less pleasant aspects of worlds which had not been retarded by cosmic accident. She was in the midst of men and machines belonging to a regimental combat team of nineteen hundred years later.

To her left, mechanics were working over a row of some two dozen tri-di caterpillar cannons of the latest design. Armored pipits were lined up four deep to her right, and smaller groups of other armored units scattered about the four-acre area. All vehicles wore the airy massivity that proclaimed their ability to fly through the air or hover, as well as to travel in water or on land. Their gun-snouts, swathed in plastic protectors, looked like ugly stunted poles.

The men who lounged about the area or worked on their machines were clad in slate-gray coveralls and long-brimmed fatigue caps and the heavy, high-laced boots of the military of an era far removed from the brief tunics, greaves, breast-plates and helmets of Roman soldiery. The language they spoke was English rather than Latin.

Their presence, in the abandoned palace of the Claudian favorite on the Aventine hill, stunned Elspeth, who moved through them toward the palace proper as if in a dream. Never before, in the missions among worlds she had performed for Mr. Horelle and the Watchers he represented, had there been occasion to transfer from one world to another any such sizeable unit of force.

If force were needed, usually it was obtained through

placing a weapon, taken from some other world, into the proper hands. Thus the Watchers maintained the cosmic balance between the myriad existences of Earth.

There were other causes for wonder at such action. Usually it was the policy of the Watchers to maintain secrecy at all costs. They usually operated through sparsely settled agents in residence and small teams of two or three travelers. Only a few, a very few persons on each version of Earth, were held sufficiently educated, intelligent, imaginative and well-balanced to be permitted to make transfer between worlds. Yet here was a force of several hundred officers and men transferred in bulk to a world that, save for its having been retarded in development, seemed to be following the normal course of history. Elspeth could not help but wonder why.

They entered a gloomy, half-lit hall of the sequestered palace, in which unshaded electric bulbs gleamed as occasional anachronisms. Elspeth let her thoughts range backward three months to the briefing Mr. Horelle had given her for the assignment on *Antique*.

She did not have to close her eyes to see the Chief Watcher's alabaster skin, his wise and gentle deep-set eyes. In her thoughts the alabaster texture and color of his paper-thin old hands rested upon the top of his magnificent study desk, flanked on one side by a terrestrial globe, on the other by a celestial one.

Only now, faced with this appalling anachronism, did she recall clearly the warning he had given her at the time. He had said, "Elspeth, I'm sending you out for the first time."

Her reply had been a prompt, "Good!" Ever since their first trip to other worlds, she and Mack Fraser, a tough materialistic and mechanically minded ex-photographer, had worked together on jobs involving transfer between worlds.

Their relationship had been a stormy one—and other was impossible between their varied natures. Elspeth was sensitive to beauty of thought as well as vision, frequently moody, apt to drift off into reverie on the wings of her imagination, with a poet's instinctive love of the bizarre, the colorful, the exotic.

Mack was strictly a down-to-earth character—an ex-prizefighter and engineeer who thought always in black and white, whose frequent shrewdnesses and insights were the more annoying because they emerged inexplicably from such a drab exterior. At the time Mr. Horelle assigned her to *Antique,* Elspeth and Mack had been indulging in one of their most angry feuds—of which the most bothersome factor to Elspeth was that, in the heat of the conflict, she had utterly forgotten its cause.

"This way, madam—are you okay?" Sergeant Carhart took her arm solicitously, as, in her consideration of the quarrel with her former partner, she went blundering past an open doorway.

"Sorry, Sergeant," she stammered, abashed as always by her ineptitude. Turning, she remembered Mr. Horelle's warning before he had sent her on the flight across the Atlantic, that brought her to the transfer point.

"I want you to look for anachronisms, to seek out whatever seems to you wrong. I hope I am making myself at least partially clear."

"You are, sir," she had replied, in perfect rapport. "And Mack isn't going along on this job?"

Mr. Horelle had shaken his head, told her, with the trace of a smile, "No, Elspeth, while his engineering talents might find much interest in this, we know most of the secrets of the Roman builders. What we have lost is much of their culture, their everyday use of the language, the way they thought and felt and behaved."

These were the words that had registered most deeply with Elspeth at the time. The warning reminded her of Gnaius Laconius and his references to things of which he should not have known.

Perhaps Gnaius was part of the suddenly distorted picture, for some distortion must exist to account for the unprecedented show of force. She watched a stocky, half-handsome man wearing a fourragère and the crossed batons of a commander rise from behind the desk and extend his hand.

He said, "Miss Marriner, Mr. Horelle asked me to extend his compliments. I'm Commander de Mestres and I hope you've been briefed on the situation. From where I sit it looks impossible."

II

Looking at Commander de Mestres, Elspeth decided ruefully that her character analysis of the soldier through his handwritten note was a number of kilometers off-base. Certainly he was not French. His accents bore the homely twang of the North American Midwest. And while his face and bearing were stamped with the imprint of a lifetime of conformity to the discipline required of a career military man, the sensitivity of his mouth, the alert twinkle of humor in his eyes, above all a sort of rakish unstarchiness of apparel—these bespoke a man capable of detachment, if not of revolt, from the restrictions of his chosen profession.

"I'm afraid my briefing must have preceded this situation to which you refer," said Elspeth. "I have received no messages since I came here—which was three months ago."

De Mestres hunched his shoulders briefly, causing his orange and silver fourragère to drum three times in silence against the short ribs beneath his shirt. He said, "A hell of a lot has happened since. If only you could have been tipped off. But you weren't and that's that." He regarded her mournfully across the desk.

"Suppose you tell me about it, Commander," said Elspeth. "I might have picked up something helpful. But mine was ostensibly a cultural mission."

"As you know," he began, "the very existence of this anachronistic planet is unprecedented." Then, at her nod: "It represents the most completely untouched mine of raw materials at present known to any of the worlds. And those that have achieved space-travel have yet to make it productive.

"However, *Antique* seems to have a corollary," de

Mestres went on. "Call it an opposite number if it's easier."

"Commander de Mestres," said Elspeth half angrily, "I may be a poet by profession and I may have flunked Algebra Two in school—but I did pass plane geometry. And I do know what a corollary is."

He brushed back his graying hair, gave her a quick grin, saying, "I had a hell of a time with algebra myself, Miss Marriner. I'm sorry, but you get like this in the service—too many numbskulls on top. You don't have to worry about the men beneath you."

"A soldier's life," Elspeth paraphrased, responding at once to de Mestres' amiability. He gestured idly, went on.

"The damned space-berg or whatever it was that all but wiped out life in this probability sector and which created *Antique* seems to have produced a counter-effect in a probability sector directly opposite. Here the normal blocking out of the sun's heat was weakened and a flock of Earths were burned to a crisp.

"However, one among them survived. And having had its last ice age practically eliminated, it developed, as the storybook boys used to say, apace. In short, it is presently on its last legs. Most of its land surface has been radioactive for centuries as a result of this precocity. Its late discovery by the Watchers hasn't helped, either. The name of this Earth is Heartland, for only in an area roughly corresponding to Western Asia, Central Europe and the Mediterranean regions does life remain."

"A return to the womb," said Elspeth breathlessly.

De Mestres looked briefly puzzled, then nodded. "Correct," he told her. "With a few variations only the original fount of what we laughingly call Western Civilization is left. And by way of carrying the analogy further, such civilization as remains seems to be a matriarchy. When the men had been pretty much killed off, the women got fed up with the whole sorry business and took over."

"Sounds like an ideal world," said Elspeth quietly.

The Commander looked at her and his grin was quick and warming. He said, "Take my word for it, it isn't. Our people are doing what they can to bring Heartland back to self-sufficiency, but a couple of primary mistakes were made by the first agents to visit it. The matriarchs played it cute and a man was made resident agent."

"Sounds just like a bunch of males," said Elspeth mercilessly. "Taking it for granted the men were superior."

"Scourge me with whips if you wish," said de Mestres, "but I wasn't even there. It was just one time the percentages failed to pay off. If we'd sent a woman agent—but we didn't."

"And is this Heartland the reason for your military mission to *Antique?*" asked Elspeth, frowning at him.

"It is," was the prompt reply. De Mestres sighed and told her. "The master chart has revealed the operation of gateways on both Heartland and *Antique* that are not known to the Watchers."

Elspeth thought this over as de Mestres gave her time. The significance, as it sank home, became appalling. One virgin planet, one planet virtually stripped of raw materials—add the vagaries of a matriarchal civilization and open gateways on both planets unknown to the Watchers. She said, "You mean Heartland is raiding *Antique?*"

"Exactly," said de Mestres. "My men and I have been sent here to stop it—by force if necessary. We effected transfer at night via one of the new Z-type submarines and flew our machines in here last night. We're here; we want to get to work. Not more than a handful of my men have the slightest idea of what we're doing. They volunteered for a punitive expedition at triple pay. They were selected more for ability to keep their mouths shut than for anything else."

"It must have been an incredible transfer," said Elspeth. In her mind's eye she could visualize the interior of the giant undersea vessel, stricken with the darkness of the void that attended all transfers between worlds. She saw its long lean deck, a black streak on the night waters of the strait, lying awash as vehicle after vehicle emerged to rendezvous in the sky above her and head north toward Rome in the silence of muffled motors. Suddenly she realized the Commander was talking to her.

". . . must understand the considerable difficulties of our assignment," he was saying. "Until we get a clue to the missing gateways or actual illicit operations, my men are confined to the palace and its yard. They're human, unfortunately. They know they're in a city and they'll want to see it. Some of them will. I risked sending you Sergeant Carhart this afternoon simply because I could not leave here at the moment. I received a visit from the resident Watcher."

"Pliny the Elder?" said Elspeth, her mouth curving upward. "According to my schoolbooks he was a dreadful old bookworm who never spent a moment away from his work. Actually he's a charming old scoundrel with a flock of slave ghost writers from Greece."

The Commander laughed. "I must confess I thought for a few minutes he must be an imposter," said de Mestres. "He proved quite convivial. By the way, Miss Marriner, can I offer you a drink of whisky?"

"You may and I accept—the next time we meet," replied Elspeth promptly. "I'm so sick of Roman wine I'd literally give my shirt for some decent Scotch. But I'm going to a wingding tonight and I don't want to fall flat on my unpretty puss."

"I'll take a raincheck," said de Mestres, who seemed to be becoming less formal by the moment. "Unfortunately it's bourbon. In my world America is not under British dominion as it is in yours."

"Do any of us really have home worlds?" Elspeth asked him. Then, without waiting for a reply: "I gather you want me to keep my shell-pink ears open and look for clues."

"If you don't," replied the Commander, "we're sunk. And if a world—Heartland—succeeds in betraying the Watchers and embarking on a successful career of polyworld conquest, the entire cosmic balance will be knocked into the proverbial cocked hat. You and Pliny are the only contacts we've got here—and remember, he's an admiral."

"Remember, Commander, the Navy brought you here," said Elspeth with a trace of mockery. And before de Mestres could reply to the gibe: "I may have a clue; it's so tenuous as yet that I'm not going to mention it. But I have stumbled on an odd human anachronism."

"Good," said the Commander, his eyes suddenly bright. "Now, Miss Marriner, what about *Antique!* You've been here longer than any traveling agent to date—what's it like?"

"So far," she replied slowly, marshalling her thoughts,

"*Antique* seems pretty much to follow the main thread of basic probability. It has its peculiarities, of course. The Etruscans have remained stronger, and trade with China is far more extensive than on most other planets in this era of history.

"But the main thread is there. They've had their civil wars: Marius and Sulla, then Caesar and Pompey, and Octavius and Anthony against Brutus and Cassius, finally Octavius against Anthony and Cleopatra. Augustus developed the Empire; Christ was born but His influence hasn't been too much felt yet; the Claudians performed all their excesses and Nero was assassinated ten years ago.

"The city is still uneasy, even under Vespasian and with Titus coming up. But it's building—Lord how it's building! If you haven't seen it, get Sergeant Carhart to tell you about it. He seemed rather impressed while escorting me here. By the way, I'm due at a party Berenice Agrippina is tossing for Titus tonight. I'd try to take you, but I'm going to be otherwise busy."

Commander de Mestres glanced at the watch on his wrist, said, "I'll escort you to your villa myself. It might be wise for me to get acquainted with Rome."

"Thank you, Commander," said Elspeth, dimpling. "But you'd better bring along the sergeant and a few men. It isn't safe to walk alone in Rome after dark."

"In what way?" the Commander asked with a faint hint of a smile.

"In any way," said Elspeth unequivocally. Then, as she had already told Sergeant Carhart: "This is a pagan city, Commander."

At first the journey was through the twilight shadows of the narrow Roman streets, then continued by torchlight at the rapid fall of night. Elspeth's escort was successively appalled and roused by sniggering comment by the early evening activity about the crumbling Murcian gate, struck spellbound by the torchlight magnificence of the Forum with its dizzying background of Palatine palaces and temples, silhouetted at the top against a yellow tea-rose afterglow. They were even forced to engage in a brief struggle as footpads tried to raid Elspeth's litter at the first rise of the Clivus Suburbanus.

Leaving her at the entrance of her villa, Commander de Mestres pulled his toga tight about him against the cool evening wind and said, "It's been a pleasure, Miss Marriner."

"Marina Elspetia, please, Commander," she replied in Latin.

Flawlessly, in the same tongue, he said, "My apologies. I'm afraid my professional sang-froid is bubbling a bit." Then, in English, looking about him at the litter bearers and including the whole city in his gesture: "Lord, but they're small. I've always thought the Romans were a tall sort of master race."

"Average Roman man, five feet two," replied Elspeth. "Average woman five feet. I'm something of a giant freak."

"A very charming one," said the Commander gallantly.

"Commander!" replied Elspeth, "remember your wife and children."

"Not just now if you don't mind," he retorted, smiling. Then, serious once more. "I hope you uncover something soon. Old Pliny may be a wonder boy in this age, but he wouldn't know a minor deviation from a major time flaw, I'm afraid."

"Don't be too sure of that," she replied. Then, with a salute to Sergeant Carhart, she slipped into the villa. For a moment she listened to the measured tramp of the soldiers' feet as they marched off down the steep slope of the Clivus Suburbanus.

She found Lamia peering out one of the narrow atrium windows at the receding backs of her escort. Reluctantly the girl turned at her mistress' summons, saying, "Madam, where did you ever find so many *big* men? And couldn't you have asked them in for a little?"

"You know there's no time if I'm to reach the party," Elspeth replied, eyeing her little slave.

"Is madam well?" the slave-girl asked her.

The poetess smiled, told Lamia she was quite well and ready for her bath. In the chill of the Roman evening she was grateful for the hollow tiles through which a basement hot-air furnace dispensed heat evenly through floor, walls and ceiling—far more effectively than in the latter-day

English style country houses which had been her own early environment.

She still found it somewhat uncomfortable to bathe under the sad black eyes of the Nubian eunuch who poured the water into her tub, to submit to Lamia's washing and drying. Yet this was Roman custom and to reveal her embarrassment would have been to betray her status as an alien in time.

Since the occasion was an important one, she had Lamia procure for her a gown of gauzy white linen fringed cloth of gold. There had been no time to try it on, and she was briefly dismayed to discover that, in the fashion then considered chic, it was scarcely concealing. Yet the steel handmirror informed her that it set off her figure enchantingly.

She tilted the mirror to look at her hair and sighed. Elspeth, like many ash-blondes, was in beauty-parlor parlance, a dough-head—her hair so fine that it was virtually impossible to set. She complained of her problem to Lamia, who said, "I'd give up seven nights with a Gothic chief to have hair such as yours—so silken, so light in hue. I have been studying your problem. If madam will sit down . . ."

She went to work at once, using numerous combs and a lacquer that worked wonders at keeping her stubborn curls in place—though Elspeth did not dare inquire as to its ingredients. Some of the Roman beauty aids were appallingly primitive in their composition.

Midway during the coiffure a house-slave brought word that the litter and escort sent to bring her to Berenice's palace had arrived. Lamia worked fast but carefully, refusing to let her mistress depart until she was satisfied with her work. Then, putting in place a final pin of ivory inlaid with gold, she said: "There! If madam is not careful she will catch the eye of Prince Titus himself."

"And get my throat cut by some of Berenice's bullies," said Elspeth. She made a move to disarrange her hair, causing Lamia to squeal with dismay. Then she smiled and left it alone, adding, "You've made me look like a lot more than I am."

"Oh, madam!" said the slave reproachfully, "if you had

but known some of the women I have served in this villa you'd not say it."

"All right, then," replied Elspeth, rising and letting the Pamphylian girl adjust her blue and silver evening stola, "I'll not say it. Be a bad girl while I'm gone."

"I'll try, madam," said the girl, revealing twin dimples in her full cheeks as she smiled.

Elspeth climbed into the heavy ceremonial litter that awaited her in the narrow street and wondered a little at her risqué remarks. Certainly Mack Fraser would disapprove heartily of this pagan world in which she was living so light-heartedly.

But Mack was full of disapprovals, though on occasion he could barely match a tomcat for morals himself. It was, she decided, this odd brother-and-sister relationship which had sprung up unwanted between them that underlay much of their quarreling. Though they were far from being lovers, neither could escape a sense of responsibility toward the other. She wondered briefly on what world Mack was working at the moment.

As the litter swayed over the uneven pavement she again considered herself and the anachronistic city about her. Certainly the Romans were shocking to one from a world nineteen centuries further developed. Their utter lack of conscience, their open immorality, their venality, their love of violence—all these were terrifying to a person reared in a neo-Christian morality.

Yet they lived with a gusto denied those in whom a sense of guilt had been implanted from birth. And the very openness of their wrong-doing had a certain element of charm. And certainly the resulting freedom of spirit and intellect made such poets as Horace and Sallust possible, and such unchanneled scientific speculation as Pliny's acceptable in the most pedantic circles.

They were small in body and generally brief in lifespan—but while they lived, they *lived*. There was a robust devil-take-the-hindmost quality to their existence that struck a sympathetic chord somewhere in the Irish blood that partly filled her veins.

She considered what would happen if folk from a plundered planet were to strip them of their resources, ultimately of their gusto. It was not a pretty thought, for here, in *Antique* lay a world whose potential seemed almost limitless. No other Earth had been discovered by the Watchers so early in its development. Under the wise invisible guidance of Mr. Horelle and his successors and colleagues it might be possible to spare it the worst of the man-made cataclysms, such as Ghengis Khan, the Crusades, and, later, Charles the Twelfth and Napoleon, Hitler and Stalin, that had wrought so much destruction in so many other worlds, not only of human life and spirit but of the very elements themselves.

As the litter approached its destination, Elspeth ceased her speculation at sight of the torch-bearing Praetorian Guards, tall for Romans, and made taller by their high-crested helmets. They lined the walled street for a hundred yards in either direction and held back the mob of curious. Elspeth's bearers were delayed a good twenty minutes by the press of other litters and chariots arriving.

It was the first party she had attended which was graced by a member of the Imperial Family—though Berenice herself was attached in highly personal if unofficial manner to both the Claudian and Flavian houses. Knowing well the tragedy that almost certainly lay ahead of the proud yet appealing Judaeo-Roman princess, the poetess had been drawn to her as if by a magnet.

Perhaps sensing some answering exoticism in Elspeth that lay beyond her uncommon height and fairness, the demi-Oriental princess had responded with a sudden warm friendship that had made the poetess' cultural mission both simpler and more complex than she might have wished. It was made simpler because, through the Princess, Elspeth could obtain introduction to virtually anyone she wished in Rome; it was made more complex because of the numerous social obligations it entailed.

Though Elspeth had been inside Berenice's palace on almost a dozen occasions, she was unprepared for its formal splendor when readied for a fete. Its usually cold-looking walls were hung with brilliant Oriental rugs of immense size; its high-ceilinged and frequently colonnaded rooms, usually dim after sundown, were ablaze with wall flambeaux. The atrium was awash with the colorful togas and tunics and gowns and stolas of the guests—and by the slaves, almost as magnificent, who attended them.

There was silence when the poetess entered and handed her stola to a tiny black girl naked above the waist, whose eyes were as wise and corrupt as the eyes of a dowager Empress. Elspeth, feeling like a pale giant among the tiny dark women, could sense the hatred that stemmed from them. She smiled at two of them she had met, sat down and allowed another slave to check her coiffure.

Slowly conversation rose around her—conversation much like the talk that had passed among women in such chambers since humanity first emerged from caves. There was much laughter in which neither Elspeth nor the slaves joined.

Elspeth, sensing antagonism directed against her alien blondness, and size, finished her toilette and let herself be escorted to pay her respects to her hostess.

A nervously arrogant girl not as old as Elspeth, Berenice Herod-Agrippina was possessed of a fierce voluptuousness of feature softened only by the quick response of her well-cut but unexpectedly wide mouth. She looked truly regal in a gown of blazing silver, her arms, neck, fingers and raven-black hair ashimmer with rubies and sapphires.

When Elspeth curtsied before her, the Princess bade her rise and whispered with a brilliant smile which revealed one of the few complete adult sets of teeth in Rome. "Stay close to me, Marina Elspetia—the Prince will soon be here and I wish you to meet him."

"Am I then a Gothic princess?" the poetess asked, recalling a story of the Prince's romantic inclinations.

"I shall be close," said Berenice. Elspeth had barely stepped from the platform when large male fingers gripped her upper left arm. She turned to find Gnaius Laconius enveloping her own perfume in his own redolent aura.

In tunic of poppy red and gold edging and belt, his flat curls replaced by wood-shaving ringlets, his bare knees knobby and slightly bowed, he looked in Elspeth's opinion like something out of an early Hollywood movie. But she managed to suppress her desire to laugh in his face, and to turn to him eyes she hoped were limpid.

He whispered fiercely, his rouged lips close to her ear: "My darling, we must slip away from this occasion together as soon as we can. I have been counting the moments since I left you."

"You!" she countered mockingly. She thought she had never seen anything more repulsive than the poet in his present get-up.

"What sort of talk is that?" he countered. "Marina, you must be mine tonight or I shall die. I'll blast myself if you refuse me."

The word "blast" did it. Only in the most advanced of the parallel worlds were blasters coming into use, blasters and the word *blast*. Added to the anachronisms she had already noted and Commander de Mestres' statement of the situation, it made Gnaius Laconius a worthy subject for investigation. Thinking, *Well, here I go for dear old Mr. Horelle and the many worlds,* she said, "Later, Gnaius."

His face glowed beneath the paint that covered it. "You mean . . . there's hope?" he whispered, his voice trembling.

"I mean I'll go with you afterward—not yet. Berenice wants me to meet the Crown Prince. Afterward . . ." A night with Gnaius was scarcely anything for a girl to wax romantic about. Besides, if Lamia were right about him—and she was seldom wrong in such matters—Elspeth had little to fear . . .

III

The emperor-to-be was of no more than average height for a Roman. But as he strode toward his hostess through twin lines of bowing and kneeling guests, Elspeth received an impression of height. Perhaps it was caused by the fact the others present were lowering themselves; perhaps it came from the life-long habit of command; perhaps it was inherent in the man himself. Despite his mere five-feet-two or three inches, the Crown Prince dominated the brilliant assembly.

Upon the platform, his greeting to Berenice was affectionate. He quickly lifted the deeply curtsying Princess to her feet, smiled upon her with quick affection, then moved to the throne-chair which had been awaiting him at the platform's rear. Berenice, dark and graceful as a dancer, moved to a stool at one side of the throne.

Almost at once the entertainment began. And Elspeth, who had never been fond of such cheesecloth and plump-lady exercises as folk dances, found the dancers incurably boring.

Mercifully, however, Gnaius seemed entranced. The poetess watched him covertly, unable to believe his enjoyment was real. Yet something in the endless ritual struck a responsive chord in his bosom and for the time, at least, he forget to press his suit.

Relieved, she turned toward the platform and discovered that Berenice and her royal lover had slipped away, evidently through the heavy drapes behind the throne, thus leaving the other guests to amuse themselves as they wished without imperial restraint.

The little Nubian slave-girl with the wise eyes slipped through the crowd, plucked at Elspeth's gown and whispered, "My princess wishes you to follow me."

Elspeth turned to make her excuses to Gnaius, but he was regarding the gyrations of a lithe and singularly effeminate saber dancer. She sighed at the evening in prospect for her and let the tiny slave-girl lead her skillfully through the press of onlookers to a curtained door at the rear. It was guarded by a pair of Praetorians with pikes.

Inside, save for a scattering of other slaves, Berenice and Titus were alone, reclining side by side upon a double couch, flanked by tables upon which stood flagons of rare wine, the inevitable roast suckling pig and baby lamb, and a centerpiece of roast peacock complete with plumage spread like a gigantic fan of blue and gold.

Her hostess beckoned to Elspeth. As she bowed again before the Crown Prince the poetess felt a sudden surge of envy for the Princess, despite the tragedy that almost certainly lay in wait for her in the near future.

Her own life, despite the fascination of being a traveling agent of the Watchers, seemed bare and sterile by comparison.

Resting a hand on her royal lover's shoulder, the Princess said, "Carissima, this is my new friend, Marina Elspetia. She is a protegee of Pliny the Elder and puts our finest poets to shame. Surely she is fairer than any of the princesses of Gaul."

Titus regarded her with good humor and remarked with a smile, "I am happy to agree, Berenice, but you neglected to include the princesses of Britain. She resembles them more than any Gaul I have met."

It was a pointed gibe for all its amiability—intended to point out to his mistress not only that she must not heed court gossip but that such gossip never included all possible facts. A shadow passed quickly over the face of the dusky granddaughter of Salome.

Noting it, the Crown Prince laughed and lifted her lips to his and kissed her. Then, to Elspeth and smiling, "My Princess has spoken well of you, Marina Elspetia. Perhaps soon I shall have the pleasure of hearing your verses—and certainly Rome has need of a Sappho it can claim as its own. But for the present, I fear, I must reassure my Princess that it is to her I have run, rather than fled from any rude lady of the northern forests."

Curtsying again, Elspeth backed out. She had a curious feeling of dissatisfaction with herself. Even though Berenice had carefully stacked against her any cards Titus might have been moved to deal her way, the poetess sensed the evident lack of interest she aroused in the Emperor's heir. True, Berenice had not had her brought in until she had eliminated all competition—and Titus was doubtless not eager to incite his mistress' wrath by showing interest in anyone who even faintly resembled a Gallic princess—yet Elspeth was convinced that his lack of interest was genuine and final.

Why, she wondered, did she repel such dynamic figures, and draw such oddities as Gnaius? Was she fated to go through life in such fashion? Her thoughts were not happy as she returned to the main reception room. Had it not been for her promise to Commander de Mestres, she would have slipped out and ridden home by herself.

Gnaius was awaiting her, both angry and frightened by her absence. "When are you going to see the Crown Prince again?" he asked her, the fierceness of his voice marred by its querulous uncertainty.

Repelled by his possessiveness, Elspeth was coy. She said with lifted brows, "Really, Gnaius! Isn't that up to the Crown Prince? After all, we are both his subjects!"

"Fantastic backward world!" exploded Gnaius. He took her by the arm and led her toward the anteroom beyond the banquet hall.

Elspeth had been on the verge of refusing to go with him but this further evidence of the poet's alienness tipped the scales in his favor. A small escort of Praetorians to attend to such services, marched them to Gnaius' white stucco villa on the Caelian Mountain, close to the old-wall gate.

It was Elspeth's first visit to her would-be lover's home. It was built around a poplar-lined patio. He led her to a sort of combination dining and living room, equipped with tables and couches and murals in brilliant color depicting aspects of the gods and goddesses at play that had been carefully excluded from her textbooks on mythology.

Regarding these, Elspeth felt a pang of regret that her twentieth-century upbringing prevented her from becoming truly acclimated in this alien world. It caused her to feel a sharp and disappointing sense of failure.

"Carissima, you have left me!" Gnaius stood in front of her, proffering a huge gilded flagon of wine. She smiled at him and took the drink and sipped its contents—more of the sharp Marsala she disliked—then handed it back for him to quaff.

"A true loving cup!" he exclaimed and drank deeply. Then he set it down and led her to a couch. "Where do you go when you withdraw so completely, Marina? Beyond your strange fair loveliness and intelligence, I believe it is your trick of turning in on yourself that so fascinates me. My mother . . ." His voice trailed off and, hesitantly, he laid his fingers on hers, then withdrew them as if they had touched dry ice.

She said, forcing herself not to show the wave of repugnance that coursed through her at his touch, "Tell me about yourself, Gnaius. After all, I know very little about you. Where is your home?"

"My home?" He laughed without mirth. "My home is the world, a world of my own imagination, a world far different from this primitive jungle of sword and statue, slavery and stupidity."

"Nice alliteration," she murmured, wondering how he could be aware Rome was primitive if he came from *Antique*.

Anger flickered over his weak features and his fingers tightened painfully on her arm. He said savagely, "You make fun of me, Marina. You should not. I cannot help it if I find women frightening—though yourself least of all."

"Thanks for those kind words," said Elspeth icily, striving to rise from the couch. But Gnaius, revealing unsuspected strength, held her with a grip of iron. His rouged lips came down on hers and the ardor of his embrace was not to be denied. There was nothing Elspeth could do to stop him, not without betraying Commander de Mestres and the Watchers. She had one annoying thought that, for once, Lamia had been wrong. . . .

Afterward, watching him struggle to mask his disgust, she knew she had not misjudged him. While passion ruled him, Gnaius had spoken strange syllables in a language she did not recognize. Yet his reference to his mother—

Elspeth understood suddenly, and, with understanding

felt a certain amount of pity. Gnaius' eccentricities were all the result of his formative years, and he had all too evidently been ruled by his mother in an unhappy fashion.

His was, after all, scarcely an unusual psychological affliction, even in her own world, Elspeth thought. Then she remembered what de Mestres had told her that afternoon about the decadent survivors of Heartland's wars of extermination being a matriarchy. At the moment this was the final piece in the jigsaw puzzle that had been Gnaius Laconius. At once she began to plan.

Elspeth fed him more wine and stroked his head, which she held against her bosom, until he began to snore regularly.

She waited five minutes, to make sure he was really asleep. Not once was the regularity of his breathing disturbed. Then, with care, she placed his head on the roll-end of the couch, slipped her left arm from beneath him and stood up.

What she was looking for she did not know. Evidently, Gnaius had dismissed his slaves for the occasion, or sent them downstairs to their cellar quarters. This in itself was almost sufficient to brand him as un-Roman. The need for privacy was virtually unknown among these people.

Gnaius grunted and stirred in his sleep, causing Elspeth to catch her breath and return her thoughts to the specific issues at hand. Surely, if Gnaius were a transferee from Heartland, he would have brought with him some indication of the land of his origin, some device to be used only in dire emergency, some gadget to head him back to the point of transfer that had brought him here.

He could scarcely have used the Straits of Messina gateway. If he had, the Watchers would have known it; they had apparatus that recorded interworld transfers through all known portals. The fact that someone was using a gateway of which the Watchers had no knowledge restored Elspeth to awareness of the seriousness of the situation.

Where, she thought, would Gnaius have hidden any such device? Presumably in his bedroom, so that it would be handy in case an emergency arose while he slept. Thanks to her new-found knowledge of Roman interior housing, Elspeth had little trouble in finding the poet's chamber. It was on the other side of the house, with windows only on the courtyard, thus offering maximum quiet and security.

She also saw why Gnaius had not taken her there but rather to his dining-living room. One whole wall was a sort of open closet, hung with stolas and gowns in all cuts and colors. At one end, in a tiny minority, were men's clothes, most of them familiar. Above and encircling the walls were more suggestive murals. Regarding the pictures briefly, Elspeth brushed back a lock of blonde hair and murmured, "Never the twain shall meet."

Gnaius was ashamed of his eccentricities. Elspeth thought she would hate to be hated by anyone as much as his mother must be hated by him. Then she got down on her hands and knees and began her hunt for the unknown.

It took her a little while. In spite of her suspicions of Gnaius, she persisted in thinking of his mental processes as typically masculine and looked first in masculine hiding places: under the bed, in hidden wall recesses, in the bottoms of his sandals. She found nothing.

Then, realizing the probability of her error, she began methodically searching the gaudy stolas that hung along the wall. And by the time she had finished with the last of them she had found two items to justify her search: one was a map; the other was a weapon.

The map was no product of Roman civilization. It was a highly machined and scientifically accurate result of far, far more advanced civilization. It showed rivers and lakes and forest regions, unmarked by any vestige of roads or towns or other hints of civilization. It was printed on some sort of plastic which was thinner than India paper and tougher than vellum.

The weapon she judged to be some sort of blaster. It was of a dull black alloy and its body was disc-like in shape, with a narrow, belled snout protruding from one of its edges. Apparently it fitted into the palm of the hand, was fired by squeezing the hand and emitted some sort of bolt or ray discharge through the tiny barrel. It was, she surmised, only useful at close range.

Elspeth managed to stow the objects safely away in the blue-and-silver stola. Gnaius had removed it when they entered and placed it over a side table in the living-dining room. Certainly her gown offered no slightest place for concealment. Finished, she returned to the couch on which her host slumbered and looked down at him.

She said, "Gnaius, it's growing late. I think I had better return home." Inwardly she cursed the lawlessness of the pagan city which made it impossible for her to pass through the streets alone.

He opened his eyes and stared up at her without recognition. Then he rose hastily and, falling to one knee, pressed the hem of her gown against his lips. "Forgive me . . ." he began.

"I do," she said, barely controlling the revulsion with which he inspired her. "I want to go home now."

He made no protest though he did have the courtesy to accompany her—this despite the fact that being abroad in the early morning hours evidently made him uneasy. They made the journey without incident of any kind, and Elspeth left him outside, alone in the litter, surrounded by four sleepy slaves.

Within her own villa, Lamia was curled up in a curved-bottom Greek chair in the foyer. Her mistress studied the voluptuous little Pamphylian, then moved silently close to her and kicked the edge of the chair.

The girl screeched and tumbled to the floor with considerable display of her short but shapely limbs, then scrambled to her feet with an air of sleepy but outraged dignity. "Madam," she said reproachfully, "surely I did not deserve such treatment."

"Surely you did!" said Elspeth resentfully. "You told me Gnaius Laconius was harmless as far as women are concerned. You were wrong."

Lamia clapped both hands to her mouth and her eyes went round with surprise. Then they closed and she began to shake; for a moment the poetess feared she was crying. And then she saw that her slave was convulsed with laughter.

"I want you to understand right now," Elspeth began angrily, "that I am not a woman who—" All at once, to her own mixed horror and relief, she found herself laughing with Lamia. *Heavens,* she thought, *what is this world turning me into?* But she kept on laughing till the tears rolled down her cheeks.

But there was little time to wallow in any sort of reaction to her experience, as it was imperative that Elspeth get her loot to Commander de Mestres at once. Not only might time be all important, but there was a distinct possibility that Gnaius might discover the theft and come after her with his slaves to recover the map and weapon she had stolen.

While Elspeth changed into warmer and less conspicuous attire, the slave-girl roused her litter-bearers from slumber in their quarters. By the time the poetess was ready, her Iberians were waiting in the atrium with the litter. Beside them stood Lamia, wrapped in a dark blue stola of warm wool.

"Please, I feel I should accompany you, madam," begged the girl. "It isn't proper that you should go out attended only by these Spanish dogs—not at this time of night."

Elspeth cast a quick glance at her men-slaves, who were waiting sullenly by the litter poles close to the door. Never before, she thought, had they looked so forbidding. Then she eyed Lamia, noted the alert resourcefulness of her expression and bearing. She supposed fondness for the girl was making an idiot of her.

Drawing the girl well away from the bearers, she said in low tones, "Lamia, if I let you come with me I want your promise to keep your lips sealed, no matter how strange the sights you are about to see. And I want you to keep your mind only on service to me. Do you understand me?"

"I understand," said the girl, with what appeared to be utter simplicity. "Thank you, madam, for letting me come. Left here in the house I should have worried for you."

"You may worry a lot more for coming," warned Elspeth. They went outside with the Iberians into the narrow street. Shadows slithered like lurking assassins from the attack of the torches carried by the bearers. The women got into the litter together and Elspeth told the leader of her slaves. "To the Aventine palace we visited this afternoon. As rapidly as possible."

The slave bowed and they got under way. Once, while passing through the Forum, they heard the clash of iron on iron, followed by a sobbing scream as some man died in quick anguish. Elspeth shuddered and felt Lamia move quickly by her side, but neither woman spoke.

Not until they had passed the Murcian Gate were they

molested—and then the attack came furiously and without warning. All at once a bearer cried out and the litter thudded unevenly to the pavement. Swift footsteps sounded about them, followed by a hoarse cry and the sudden yelp of a man in pain.

Lamia, plucking a knife from beneath her stola, slipped out of the litter, leaving Elspeth alone. There was a horrid bubbling gurgle as another man died, followed by sounds of panting breath. Somewhere close Elspeth could hear the snap of a bone, followed by a hoarse scream of agony.

Suddenly, on the far side of the litter from that through which the slave-girl had moved into the fray, the curtains were thrust rudely apart. The interior was flooded with erratic light from a torch that still flamed on the pavement outside. A man thrust his head through—a horrid filthy unshaven head with broken nose and one empty eyesocket and sweat-stained pock-marked cheeks. The brigand's one good eye gleamed at her with an unholy expression of pure lust.

Elspeth shrank back and opened her mouth to scream—but no sound issued. In the sheer horror of the moment she became possessed of a sort of hyperacutia, noted every scrape of sandal, every grunt, every exhaled breath in the struggle that still raged beyond the other curtain. Everything seemed to happen in slow motion.

But her thoughts were racing. While the one-eyed brigand revealed a hand whose filthy fingers gripped a rude stiletto already dripping crimson, she felt an instant of sheer panic. And then she recalled that she was not really a helpless Roman matron, beset by footpads in the ancient city. She was a free-wheeling and supposedly resourceful agent of the Watchers, selected from among hundreds of millions as best able to persevere on her assignments among parallel worlds.

She felt a moment of regret that she had not brought with her the blaster she kept concealed in the strongbox in her chamber. Then, as face and hand and knife drew inexorably closer, she thought suddenly of the strange gun she had stolen from Gnaius Laconius—if it were a gun. Fumbling for it beneath her stola, she realized with odd detachment that she was going to learn in a hurry just what it was.

The robber's hissed syllables made no impression on her

consciousness. All her awareness was concentrated on the knife approaching her bosom. The lust in the brigand's one eye was evidently not for her person but for the jewels he supposed she was wearing. She felt the odd, disc-shaped weapon fitting into the palm of her hand. She said a quick prayer lest there be some sort of safety attachment, pointed the nozzle toward that ghastly face and squeezed.

She felt the little disc leap in her palm, but no flame emerged from the belled nozzle and for a moment she felt disappointed that Gnaius' weapon had proved a failure—not fear, just disappointment. Too much was happening for her emotions to react with the logic expected of less abnormal situations.

Then she looked up at her attacker—and felt fear. The man's hideous face had vanished, to be replaced by a bubbling, smoking, stinking thing of burning flesh and bone that crackled as it seared. His bloody knife fell harmlessly on her stola as he tumbled backward beyond the curtains.

"Good God!" exclaimed Elspeth in English. The litter began to rock and, holding the alien weapon, she plunged through the curtains. One of her feet came down solidly on the body of what had been the one-eyed attacker, and she leapt clear just as the litter toppled over on his gruesome remains.

There were no other attackers on the near side of the overturned litter, but Lamia and the surviving two of her Iberian slaves were penned in by a half-dozen ragged bandits, whose knives flashed in the torchlight as they closed in. At least as many bodies, lying like crumpled heaps of discarded clothing on the pavement, testified to the fact that her slaves were resolved to defend her with their lives if need be.

Elspeth slipped along the wall behind her as the footpads closed in for what was meant to be a final rush. She rounded the litter and pressed Gnaius' weapon against the side of the nearest bandit. He screamed as the blast burned him almost in two, then collapsed like an airless balloon.

Quickly Elspeth eliminated the next bandit and the next, as a fourth fell before the short sword wielded by one of the surviving Iberians. The remaining pair of attackers, seeing the carnage about them and finding themselves unexpectedly outnumbered, fled crying into the night.

Returning the weapon to safe concealment within her stola, Elspeth surveyed the situation and said, "We shall walk the rest of the way. Come on—let's go. We're not yet out of the woods."

One of the surviving Iberians was wounded, and Elspeth put a tourniquet about his upper arm to stop the bleeding of a torn wrist artery—an operation the slave endured stoically but which filled Lamia with admiration.

The Pamphylian girl, who had wiped her crimson blade on the ragged tunic of one of the dead attackers, picked up a still-flaming torch and handed it to the sounder of the Iberians. As they proceeded past the gate toward the Aventine palance, she walked close to her mistress, regarding her intently from time to time with awe.

"Why are you looking at me like that?" Elspeth finally asked.

"The way you stopped Janisius from bleeding to death!" she exclaimed. "The way in which you struck down the bandits with bolts of black lightning. Madam, you didn't tell me you were a witch!"

Elspeth smiled at the reproach in the slave-girl's tone. But she said, "Keep up with me, Lamia. You have a lot to learn."

"I didn't think so," said the girl with disbelief. "Not until just now." And Elspeth only then remembered that, in Roman folkways, a witch was no broomstick-riding hag but more or less synonymous with a goddess. The thought made her feel better for reasons she didn't wish to explain to herself.

IV

Throughout the fight in the street, Lamia had shown no trace of fear. But once they were inside the palace yard she shrank against Elspeth, muttering some invocation to the Pamphylian gods in her native tongue. The big war-machines, the size and uniforms of the sentries, the alien words Elspeth exchanged with the corporal of the guard combined to fill her with terror.

Not until Sergeant Carhart's large and sleepy countenance reflected the glow of a flashlight did she recover herself. Then she said, "Ah, the slave messenger of this afternoon."

Apparently the sergeant's Latin was better than his speech implied. Interrupting himself in a series of low-voiced orders to take care of the damaged Iberians, he swung on Lamia angrily and tried vainly to express himself in Latin. Then he said to Elspeth, "Ma'am, tell this creature I'm no slave!"

Elspeth explained the situation briefly, and the girl regarded the sergeant with new interest and respect. As they were conducted into the palace after the wounded had been arranged for, the poetess drew from her stola the map and the little hand blaster that had served her so well in the street fracas.

Lamia, with a little cry, offered a mate to it, said, "Here, I have one too if you want it, madam."

Stunned, Elspeth stopped in her tracks, said, "Where'd you get it?"

"Oh, I plucked it from the robe of one of those barbarians who tried to slay you, madam," was the girl's reply. "He'll never have use for it again. I thought it an odd trinket."

"You don't know how odd," replied Elspeth, freezing

at the implications it presented. She had the girl wait outside while she went into the office where Commander de Mestres, sipping a cup of coffee, awaited her. There she gave him an account of what had happened, omitting only the details of her rendezvous with Gnaius Laconius.

"Evidently the attack was planned by him or by someone to whom he reported the theft," said the Commander. "What's your bet?"

My guess is someone else did it," came the reply. "What I don't understand"—Elspeth shuddered, paused briefly—"is why, if the supposed bandits had such weapons they didn't use them on us."

De Mestres regarded her thoughtfully, sipped his coffee, made a face as it scorched his tongue. "Probably," he suggested, "only the leaders of the group were so armed. You say their attack was going well until you caught them in flank with the blaster?" And, at Elspeth's nod: "It probably never occurred to him you'd have enough savvy to use the weapon properly." He eyed it distastefully where it lay with its mate on his desk and added, "Nasty looking little gun!"

"Do you think it's a Heartland weapon?" Elspeth asked.

De Mestres picked up the nearer one gingerly. "From what we know of their culture it fits," he said. Then, rising from behind his desk, he said, "But we can soon find out for sure."

He crossed the room, unlocked an oblong metal box that stood on a table against the wall and lifted its case to reveal a transferometer. Seeing it Elspeth said, "Good!" and leaned forward to watch the proceedings. She was a little frightened at the reassurance she received from de Mestres' unshakable poise, from the homely twang of his Midwestern American accents. It made her realize how close to the margin of fear she had been living now for three months.

She was well acquainted with the marvelous instrument the Commander was operating. Each of the myriad Earths, existing in parallel space, had a slightly different atomic variation from all the others—a trade-mark that remained the same no matter how frequently an object or person from such a world was transferred to others.

The transferometer, whose face resembled the front of an old-fashioned radio in the multiplicity of its dials and indicators, was built not only to check the world-source of such an object. It also located any alien object to which it was tuned. At the moment its use was the simpler first of these.

Suddenly de Mestres swore and Elspeth asked what was wrong. Turning to face her the Commander said, "Apparently Heartland is so newly discovered that its atomic gauge is not listed. We'll simply have to content ourselves with whether this weapon is alien or not to *Antique*."

It very definitely was. And since the A-gauge was not that of an object from any of the listed worlds, both Elspeth and the Commander thought it safe to assume they had captured two Heartland weapons. They returned to the desk, where de Mestres unfolded the map Elspeth had filched from Gnaius Laconius.

"Any idea where it is?" Elspeth asked him.

De Mestres shook his head, told her, "No . . . sorry. But I've got a lad here who knows most of Europe by heart. And from what we know about this problem it's Europe odds-on. The Mediterranean Basin is much too settled not to show some roads or towns. My guess is that it's somewhere in Western Germany. There's a hell of a lot of forest."

A few minutes later a slim dark young captain, wearing his combat jacket over striped pajamas, entered rubbing his eyes. He regarded Elspeth with sleepy appreciation and helped himself to coffee from the Commander's silex. Elspeth, who hated coffee, again wondered when, if ever, she would get a cup of tea.

At work on the map, the newcomer, whose name was Johnson and who spoke with a definite Southern drawl, quickly proved his commander to be wrong. After rubbing a bristly chin he said, squinting at the map, "That looks like Silesia to me. I'll check."

"It couldn't be the Rhineland?" de Mestres asked plaintively.

"Nope. Sorry, Commander, but that smaller stream looks familiar." At his request an ordnance map of Silesia was brought in, and Captain Johnson located the area shown on the stolen map. "This cross marked on it," he told them, "is about six miles above the junction of the Meisse and Oder Rivers in Silesia. It's not far southeast of Breslau, closer to a little place called Brieg."

He paused, fingered the material of which the stolen map was made, said, "I wish we put ours on something as good."

"Thanks, Johnson," said de Mestres. "That does it."

Reluctantly, the captain withdrew, casting sheep's eyes at Elspeth, whose ego derived an almost juvenile lift therefrom. When Johnson had gone, de Mestres said, "I think we should check that marked area. How do you feel about it?"

"Perhaps we should inform the resident agent," she said.

"I don't think there's time," was de Mestres' reply. "After what happened on your way here they're bound to get the proverbial wind up sooner or later. I'll send him a message, of course—but I have a hunch we ought to investigate right away."

"Why not check on the transferometer just to make sure," said Elspeth. "I'm afraid you're right about Pliny. He's with the fleet at Misenum." She watched while de Mestres put the instrument to its use as a locator, retaining the A-gauge previously revealed by the hand weapons.

"This is it, all right," he said a minute or two later, revealing the coincidence of indicators. "Both direction and distance check—north northeast and about a thousand kilometers." He glanced at his watch, uttered a curse, said, "It's close to dawn. I wouldn't dare send out a flier this near daylight. It would be spotted for sure. "We'll have to wait till evening."

"That should be soon enough," she said, "unless they have radio or fliers themselves."

"We don't know what they have," was the reply, as de Mestres paced the floor, frowning. "What's more, I don't know who to send. I daren't go and I'm the only person sufficiently briefed at present."

"What about me?" Elspeth asked promptly. "I can fly a pipit."

The Commander stopped short, peered at her as if seeing her for the first time. "It's those damned clothes," he told her. "I keep thinking of you as a Roman matron."

He hesitated, then said, "I hate to think of asking you to risk your life, but if you really feel you can handle it—after all, this is an emergency."

"I've handled some tough ones," Elspeth said simply. "And in view of what's happened I'll probably be safer on the move than hanging around Rome, waiting for another attempted murder."

"You'd better stay right here," said the Commander, pressing a buzzer. "I'll see you and your woman get quarters. By the way, I hope she won't let the men frighten her."

Elspeth burst out laughing—she couldn't help it. The idea of Lamia being afraid of any man! The worst of it was she couldn't very well explain it to the Commander without giving him all sorts of ideas about her. He looked bewildered, slightly aggrieved, but accepted her apology and said, "I might send Johnson along if it's all right with you. He's the best navigator-flier I've got."

"Glad to have him along," replied Elspeth. Then: "By the way, Commander, am I under your orders or what?"

He regarded her somberly and told her, "According to Mr. Horelle we're in different command echelons. We're supposed to work together."

"It's a pleasure, Commander," she told him. Unexpectedly he offered his hand and she took it. She hoped he never found out about Gnaius Laconius. She felt no sense of guilt at being a thief, it was the other matter that troubled her conscience.

A pair of army cots were set up in one of the smaller and less-eroded rooms of the crumbling palace, and Lamia exclaimed at the miraculous softness of them. Finally, however, she decided to sleep on the floor lest the cot give her a backache.

Lamia regarded her mistress with somber speculation and said, "Madam, those men are soldiers—but soldiers of a sort my world has never dreamed of. They could destroy or capture Rome in a day with their weapons." She shivered. "Madam, it may not be my place to ask—but why are they here?"

"To save your world from far more vicious invaders," Elspeth told the girl. "Remember, you are vowed to secrecy. And your master is a party to the plan. He'll have you flayed alive if you reveal a word of what you've seen except to him or me."

Lamia snorted. Apparently, Elspeth decided, the elder Pliny was not too stern a master. Yet the poetess sensed that the Pamphylian girl could be trusted. Beneath the undiscipline of her morals lay a solid base of integrity that had revealed itself in a hundred different ways over the past eight weeks. It was, Elspeth decided, time she got a few hours' sleep while she could. A long night loomed ahead.

Commander de Mestres did not rouse the women until close to noon. Then he sent Sergeant Carhart to rap on their door. Lamia peered around it at him. Elspeth, awakening, heard the sergeant say, "Hello, honey, here's some duds I rustled up for you and the lady. I hope they ain't too big."

"What did you say?" Lamia inquired in Latin, and the sergeant began to stammer awkwardly in the alien tongue. Elspeth told the slave girl to accept the clothing, then assured the sergeant in English that it was all right and they would both be down shortly.

The clothing both fascinated and repelled Lamia. Measuring against herself a pair of battle dress trousers that reached from bosom to toe of her tiny body, she cried, "Barbarian clothing! But see how well-made it is. Feel how light!"

Without thinking, Elspeth plucked a cigarette from the package Sergeant Carhart had thoughtfully stuck in a breast pocket, and lit it.

"Madam!" cried the girl. "You're on fire!"

"Just smoking," said Elspeth, inhaling with joy. It was her first cigarette in three months. Evidently Commander de Mestres was not a smoker and she herself had been too agitated and too accustomed to doing without to ask him for one during their earlier sessions. Regarding the girl, she said, "Better get dressed."

"I'd prefer to keep my own clothes on," Lamia replied thoughtfully. "Madam, you are big and blonde, and the gray-blue goes with your eyes. Me, I should look like a pig trussed for roasting."

"Suit yourself," said Elspeth, seeking a non-existent

mirror to check her own appearance. She had a feeling of being at home in the uniform, even though military dress was new to her. At least the things came from her own time, if not from her own world. She reminded herself to ask Commander de Mestres, the next time she saw him, just which of the worlds he was from.

"Madam," said Lamia plaintively, "I don't pretend to understand any of this, but it is evident that you are a witch of great power."

"I'm no witch," said Elspeth, dropping ashes on the floor and pushing a stubborn lock of hair back from her forehead. "I'm just—well, let's say I'm from a very different place. Outside of that I'm merely a woman like yourself—perhaps not quite as much so."

"Don't say so," countered the slave-girl. Then: "And this strange tongue you speak—what language is it?"

"Believe it or not we call it English," replied Elspeth.

"Then you must come from Britain," said Lamia, happy at having found an explanation that satisfied her. "Perhaps from the mysterious provinces of the north. They say there are many fair women there."

"We thank you," said Elspeth, "Let's just say again I come from a very long way off. Now, let's see if we can eat."

To Lamia's evident disappointment they were not permitted to share their mess with the soldiers but ate in the Commander's office, served by Sergeant Carhart.

Lamia, of course, was astounded by the alien food, though she managed not to make too much fuss about it.

The meal finished, Elspeth asked permission to visit her wounded littermen, whom she found stunned but comfortable in a jury-rigged dispensary at the other end of the palace. They greeted her appearance with something close to terror, and Lamia, more conventionally clad by their lights, had to reassure them all was well.

"They think they have died and been conveyed to heaven," the slave-girl told Elspeth outside the dispensary. "They think the illumination is bits of sunlight stolen to give them warmth."

"What do you think?" Elspeth asked the Pamphylian girl.

Lamia shrugged her shoulders and said, "I've stopped

trying to think. I'm merely trying to learn and see. And I'm glad you are here to protect me against things I do not know or understand."

"I'm leaving you tonight for a bit," Elspeth told her. "And while I'm gone—don't be an idiot, you'll be all right—I'm leaving you in charge of those two poor littermen. And I want you to behave yourself. Do you understand? I shall probably be busy from now on."

She spent most of the remainder of the afternoon closeted with Captain Johnson and the Commander, completing plans for the trip to Silesia. It was agreed that they should take off in a light combat car as soon as darkness had fallen, be back before dawn or wait over until the next night if there were any question of flying over Italy by day. No check-up or relief would be sent them unless they failed to return within thirty-six hours.

"Fair enough," said Elspeth, a cigarette in her mouth. "Now, how about route? That's in your province, Captain."

"Call me Bill," said the flier-navigator with his boyish, disarming grin. Elspeth shot a quick glance at Lamia, who sat curled on a bench, silent and uncomprehending.

That evening, after dining on steak and French fried potatoes, she and Captain Bill Johnson took off in a helipipit whose thin coat of light gray armor and caterpillar treads proclaimed it to be a light combat car. Before they rose from the ground, the Commander said to Elspeth: "Try to get back here by morning. I can't keep my men cooped up here much longer. They want action."

"They may get it," said the poetess. She clambered into the cockpit and sat down beside the captain, waved through the window at Lamia, who looked on, apparently expecting the worst.

Bill pressed the starter button and Elspeth could feel the faint vibration as the wings above them began to whirl. Once they had risen clear of the city the pilot would switch in the jets, and the rotor vanes would fold neatly into the cabin roof above them. All in all, Elspeth decided, it was a very neat vehicle, improved upon its opposite numbers in her own world. But then, for the moment, her world was not threatened with large-scale warfare.

They lifted easily and, looking down, the poetess saw Lamia standing there, stricken by her mistress' airborne departure, a hand pressed against her mouth. Even as the beamed light was turned off, killing the view, Elspeth saw Sergeant Carhart's bulky form loom up behind the girl and place a reassuring arm on her shoulder. She smiled to herself in the darkness—Lamia was going to be all right.

According to plan they flew due east, thus passing only over the southern outskirts of the city. But even from this angle, Rome was impressive. The Forum was lit like a volcano, its facades reflecting in pink or white or lemon yellow the bright lights of the huge torches that shed their smoky glow upon it.

But soon the Eternal City was a mere spot of light in the distance behind them as Bill Johnson guided the helipipit's passage over the lower Apennines before swinging due north. They flew across the Adriatic, Illyricum and Pannonia to their destination, in the supposedly uncharted northern forests of this primitive world.

At seven thousand feet he cut in the jets and seemed, until Elspeth grew accustomed to the greater speed, to be taking leave of the world. The poetess looked up at the stars and wondered what it was like to travel in space.

Not that any person or group on any of the known planets had succeeded in reaching the stars. However, certain of the more advanced parallels *had* succeeded in reaching the planets—though not as yet with spectacular results, economically at any rate.

A star, she thought. *I am a star whose beam extends its slender glow beyond galaxy's rim, a star chained to the rhythm of the universe, a universe which must be cold and whirling ash before my light is seen by men or other galaxies.*

"What's on your mind, Elly?" Captain Johnson asked, bringing her abruptly out of her self-imposed spell.

"Oh," she replied, "I was just thinking what it must feel like to be a star—a little gay, a little sad."

"It'd be mighty hot," said Johnson. "You sure you feel okay?" he asked.

Elspeth laughed and told him, "Don't mind me—I used to be a poet before I got tangled up in this business."

If anything this statement frightened him more than her previous one. He said, "A poet! But what in hell can a poet . . ." His voice trailed off in something approaching Donald Duck frustration.

"I know," she said with moderate sympathy. "It's frightening. But sometimes poets are able to view people with a certain amount of detachment. And oddly enough, no matter how many worlds the Watchers attain, all of them seem to be more or less full of people."

"I hadn't thought of it from that angle," mused the young captain. Then, evidently at last aware of his lack of tact, he said, "When I saw you with the Commander last night I thought maybe he was off his rocker. I thought you were one of these dames from the city in that get-up. Then when I heard you talking American I felt better."

Elspeth decided to make him suffer. She said, "It might interest you to know that I'm a British subject. In the world I come from, the United States belongs to the British Commonwealth."

There was uneasy silence. Then, in a small if not still voice the Southerner drawled plaintively: "I reckon I've got a whole lot to get used to in this business. You see this is the first time I've jumped worlds and it's all a mite strange."

"I understand," said Elspeth in more kindly fashion. "Making transfer by submarine must have been quite an experience. That's one method I haven't had to use yet."

"Elly, it was downright frightenin'," said Bill Johnson. He went on to give her some of the details of that fantastic change of worlds. Meanwhile, he piloted the plane expertly northward over the barren hills of the Northwest Balkans toward their destination.

Under full jets the helipipit was capable of speeds up to six hundred kilometers an hour—not fast for fighter planes in its own world but more than respectable for a combination vehicle. They had taken off at nine o'clock and their route was about twelve hundred kilometers each way. They had, according to Bill, encountered no appreciable air currents in any direction.

"If we were a sailin' ship we'd be sittin' in the middle of the pond," he informed her as the clock on the instrument panel registered six minutes of eleven.

"If we're on course we ought to be seeing something soon—if there's anything to see," said the poetess.

"We're on course!" There was outraged pride of profession in the captain's voice. He might not, Elspeth thought, appreciate poets and poetry, but he certainly could handle a flier with more dash and finish than anyone she had ever flown with—even Mack Fraser.

"Look down there—at two o'clock," he said a moment later. His questing eyes were on the silver tape of a river winding far beneath in the moonlight. "That's the Oder. Just a little beyond the Meisse conflows with her. After that—well, we'll see."

He began to bring the ship down in a gentle glide as it passed above the juncture of the rivers. Peering out at the ground below, Elspeth thought she had never overlooked so desolate a panorama. As far as the eye could see in the semi-darkness of the moonlight, forest rolled unbroken like some mighty land-ocean. Nowhere did pinpricks of orange or yellow break the stretch of darkness. It was utter blackout.

Elspeth felt certain depression seize her. The road had been too easy, too clearly marked. They were, she felt sure as she let her gaze follow a moon-bathed spur of rock that jutted up through the dark carpet below, doomed to a wild-goose chase. The Heartlanders, if it was those unfortunate people who were responsible for the invasion, had been too clever for them. If she and Bill found a thing beneath that forest sea, it would be a decoy, perhaps a booby trap.

At the sound of a click she turned abruptly, said, "Why are you turning off the cockpit lights, Bill?" She had a fleeting suspicion of his motives.

But all the Southerner said was, "Look ahead."

Elspeth peered vainly through the plastic windshield, and then she saw it: a dim bluish glow that came not from the moon's reflection but from some source still hidden by distance and the trees.

Perhaps it was not going to be a wild-goose chase after all.

V

Captain Johnson cut the jets and again the helipipit vibrated gently to the silent swirling of the vanes. The bluish glare increased as they approached it at an altitude of about a kilometer. Conscious of a movement at her left, Elspeth saw her companion, his lips compressed, checking levers on the instrument panel.

He caught her glance, grinned quickly, said, "Just in case, maybe we could lay an egg on them. I've got a hundred-pound sodium bomb aboard. Maybe we can mop this whole business up right now."

"As you were," said Elspeth sharply. "You may be the pilot, but I outrank you on this trip." She had no idea whether she did or not, but she sensed and feared Johnson's eager-beaver enthusiasm. "We came here to observe, not to destroy."

The Southerner actually pouted, and Elspeth had to explain. "Bill, we don't know enough to show our hand yet. This may be only one center of operations. Besides, dropping a sodium bomb on that layout would be like attacking a hornet's nest with a spitball."

They were well within sight of their target and it was evidently a large-scale mining operation, covering ten times the area one small bomb could affect. She surveyed it, frowning at its odd circular prefabricated domes, its evidence of round-the-clock activity, its number of men over machines.

This feature puzzled her until she considered the fact that these interplanetary pirates were new to transfer between worlds. Undoubtedly, they had not yet had time to test the limits in size and tonnage of what could be sent from their own world into this one. Also, much of their machinery might be below ground. Such of it as did show impressed her untechnical eye as being compact and efficient, perhaps beyond that of any world she had seen.

"Okay, General," said Captain Johnson, "We've seen it and I've had the infra-red cameras on it. Want to go back now?"

"Sure you've photographed it all?" Elspeth asked. At his nod, she said, "I suppose we might as well. Commander de Mestres wants us back as soon as possible."

"It's your red wagon," drawled the Southerner, giving the wheel a twist. "What the hell!" he suddenly cried as a bolt flashed past their wing, exploding above them in a rocket-like shower of varicolored blazing trails.

Elspeth cried out as something burst through the cockpit behind them with a sizzling roar, leaving a smell of burning ozone behind it, cutting through the thin armor of their flying vehicle as if it were butter.

At once the plane began to buck like a mustang out of control while the Southerner, swearing softly but fervently, strove to reassert his mastery. Flames flickered in the fuselage at their backs and the dark forest tilted and rose until it filled half the sky.

Elspeth had always supposed herself to be a physical coward. All her life she had fled from the threat of physical violence and pain. In her creed violence belonged only to nature, while pain was a part of the ugliness that belonged to the foul family of death and sickness and the filth that bred them.

Yet now, for the second time within twenty-four hours, she found herself acting promptly and efficiently in the face of probable pain and possible death. Her hands flew without volition to the extinguisher that was clamped to the instrument panel. Bracing herself so that the violent gyrations of the helipipit would not send her on her ear, she sprayed the spreading flames, which were licking angrily at paint and upholstery, with fire-killing foam.

Heat seared her face and a sudden pseudopod of flickering yellow licked at the wrists of her coverall. She swore as efficiently as her companion and put out the last flaming assault with a last burst of extinguisher foam. Her knees felt like eggs in a waterglass, and little imps were snapping rubberbands at the backs of her eyeballs.

"I guess I'm as brave as anybody," she said aloud, "as long as I don't have time to think."

"Good gal!" said Captain Johnson, darting a hand from the controls to give her near knee a quick pat. Then, grimly, he said, "But I reckon we aren't out of the woods yet—that's for sure."

"Or rather we're still in them," said Elspeth with a pitiful attempt at humor. The helipipit was still rocking but less violently. They were well-away from the blue-lit mining camp now and the tops of the trees seemed to be reaching up to embrace them.

"If I can clear this next hill," drawled the Southerner from between set teeth, "we should be able to ditch in the river."

"Here's hoping," said Elspeth, mentally crossing her fingers. To her annoyance, her teeth were actually chattering.

Though Johnson was racing the motor for all it was worth, the helipipit was still losing altitude—and he was far too low to cut to the jets. Worse, if he tried to while the vanes were still whirling, he'd strip them and inevitably crash in the trees beneath.

Desperately he worked with the plugs on the instrument board, turning them, pressing buttons savagely. Then, as Elspeth braced herself for the inevitable crash, the lagging motor seemed briefly to catch hold again. The helipipit lifted some fifty feet, barely making the rise. The hill fell away on the other side and the silvery Oder curled broadly before them.

"Mother always said I'd make the grade if I ate my oatmeal," muttered the flier. Elspeth felt such a surge of relief at the narrowness of their escape that she was unprepared for the shocking jolt of their striking the water in a sheet of spray that momentarily shut out the world.

The poetess had one quick watery glimpse through the windshield of the dark shore rushing toward them. Then there was a shock that left her lying bruised and shaken on a tilted cockpit floor. They had missed one crack-up to fall into another.

Suddenly fear of fire returned to bring Elspeth out of her punch-drunk condition. If Bill had not cut the switch before they struck, they might be incinerated. Pulling herself onto the seat, she checked the instrument panel. She felt sobbing relief as she saw that, with his last conscious gesture, the Southerner had cut off the engine.

For Captain Johnson was definitely out. He lay across the wheel like a collapsed drunkard, blood trickling from his right ear and from an ugly bruise on his forehead. For a minute or so Elspeth sat paralyzed, thinking him dead. Then, without warning, he began to snore. The poetess found herself giggling like a hysterical schoolgirl, for the moment unable to do more than sit there.

She found herself eying the unconscious pilot with a dislike she knew to be utterly unfair. After all, he had done a magnificent job. Yet, annoyingly, a voice within her kept repeating that Mack would never have got them into such an impasse, that he always managed to come up with a way out no matter how hopeless the situation seemed.

Yet Captain Johnson needed attention. Though she was aching and bruised from the smash and her wrists were blistered from the cockpit fire, she was going to have to do something for the Southerner. She considered getting him out of the helipipit, but a look at the forbidding forest border in which the vehicle had wedged itself caused her to decide such a move was beyond her at present.

The rear of the cockpit, penetrated as it had been by the incendiary charge, was out of the question. So the poetess managed to pull and tug at her companion until he lay on his back across the seat. He had stopped snoring, but blood was still trickling from his ear. His forehead was beginning to purple.

All she could do, she decided, was to bind up his head. She did so, then threw over him a half-burned seat cover from the rear of the cockpit. She wished she had managed at some time or other to learn medicine, or at least to have got some nurse's training. She had no idea whether her pilot was dying or not.

She opened the cabin door and stepped out into icy water that rose to her knees. Its chill was unpleasant but helped to restore her senses fully.

The helipipit itself was battered but still looked serviceable. Its blunt nose was driven almost a foot into a high bank of moss, loam and underbrush, but did not look hard to pull out. Elspeth's spirits rose as she toted up the damage. Then she scrambled up out of the water onto the bank and saw the vanes—and her morale plummeted.

Only three of them were intact. The fourth looked like a piece of taffy at the wrong end of a taffy-pull. Grotesquely twisted and torn, it hung forlornly from its mooring. No wonder, she thought, that the machine had behaved like a sailor three days in port.

As nearly as she could calculate, Bill Johnson had come down in a curve of the river. This had caused him to run the helipipit into the bank on the same side as the factory they had seen from above. She wondered if those same forces that had shot them down would institute a search. She decided they probably would.

Overhanging trees hid the vehicle against air search fairly well. But if the miners had scanning or other search equipment to match their other machinery, it seemed unlikely to her that she and Bill could hope to escape detection.

She lit a cigarette and looked about her in the moonlight and thought, *So this is the forest primeval!* Then, as some creature made a rustling in the trees beyond the bank, she checked her blaster, made sure it was in order and ready for use. There was no point in doing anything until morning, so she crawled back into the helipipit and tried to doze in the charred rear of the cockpit. In the front seat the unconscious Southerner was snoring again.

Elspeth managed to get a few hours of broken sleep. But when at dawn the forest awoke to a chattering of birds and other animal sounds, she scrambled out of the damaged vehicle to the bank. She was determined to scout around before trying to restore Captain Johnson to consciousness.

Once beyond the barrier of thickets that lined the river bank, the forest thinned out to become almost a grove. Elspeth found herself treading upon a soft carpet of pine needles, and her poetic soul responded to the natural Gothic cathedral created by nature around her.

The growth of new timber thickened as she went on, until she found herself walking along a sort of path. It was no more than four feet broad, banked on either side by baby firs, struggling for life amid the great strangler roots of the older, taller trees that seemed to ignore the upstarts striving to rise against them.

Even here in the untouched forest, she thought, the dog-eat-dog struggle for survival went on, intermeshed as always in the very warp of existence. She turned a corner and barely suppressed a gasp, as, in a little clearing, three savages, half-clad in animal skins, clustered busily about another.

Her hand darted to the blaster at her belt. Some inadvertent sound must have betrayed her, for the wild men turned like one, their mouths agape, their dark eyes staring. Elspeth had only time to note that their faces were shaven before, with queer unintelligible utterances, they took to their heels and fled toward the depths of the forest. They left behind them the object that had drawn their attention.

At sight of it Elspeth gasped. Dangling upside down, his ankles caught in the simplest sort of rope-trap, was Mack Fraser. He looked slightly the worse for wear, and his blood, rushing to his face, had given his complexion the hue of a cocktail cherry.

His choked, angry voice brought her out of her surprise. He said, "Dammit, Elly, get me the hell out of this, will you?"

So unexpected was the sight of her erstwhile partner in such a scrape, that she could not suppress a giggle as she moved forward to blast the rope from which he hung. He landed with a thump on the pine-needle floor beneath.

He said, "Shut up, you idiot—it's not funny!"

She said, "Dr. Livingston, I presume," and got a dirty look. Impulsively she offered him a cigarette.

Inhaling it with unspoken gratefulness, he got up. Testing his limbs and finding them all there, he told her, "You've got to get out of here in a hurry. The Heartlanders are scouring the woods for your ship. I figured you'd have come down around here and tried to get here ahead of the Martinez when those damned nature boys bushwhacked me."

"Come on—I chipped a few trees so I wouldn't get lost. My pilot ditched us in the river after the ack-ack got us."

"How badly are you damaged?" asked Mack, ever pragmatic. He shook his head doubtfully, when Elspeth told him as best she could. "If you can't get out of here it's going to be a hell of a mess. The Martinez and her gang are mining and transferring uranium by the ton, and they aren't going to let you or me or anyone else stop them."

"What's the Martinez?" Elspeth asked him, feeling unaccountable security in the nearness of Mack and stealing a look at his tough rough-hewn, handsome-homely countenance.

"You'll be lucky if you don't see her," was the reply. "She's the boss of this operation—and just about runs Heartland as well. Ana Kai-Martinez—she's the toughest, smartest, best-looking Amazon in a world of Amazons. How those women treat their men!" He shook his head.

"You seem to be doing all right," said Elspeth. "If you weren't why should those phony cave men have tried to do you in?"

"I'm in a hell of a spot," Mack said ruefully. "Men on Heartland are an inferior sex. They get no practical education, are given no hand in politics. The women run the show. But I'm supposed to be a phenomenon because, although I'm a man, I know a little engineering. So I've been getting privileged status on this deal and naturally the rest of the men hate my guts. They're being treated like beasts of burden. This hunt for your ship gave them a chance to get me."

"And you fell into a rabbit trap!" gibed Elspeth. "Gracious, Mack, do you suppose the condition of these Heartland men is contagious?"

"Shut up," snapped Mack. Then, softening: "I suppose I ought to thank you for getting me out of that mess. They were just figuring what they were going to do next. None of their ideas was . . . pleasant."

They reached the river bank, and Mack studied the ruined vanes of the helipipit. Then he went inside and looked at Captain Johnson, who was still unconscious and snoring again. He gave Elspeth a look of reluctant admiration and told her, "Looks like a good first-aid job, Elly, even though I hate to admit it." Then, glancing into the rear of the cockpit, he said, "Kind of a mess-up, isn't it?

Doesn't look too bad though. How come you idiots flew right over the mine?"

"We had no instructions it might be defended," said Elspeth.

Mack frowned and said, "These Amazons aren't fooling. They've made a hash of their world and now they think they've got a chance to reclaim it. It's big stuff, Elly."

"How come they don't use sodium if they're so short on uranium?" Elspeth asked curiously.

"Believe it or not, they don't have enough radioactives left to trigger a pile of radium itself," said Mack. "Come on, let's take another look at that busted vane. Got any tools?"

She sat on the roof of the helipipit, handing Mack the instruments he needed while he worked to put the vehicle in operable shape. After a while she asked him, "Mack, how does it look?"

"Can't tell yet," was the reply. "But if I can get rid of this damned vane and this whoosit can fly on three instead of four, you may get her out of here by sundown." He paused, squinted down at her and added, "Gee, but you look beautiful today, Elly."

Well aware that she was smooched with grease and in a general condition of disarray, she said, "You're lovely too, you big creep."

He grinned briefly and blew her a kiss, then got back to work. Finally, as the shadows of later afternoon were beginning to cover the top of the vehicle and inch out across the water, he rubbed his hands on the sides of the overalls he was wearing. Sitting down beside her, he said, through puffs on a cigarette, "Well, that's it, Elly. Back her out of the bank in full reverse, head her upstream and take off. Cut in the jets as soon as you can. Those damned vanes took a beating."

Grease and all, Elly leaned over and kissed him. For a moment one of his strong arms tightened around her shoulders. Then he sat back and said, "The Martinez would have a fit if she caught this."

"Oh!" said Elspeth, drawing a little away from him and hating herself for being so vulnerable. Then, in a small voice: "What does this Ana woman look like?"

"Like a king-sized Diana with red hair," was the reply. "She's good, too—knows a hell of a lot about running this show. But she made a mistake when she gunned your ship. I knew it was a Watcher's plane and tried to tell her. But she said it would teach them a lesson and cut in the automatic cannon." He paused, wiped his greasy face with the back of a hand, added, "How much of a show have we got in this damned world anyway?"

"A big one," replied Elspeth. "The biggest I've ever seen. We came up here to check the location of the gateway and to get a line on the extent of the operation if possible."

Mack grunted, then said, "Stationed in Rome, I suppose? It must be quite a job to keep things out of sight."

"It is," replied Elspeth. "But it's being done. Well, I've got to get Bill Johnson back in one piece if I can."

Mack looked at her oddly. He said, "Good-looking guy—if you care for the type."

"Thank you, Mack," said Elspeth sincerely. She gave him another quick kiss, and, before scrambling down off the helipipit: "Better get rid of that grease, honey. Your Martinez might wonder how you got into it out here in the forest primeval."

"Good idea," he said grudgingly, handing her the tools, which he had assembled before sliding down. "Thanks again for getting me out of that jam in the woods."

"Think nothing of it," she said airily. Then, more softly: "Mack, it's nice to know we're on the same job—even on opposite sides."

He gave her a half-grin, scratched his grimy nose and said, "Yeah—remember, full reverse, then upstream, then up. You ought to make it okay, if nothing else happens."

"I know we will, Mack. Good luck." He was still standing there, half-merged with the shadows of the underbrush, as she pulled the cabin door shut. Propping Captain Johnson in the other corner of the front seat, she was able to get the engine going.

There was a sucking jar as the vehicle asserted its power and came clear of the bank. She cut in the vanes once they were clear of the overhanging shrubbery, felt the unrhythmic vibration as they caught hold of the air in three-quarter time. Looking down as the ground fell away beneath them, she could not see Mack at all.

She cut in the jets and headed due south, thinking over the eventful scouting trip on the way. Poor Mack! She could not help smiling to herself in the darkness as the helipipit sped through the night, recalling him, hanging upside down in the super-rabbit trap the false barbarians from Heartland had rigged for him.

She wondered why she had seen no evidence of the real Goths and Germanic tribes who presumably roamed the Silesian forest. Probably, she decided, there were too few of them over too large an area for her to have stumbled on any natives save through merest chance.

Yet the fact the Heartland Amazons dressed their men as primitives while touring the woods suggested another idea. The natives might be in the vicinity, but could have been scared out of showing themselves by the weapons and threats of the planet-looters. The skin costumes could have been adopted to prevent barbarian rumors of the invaders from seeping south to the borders of Dacia and Pannonia, thence to Rome and, perhaps, to the ears of the Watchers.

Elspeth reached the Adriatic coastline before she realized she was lost. Looking down, she had not the slightest idea whether she was over Aquilacia or Salona. However, she continued to head south, diagonally across the long narrow sea, resisting the temptation to veer west and fly down the boot of Italy to Rome. It would never do to risk being spotted from the ground.

The moon passed under gathering clouds at that moment, which helped her not at all. For the first time since being airborne, Elspeth felt the clutch of fear beneath her breasts. Having come this far with the wounded man, the photographs and a report of her conversation with Mack, she had no desire to mess up the trip.

Beside her Captain Johnson stirred and mumbled in his sleep. She hoped that he would not recover consciousness and be out of his head. However, she certainly could use his navigational help. She was debating the wisdom of trying to wake him when a *blip-blip-blip* sounded from the instrument panel. Commander de Mestres was operating a radio beam for her benefit. She all but laughed in relief.

From then on it was easy. Less than an hour later she had cut the jets and was hovering uncertainly over the courtyard of the Aventine palace. During this peaceful last leg of the journey, she had had time to wonder about a number of puzzling factors.

Why, for instance, had not the Heartland invaders transferred to the Congo, or the Urals, or one of the other really great uranium deposits instead of mining the relatively low-grade ore of Silesia? Several answers occurred to her. One, in this world the Silesian ore might not be low-grade. Two, perhaps in decadent Heartland all record of the Congo deposits might have been lost. Three, no convenient transfer point might have been discovered.

Another possibility entered her head: Perhaps the Heartland pirates might be engaged in looting other uranium deposits on Antique, unknown to the Watchers. But this was unlikely—certainly transferometers must have scanned this and all adjacent worlds.

A searchlight beam illuminated the palace courtyard beneath her, and she brought the limping helipipit gently down, managing to mangle the landing so that the craft bounced twice before coming to a halt. She scrambled out in a hurry, all at once feeling dead tired.

As she was lifted down to the ground by the strong arms of Sergeant Carhart, Captain Johnson sat up and looked around, a puzzled expression on his bandaged face. He scowled at Elspeth and said, "For Pete's sake, get in. We're already late for the take-off."

Elspeth smiled and turned away, willing to let someone else do the explaining. She felt her knees hugged and looked down into Lamia's upturned face. The slave-girl was crying and saying in Latin, "I was sure you were slain, madam. I was sure you were slain."

She managed to reassure the girl, who was in a state of happy collapse, by the time she reached the Commander's office. There she made her report as concisely as she could, omitting only the portion in which Mack had been strung up by the Heartland men.

He heard her out in grim silence, his lips tightening as she described the effect of the weapon used to bring down the pipit. When she had finished, he looked at his folded hands, then at her, and said quietly, "You know what this means, of course, Miss Marriner—it means war for the first time between different versions of Earth. It also means things are coming to a boil."

"Yes, sir," said Elspeth meekly. "What do you want me to do?"

"I want you to return to your villa," replied de Mestres. "You must get in touch at once with the resident Watcher and inform him of what had happened. And I want you to keep an ear to the ground for anything untoward that goes on in the city."

"Why? What could happen?" Elspeth asked.

"I don't know," was the reply. "But I must remind you that my men and I are in a highly precarious situation here. Oh, we can defend ourselves, never fear—but whether we can do so without destroying our chances of accomplishing our mission is the problem. I shall call on you tomorrow, when I return from transfer. I fear a conference with Mr. Horelle is in order."

"Give him my love," said Elspeth, thinking of the kind, wise, old man of Spindrift Key, with the weight not of one but of hundreds of worlds on his slim, stooped shoulders.

VI

It seemed strange for Elspeth to awaken the following morning in her bedroom on the second story of the Cispian villa. Moving in and out among staggered time-tracks was, she decided, a great deal more demanding than the transfer between worlds, to which she had, after a fashion, become accustomed.

The effects of the Silesian crash were still with her: her body remained stiff and sore from neck to soles and her fair skin was marked with a number of purple bruises. She stirred and looked around and saw Lamia standing over her, a hand extended to shake her awake.

"Don't . . ." she murmured to the slave-girl, her tender body shrinking from any contact. The girl informed her that a messenger had arrived from Pliny, announcing that, in response to her night-sent summons, the resident Watcher was proceeding to the city and expected to dine with her at noon. Inquiring as to the time, Elspeth was informed she had scarcely two hours to prepare for her guest.

"Princess Berenice Agrippina also sent a messenger," Lamia informed her. "She wishes you to meet her at the Bath this afternoon."

"I'll be there," said the poetess, placing her feet on the floor and slowly standing erect. In keeping with the custom of the city, she wore no clothing while in bed. The slave-girl's dark eyes widened at the sight of the bruises on her body.

"You have been hurt, madam," she exclaimed.

"You should have seen the other guy," replied Elspeth, smiling again at the memory of Mack Fraser dangling upside down in the trap.

Eyeing her askance, Lamia busied herself expertly with giving her mistress an oil massage that, within an hour, worked much of the soreness and stiffness from her limbs.

Later, while the poetess was relaxed languidly in her bath, Lamia eyed her sternly and said, "I don't understand what is happening. What are these strange soldiers in the Aventine place and what was this wizard's machine that carried you to the clouds?"

Elspeth sat up in the tub and studied the girl before saying, "Lamia, I cannot explain now, but witchcraft and wizardry have nothing to do with it. I have been sent here to help your world against enemies of which it is not as yet aware."

"I do not doubt you, madam," was the slave-girl's response. "I only wish I could be of more assistance."

There was no mistaking the sincerity of her wish. Elspeth hesitated, then said, "There is a chance—just a chance—that if all goes well I shall be able to take you with me when I leave. You would, of course, no longer be a slave, for there are no slaves in the land I come from. You would have much to learn, much hard work to do. Do you think you would like it?"

"Oh, madam!" cried the girl eagerly. "I will gladly be your slave forever."

"That's just what I don't want you to be," replied Elspeth. "I believe, in time, you might be a very valuable person. What's more, I like you and I want to see you get the chance. But this is not a promise. Many things might happen to prevent its fulfillment."

"I shall help you in any way I can," the girl said simply.

Bathed, Elspeth refused breakfast in consideration of her coming dinner with the resident Watcher. Lamia, she discovered, had already arranged the meal with the chef. Since both were former slaves of the Admiral, she had no worry that the meal would not suit him.

It was, for that era and for a man as important as Pliny the Elder, a most simple repast, fitting to a life-long scholar and sailor. There was soup flavored with vegetables and the bird's nests of China, a baked carp in aspic, adorned cunningly with colored flowers by the chef, a saddle of baby mutton roasted in herbs and wine. For dessert, fruit, biscuits and a small cheese from Malta were served. A flagon of the Admiral's finest Falernian accompanied the dinner.

Gaius Plinius Secondus, who had arrived shortly before noon with a small escort of horsemen, was small even for a Roman. A man of modest mien and nervous mannerisms, he seemed to resent each minute that moved, like a link in some immutable chain of time, into his past. Yet, despite his restlessness, he discussed during the meal his wife and son, still in his villa at Lake Como; the state of his vineyards; the excellence of the food, the recent indisposition of the Emperor, and the strength of a new Scythian hemp in the fleet hawsers.

His speech was slow and precise. Yet, underlying the almost terrifying gravity of his preoccupations lay the half-laid pavement of self-mockery that made the man, to Elspeth, at any rate, far more a dear than a bore.

He paused while describing to her the problems of Roman ship-architects in designing a rigging that would be of help to the oarsmen between decks while heading into a wind. And somehow she sensed that he was not hesitating merely to arrange his words in order but in the hope that she might give him some advice on the problem.

"Sir," she told him, "you know that I am not permitted except in emergencies or under special orders to give you information that belongs not in this era. However, have you considered the advantages of a sloop rigging on a large vessel—or of using more than one mast?"

Pliny pondered the statement gravely, then with a spark of excitement. He held a dripping piece of mutton skewered on his knife and said, "But would not that make the vessel cant dangerously in a heavy wind, Marina Elspetia?"

Elspeth shrugged, then added, "I have said too much—but have you also considered eliminating oarsmen entirely? With skilled rigging and hull design you can do better in all weathers with sail alone."

The admiral-scientist dropped his knife with a clatter, staring at her in disbelief. Then, his voice low, he muttered, "And what if such a vessel should be becalmed?"

Elspeth wrinkled her nose and told him, "I'm no sailor, but I believe in that case small boats with oarsmen can use tow-ropes."

Her visitor-host remained silent while digesting her radical suggestions along with the rest of the meal. Then, after dismissing Lamia and adjourning to a secluded chamber where they could not be overhead, she told the resident Watcher something of the situation. She ended with, "We have reason to believe that, now the Heartlanders know we are aware of what they are doing, they will take more drastic action. What we don't know is where the move will come."

Pliny pondered her statement, then said thoughtfully, "Were I in their situation I should seek to take advantage of the Emperor's sickness and do my utmost to attain influence over Titus. It would be difficult for your people, my dear, to move if the Emperor's son and heir were against you: The Princess Berenice we can trust. But I like not the rumors of Titus' alliance with a northern princess!"

"Princess Berenice has been quick to reassert her claim," said Elspeth, recalling the scene of her introduction to the Prince. "She has asked me to meet her at the Baths of Agrippa this afternoon."

"Then go to her," adjured the scientist-sailor, "and impress upon her to the best of your persuasive abilities the importance of ensuring the allegiance of Titus."

"I doubt that I shall have much persuading to do," replied the poetess. Then, because of something in Pliny's tone: "Have you any definite indications of what they plan in this direction?"

"Nothing definite," was the reply. "Yet there is a rumor among the officers of the fleet that Titus is far more attached to his barbarian princess than is generally supposed. Some of those who saw her during the recent trip have described her as a blaze-haired giantess, whose beauty is that of a goddess."

"I shall do my best," said Elspeth, as a sudden thought occurred to her. The mysterious Gallic princess, as described by Pliny, seemed to fit uncommonly well with Mack's description of the Amazonian leader of the Heartland invaders. She said, "What is her name?"

Pliny gestured his indifference and told her, "It is some barbarian nomenclature—Anna Martiana is the closest Latin equivalent."

"Why do you suspect her?" asked Elspeth, sure now

that the Heartland leader and Titus' new flame were the same woman.

"I did not say I suspected her," replied the scientist precisely, after pausing to bury his face in the crimson juice of a pomegranate. "However, I mistrust anything out of the ordinary in the present circumstances. And this princess is reputed to come from the wilds of the East, where beauty such as hers is not known to exist."

"I'll find out what I can about her," said Elspeth.

"It might be wise." He slurped up more of the fruit, pointed his knife at her and added, "Would that I could know more of the strange machines and vehicles you and your people have brought into this world to help us defend ourselves. I feel like an orphan lad not invited to share in an imperial banquet."

"They would, I fear, be of little use to you, sir," said Elspeth. "I'm not impugning your intelligence or learning, but the techniques of centuries to come would look more like magic than science."

Pliny sighed and wiped his face on a towel. "I suppose you're right," he told her wistfully. Shortly afterward he took his leave and Elspeth, in company with Lamia, prepared to visit the Baths.

To Elspeth the Baths were the most impressive of all the impressive structures of *Antique*. It was rigid custom that, while men and women thronged together as bare as when they came into the world, no allusion to this general nakedness was ever made. Oddly enough, although Elspeth had found it difficult to keep her eyes from wandering during her first few visits to the Baths, she was becoming more and more adapted to the customs of Rome.

She took a quick plunge in the cold pool, then moved to the corner of the huge central pool, where Berenice as usual was holding court. The Princess was reclining on special cushions brought by her attendants, her magnificent little figure on proud display. At Elspeth's approach, she looked up curiously. Her dark eyes narrowed and she said, "We have missed you since the fete. You look as if Gnaius Laconius had shown you more of the beast than we thought was in him. Tell us, what have you done with the poor creature?"

"I?" Elspeth was surprised. "Why nothing. It's true I

did leave your fete in his company, but I have not seen him since."

The Princess' mocking eyes seemed to count in detail the bruises on the blonde girl's body. She said, "Then truly it is odd that both of you should vanish at once, and he in such a passion for you. Now only one of you has returned."

Elspeth was annoyed. She said, "Your mood is scarcely a pleasant one, Highness. Did you invite me here to abuse me then?"

At once contrition patterned the Princess' face, which became a mask of tragedy. She said, "My apologies, Marina. I had hoped sight of you would cheer me. Surely you have heard the news?"

Elspeth felt a stab of alarm. Something, she sensed, was going very wrong for the Princess. Under the circumstances it probably meant something was not going well for herself. She said, "I went to the country for a brief rest. I have heard neither news nor gossip."

"Then I might as well tell you," said the Princess, who had dropped her royal *we*, "my lover's barbarian princess arrived in Rome this morning. I am of a mood to pay him back in kind."

"Which would only lose him to you forever," Elspeth said promptly. Berenice's face crumpled, and for a moment she looked about to burst into tears.

Then, rallying with a magnificent display of hatred, Berenice said, "You're right, of course, Marina. I shall have to gain vengeance through *her*. She is expected to visit the Baths this afternoon. That is why I wanted my own friends at my side." She gestured about her and Elspeth realized with pity that, save for slave-attendants, the proud Princess was alone.

Thinking of Mack and his problematical relations with the red-headed Amazon, who had become such a sudden and threatening menace, she said, "I have my own axe to grind in this contest, Berenice. And then when we have won the others will come trooping back."

"A neat phrase—axe to grind," said the Princess, seizing on the cliché. But Elspeth's thoughts were elsewhere. If the redoubtable redhead had journeyed so swiftly from Silesia, the Heartlanders must be equipped with vehicles to match those of Commander de Mestres. She felt a sudden dart of illogical relief that Mack at any rate had apparently been separated from his outsized female protector.

And there was something to consider in the arrival of Ana Kai-Martinez, or Anna Martiana, at the capital. The fact that she had felt impelled to leave the mining operation so vital to her planet and come to Rome to assert her influence meant that affairs were definitely coming to a head.

Elspeth, essentially a dreamer, felt the little knot of fear within her that always came at the prospect of violence. She wondered if the newcomer would be able to force Titus, virtually in power now with the Emperor ailing, to get his legionnaires to storm the Aventine palace. The prospect was surely a fearful one.

What would Commander de Mestres be able to do?

He had expressed no fear as to his detachment's ability to defend itself against any odds. But under the assault of tens of thousands of Roman troops they might be overwhelmed, notwithstanding the immense superiority of their weapons.

They could take off, of course. But that would mean defeat of the Watcher's purpose, would give the Heartlanders a start on what might be an unparalleled course of conquest among the hundreds of worlds. Elspeth shivered, wondering illogically what had happened to Gnaius and what his role in the whole proceeding could be.

She said to the Princess, "Highness, you have really had no word as to Gnaius Laconius' whereabouts?"

The Princess, whose attention was focussed on the entrance diagonally across the central pool, shook her head and said, "There is some fear he was slain two nights ago in a footpad scuffle close by the Murcian wall. I scoffed at the rumor, feeling that he was with you. If he was not, perhaps he is dead. A pity, for he showed promise as a composer of small satires."

Elspeth wished to ask more questions, but dared not. She had seen no sign of Gnaius in the fight on her way to the Aventine palace either among the survivors or the corpses. Yet such a rumor could hardly have been started had he not been seen by someone near the battle. A sense of alarm and guilt swept through her.

THREE FACES OF TIME

If anything had happened to the poet it must have come as a result of her theft of the map and weapon from his bedroom. She felt an unexpected shaft of sympathy for the sadly confused young man who had forced his attentions upon her—or was "forced" the correct word? She pondered the problem. Certainly, in view of her own assignment, Elspeth had encouraged his suit once she became aware of the odd anachronisms in his speech. Such thinking made her feel only the more guilty.

She was thus wrapped in wretched thought when a stirring of excitement about her, a sudden tenseness on the part of the Princess, caused her to look around.

A group of attendants, wearing Imperial Household insignia, had entered and were clustered just within the main entrance. Dividing into two groups, they moved on either side of the portal. The entire population of the huge structure buzzed and grew attentive at the spectacle, looking, the poetess thought, like a collection of hairless pink seals alerted by an approaching grampus whale.

First member of the Imperial party to enter was Prince Flaviaus Domitianus, younger brother of the Crown Prince. He had been recalled from the pleasures of Nicaea, close to the Ligurian-Narbonensian border on the Mediterranean, by his father's severe illness. He peeled off the towelling robe he was wearing to reveal a magnificent compact muscular body, as well-conditioned as that of a gladiator.

Next came Titus himself, smaller, more nervous, more dynamic. His wiry slimness was marked by the scars of years of strenuous campaigning on the northwestern frontiers where the restless German tribes were forever probing and pushing against the walls of men and masonry that forbade them the loot of soft, civilized peoples within.

The Crown Prince paused for a moment, unembarrassed by his nakedness, turned and looked up at the next entry. In Elspeth's ears, as she watched the unfolding drama, the sudden exhalation of Princess Berenice's breath sounded like the hiss of a snake.

Magnificent was the word for Ana Kai-Martinez—Anna Martiana. A murmur of something like awe coursed through the hundreds of pink hairless seals on the scene—

of awe mingled with sheer appreciation of an object of beauty whose magnificence put it beyond mere mortal desire.

The supposed Gallic princess towered over men and women alike that stood around her. Elspeth estimated her to be at least an inch over six feet in her unsandaled feet. Long-limbed, full-hipped and deep-breasted, strong, slim of waist, here was a goddess indeed.

Nor did she fail from the neck up. Her head, held erect, was perfectly in proportion with the rest of her, its features commanding, passionate, beautiful. The mouth was full but firm, the nose just missed the stigma of straightness, the cheekbones were sufficiently wide to give the eyes an almost Slavic tilt. The eyes themselves, even from a distance, seemed to flash green fire. The hair that framed this arresting face, rising from a broad, low, intelligent forehead in a provocative widow's peak, was cut short. Unlike Elspeth's shoulder-length dark blonde tresses or the long black hair of the Roman matrons, it flamed like a copper helmet on her perfectly shaped head.

Here, Elspeth sensed, was a woman who could love or kill or reward or torture, as the spirit moved her—a spirit directed always by the cold intellect that lurked behind those eyes of green. Elspeth thought, *Poor Berenice!* Quickly she looked at the Princess, who was studying her rival with a malevolence unmatched in the poetess' not inconsiderable experience.

The Princess caught Elspeth's covert glance, and her dark eyes returned the gaze unconquered. Thin lips curled in a faint, mirthless smile, and she said, "In truth, my love has been taken by a cannibal queen. We must save him from the stewpot."

Elspeth managed a slight nod and said, "I fear not many men would be averse to such a fate."

"My lover is no fool," was the unconvincing reply. "Nor will he risk an empire by alliance with such a barbarian." To Elspeth, it seemed that her royal friend was whistling in the twilight of the Baths.

She watched the progress of the Imperial party, which seemed headed directly toward them. To her amazement Titus, his face composed as rigidly as if he were personally leading an assault against a phalanx of Scythian swordsmen, strode up to Berenice, stood before her and said: "Princess Berenice—Princess Anna Martiana. We are extremely anxious that the two of you be friends."

The devil! Elspeth thought as Berenice, refusing to rise and display her tininess along the unadorned king-sized red-head, managed a nod and a formal acceptance of her lover's charge.

In a deep husky voice that merely added to her charms the newcomer said in perfect Latin: "His Highness gives me to understand that you know him very well. I shall be grateful for whatever information toward his pleasure you can give me."

It was war at first sight, of course. For a moment Elspeth wondered if the Crown Prince were actually a fool. The idea of asking his current love to brief her successor seemed at first thought idiotic. Yet no Roman leader, she had come to discover, was ruled by women. If he let himself be hen-pecked his leadership was soon discarded.

Even Marc Antony, reputed to have cast away the Empire for love of Cleopatra, had considered women mere playthings, companions and potential mothers, rather than objects of undying affection. At the close perspective given her by *Antique* she had discovered an entirely different version of the Antony-Cleopatra myth than what she had acquired in her ancient history schoolbooks.

The purpose for which first Caesar, then his erstwhile lieutenant had married the Egyptian queen had been political and economic in basis rather than romantic. The facts of the so-called great romance, Elspeth had learned, had been a matter of political haggling, or straight power politics, with the body and heirs of the Egyptian queen an important factor in the dealings.

Only its near-success had been the foundation of an empty, romantic legend. Politicians, not poets had cleverly created the legend to discredit Antony rather than to idealize him in the eyes of such of his followers and sympathizers as remained.

To the average Roman of good family, the idea of permitting love of any woman to stand in the way of his duties toward country or career was both shocking and degenerate. *Antique* was a pagan world, where physical love was abundantly available for all; emotional love was a suspect rarity save when constricted within the rigid limits of the ancient Roman marriage laws.

Even in a later looser age of Empire, where emancipated women made willing bankrupts of their admirers and divorced unwanted husbands as frequently as they themselves were divorced, no woman in her senses tried to steer the ship of state. The idea was as alien in this retarded world as, in Elspeth's own, would be the idea of a ruler selling out his state through unnatural passion.

Hence she doubted the seeming idiocy of Titus in asking friendship between the two warring princesses. And, regarding his expressionless countenance, she sensed that he was putting both women to a cruel test.

He was deliberately setting them against one another, with himself as prize, probably preferring to let one of them destroy the other rather than let himself be torn between them. Sympathizing with the odds against which her friend Berenice must contend, Elspeth felt swift anger at the Emperor-to-be. Yet, mingled with anger was reluctant admiration. For truly here was an Imperial maneuver, even if limited to the confines of the Emperor's domestic life.

Berenice, choosing to ignore the magnificent redhead as much as possible, addressed Titus directly, saying, "Such news as we have of your father, Highness, is not reassuring. I hope he soon turns for the better."

Titus shrugged, replied, "My father is old and much worn by campaigning and the affairs of state. I fear I cannot hold out much hope for his recovery. Hence it is the more important that those close to me unite in friendship and mutual support."

"We hear, Highness," said Berenice. Elspeth followed her dark glance toward Anna Martiana and Domitianus, who were now standing a little back behind Titus. She caught the speculative glance the Gallic Juno cast at the younger brother, the matching speculation with which it was returned.

There was relief in Berenice's voice as she went on with, "We shall do our best to serve Your Highness in every way possible."

Which, thought Elspeth, did not bode well for the newcomer to the Imperial family circle. Berenice, sensing the treachery of Anna, knew it also an opportunity for herself and her cause. She was rallying and would fight with all the ruthless wile and cunning a granddaughter of Salome possessed. Realizing this, Elspeth felt better.

Finally the Imperial party moved away toward the side of the pool and prepared to bathe. With their recession some of the retainers behind them became visible—and Elspeth suddenly felt herself blush. She was staring directly at Mack Fraser, and Mack was as bare and blushing as she was!

VII

For one startled moment Elspeth felt like diving into the pool. It was one thing to wander naked among people who were, after all, strangers and to whom nakedness under such conditions was the accepted condition. It was another to encounter Mack in public with neither of them wearing a stitch.

She saw something close to sheer terror flicker across his somewhat battered countenance. It was followed by excruciating embarrassment as the humor of the situation struck home to her. It was with difficulty that she managed to suppress a snort of laughter. And the increased discomfort with which he regarded her barely concealed mirth only added to her enjoyment.

She thought, *I'd like to paint ugly little Tobey-jug faces on those knobby knees*. Something of what she felt must have showed in her face, because Mack ducked partially out of sight behind Domitianius and glared at her over the Prince's brawny shoulder. Seeing that no one was paying either of them any attention, Elspeth stuck out her tongue at him. Mack looked shocked at her brazenness.

The Imperial party having moved off, Princess Berenice summoned her slaves and allowed her robe to be draped around her. She said to the poetess, "We are grateful for your support, Marina." Then, dropping ceremony: "Come and see me tomorrow." With a quick squeeze of her hand the Princess moved gracefully toward one of the side entrances.

Mack, still looking thoroughly abashed, lingered behind his party as it moved off in the other direction. Approaching Elspeth with the diffidence of a teen-ager forced to ask a wall-flower to dance, he said: "Get into the water!

can't talk to you like this. And there isn't much time."

Playtime was ended. Elspeth slipped quickly into the pool and turned in time to see Mack diving in beside her in graceless belly-flopper fashion. He came up alongside her, close to the edge and out of sight of the Imperial party. He muttered in English, "What the hell kind of a world have you got yourself into, Elly?"

"I could ask the same of you," replied the poetess, nodding her wet head in the direction of the red-headed Martinez.

"Okay." Mack was all business. "I'm glad as hell to see you. The Martinez brought me down here in an air-car yesterday. It seems things are about to pop. She's set to make a deal with Titus, allowing her to loot *Antique* in peace and freeze out the Watchers."

"How do you figure in it?" Elspeth asked softly.

Mack shrugged, looked faintly embarrassed again as he always did when asked to give himself a pat on the back. He said, "The men in Heartland are so hopeless that these she-zombies seem to think I'm an engineering genius. I'm going to be lend-lease and help the Romans put up a few new aqueducts or something as part of the deal." His modesty became grimness as he added, "These Heartlanders are loaded for bear. Your trip the other day put their wind up properly. You'd better get word that things are warming up."

"I'll pass the word. How much freedom have you got on this job?"

Mack shrugged, wagged his head. "The Heartland men are so cowed their women simply don't expect them to breathe without asking permission. They think I'm a throwback. I can get around, I imagine, if I want to—inspect something or other, maybe."

"They could be right about that throwback business," Elspeth said tartly. Then, more seriously: "Try to inspect a palace on the Aventine Hill tomorrow afternoon. I'll meet you there."

Mack's brow furrowed. He said, "If it's the palace you mean, I know where it is. That's the place my gang is out to get."

"It's Watcher headquarters," Elspeth told him. "They

may get more than they bargain for."

"I'll be there," Mack told her. He added with a trace of mockery. "How will I know you with your clothes on, baby?"

Elspeth splashed water in his face and scrambled out of the pool before he could reach her. Fortunately he was wise enough not to follow her, thus perhaps calling attention to their being together. She half waved at him as she slipped out of sight to where Lamia waited with her robe.

The slave-girl said, "Who was that man you talked with?"

"An old friend," replied the poetess. Catching a certain gleam in the Pamphylian girl's dark eyes, she said, "Hands off, Lamia." She wondered, not for the first time, what it was about Mack's generally unlovely exterior that seemed to attract so many women. Of course, if they knew the fine realistic sturdiness of the soul within . . . But the attraction she was considering had nothing to do with soul. Perhaps it meant something—but past experience suggested his concern was more fraternal than passionate. She led the way to the dressing room in silence.

On her return to the Cispian villa, Elspeth was informed by a house slave that a woman was awaiting her in the anteroom. Her first thought, as the visitor rose from the curved Greek chair on which she had been seated, was that here was a remarkably tall woman for a Roman, even in comparison to the red-headed Heartland leader masquerading as a Gallic princess. Alarm bells rang again within her at the thought that perhaps this was one of the invading Amazons, sent to do away with her.

Instinctively Elspeth's hand flew to her waist, where during the flight to Silesia her blaster had hung in its holster. Her fingers brushed the soft material of her stola. Nor was her alarm abated when the visitor leaped toward her and all but smothered her in a fierce embrace.

Elspeth struggled vainly to extricate herself for several seconds before she realized that not a woman but a man was holding her. She jerked back the parka-like hood that shadowed the stranger's features and found herself looking into the eyes of Gnaius Laconius—eyes as frightened as her own.

"You must fly with me," said Gnaius, still holding her close. "I've come to take you away from here." Then, as Elspeth opened her mouth to express surprise, his hand quickly muffled her and he added with angry despair, "Had you not taken advantage of my hospitality, I should not have had to flee."

Elspeth sputtered and finally was able to say, "I'm not going to give the alarm, Gnaius. But you must be mad."

"I plead guilty to such a charge," he replied, suddenly sorrowful. "Only a madman would seek you out after the irreparable harm you have done me. But without you I am lost."

Elspeth rallied, her mind beginning to function. She said, "I know now what harm I have done you. Surely the two poor mementoes I took were small return for what I gave you willingly."

Her innocence seemed to stop him in his tracks. He stared at her, gave vent to an ironic laugh, released her and smote his brow. "Truly," he exclaimed, "fate plays curious tricks with me. I had thought myself the victim of conspiracy, with you, Marina, its most treacherous jewel. Now I find myself the victim of mischance."

"Suppose," said Elspeth, "you make yourself a trifle—"

He cut her off with a tragic gesture and told her, "All the more reason, since it was not you but some petulant goddess that betrayed me, for you to fly with me from a world in which such persecutions can exist." He seized her hands, looked deeply into her eyes.

There was something close to pathos in the floridness of his declamation. She averted her laughing eyes as if in perplexity. Unexpectedly she saw that his right hand was clutched tightly around some object whose tiny snout protruded from between the covering knuckles. Suddenly she became aware of the extent of his desperation.

His intention had been to take her with him or slay her if she refused. Her false innocence, she suspected, had momentarily put him off his purpose. For, she remembered, Gnaius Laconius—whatever his name in his true planet home—was one of the Heartland men so despised by Mack and their own Amazonian womenfolk.

Just how he had managed to reach the Rome of *Antique*

was a question she could not answer. But she had an idea the answer was a vital part of the problem facing the Watchers and she intended to learn the facts.

The reason behind Gnaius' disappearance was more easily guessed at. Evidently he had awakened shortly after she had left him. Or perhaps he had been roused by an agent of his own people. The theft had been discovered, the other agent and a crew of professional footpads had probably been sent to her villa. Finding her already in progress toward the Aventine palace, they had ambushed her party near the Murcian Gate.

Berenice's remark that Gnaius had been seen within range of that sanguinary combat seemed to Elspeth to prove the point. Doubtless he had held himself well out of harm's way and had fled when the bandits had been so disastrously defeated. From that time on, of course, he was probably in great trouble with his own people—while she herself must have become a thoroughly marked woman to the Heartland leaders.

Disguised as the woman which his society favored, Gnaius must have lurked hidden in the sprawling city. Frowning, she said, "If you are in such danger, Gnaius, why have you lingered in Rome? Surely, if flight lay open to you—"

"I could not flee until I had seen you, either to take you with me or to decry your guilt and slay you," he replied dramatically. "Now that I know your innocence, I must have you with me. Lacking your strength, I am lost."

Elspeth made up her mind to go along. Gnaius, she felt certain, was much too poor an actor to be baiting some trap set by others. She said, quietly, "Very well, Gnaius, where to?"

Her acquiescence took the wind completely out of his spinnaker. He sputtered, seeking to continue his course of persuasion. Suddenly he stopped speaking to regard her incredulously and say, "You'll come?"

"Of course," she replied. "If I have caused you unwitting harm it is only right that I should make amends."

He looked at her, horrified, and cried, "You come with me but through pity! And I will not be pitied by any woman."

Cursing him for an incorrigible egotist, she sought to

mend her fences by melting against him, stroking his arm and saying, "Your heart should tell you pity has no part of what I feel for you." She did not trouble to explain further that her chief feeling toward him was and had always been repugnance.

It worked. He folded her in his ridiculous woman's garment and kissed her with lips that were for once unrouged. Taking her hand in a firm grip, he said, "Come—this way. My litter awaits."

It did, drawn by four burly ruffians, who looked as if they had been culled from the sewers of the city—and smelled the same way. Noting her distaste, Gnaius said: "They are safe enough."

"Very well," said Elspeth, subsiding beside him within the sheltering curtains of the litter. "Where are we going, my dear?"

He peered at her intently, and she saw that he needed a shave. He said, "My dear, I must ask you not to be frightened by any strange or wondrous things we encounter. Truly I am taking you with me on a fabulous voyage—a voyage to a land where I am of royal lineage."

Like the sons of the kings of Ireland in my world! thought Elspeth suspiciously. But with a stir of inner excitement she sensed that instinct had not played her false. Gnaius was planning to take her with him to his world—perhaps through a gateway as yet unknown to the Watchers. She decided to keep track of the route as the litter was borne through the Esquiline Gate.

"I shall try not to be frightened," she told Gnaius gravely as they turned right beyond the turreted portal. "But where is this land you speak of as yours? Surely it cannot be far from the city."

"It is both far and near," was the reply. "We must pass through a portal of night whose secret I alone know. Once we are safely past its barrier I shall spirit you to a warm ocean island, far from the meretricious intrigues, where together we can compose verses to express the twin glories of our souls."

"You flatter my poor talent," said Elspeth. Meanwhile, she noted that they turned left on the Via Tuscalna, proceeding directly away from the city into the tilled and landscaped story-book countryside that seemed to lap in waves of green grass and brown earth against the very walls of Rome. She began to speculate on whether the matriarchy of Heartland might not implant unexpected weakness in the female sex as well as in the male, thereby leading to a means of bringing failure to the trimphant Anna Martiana.

"My story is truly a strange one," Gnaius confided. "So strange that I have dared tell no one in Rome about it. To them I am merely a young man of means who has come to Rome from Utica. Actually, I am from a world both like and different to the world you know."

"Hades, perhaps," offered Elspeth, playing her part.

"Nay, not Hades nor any other land of legend," was the poet's response. "My world is very real. Only by a miracle was I able to find my way into yours—a miracle and a dispensation."

He went on with his story—how, although a prince, he had been held in bondage of sort by the Amazons who ran his version of Earth.

Elspeth offered at this: "Then you come from the land of these fierce women warriors? You would take me and deliver me into their hands?"

"Nay," he replied again. "It is from them I flee." He told her how he had been quietly approached by a stranger—Gnaius called him a son of the gods to make him more comprehensible to Elspeth—and given instruments that enabled him to make passage between worlds. And, in conclusion: "But my secret, or part of it, was discovered before I could put it to use. But one of the gateways remained in my possession and through this I fled to your world. I longed to escape the bondage of my sex."

"You seem to have done pretty well," said Elspeth, regarding the woman's raiment her companion wore.

Mercifully, he misunderstood her and replied, "But they have followed me and seek the few remaining possessions I brought with me. When you took them from me through mistaken desire for a memento of our love, my life became forfeit. Now I must flee again."

"How do you expect to escape death in your own world?" Elspeth asked him, puzzled.

"Because, once through the portal, I know where to hide," was the reply. "Great portions of my world were laid waste by war long before my own time. Yet in the heart of some of these wastelands lie regions untouched by the holocaust that all but destroyed my world. Like oases in the desert they are green and fruitful—and unmarked on any map. It is to one of these that I would flee."

"I see," said Elspeth drily, contemplating with a shudder the dismal thought of playing Virginia to Gnaius' Paul in a radioactive-locked Madagascar. She all but blurted *Adam and Eve* before she recollected that she was scarcely supposed to know that myth.

While her companion continued rhapsodically to paint the life they were to live together—with herself, she gathered, doing most of whatever heavy work was to be done—she considered the coincidence of Gnaius and herself, two aliens in a city of perhaps a million souls, managing to land together in such a situation.

Yet, on second thought it was scarcely remarkable. Elspeth had been on the alert for any alien indications, and Gnaius had given her plenty. It was natural for each of them to seek the highest possible circles in the Eternal City, thus to be thrown together in what was actually a small and close-knit society. There her own alien detachment must have drawn him in the same way as his own out-of-place modernity interested her. About the only true coincidence, she decided, lay in their both being poets.

Three miles southeast of the city, they were borne, in response to a sharp command from Gnaius, off the paved roadway for perhaps two hundred yards. The littermen stopped over the brow of a low hill. There Gnaius, after helping Elspeth to alight, paid off the litter-bearers and stood within the shade of a tall poplar. He kept his arm around Elspeth until they had vanished.

"Come *carissima*," the poet said, the softness of his voice underladen with excitement. "We are about to seek the portal of another world. Come with me."

They walked perhaps a quarter of a mile over uneven terrain through the oncoming dusk. Then they came to a ruined farmhouse, an unreconstructed casualty of the civil wars, whose fields were shaggy and overgrown and gone to seed. Gnaius led her to a barn whose thatched roof had partly fallen in, leaving skeleton rafters silhouetted against the pale western sky.

The ship, no larger than a pipit in Elspeth's own world, lay on the dirt floor. Except in size it was very different from any vehicle she had ever seen. Evidently designed primarily for flight rather than surface use, its wheels were many and small. In shape it was something like a sea sledge, with sharply pointed bow and a flat stern from which rocket tubes protruded.

The cockpit was small but held them both comfortably. The instrument panel was remarkable for its simplicity. Half-reclining in her seat, the poetess watched her companion narrowly as he got the vehicle running. He cast her a quick glance, laid a reassuring hand upon her wrist and said, "Don't be afraid—there is nothing to fear."

Deftly handling the few instruments, Gnaius backed them easily and almost silently out of the barn, swung the sharp nose around and, with a quick burst of power, sent them soaring aloft. Aware of the neatness of the machine, Elspeth understood Mack's concern about the possibilities of a Heartland victory over the Watchers. Certainly it was far more advanced than anything she had ever seen or heard of in any of the other worlds.

There was almost no sense of acceleration, almost no sound, virtually no vibration. They soared high over the vast Pontine marshes and, briefly, out over the Mediterranean itself. In a mere matter of minutes, through the fading twilight, they swung back toward land over the Bay of Naples.

Only then did Elspeth feel fright. For it seemed to her that Gnaius planned to crash them against the sloping side of Mount Vesuvius as he rapidly slanted the vehicle downward.

He must have sensed her sudden tension, for he cast her a quick smile of reassurance. "I promise," he repeated, "there is no cause for fear. You are being a remarkably brave girl, *carissima.*"

"Sure," said Elspeth, holding tightly to the edge of her seat as the rock mountain swept up toward them, "I'm a whole flock of heroines rolled into one. Well, here goes nothing."

He frowned at her as he slowed his aircar until it hovered above the rim of the gaping crater, and said, "You puzzle me at times, Marina. You are so brazen, so unlike yourself."

"Well, the real me has no desire to commit suicide—not even in a volcano," she replied, letting out a yelp as the walls of the crater itself rose slowly around them. She had a sudden new sense of the date of her mission. As nearly as she had been able to compute it was close to 80 A.D. in *Antique*. For the first time she remembered that the eruption of Vesuvius which destroyed Pompeii and Herculaneum in most of the other worlds took place in 79 A.D. The recollection was scarcely a reassuring one, especially as a curl of subterranean steam took the moment to rise ghostlike past the windows, yellow and sulphurous in the searchlight beam Gnaius had switched on.

She was just about to make an effort to overcome her companion and lift the aircar out of the crater when they moved slightly ahead and came to rest on a sort of shelf projecting from the huge shaft. She cast an inquiring glance at her companion, who was squinting as he studied what appeared to be a clock on the instrument panel. It was marked for twenty hours in numerals which bore only a faint resemblance to the familiar Arabic figures of her world.

"What now?" she asked him, wondering if he had gone mad.

"For a little while we must wait—then, a new world!" was the reply. He reached for her, drew her close, kissed her.

Her response was scarcely electric. The full enormity of undertaking interworld transfer with such a practical ignoramus as Gnaius scared her out of her wits. She had been informed, before going on the mission to *Antique*, that the worlds of *Antique* and Heartland were in a condition of parallel alignment which made direct transfer between them possible.

It was not difficult to visualize Vesuvius as a transfer point; surely the ancient mountain bore both the geologic and animate historical violence that made transfer possible. Wondering briefly what had happened to the forests of Silesia to create such a portal in that desolate region, she decided the story belonged to pre-history.

Then she felt the sudden taut tingling of nerves that reminded her of a cat on the eve of a thunderstorm. Idiot or not, Gnaius had timed his expedition well. They were going into transfer almost immediately. Somewhat to her surprise she found herself still in his arms. Pulling clear of them, she set herself for the ordeal ahead.

Then the darkness was about them—not the dark of night nor of the crater, but the almost palpable darkness that was the passage between parallel worlds. It seemed to Elspeth, as always, that she was unable to breathe, yet breathe she did as the unseen moments crept slowly by. At her side she could hear her companion's teeth chatter; she resisted an impulse to tell him there was nothing to be afraid of.

Then, when it seemed no longer endurable, the darkness was gone. They were resting on the lip of an eroded Vesuvius with the moon and stars giving them light and revealing a washed-out and eroded panorama about and beneath them. Far below, in the great arc of the bay, gleamed a few sparse lights—few even by the standards of the *Antique* Roman Naples over which they had so recently flown. There was a desolation to the landscape reminiscent of Walpurgis Night. Gnaius suddenly laughed, ringingly, triumphantly. He cried, "At last, carissima—this is my world!"

"It doesn't look much like an oasis from here," said Elspeth, evading his hungry arms and lips. "It looks desolate."

"And so it is, Marina," he replied. "So it is, save for the few forbidden spots in the great wasteland. Come—let us take off and fly to our private paradise."

Elspeth began to be truly worried. Now, she told herself, was the time to escape. She had found a gateway, passed through it. Her job now was to get back through it, back to Rome and Mack and Commander de Mestres, so that she could report the portal's presence.

She opened the door at her side and slipped from the aircar, barely escaping the poet's clutching fingers. He cried out in perplexity and she saw him emerge, reaching for his tiny hand-blaster. She wondered fleetingly if it could be in his heart to kill her.

There was small sense in giving him the chance. As his

feet touched the ground, she tripped him, pulled his stola over his head, seized his hand while he was struggling in its folds and bit it until the dangerous and ugly little weapon fell clear.

By the time he had unwrapped himself, Elspeth was holding the blaster, pointed at his belly. Speaking English, she said, "All right, my fine Heartland friend, not another move."

He looked at her in horrified perplexity and she realized he didn't understand. She repeated her command in Latin and felt a pang of regret as he crumpled under the impact of her words.

Pale in the moonlight, he said brokenly, "So you were merely pretending all the time."

"Pretending Hades," she exclaimed. "I was performing a dangerous and disagreeable du—" Her voice trailed off as she saw another aircar approaching.

So fast did it come that she had barely time to slip behind the poet's vehicle before it had landed alongside with a faint scrape of gravel. A couple of tall women got out, said something to Gnaius that seemed to paralyze him. He stammered, tried to speak, could not.

One of the women, apparently the leader, laughed. She said a few words to her companion, in a language Elspeth could not understand. Then, walking forward, she felled Gnaius with a single blow that a slaughterhouse slayer might have envied. The two women bundled the unfortunate poet into their car. Then the leader got in and took off, leaving the other to guard Gnaius' vehicle. They had been unaware of Elspeth's presence.

VIII

The Amazon guard leaned against the other side of the aircar behind which Elspeth was hiding. After a while she began to hum a tuneless sort of melody in a low contralto. The poetess wondered briefly what fate lay in store for Gnaius Laconius. Probably, if he were a member of an important family, as seemed true in view of his having been singled out by the first Watcher visitors to Heartland, he would be spanked and confined somewhere. For this Elspeth felt small regret. The poet was too unworldly, too undisciplined emotionally, to be a safe factor if allowed to roam loose among the worlds.

A foot scraped on gravel, then another. The humming stopped. The guard was about to walk around the ship. Elspeth battled an intense desire to take to her heels in flight. She steeled herself, raised the hand-blaster, tried to tell herself that she should have, under the circumstances, no compunction in killing her foe.

Yet, when the Amazon appeared around the nose of the aircar, Elspeth could not put on the pressure that would release the deadly beam of heat. Both women stood there, frozen, for a long second. And then the Amazon's right hand darted for her own belt.

Elspeth fired then—and turned away from the sickening charred mess that lay on the ground in front of her. She scrambled into the aircar, tried desperately to work the strange controls to turn the vessel about. She felt, however illogically, that unless she could turn it around she would never achieve transfer back to *Antique*. She knew something of the two-way oscillation governing the transfer process but, while her mind trusted the knowledge, her emotions refused to.

However, the controls were beyond her mastery. She did not dare try to work them all lest she plunge the machine into the now-dead volcano; she might even send the craft soaring in wild flight, hopelessly away from the interworld portal. After a few desperate moments she sat still, shivering.

It was then that she saw the lights of approaching aircars, heading with definite purpose toward the mountaintop. Evidently Gnaius had talked—and they were coming for her. Feeling as if she were trapped under a falling skyscraper, Elspeth sat helplessly watching their rapid approach. She felt herself in a paralysis of resignation.

Her fate depended upon the pulse of the interworld rhythm. A transfer would probably occur within minutes— but it could be a matter of days or weeks. Its timing depended upon the frequency of the portal itself, which in turn depended upon its importance as a probability point of decision. Sitting there, with the lights of the approaching flotilla coming rapidly closer, she felt suddenly damp with perspiration that trickled chillingly down her spine and breasts.

If—rather when—they reached her, she would be in for a bad time. Heartland was at war with the Watchers and she was an alien spy. Furthermore, in a world dominated by women, her sex would scarcely be a protection—quite the reverse. She thought of Mack and, in sudden rage and frustration, struck a useless blow at the instrument panel in front of her.

She hit something that swung the aircar slowly about. Noting the motion, flame flickered from the nose of two of the leading ships and bits of the mountain below her blazed with sudden fire. She looked at her tiny hand-blaster and flung it to the cabin floor.

The aircar stopped moving—and the blackness was around it once more as the very gravel around her seemed to burst into flame. She shivered and thought of Mack and wondered if she would ever see him again. The whole course of their odd, combative relationship passed before her, and she all but wept at the uselessness of their squabbles, the stubborn idiocy with which they had each fought dependence upon the other. For surely, if two people were ever meant to be perfect complements, she and Mack were that couple.

She resolved, if she ever did see him again, to reveal the true warmth of her feelings toward him, her trust in him, her—yes, her love. And then the blackness was gone and she was back on the ledge deep within the crater of the *Antique* Vesuvius—and the aircar was still turning, turning toward the edge . . .

Elspeth screamed and scrambled out just before it dropped from sight in the bottomless crater beyond. For a long moment she leaned against the volcano wall behind her, trembling and weak and unable to lift a finger.

Then, cursing the awkwardness of her Roman woman's garb, she began the long difficult climb out of the volcano, sure that at any second it would erupt and engulf her in boiling lava. Sulphur fumes made her cough and weep, and sharp stones scraped her legs and body and caused her hands to bleed.

Somehow though, under the press of desperation, she made it. Finally, she lay full length on the ground outside the immense shaft that had all but swallowed her alive. After a while she got to her feet and began a staggering progress down the side of the mountain.

Unaided by Gnaius' aircar, she took the better part of two days to get back to Rome. She might not have made it at all had not a kind Senator, proceeding to an emergency session in the capital, taken pity on her and given her a place in his suite. He was a plump, perturbed man of middle age, more concerned with animal husbandry and his olive crops than with the intrigues of the city.

But the Emperor was dying and it was necessary for the Senate to meet in rubber-stamp fashion, to appropriate the monies needed for the funeral, to confirm Titus as his successor, to preserve the outer form of a republican process long since moribund. He seemed much interested in such gossip of the city as Elspeth could give him.

Once he said, wrinkling his forehead almost to the top of his bald pate, "I must confess I do not like what you tell me of the Crown Prince's new favorite. Just now a willful barbarian might well tear Rome apart more fully than Cleopatra herself. But I fear the populace will never consent to an alliance with Princess Berenice. Their distrust of all Asiatic rulers is too deep-seated to allow it."

"Poor Berenice," said Elspeth, feeling sympathy for her semi-royal friend. Truly, her life had been incredible, with three marriages before she was well into her twenties. Indeed, Berenice was in a most precarious situation, not only because of popular feeling but because of the rivalry of the Heartland princess.

It was late the second afternoon after her escape from the crater when, weary, tired and bedraggled, the poetess stood once more before the bronze doors of her Cispian villa. Yet, as one of her Iberian slaves admitted her, she was nerving herself, rallying her energies for what she had to do. She must get at once to the Aventine palace to report to Commander de Mestres. The Vesuvian gateway was no longer a secret to the Heartlanders and, being so close to Rome, might well be the portal to a new invasion of Italy itself by the Amazon warriors of that tired but aggressive world.

And there was Mack, of course. He would probably be angry with her for having stood him up the day before—until she explained what had happened. Then, she foresaw with rosy anticipation, he would give her the devil for taking such chances by herself. This would be followed by the scene of which she had dreamed while making the return transfer from Heartland: the fond declaration that would end their long feud.

Wondering where Lamia could be, she strode toward her own second-story chamber—and stopped short on the doorsill. Lamia, clad only in the briefest of wispy shawls, was reclining beside Mack on her own couch. A table was pulled up alongside, and on it were two flagons of Pliny's choicest Falernian—one obviously empty—and a bowl of fruit, much of it evidently eaten.

Mack saw her first and lifted a hand in salute. He was evidently feeling the wine, for he grinned with lazy impudence and said in English, "Better late than never, Elspeth. Come on in and join the party."

Lamia saw her mistress then and leapt from the couch with a little scream. Then she stopped, taking in the poetess' torn and bruised condition. Solicitude replaced fright on her provocative little face. She gasped, "Madam, you're hurt!"

"You're telling me!" countered Elspeth. She slapped

the girl and sent her sprawling, then faced Mack, her eyes blazing and said, "What the hell are you doing here?"

"As a matter of fact," he replied cheerfully, "I'm hiding out. Pal Ana seems to be onto me and I had a devil of a time getting here at all. The whole city's upside down with the Emperor dead." Then, squinting: "Hey, Elly, you do look a bit banged up. Better have a snort to pull yourself together." He offered her the unfinished flagon and she knocked it out of his hand to the floor.

Lamia, on her knees, cried, "Madam, I didn't want to, but when Macronius Frazius came last night he demanded entertainment."

Elspeth felt her anger toward the sobbing girl dissolve. She lifted her up and said, "Get my bath ready." Then, turning on Mack when the girl had darted from the room, she said, "I'd forgotten what a tomcat you are."

On his feet, he shrugged and replied, "She's a cute little dish. What did you want me to do while you wandered off with that cute poet of yours? You know I can't even read in this language."

With great effort she put personal problems behind her. She said, "I've got to get to Commander de Mestres at once. I've been through a new gateway in Mount Vesuvius."

"*In* Mount Vesuvius!" The fumes of wine seemed visibly to fade as his alert practical mind seized on the problem they faced. "You mean you've been into Heartland and back through the crater?"

She nodded and said, "What's more the Heartlanders know of the gate there now. They may decide to use it themselves."

"It wouldn't surprise me if they already have," said Mack quietly. "My brick-topped girl friend is really making things hum. That's part of why I had to get out. But how in hell we're to get into the Aventine palace beats me. Titus camped four legions around it this morning." He paused and added, "Nice fellow, that de Mestres."

Elspeth made no response. The neatness with which Ana Kai-Martinez, or Anna Martiana, had used her influence over the heir to *Antique* Rome stopped her cold. She had news of vital importance to convey to Commander de Mestres. But if the Aventine palace was under seige, a

Mack implied, there was no way of getting word to the forces of the Watchers.

The problems remained unsolved during her bath—which though the water was hot, suffered from a noticeable coolness between mistress and slave. Elspeth, abstracted and unhappy, spoke only when necessary to the Pamphylian girl, who waited on her in silence.

Not until the massage was finished did Lamia blurt, "Madam, if I have offended you, I am heartbroken."

Elspeth rolled over on the sheet-covered massage table and smiled at the anxiously alive little face above her. She said with an unexpected sense of relief, "I'm not angry with you, Lamia, but I'd like to wring the neck of our mutual friend in the next room."

And then, remembering the girl's resourcefulness, an idea struck her. She sat up and said, "Lamia, do you think you could manage to carry a message to the Commander of the force within the Aventine palace?"

Eagerness and excitement flooded the little slave-girl's face. "If it will be of service to madam . . ." said the girl submissively, but her eyes were aglow at the prospect of adventure. Elspeth then wrote a brief note in English to the Commander, telling him of the Vesuvian gateway and her fear lest the Heartlanders should employ it to launch an expedition to Italy proper.

When Lamia had left and Elspeth was clad once more in tunic and sandals, she went down to the dining chamber where Mack was awaiting her. He had sobered up considerably and was looking both sheepish and a trifle hung over. He said, "I hope you weren't too hard on the kid. I was way out of line, but I didn't know this poet character was part of your assignment."

"Lamia's merely running an errand for me," said the poetess. Then, as the first course was brought in, she said, "Mack, what about these people? How long have you been on this job?"

"About four months," he told her. Then, slashing into the suckling pig and smearing both face and hands, he sighed. "This is living, Elly. If I hadn't stolen time off to get some game, I'd have had to live exclusively on bran muffins and yogurt. You've been having it good."

"You haven't done so badly yourself," said Elspeth a

shade tartly. "What about the Glamazon boss of yours?"

Mack had the grace to blush.

Elspeth laughed. She couldn't help it. The picture of Mack being reduced to inferior status by a proud woman who outstripped him physically was salve to her own recently bruised ego. But she said, "Poor Mack. How'd you ever manage to get established with them anyway?"

"It was pretty much makeshift all the way," he replied in English, since a classical education had not been part of his training. "The first Watcher who reached Heartland walked into a radioactive zone before he knew it and came down with a fatal case of poisoning. If he hadn't been half out of his head, he'd never have selected a man as resident Watcher. But he was dying and handed the torch to some decadent prince, who tried to use the gift for his own ends."

"I know," said Elspeth quietly, thinking of Gnaius.

"You don't know what Heartland is like," was Mack's reply. He seemed to shudder visibly, then went on with, "It's the used-up end of a world that's knocked itself out with war. There's life in some of the forbidden areas—and they comprise Asia, Africa, both Americas, Australia, England and Antarctica—but you wouldn't want to see it."

"Mutations?" Elspeth asked, shivering herself.

He nodded. "Some beauts—and every one of them recessive. It's a starving world that's forgotten most of its own existence. But they've got machines left—some lulus. You've had a taste of their technical stuff. The trouble is they operate by rote. They've lost the knack of new ideas—probably scared to death of them after the destruction their planet has taken.

"So I got through the Silesian transfer point and made like a character from one of the borderland provinces," he said, half piling his plate with greens. "Anyway, I fixed up a couple of gadgets that were out of whack and got myself marked as a genius, masculine gender."

"Clever, clever fellow," said Elspeth. Mack glowered at her, then went on.

"Understand, no man can rate as an equal with the Heartland ladies, Elly," he said. "I was just a talking horse with them. So they kept me warm and fed and discussed me as a potential menace if more like me turned up.

Finally, just as I got the Silesian mine job, I began to get hep to what was happening.

"The damned fool our pioneer made resident-Watcher had spilled the beans, of course, then taken a powder through another gateway. Which left just the Silesian portal. But that was enough. It was right on top of Heartland's last worked-out uranium bed and the Martinez got the idea of bringing through an expedition and replenishing her planet with radioactives pirated from this world.

"I made a quick transfer and outlined the setup to Mr. Horelle and he sent me right back and told me to go along with it. So I did. I helped get the diggings working, while the Martinez was looking around and discovering this world wasn't full of deadly continents and might have a lot more uranium mines. Needless to say, I didn't tip her off to the Congo or Northwest Canada.

"She took a trip and tied up with this Titus in France—or Gaul," Mack went on, "and from then on things went into high gear. She sent a few spies to Rome—a few of the Heartland men make good undercover operatives—and found out her missing Prince was hiding out here. And from then on the operation was stepped up."

Elspeth nodded and, over dessert, they chatted about their problem. Shaking his head, Mack said, "Somehow we've got to get word to de Mestres. I was lucky to have a chance to talk with him before my lady-boss got suspicious of me. One of her damned spies saw us talking in the pool and it seems you're already suspect."

"Sorry," said Elspeth. "But I wonder why they haven't made an attack here yet. Surely they must know you're with me."

Mack shrugged, then said, "You haven't seen the city for the past couple of days. Ever since the Emperor died it's been a madhouse: crowds, games, public sacrifices, parades, street-corner speeches, drunks, bandits—a real bedlam. I've got a hunch they haven't many operatives here—and those they have have been too damned busy to bother much with a couple of minor issues like us."

"They'll get to us in time, never fear," said the poetess.

"I don't," was the far-from-reassuring reply.

A round-eyed slave interrupted the meal with word that the Princess Berenice requested entrance. Elspeth issued hurried instructions in Latin and, when the slave had departed on the run, Mack looked at the poetess with reluctant admiration. "You certainly know how to spout this damned lingo around here," he told her.

"Advantages of a classical education," she retorted. "In spite of your scorn for dead languages they do come in handy at times."

"Maybe," replied Mack, "but it took a freak cosmic disaster to turn the trick!"

The Princess came in without ceremony, brushing quickly past the slaves. She sank onto a couch saying, "Thank Astarte, I'd forgotten there was such a thing as food."

Not until she had satisfied the sharp edge of her hunger did Elspeth have a chance to introduce her to Mack, who nodded gravely, saying nothing. He looked, the poetess thought, absurdly like an unwilling guest at a costume ball in her own world.

After studying him briefly the Princess said, "Is your guest a mute barbarian that he doesn't talk? He must be a relief after poor Gnaius. Have you heard anything from him?"

"Nothing, Highness," said Elspeth. "I fear for his fate." Then, with a sidelong glance at Mack: "Macronius Frazius is an old friend. He is not a barbarian, but he does not speak Latin."

The Princess said with some surprise, "Not a barbarian, yet not able to speak the language of civilization? Perhaps he comes from Cathay?"

"What in hell are you talking about?" Mack asked in English. His head had been turning back and forth between the women like that of a sideline spectator at a tennis match.

Elspeth laughed and said to him, "Princess Berenice is curious about you. I'm trying to explain."

"You'd think I was a freak or something," growled Mack with a surly expression.

"What is this strange tongue you speak with your friend?"

"It is a dialect from a distant part of Britain," the poetess said. "Macronius hails from there and we shared the same slave-tutor as children."

"It is a rapid tongue," mused Berenice. "But Rome is full of strange tongues at present. Is not this the young man who appeared in Princess Anna Martiana's suite at the Baths?"

"The same," said Elspeth. "But he is no friend of hers. He is, in fact, hiding from the Princess and her followers."

"So!" said Berenice, after a thrusting glance at the subject of the conversation. Then, with a shrug: "Perhaps he can be of service, as I hope you can, in my campaign against this barbaric invader. For I fear for my place in Rome if her power over the new Emperor is not sapped. Titus has stripped me of half of my suite, and there is gossip abroad that he plans to install this . . . barbarian witch in my palace."

Save for the slight hesitation in her last sentence, Berenice spoke with a calm matter-of-factness that wrung Elspeth's heart.

Turning to Mack she said, "Princess Berenice is in danger of being ousted from the Emperor's favor by your ex-boss. Do you know any chinks in her armor? We've got to do something, for our own sakes as well as hers. Can you think of anything?"

Mack looked thoughtful and said after a long moment, "Damned if I know any—unless it's her contempt for me. You might be able to humiliate the Emperor."

It was Elspeth's turn to think. She frowned, saying, "The chances are she won't show her hand until she has the game in hand—and we can't wait that long. Darn it!" She frowned, and then, out of nowhere, an idea occurred to her.

She saw in retrospect, without closing her eyes, the mutual speculative glance exchanged at the side of the pool between the red-headed menace and the new Emperor's younger brother. Domitianus, she knew from rumor, was both jealous and ambitious, a young man who was impatient of his chances of sitting on the throne. Perhaps something could be made of that.

She glanced at Berenice. Reading the curiosity in her eyes, she said, "I wonder—if Domitianus received a note from her asking him to come to a rendezvous at a time and place we know Princess Anna Martiana will be present, and some trusted servant were to warn Titus at the last minute . . . But no, it is a clumsy subterfuge."

"You noticed too, at the Baths," said the Princess

Berenice, her face alive with eagerness and renewed hope. I thought my eyes must have deceived me out of wishfulness. Marina, you are indeed a friend. Though why my poor wits could not supply the answer—"

"You'd have thought of it, Highness," said Elspeth consolingly. Suddenly she felt quite proud of her newly developed talent for court intrigue. It felt so—Persian was the only suitable word. There was another word, too, of course, one far less romantic—Machiavellian. But, she reminded herself, when in Rome . . . Certainly Mack seemed to have accepted Roman hospitality with unequivocal enthusiasm.

Princess Berenice rose and moved around the table and embraced her. Elspeth felt surprise at the frailty of her guest's body. She marveled at the indomitable will that had maintained her close to power for so long, when stronger men and women and far greater reputations fell almost daily.

She accompanied Berenice to the door, Mack trailing uncertainly behind. Seeing her to her well-guarded litter, which all but blocked the narrow street outside, the poetess remained to wave farewell to the jeweled and shapely arm which saluted her through the rift in the litter curtains, which were gay with the lion of Judah and the eagle of Rome.

Thus she was still standing in the lighted doorway when the bundle, hurled from somewhere in the darkness beyond the oval of torchlight, landed with a horrid thud in front of her feet and brushed her ankles as it bounded past her and rolled into the doorway. Involuntarily she shrank back with a slight scream.

Moments later, her eyes bulging with horror, she watched disgust followed by deadly anger cross Mack's familiar face as he opened the bundle to disclose the bloody, severed head of Lamia!

IX

The happenings of the next few hours were, to Elspeth, like passages in a nightmare—dramatic, terrible, unescapable. For even in that ghastly moment, while she and Mack gazed at the lifeless head of the slave-girl who had once been so vividly alive, Elspeth knew that they were trapped.

The Heartland invaders appeared to have every contingency covered. With a new transfer point close to Rome, they could easily counter-effect the strength of the Watchers' contingent in the Aventine palace. With the support of Titus and his legions in the capital itself, thanks to the Martinez' successful intrigue, they had sealed off de Mestres' forces so that it was impossible to get word to them of what was going on outside the crumbling walls of their citadel.

Any haphazard show of force by the Commander's troops would inevitably turn the rulers of *Antique* even more strongly against the Watchers and would place them more securely in the hands of the planet-looters. Elspeth felt sick, not only at the brutal slaying of Lamia, but at the prospect of the matriarchy in full control of *Antique*.

It would not take them long to discover the huge sources of untapped mineral wealth in the retarded planet—even in regions so long poisonous in Heartland that their existence had been all but forgotten by the people of that unfortunate version of Earth.

Mack, suddenly the grim-faced man of her own world, said, "Come on, Elly—we've got to get the hell out of here."

"Where can we go?" the poetess asked helplessly.

"We've *got* to get a message to de Mestres," said Mack.

"And if I have to, I'll *blast* a way through to the palace myself."

Elspeth moved uncertainly to her room. But once out of sight of the ghastly relic of Lamia, her thoughts began to organize themselves. She said, "You haven't a chance—*we* haven't a chance just now. I suggest we entrust that part of the job to Berenice. She still has some friends and influence. If anyone can get a message through to de Mestres, she can. Maybe not for a day or two but soon—with the city demoralized as it is."

Mack frowned. "Okay," he said. "But what do we do in the meantime? Sit here and wait to be slaughtered?"

"Mack!" said Elspeth, "Mack—we've got to get to that Vesuvian gateway and block it somehow. Suppose no one can get word to de Mestres in time—it's up to us."

"And what do we use for transport?" countered the more practical member of the team. "Besides, don't tell me our friends won't have every road from Rome blocked—at least to us."

"There is still Pliny and the fleet," she said.

"Too damned slow," was the discouraging response. "Even if we made it we'd never be in time."

"But it's the only way left," said Elspeth. She felt the sudden reaction from her slave's tragic murder, felt tears well up unwanted behind her eyes. Suddenly she could restrain her grief no longer. The pressures of recent days, Lamia's death, the hopelessness of the position—all united and burst from her in weeping.

Mack offered her clumsy comfort, repeating over and over again, "Come on, Elly, snap out of it. We've got to get going!"

Red-nosed and sniffling, she finally managed to write a note to Berenice in Latin, and one to the Commander in English, apprising him of the situation outside the walls of his palace prison. Enclosing one within the other, she entrusted the mission to the stoutest and most resourceful of her remaining Iberians. Ordering him to leave by climbing the portico balustrade and climbing down the face of the Cispian hill on which it fronted, she hoped he would be able to evade the spies and sentries at the street entrance.

"We'd best leave together," said Mack. He had pulled from under the bed a small but apparently heavy suitcase and was checking its contents. He noted Elspeth peering at some of the odd gadgetry it contained—gadgetry utterly alien to her experience. He said, "I was going to turn this stuff over to Mr. Horelle, but if we're going to blow up Vesuvius we'll need a few explosives."

"Heavens, Mack, I'd forgotten!" said Elspeth, realizing the futility of her swift planning unbacked by Mack's practicality.

"We'll give 'em something to remember us by," Mack said grimly, closing the case with a snap and checking its fastenings. "It's a good thing I brought a few samples with me when I scrammed."

"Yes, Mack," she said, wanting desperately for him to hold her in his arms and give her, however briefly, the illusion of safety.

But Mack's mind was not on her. It was on avenging Lamia's murder and, more intently, upon their making a getaway. He eyed Elspeth's clothing, then his own, shook his head. Then, from another suitcase, he procured coveralls of some light, warm material, evidently of Heartland origin. He tossed her a pair.

They quickly got into the more practical garb of a more advanced version of that on her own Earth. The Iberian procured a stout rope and after fastening it to a pillar of the balustrade, they began their descent.

The cuts on Elspeth's hands from her climb out of the crater a few days earlier were quickly reopened by the coarse fibers of the rope and the rough bark of the trees that got them down the hill. But she barely noticed the injuries in her desperate hurry. The Iberian led, with Elspeth second, and Mack and suitcase bringing up the rear. Each time the Iberian reached firm footing, Mack would hand the bag down to Elspeth, who would transfer it to the slave below. Then they would begin the slow progress all over again.

They parted company on the Via Subura, the Iberian darting into an alley to work his way toward Berenice's palace. Mack and Elspeth, their coveralls now hidden by toga and stola, carried the suitcase toward the river and the small naval basin on the Tiber River island across the Pons Fabricius. As far as they could discover, their flight had not been watched and they were not followed.

The nightmare continued for Elspeth as they fought and pushed their way through foul-smelling, half-drunken street crowds. They worked around the fringes of the great Forum to avoid being spotted by agents of their foes.

Once they had to pause while a legion, recalled from the provinces, marched across their path on their way to the Palatine. And despite the urgencies of their situation, the poetess could not help but thrill at the sight of the eagles and fasces, the reflections of torchlight on glittering bronze-and-steel armor and helmets and weapons, the raw stirring notes of the immense curled horns and the measured tramp of heavy service sandals on cobblestones.

Mack shook her roughly to snap her out of her reverie as the last detachment of legionnaires marched past. "Come on," he urged, "let's step on it."

When at length a sentry challenged them at the Fabrician bridge the game was up to Elspeth entirely—for Mack, of course, could not speak Latin. Asking to be taken to the Admiral, she was informed that he was asleep on his flagship and could not be disturbed. But she finally managed to be taken to the officer on the watch aboard; there she raised such a clamor that at last old Pliny appeared, blinking away sleep. Immediately he had Mack and herself taken to his cabin.

"Nice going, Elly," Mack said softly, and she felt much like an Arthurian knight just promoted to Round Table status.

Within half an hour they were under way, the gilded wooden flagship with its single bank of muffled oars, shipped mast and furled single sail cutting through the smooth water in magic silence. Standing on the poop, with Mack at her side, the poetess watched the glowing reflections of a city alive with torches and flambeaux as they barely made clearance with shipped oars under the low Tiber bridges.

She caught a glimpse of the eroded walls of the Aventine palace, silhouetted against the glowing night-sky of the city. All about it glowed the fires of the encamped legions, supposedly bivouacked for the funeral and coronation processions, but actually sealing de Mestres' men and machines with an airtight ground blockade.

She wondered what would happen if de Mestres decided

to take action and sent his flying armor over the walls, spitting flame and missiles at the primitive weapons of the legionnaires. It would provide a spectacle never before recorded in the history of any of the worlds—a spectacle far more horrible and magnificent than any the new-built Colosseum of Rome would ever know.

"I hope the Martinez can get Titus to keep his boys in hand," said Mack looking worried. "A blow-up now would queer the works."

"I wish we had your pipit," replied Elspeth illogically.

"You and me both," replied Mack. "Look at the way they make those poor devils sweat!" He nodded toward the half-open decks ahead and below them, in which they could see the scarred and sweating backs of the oarsmen, bending to with a will under the threat of the lash.

"It looks like a cinema," said Elspeth. "It can't be real."

"It's real, all right," said Mack gloomily. "And if we don't knock these Heartland so-and-sos out of the picture these people are going to be in for a lot more of it. Our friends didn't wreck their own world by being humanitarians."

"A pity!" exclaimed the poetess. "Think of the chance to watch the culture of a world develop, to see its artists at work, its builders, its philosophers, its spiritual leaders! Think of the understanding it would give us for all other worlds!"

"Yeah," replied Mack drily, "and think of all the famines and torturing and wars and pillage and rape and disease this world will know if we don't step in and give them a few of our benefits!"

"It might be worth all that," said Elspeth defensively.

"*You* can say that," Mack retorted, "because you aren't one of them. How would you like to starve or die of some plague or—or have your head cut off simply because we didn't step in and speed up the growth process? Would you really enjoy it?"

"You're right, of course," replied Elspeth, a trifle sadly. She thought of Lamia, who had died for her so recently, of some of the inhuman horrors she had been compelled to witness at games in the Colosseum.

They reached Ostia well before dawn and without incident. There they transferred, along with the Admiral, to a huge swift trireme, whose prow and stern were too lofty to pass under the Tiber bridges and whose oarsmen were fresh and unwearied by the pull downriver.

Dawn was rising when they put out from the harbor at the mouth of the famous stream. Behind them were the still-dark fronts of the surprisingly tall four-and-five story warehouses and apartment buildings along the waterfront. They moved serenely among the scores of galleys and smaller craft, the bright colors and giltwork of their ornate sterns and figureheads reflecting the first rays of early light.

But once in the open water of the Tyrrhenian Sea, they struck rough water and favorable winds. The great sail went slowly up the mainmast, billowing like some immense pink parachute as it filled. Oars were shipped and the big war vessel plunged through mounting waves at a good clip without manual aid.

Elspeth descended to an aft cabin, where Mack, under the inquisitive regard of the Admiral, was assembling a bomb from materials hastily brought aboard before they left Ostia. He seemed unmoved, as was Pliny, by the rolling and pitching of the galley and went about his work with methodical efficiency.

Elspeth was forced to act as interpreter between the curious Pliny and her colleague. "What sort of a machine are you making?" she asked. "Our pal here wants to know."

"Tell him," said Mack, rubbing an arm across a grimy face, "that I'm trying out a sort of gun cotton to be triggered by a couple of Heartland percussion caps. You might ask him if he hasn't an atom bomb stowed somewhere in his hold."

Elspeth repeated this message in Latin as best she could. Turning to Mack, she asked. "Do you think it will do the work?"

"It ought to kick up a bit of fuss if Vesuvius is active at this time on this world," he replied. He added, *"And* if we can detonate her deep enough down the shaft. Now shut up and let me work."

Later, lying on a bed of torment because of the unfamiliar rocking of the boat, the poetess felt intense homesickness for Lamia and the care and service to which she had become accustomed in her nine-odd weeks of residence in the Admiral's Cispian hill villa. Tears rolled down her face as she recalled the slave-girl's gaiety, the unswerving devotion with which she had sacrificed her life for her mistress.

After a while, mercifully, Elspeth slept.

Thanks to the following wind, which stayed with them all the way, they were able to make the harbor at Misenum late the following afternoon. While the galley was rowed through the calmer waters of the Bay of Neapolis, Elspeth recovered somewhat from her malaise of the night before and, after downing a bowl of broth, managed to pull herself together and stagger up on deck.

There the fresh salty air revived her further, as did the magnificent sweep of the bay, dotted with villas of pink and white and pale blue and backed by the Fuji-like cone of the big volcano. The panorama reminded her of murals in a Chelsea or Greenwich Village Italian restaurant with its gay bright colors and knife-sharp contrasts between dark and white.

Truly, she thought, there was beauty in this fantastically retarded world—beauty of spirit and feeling as well as in outer garb. Her own emotions soared anew and she watched Mack directing a quartet of brawny picked sailors as they gathered the explosives together.

"Think you're up to the climb," Mack asked her when they stood on the pier. She nodded. After a doubtful moment he said, "Good—after all you've been up there and I haven't. I'll get you a burro."

Slowly they made their way up the foothills of Vesuvius as the sun set behind the massive shoulder of the sea in back of them. As twilight thickened into darkness, Pliny exclaimed when Mack produced a powerful electric torch to light their way up the mountain. His aide and the three sailors who made up the rest of the party murmured uneasily at this sudden magic.

"Tell them it's okay," said Mack. "I'd let them use torches. But if our Heartland pals should come through, I want to turn this light off in a hurry. Tell them it's good magic."

Elspeth did as best she could. Their initial surprise over, the men seemed to accept the flashlight with increased faith in the purpose of their mysterious assignment. But

Gaius Plinius Secondus' questions were a lot harder to answer. Ultimately she had to serve as harassed interpreter while Mack tried to explain the functioning of an electric flashlight to the scientist-admiral.

They were within a few hundred yards of the near rim of the crater when a droning sound from within it caused Mack to douse his light quickly. He snapped an order to Elspeth to tell the others to hold still where they were. She had barely repeated it when a beam of light rose from the crater and a sharp-nosed Heartland aircar came bursting out of the mountain and rose rapidly in the heavens.

"Damn!" Mack exploded. "We're too late."

"Wait—we'd have seen them all coming through if they were really operating," replied Elspeth more hopefully. "If this is a single scout it will go back for information and further orders."

Mack ignored her suggestion and burst into lurid profanity as the picked sailors, terrified at the sight of the Heartland aircar, decamped noisily, shouting their alarm as they stumbled and ran down the side of the mountain. Mack, the Admiral and Elspeth remained alone with the burros.

"Some mob you've got!" Mack exploded at the Admiral.

Elspeth, not wishing to make a bad situation worse, said in Latin, "It's a pity your men are not as staunch as yourself, Admiral."

"They have not been educated to the scientific mind, which is curious rather than afraid of the unknown," replied Pliny shortly, through the chattering of his teeth. Admiring his bravery in terror, Elspeth felt warm sympathy and liking for her prosy and somewhat dull little sponsor in the Eternal City.

"You may be right, Elly," said Mack suddenly at her elbow. He pointed at what seemed to be a shooting star falling toward the top of the mountain. The Heartland craft was that of a scout, after all. It was returning to the transfer point to report its successful passage into *Antique*.

When at last it vanished below the rim of the crater, Mack said, "Come on—let's put the show on the road. Elly, skin a couple of those damned mules. At least they didn't run."

"Burros—not mules," said Elspeth, as she grabbed hold

of a couple of halters. Moving at a fatiguing pace, Mack led his two remaining companions rapidly up the steep slope that led to the shaft in the volcano.

When at last they peered cautiously down into the immense shaft, it was empty and dark as if nothing had transpired within its perpendicular walls. The Admiral stared down into it as if stunned, then said to Elspeth in his flawless Latin, "I am afraid of what you are about to do—yet I am more afraid of the machine that disappeared."

"It's got to be done," Elspeth told him practically, her own resolve having hardened at the sight of the Heartland aircar. Then, in English: "Mack, we'd better get this business over with. More of them will be coming through at the next opening of the portal."

"Right," said Mack. Then, in the act of unleashing the packs on the burros: "You know, Elly, this isn't a very good gateway from the point of view of putting a large-sized expeditionary force through. They have to come single file—not all at once like Commander de Mestres and that force of his."

"I hadn't thought of it that way," said Elspeth, staggering under a bulky package which Mack shoved into her arms. Yet his optimism did much to lift her own spirits. Mack's usual approach to any problem was in a mood of skeptical pessimism.

He took at least a quarter of an hour to assemble his bomb and encase it in three layers of beef-hide to protect it from damage as it rolled into the crater. He had encased the timer—a shockproof Heartland super-gadget—in the gun cotton itself as an added precaution against breakage after setting it twelve minutes ahead.

Finally, while the timer ticked faintly and ominously, he sewed the outermost of the hide coverings together. This done, he gave the outsized volleyball that resulted an almost careless push that sent it rolling over the edge and deep into the bowels of the Earth.

"Here's hoping she works," he said with a smile, holding up crossed fingers. "If she doesn't—"

"Look!" Elspeth pointed down into the crater, where the familiar shelf was suddenly ablaze with artificial light as a Heartland air-cruiser suddenly appeared. It was an ugly-looking ship, boasting a number of turrets and gun emplacements from which protruded the ugly muzzles of exotic cannon mounted singly and in pairs.

"By all the gods, including even the Christian!" exploded Pliny, gazing at the scene below with his mouth agape. "What manner of thing is that?"

"A very bad manner of thing," said Elspeth. Mack, she saw, had removed his toga in favor of his coveralls and she did the same. Then, moving swiftly and letting the burros roam as they would, the three of them began their descent down the steep side of the volcano.

"The further away from that ship we get the happier I'll be," Mack panted. "What a deadly looking job! I've never seen that one before."

"I hope they haven't got many like her," said Elspeth.

A little further on, as they stopped for breath, she felt a faint jar in the volcano beneath them. "She went off," said Mack. "Now we'll see what—"

He stopped talking as, after a long moment of silence, the mountain began to shake more violently and a hissing roar sounded through the thickness of its side. Almost at once a shriller sound made itself heard—or rather felt.

"What's that?" the poetess asked, beginning to be frightened.

"A ship—trying to get altitude in a hurry." A grin flashed across his battered face. "We must have kicked up some hell with that gizmo." He laughed and added, "Hell, it was put together with spit."

The Heartland cruiser suddenly appeared above the rim of the crater, from which a redder glow than the vessel's headlights was beginning to make its fitful appearance. The ship shot directly upward and seemed to hang in the air perhaps a hundred yards above the summit of the volcano, its rocket tubes ablaze.

Then, with a roar too loud for human ears, the mountain seemed to explode. A sudden burst of bright white flame shot directly upward into the sky. It caught the Heartland cruiser and, for an instant, there was a blob of extra brilliance in the pillar of heat. Then—nothing but nature blowing her top.

X

Elspeth ceased playing the role of spectator as panic overwhelmed her. Racing, she stumbled and rushed down the mountainside. More than once she fell, only to pick herself up, panting, to continue her flight.

To her left a blazing fragment seemed to settle slowly to the ground—only to land with a crash that sent flaming tracers rising in all directions. She cried out and flinched as something stung the side of her neck. Her racing footsteps veered to the right, only to be turned again as another ball of fire struck and flared up almost in her face.

She shook free as a hand gripped her shoulder; she struggled against arms that swept her off her feet. But she relaxed when Mack's voice penetrated her terror with, "Not a chance that way, Elly. Here!"

She was being carried upward, then across level ground, then dumped unceremoniously under a sheltering rock overhang. Mack scrambled in beside her and held her close against his chest until some measure of rationality returned. At last, utterly wrung, and for the time being, beyond terror, Elspeth finally managed to say, unevenly, "Sorry, Mack—I didn't mean to—"

"You and me both," he replied. "If I hadn't seen you running right into those fireballs I'd still be running myself."

The area was still being bombarded in a display of cosmic pyrotechnics. Fascinated, Elspeth watched it, then said: "At least it doesn't look as if Pompeii and Herculaneum were going to be buried in hot ashes this time."

Mack shrugged, replied, "It's too early to tell yet." Then, peering at her: "You got a blister on your neck."

Elspeth felt the mark left by the blazing volcanic spark

and first became aware of the pain. She looked around, then asked: "What about the Admiral? Where is he? Is he okay?"

Mack shook his head and said quietly, "Afraid not, Elly. One of those flaming hunks of rock landed on him."

She buried her face in her hands. In a way, though she had really seen little of him, she had become fond of the resident-Watcher. Wearily she considered the deaths that seemed to be as much a part of an interplanetary mission as of a major engineering project. She wondered if the good the Watchers did in any way compensated for the loss of even one first-class life. Or did they do good?

The mountain shook dangerously beneath them, and less sharp but longer explosions sounded from the crater. "How does it look, Mack?" she said. "Think we're going to get out of this?"

Mack opened his hand and said, "I'd hate to make a bet on it. But let's take a look. The fireballs seem to have stopped."

They moved out from beneath the overhang to study their situation. Elspeth discovered that they were on a jutting outcrop from the general slope of the mountain, almost a spur. There was a level surface, a sort of tiny plateau, in front of their rock shelter. It was perhaps fifty feet in length and thirty feet broad at its widest.

Looking back at the crater, Elspeth again felt the grip of panic. What looked like white-hot liquid was spilling out over the brim, its flow blanking the stars. Even as she watched, its area spread unevenly down the side of Vesuvius. It seemed to be flowing directly toward the little plateau on which she and Mack stood.

"Mack!" she cried, pointing to it. "Let's get out of here."

He turned reluctantly and his face was grim against the light of the glowing lava. He pulled her to the edge of the plateau for answer, and pointed beneath. "Looks like we're stuck," he said, shouting into her ear to make himself heard as the mountain boomed again.

She felt her heart do a nose-dive. Another crater had been opened by the force of the induced eruption, and already lava was spreading from it down the hillside beneath them. They were cut off, isolated on the plateau.

THREE FACES OF TIME

They sat down under the rock overhang once more, finding solace in each other's company. They could do little talking, even if they were of a mind to—the volcano was making far too much noise. After a while they went out again to see how things were going. They discovered, during a lull in the sounds that had been enveloping them, that they were now on an island, completely surrounded by rising flows of lava.

"Not so good, is it?" said Elspeth, fighting the trembling of her lower lip. What she really wanted to do was bawl like a baby.

Mack didn't bother with answering. Instead he looked at her closely, almost as if for the first time. He said, "You know, Elly, now that I've gotten used to you, you're a sort of attractive gal."

"So what do we do now?" she said, inexplicably resentful of his appraisal. "Go back to our cave and make animals of ourselves?"

"It's an idea," he replied. "After all, we haven't much time."

Perhaps it was the practicality of the proposal—perhaps it lay in its coldness, in the fact that Mack had made no mention of love . . . Yet whatever the reason Elspeth, who hand for long months wanted nothing more than Mack's embrace, felt suddenly, irrationally, furiously angry.

She said, "Drop dead, will you?" At once she felt sick for her words.

Mack eyed her a moment longer, then shrugged and dropped his cigarette and ground it out carefully underfoot as if afraid of starting a forest fire. He said, "Stay out here if you want to. Me, I'm going back under the rock and try for some shuteye."

"Somebody ought to keep watch," Elspeth replied.

"For what? A fairy godmother riding on a star-beam to rescue us with a wave of her wand?" He left her.

As soon as he was gone, she felt a quick clamoring urge to run to him. Knowing him, she felt certain he had come as close to telling her he loved her as he was capable of doing. *"Now that I've gotten to know you, you're a sort of attractive gal—"* These were supposed to be words of passion to make any girl melt proudly into his arms! Yet she had a suspicion plenty of girls had so melted with even less provocation. She cursed herself for being seventeen kinds of a romantic fool. After all, she rebuked herself, she was scarcely a prize.

While she stood there, the lava continued to narrow the confines of their little plateau. The explosions had ceased for sometime, and a dark, smoke-blanketed dawn was no more light than the night had been around them.

Elspeth thought of Mack, lying there, awake and afraid, waiting for her to come to him. She thought of Lamia and the Martinez and certain others she had known about. She decided that if he really wanted her, he was going to have to call for her.

And then, in a brief clearing away of some of the clouds that swirled about them, Elspeth saw blue sky—and, crossing it, a helipipit with its rotor vanes whirling. She raced to the rock to get Mack and bring him out to help her signal. She found him sound asleep.

She tried to waken him, gave it up, then ran back herself into the open, where she jumped and danced and waved and shouted. But the helipipit sailed serenely on into the dark clouds, and the lava continued slowly to rise. . . .

"What's all the excitement?" said Mack, suddenly emerging at her shoulder. "Why'd you want to wake a guy up?"

"You fool!" cried the poetess in utter exasperation. "One of our planes just flew over. If you'd been out here he might have seen us—and—and taken us off this horrible place."

"Huh?" said Mack, squinting. Then, as awareness came: "Holy smoke! Your messenger must have got through to your gal-pal."

"And she got through to de Mestres," said the girl exultantly, herself beginning to understand what sight of the helipipit meant.

"And meanwhile we're still here," Mack said grimly, sending her recently uplifted spirits plummeting. He hesitated, then touched her arm lightly and added: "I'm sorry about the way I talked earlier, Elly. You must have thought I was treating you just like another female who happened to be here. Actually I—well, I . . ." His voice trailed off, and his already burned face reddened in embarrassment.

"Mack . . . *darling!*" cried Elspeth. "You don't have to say it. I'm the wordy one of the two of us."

"You sure are," said Mack. Without further ado, he swept her into his arms and sought her lips with his own.

An amused voice brought her out of it—a voice that said almost in her ear: "You two trying to start a volcano of your own?"

Sergeant Carhart was leaning through the door of a helipipit, hovering no more than a foot above the little plateau. As they scrambled inside, the sergeant said to Elspeth. "Lady, I didn't know you could dance. Not till I saw you down there through the smoke."

It was Elspeth's turn to blush.

According to Sergeant Carhart, the situation in the city was still a stalemate. "We could cut through them legions like butter, but the C.O. don't want us to tip our hand," he said. "He got your message yesterday and sent me and a couple other scouts out last night." He looked back at the inferno now far behind and beneath them. He added, "You mean to say you kicked up all that?"

"With an assist from nature," said Mack quietly. "What are you going to do now? Land your ships outside the city and wait for evening?" He nodded to the other two helipipits that had fallen into formation on either side of their own vehicle.

"Looks like we won't have to wait," said the sergeant, glancing ahead. The whole of Italy, from the Apennines to far out over the Tyrrhenian Sea, was shrouded in an enigmatic bank of cloud. "We'll zero right in to the palace courtyard."

"First time I ever enjoyed a fog while flying," said Mack. He gave Elspeth an odd, half-speculative, half-embarrassed look that caused her face to feel hot again, then curled up in his seat and went to sleep.

The poetess was still too keyed up to doze off—and there was little time. In a mere matter of minutes they were dropping through the mist over Rome, with jets cut off and rotor vanes whirling softly.

The troops in the palace courtyard had not been idle since Elspeth had last left them. The atmosphere had changed from one of restlessness to one of tense anticipation. Uncovered gun muzzles covered the walls, and sentries with automatic arms were posted everywhere.

In his office, after expressing relief at their rescue and receiving thanks from Elspeth and Mack, Commander de Mestres said bluntly, "Things are going to pop here any moment now. We checked a half-dozen raids on the walls last night. They've got six legions—about twenty thousand men—surrounding us now, and I'm afraid a full-scale assault is in the cards."

"What are you going to do?" Mack asked.

"You can't shoot them down!" exclaimed Elspeth. "They haven't a chance against your weapons."

The chunky Commander shook his head and said quietly, "Who said anything about shooting? We've been waiting for word about you two. Now we're going to put on a demonstration before we take off for Silesia. We're just waiting for better visibility."

"But I—" began Elspeth and checked her speech abruptly.

"Unless we bungle it you'll have plenty of opportunity to get your work assembled, Miss Marriner," de Mestres told her. "We don't intend to send all our forces north."

"Thanks, Commander," said Elspeth. "I do have much to complete of my original assignment."

"You've certainly saved the day for us on ours—you and Mr. Fraser," de Mestres said. "I'm leaving Captain Johnson in nominal charge here—he's coming along nicely now—with Sergeant Carhart in actual command. I think they'll be able to give you any protection you need. Now, what happened to the resident-Watcher?"

Elspeth and Mack told de Mestres about the death of Pliny in the eruption. They were still discussing their mission to Misenum when Captain Johnson, wearing a much smaller head-bandage than the one Elspeth had contrived for him, entered and said: "The clouds are lifting, sir—and from the look and sound of things outside the walls, a general assault is being prepared."

"Okay, Bill—stand by," said the Commander. Pulling a desk microphone close, he said "Now hear this—" and began giving his men detailed orders in a quiet, assured tone.

Johnson came over for a hurried handshake with Elspeth. Somewhat sheepishly he said, "I understand you brought me back alive, Miss Marriner. Thanks is a poor word under the—"

"It's still Elspeth to you," she told him. "Anyway, Bill, it wouldn't do to let you go to waste; you're much too good looking."

He blushed and turned to Mack and said, "I hear I owe you my life too. Maybe I can return the favor some day."

"Maybe—but I hope not," Mack snapped. Elspeth was pleased at the thought that he was actually jealous of the handsome young captain.

But there was small time for personal byplay. Things began to happen rapidly as soon as de Mestres pushed back the microphone and rose from his desk. Somehow the poetess found herself in a small observation helipipit with Captain Johnson and Sergeant Carhart. Mack had accepted the Commander's invitation to come along as a passenger in his own command-vehicle.

"Hurry, miss," said Sergeant Carhart, hoisting her into the observation pipit as Captain Johnson already had it off the ground. As she scrambled aboard, the poetess saw the plumed helmet of a Roman legionnaire appear in silhouette above the top of the wall. It was followed by other helmeted heads at a number of other points where scaling ladders had evidently been set.

There came a hoarse shout from the swarming attackers as the entire squadron of alien vessels rose slowly into the sky and spread out, hovering in formation above their astonished ranks. Horses reared at the sight of the strange "creatures" in the air.

Beyond the clustered ranks of the encircling Roman soldiery, the population of the Eternal City swarmed in the narrow streets and wide squares. They clustered like an endless insect swarm atop every building that might afford them a view of the battle.

Commander de Mestres' voice, strangely amplified and speaking rather halting Latin, said: *"Citizens of Rome—we have not come here to do you any harm. The weapons at our command are capable of wiping out your great city in a matter of minutes. Regard closely the abandoned grain elevator beyond the Capitoline Hill . . ."*

It was a beautiful maneuver. A gun lashed flame from every one of the flying vehicles as the Commander gave his signal. For a split second that seemed to hang on forever in the poetess' eyes, the indicated structure stood, apparently unharmed. Then, in a flash of flame and smoke that sent thunderous peals of sound echoing through and above the city, the elevator ceased to exist. As the fumes of the blast rose lingeringly in the air, where the abandoned building had stood was nothing but a blackened cellar pit.

"T.O.T.—perfect T.O.T.," said Sergeant Carhart ecstatically.

"What's T.O.T.?" Elspeth asked him.

"Time on target," said the Sergeant patiently. "It means every shell or charge was set to strike the same target at the same instant. I never saw it done prettier."

"Look below," suggested Captain Johnson in his slow Southern drawl. "Our little show seems to have kicked up a hell of a fuss."

The remark was an understatement. Panic was beginning to sweep the streets and housetops alike. The legionnaires were scrambling away from the abandoned Aventine palace as if they feared annihilation by devils—and their fears were communicated to the mob. Horrified, fascinated, the poetess watched a careening two-horse military chariot run over a dozen or more people in a street directly beneath. A wake of figures was left on the pavement, some struggling, some still.

"Stop it!" she cried involuntarily. "Somebody stop it!"

As if on cue, Commander de Mestres' amplified voice sounded again, sternly. In Latin, he said, *"You will cease your attempts to flee or suffer the consequences. We shall do you no harm unless we are attacked. See that you do not harm yourselves."*

They watched the panic slowly subside as, after a half-dozen repetitions of his message, Commander de Mestres finally managed to get some sort of authority over the stampeding multitude. Then, when comparative calm was restored, a large body of the squadron suddenly closed ranks and rose high in the air before cutting in jets and heading at full speed toward the Silesian mines and gateway.

A score of vehicles, including that in which the poetess rode, then returned to the Aventine palace courtyard and came to rest within the shelter of its walls. A handful of sentries, who had been left to guard the palace, greeted them curiously, wanting to know how it was going.

"Like silk," said Captain Johnson after assisting Elspeth out of her plane. "We put the fear of God into them all right."

"Where's Mack?" the poetess asked, only to realize that, deliberately or otherwise, her colleague had gone north with the Commander. She said a very naughty word that caused Sergeant Carhart to jump as if he'd been stung by a bee.

"Something you want, miss?" he inquired.

"Yes, Sergeant," said Elspeth, mustering the vestiges of her self-control to conquer angry frustration. "I'd like the use of one light vehicle and a driver. I still have work to do."

The flat roof that covered the central portion of Princess Berenice's palace was unguarded when the helipipit landed. Elspeth swung easily out onto the flagged surface.

"Wait here," she said to the soldier who had been assigned as her chauffeur. She loosened the blaster at her belt for she had no knowledge of how the attack and panic had been accepted by the city.

Princess Berenice emerged alone from a doorway and moved toward the poetess. Her face was composed but determined; her purple stola swept about her by the breeze and revealed the tininess of her exquisite person. Approaching Elspeth, after a look at the parked helipipit and its lounging pilot, she said: "I know now why you have come here, but we greet you in peace and hope for understanding."

The poetess grinned and said the Latin equivalent of "Come off it, honey—you and I are pals."

The Princess was stopped in her tracks. She peered at her visitor, first at the outlandish coverall, then at her face. A small hand flew to her mouth. Then she gasped. "Marina Elspetia—it is you! I thought you had fled the city with the Admiral."

"It's me and I'm back and we've got a lot to talk about," Elspeth said, putting a friendly arm about her hostess' shoulders. In her new guise she felt little need of standing on former ceremony.

They adjourned to the small chamber off the main ballroom, where previously Elspeth had seen Berenice entertain Titus. There, while wine and fruit were brought, the poetess explained what she could of the parallel worlds, of the Watches and of her mission. At the conclusion of her account the Princess said, "I'm honored that you have made me your friend. But why do you tell me this?"

"Because our resident-Watcher, the Admiral, died last night in the eruption of Vesuvius," said Elspeth quietly. "I want you to take his place in our service."

"I—a woman?" the Princess countered, overwhelmed. Then, looking oddly at her guest: "But of course—you're a woman too. I—it's just that I've got to get used to the idea." She paused, frowned, added: "Shouldn't such honor go to the Emperor?"

"Definitely not," replied the poetess, "It is Watcher policy of proven worth never to put such power in the hands of an individual who already has great power on his own planet. We cannot risk its being abused—as it was through an error of judgment on the planet from which comes your rival for the Emperor's affection."

Berenice murmured with a steely look, "And Anna Martiana, whoever she may be, is your enemy as well as mine?"

"Very much so," said Elspeth.

"I am glad," said the Princess. Then, with a sidelong look at her guest: "Do all women in your world dress as you do?"

The poetess laughed. "No, Berenice," she replied. "We have all sorts of costumes—including some I feel certain would meet with more approval from you. Now, what's the current situation on the Anna Martiana front?"

"She is to ride tomorrow in the coronation procession," said the Princess somberly. Then, with a glint in her black eyes: "Unless—"

"Unless what?" asked Elspeth with some impatience, tossing into a discard bowl the pit of the plum she had finished.

"Unless Domitianus keeps an appointment with her. They should be meeting within the hour," Berenice informed her.

"Damnation!" said Elspeth. "If I'd been thinking

straight I'd never have recommended such an action. With so much already going on it merely adds a tremendous uncertainty factor."

"I don't understand," said the Princess.

"You will," Elspeth told her. "On most of the other worlds your counterpart got crushed like a millstone between the Emperor and his brother. I'm not going to let that happen to you here."

"What can we do?" Berenice thus put herself entirely in her guest's hands—and Elspeth wished she hadn't.

Before she had a chance to suggest any action, a slave entered and announced breathlessly that the Emperor was approaching the palace. When he had been dismissed, Berenice rose quickly and said, "Marina, you must hide. But I want you close at hand. Quick, get behind those curtains! There's a door in back of them and you'll have an avenue of escape to the roof if you need it."

It was not difficult to read the new Emperor's mood when moments later he came striding unaccompanied into the chamber. His scowl was black, his manner aggressive, his words harsh as he said, "Why, at such a time—with the world threatened by flying devils and on the eve of my own coronation—do you intrigue against me, Berenice?" He flung at her feet the message the Princess had written his brother and added, "Seeking to turn me against my own blood!"

"Nay, sire," said the Princess. "Seeking only to retain your affection—which I have never forfeited."

"Who are you to say that?" countered the furious Caesar. "I have been advised to put you to death. Such is the proper fate of an intriguer against the Emperor!"

"If it will make you happy that I should beg for my life I will do so," replied the Princess proudly, "for your happiness is my sole concern."

Titus' right hand darted to his belt, where gleamed the of a jeweled dagger. Then it fell limply away and he bowed his head and told her, "I cannot lay a hand upon you in anger, Berenice. Would that I could, for it would be far simpler. Now I must seek some other form of punishment that, in leaving you alive, can bring only unhappiness to both of us."

"And *your* happiness, Highness, is paramount," said a

mocking voice from the doorway behind the Emperor. Elspeth felt her breath catch as the Martinez, beautiful, scornful, cold as ice, stepped into the room. She held her right hand in front of her and Elspeth knew without seeing that it contained one of the deadly little hand-blasters of Heartland.

XI

Titus spun about at the sound of the Martinez' voice. He thundered, "You were ordered to remain in your quarters. What are you doing here?"

It was, Elspeth thought during an instant of detachment, an odd situation for the new Emperor of so masculine a world as Rome to find himself in. For three women, counting herself, were at that moment deciding his destiny and that of his world.

Apparently the Heartland leader was as well aware of the nuances as the poetess. Her mocking smile widened as she replied, with a brief mock obeisance, "Seeking only to assure your happiness, Highness—by removing this source of your future grief."

"You'll do nothing of the sort," said Titus, his fury rising. Then, lifting his voice to match: "Guards! Come here at once!"

"I doubt they'll come," said the Heartlander casually. "I took the precaution of bringing some of my own people."

"Your own peo—Is my brother with you?" the Emperor asked.

Elspeth admired the Martinez' nerve. Despite the defeat that faced her, she was making a desperate gamble to hold *Antique*—even an *Antique* sealed off forever from her home planet—by control of the Emperor.

She had evidently sought to turn the trap set up for her by Elspeth and Berenice to her own benefit: first by exposing it to the Emperor, then by conspiring with his brother to take over if Titus, as the event had proved, was unable to liquidate Berenice.

"I am with her," was the reply as Domitianus appeared

in the doorway and took his stand beside the redhead. "Surely, as a Roman, it is my duty to see that the Empire is not ruled by a Caesar too weak to set aside a traitorous love."

"I am not and have never been traitorous to Rome," the Princess said quietly.

There was an awkward silence. Then, briskly, the Martinez took action. Saying, "Stand aside or share her fate, Titus," she lifted her right hand and pointed it toward Berenice.

At that point Elspeth slipped quietly out from behind the curtains, her blaster leveled in front of her, pointing directly at the Heartland leader. She said, "Take it easy, Ana—your play here is finished."

With an articulate cry of fury, the redhead pivoted and blazed away with her tiny weapon. A section of the curtain above the poetess' head and slightly to her left disintegrated in sudden flame. Then her own finger was pressing a firing mechanism and she watched her enemy crumble into ash as the blaster caught her dead center.

The Emperor stared at Elspeth as if at a ghost. He staggered back a step and all but fell over one of the dining couches behind him.

"The Princess Berenice," Elspeth said distinctly, "is under the protection of the visitors of the Aventine palace. Her person is not to be violated by anyone—even Caesar himself. Is it understood?"

Titus nodded in a dazed sort of way, then said, peering at Elspeth, "Ye gods, you're one of them! Haven't I met you before now?"

"In this very room," said the poetess quietly. "It was the night of your return from the provinces of the North."

"The woman poet!" said the Emperor. "I did not recognize you at first in barbarian garb. What have you done to Princess Anna?"

"No more than she intended for Princess Berenice," said Elspeth.

"She murdered her!" cried Domitianus, who seemed to have been reduced to a sort of statis by the horrible sight he had witnessed. "Guards—to me! To me with drawn swords!"

Before Elspeth could make another move, Titus' brother had darted through the doorway to safety. From the ballroom beyond came the thud of many feet, racing toward them. The poetess looked at Berenice and said, "Quickly, we can escape by the roof."

"We'll be trapped like wild beasts," said Titus, seeking a weapon.

"Come!" snapped Elspeth as Berenice reached her side. And to the delight of the poetess, a Roman emperor came at her summons. He refused to hurry, however, despite Berenice's entreaties. Elspeth was forced to plant another burst at the threshold, leaving it a wall of flames and blocking temporarily the entry of Domitianus' armed warriors.

Reaching the roof safely, Titus gawked at sight of the helipipit.

The Emperor's brother was just in time to throw a spear at them as the rotor vanes bit the air and lifted them from the flagged surface. The missile passed harmlessly beneath the landing carriage. The pilot grinned at Elspeth and said, "Close, but no cigar."

"We'll fall," cried Berenice, then bit her lower lip as if ashamed of showing the fear that consumed her. Elspeth consoled her, then turned her attention to the Emperor.

"There," she said, pointing at the panorama beneath them, "is Rome—Rome as no other Emperor or citizen has ever seen her before. Look well on your kingdom, Titus, and try to rule it wisely. You will have help, of course. But your reign will be one of the most difficult in history."

Terror fell away as the fascination of what he saw overcame the new Emperor. He looked long while the pilot, at Elspeth's behest, took them on an aerial tour of the Eternal City. Then she said, "See if you can bring us down safely somewhere on the Imperial palace."

Through teeth clenched tightly so that they would not chatter, Berenice said: "Marina, what a world you must come from!"

"It has its problems and injustices, like all the worlds," the girl told her. "But at least we have machines instead of slaves and almost all men and women have a chance to be educated. You will be a key figure in transition here—you and the Emperor. It will not be easy. But I promise we shan't expect the impossible."

Elspeth thought suddenly of Mack, risking his life needlessly in the expedition against the Silesian miners. Damn him! And how like a man to do exactly as he had done. She looked at Titus with disfavor.

He seemed to sense her momentary dislike, for he turned to face her and said, "I shall need time to learn my job. But while I may be wrong-headed at times, I shall always do my best for Rome." He hesitated, then added. "What of Anna Martiana—what was the witch?"

"Just a witch," said Elspeth quietly. Changing the subject she said, "What will you do with your brother Domitianus?"

Titus frowned thoughtfully out at the view. Then he replied, "I have not made up my mind as yet—nor do I intend to today. The boy merits death, if only to discourage other usurpers. Yet I am fond of him and know well the merits he possesses. If I find mercy in my heart—as I believe now that I shall—I'll permit him to prove his loyalty with an assignment on the frontier. After all was I too not bewitched by the lady?"

He looked to the southwest, pointed to a column of smoke rising above the horizon and said, "That looks to be an odd sort of cloud."

"Vesuvius is in eruption, Highness," Elspeth informed him. "I came from there this morning. It was necessary to set it off to protect your world."

The Emperor looked at her and said sadly, "I do not pretend to understand what is happening. History knows not its like. But I hope none of my poor subjects is being destroyed by the calamity."

"I trust not," said Elspeth. "The lava flow was not too rapid to block escape. But it saved you from a far worse disaster, Highness."

Titus looked at her a moment longer, then dropped his head into his hands and said no more until just before the gear of the helipipit came to rest on the Palantine palace roof. Then he said, looking at them blankly, "The coronation procession must be postponed—but not the games, lest the people riot."

Elspeth glanced inquiringly at Princess Berenice, who had moved into the seat beside the Emperor and slipped one of her slim arms about his chunky body. There was a look of pride in the Oriental girl's expression. She said, "He will be a great Caesar—far greater than the first."

"Yes," said Elspeth, regarding her friend fondly, "we'll see." *Well,* she thought, *the probability sequence is being altered early on this planet*. She rejoiced that whatever else happened, her friend Berenice's almost uniformly tragic fate on other, more advanced Earths had a chance of more joyous fulfillment.

She sat beside Berenice on a high balcony overlooking the Forum when, a week later, the coronation procession was held.

"You'll stay for the games?" Berenice asked eagerly.

Elspeth shook her head. She, who could not stomach a bullfight, had no intention of exposing her sensibilities to the mass slaughter of men and animals that was so much an element of any Roman celebration. Something, she decided, was going to have to be done about this facet of *Antique* civilization. Perhaps American football . . . ?

Doffing stola and gown for the last time, Elspeth got into the slacks, sweater and jacket in which she had first come to *Antique*. Berenice admired her costume violently, although the idea of trousers disturbed her almost as much as it did Titus. In Rome, it appeared, such garb was considered strictly for crude forest primitives.

"But in time I suppose we shall learn to wear them," said the Princess. Then, with a sigh: "We'll have to do something about our hips, though."

"You will," said Elspeth, laughing. "And Berry, dear, you'll be receiving my successor soon."

"Then I shall never see you again?" the Princess asked.

"Who knows?" countered Elspeth. "I shall try to return, if only to learn how your affairs progress."

"Your word on it," said the poetess. "Now I must go. You'll have to learn a lot of things you never even thought of, but you're going to be a fine resident-Watcher, Berry."

"I'll try, Marina."

They embraced and went to the roof, where Elspeth took off in a waiting helipipit, this time driving it herself. She proceeded to the Aventine palace, where Sergeant Carhart and Captain Johnson bade her farewell.

Johnson said, "They're leaving some of us here for a while—latest orders from home. You seem to know the ropes around here better than we do, Elly—so how about fixing a fellow with some numbers?"

"As long as you use your time to improve your Latin," said Elspeth laughing.

"Can you think of a better way to learn a dead language?" the Southerner asked. She gave him an introduction to Berenice which frankly stated Johnson's purpose; she then told him where to take it. Then she asked him what the news was from Silesia.

"None for the last two days," he replied. "The Heartlanders have been making a fight of it. They got some of their own machines through. We've lost some."

"What about Mack Fraser?" she asked, her heart skipping a beat. And, as he looked puzzled: "You know—the man who got us out of there."

"Oh!" said Captain Johnson with a grin. *"That* one. He got shipped back with the last message ship two days back. Seems he got hurt."

"Oh, no!" she cried. "Where is he?"

"I'm right here," said Mack, strolling into her range of vision. "As to what happened to me, I'd rather not say."

Captain Johnson's grin was faintly malicious as he told her, "It seems Fraser here was sent ahead to do some ground scouting on account of he knows the region like a book. When the second group went in they found him hanging upside down in a rabbit trap."

"Mack!" said Elspeth, trying not to laugh. "How'd you get hurt?"

"Oh," said the Southerner, his eyes twinkling, *"they* didn't hurt him. It seems he busted a collar bone when our fellows cut him down. He's going back with you when you make transfer tonight."

"A fate worse than death," growled Mack, and for the first time Elspeth saw the hulk of a shoulder bandage under his shirt.

"You want to change places with me, Fraser?" said Johnson. "I can assure you I'd jump at the chance."

"Over my dead body," said Mack as Elspeth giggled. But inwardly, for all the badinage, she felt a deep glow of satisfaction. She was going back with Mack, back to Spindrift Key in the Carolinas, the place she loved best in all the world, with the man she loved best in all the world.

Nor was her happiness much dispelled when, later, he said: "I don't want you to be getting ideas just because that fly-boy drooled over you. He's been shut up in that palace so long he's island happy—"

"Oh shut up, Mack," she said gently, and kissed him tenderly so as not to hurt his broken collar bone—and for once, during the blackness of transfer, she was not afraid.

AWARD-WINNING *Science Fiction!*

The following titles are winners of the prestigious Nebula or Hugo Award for excellence in Science Fiction. A must for lovers of good science fiction everywhere!

- ☐ 77419-9 **SOLDIER, ASK NOT**, Gordon R. Dickson $2.50
- ☐ 47807-7 **THE LEFT HAND OF DARKNESS**, Ursula K. LeGuin $2.50
- ☐ 79176-X **SWORDS AND DEVILTRY**, Fritz Leiber $2.25
- ☐ 06223-7 **THE BIG TIME**, Fritz Leiber $2.50
- ☐ 16651-2 **THE DRAGON MASTERS**, Jack Vance $1.95
- ☐ 16706-3 **THE DREAM MASTER**, Roger Zelazny $2.25
- ☐ 24905-1 **FOUR FOR TOMORROW**, Roger Zelazny $2.25
- ☐ 80696-1 **THIS IMMORTAL**, Roger Zelazny $2.25

Available wherever paperbacks are sold or use this coupon.

ACE SCIENCE FICTION
P.O. Box 400, Kirkwood, N.Y. 13795

Please send me the titles checked above. I enclose _____
Include 75¢ for postage and handling if one book is ordered; 50¢ per book for two to five. If six or more are ordered, postage is free. California, Illinois, New York and Tennessee residents please add sales tax.

NAME_____

ADDRESS_____

CITY_____ STATE_____ ZIP_____

SF3